Delores Fo... thor, has written ove... ...of copies of her books in print worldwide. She's received a Booksellers' Best Award and an *RT* Reviewers' Choice Best Book Award. She was also a finalist for a prestigious *RITA*® Award. You can contact the author through her website at deloresfossen.com

Lena Diaz was born in Kentucky and has also lived in California, Louisiana and Florida, where she now resides with her husband and two children. Before becoming a romantic suspense author, she was a computer programmer. A Romance Writers of America Golden Heart® Award finalist, she has also won the prestigious Daphne du Maurier Award for Excellence in Mystery/Suspense. To get the latest news about Lena, please visit her website, lenadiaz.com

Also by Delores Fossen

Silver Creek Lawman: Second Generation

Targeted in Silver Creek
Maverick Detective Dad

The Law in Lubbock County

Sheriff in the Saddle
Maverick Justice

Mercy Ridge Lawmen

Her Child to Protect
Safeguarding the Surrogate
Targeting the Deputy

Also by Lena Diaz

A Tennessee Cold Case Story

Murder on Prescott Mountain
Serial Slayer Cold Case
Shrouded in the Smokies
The Secret She Keeps
Smoky Mountains Graveyard

The Justice Seekers

Agent Under Siege
Killer Conspiracy
Deadly Double-Cross

THE SHERIFF'S BABY

DELORES FOSSEN

SMOKY MOUNTAINS MYSTERY

LENA DIAZ

MILLS & BOON

First Published in Great Britain 2024
by Mills & Boon, an imprint of HarperCollins*Publishers* Ltd
1 London Bridge Street, London, SE1 9GF

www.harpercollins.co.uk

HarperCollins*Publishers*
Macken House, 39/40 Mayor Street Upper,
Dublin 1, D01 C9W8, Ireland

ISBN: 978-0-263-32248-4

1024

This book contains FSC™ certified paper and other controlled sources to ensure responsible forest management.

For more information visit: www.harpercollins.co.uk/green

Printed and Bound in the UK using 100% Renewable Electricity at
CPI Group (UK) Ltd, Croydon, CR0 4YY

THE SHERIFF'S BABY

DELORES FOSSEN

Chapter One

The sound instantly woke Deputy Joelle McCullough, but it took her a moment to realize it hadn't been part of the dream.

The nightmare.

There were no blasts of gunshots that had killed her father. No, this had been a clicking sound like that of someone shutting a vehicle door.

Rubbing her eyes to help her focus, Joelle checked her phone for the time. Just past 2:00 a.m., which meant it wasn't anywhere near a normal visiting hour. Added to that, she wasn't exactly on the beaten path since her house was a good mile outside of her hometown of Saddle Ridge with no other houses within sight of hers.

There were no texts from her three siblings or any of her friends. None either from anyone at the Saddle Ridge Sheriff's Office where she'd been a deputy for seven years now. So, no alerts from anyone she knew well enough to contact her before just showing up at her place, but it could be a neighbor coming to her for help.

Everyone in Saddle Ridge knew where she lived, knew that she was a cop. That meant this could be some kind of emergency that had warranted a face-to-face rather than a call or text.

She threw back the covers, immediately reaching for her Glock 22 that she kept on the nightstand. Grabbing her firearm when off duty hadn't always been her automatic response. Not until five months ago when her father had been gunned down at his home. Since then, things had changed.

Everything had changed.

And Joelle no longer trusted that a neighbor's emergency—or whatever this was—wouldn't end in gunfire. Her father hadn't been armed when he'd answered his door that night. He obviously hadn't been alarmed that whoever had come calling was there to kill him.

She couldn't make the same mistake.

It was the reason she'd had a top-notch security system installed, and it was turned on and armed. If anyone attempted to get in through a door or window, the alarms would start blaring, and the security company and the sheriff's office would be alerted. Most importantly, *she* would be alerted, and she could use her cop's training to put a stop to a threat.

Despite the urgency and worry building inside her, Joelle took her time getting out of bed. She'd learned the hard way that standing too quickly would make her lightheaded.

One of the side effects of being five months pregnant.

She ran her hand over her stomach, trying to soothe the baby's sudden fluttering. Not hard kicks. Not yet, anyway. Just soft stirrings that reminded her of the precious cargo she was carrying. Reminding her again of why she couldn't risk what'd happened to her father.

Once her heartbeat had steadied enough so that it was no longer thrumming in her ears, Joelle listened for any other sounds. Nothing except for the hum of the air conditioner and the spring breeze rattling through some of the tree branches outside her house.

She went to the front window and peered out, but it took her a moment to spot the vehicle. A black car that she didn't recognize. It was parked not in her driveway but off to the side beneath a pair of towering oaks. The headlights weren't on, and the door was indeed shut.

There was no sign of the driver.

Because of the angle of the parked car, Joelle couldn't see the license plates, and she didn't waste time figuring out what was going on. Not with every one of her cop's instincts now telling her that something was wrong. She stepped to the side of the window so that she wouldn't be seen or in the line of fire, and made a call to the Saddle Ridge dispatcher.

"This is Deputy Joelle McCullough," she said, keeping her voice at a whisper just in case the driver of that vehicle was close enough to hear her. "I need backup at my house."

She wasn't sure who was on night duty at the sheriff's office, but it wouldn't be her brother Slater. He was staying the night in San Antonio, a thirty-minute drive away, since he was on the schedule to testify at a trial. If Slater had been in town, she would have called him directly since he lived just up the road from her.

After she'd done a thorough visual sweep of the front exterior of her house, Joelle went to her kitchen window to check the backyard. Thankfully, there was a full moon to give her some visibility, but there were also plenty of trees and shrubs dotting the five acres she owned. Lots of places for someone to hide if that's what a person wanted to do to try to get back at a cop.

She wasn't aware of anyone specifically who wanted to end her life or get revenge on her, but her father's killer was still unknown and at large. Since no one was certain of the reason her dad had been gunned down, she might be on the killer's hit list, too.

With her phone in her left hand and the Glock still gripped in her right, Joelle stayed positioned to the side of the kitchen window while she continued to watch and listen. Nothing.

And that in itself was troubling.

If this was someone she knew, they would have already come to the door or made themselves known. Added to that, the person would have parked in front of her house and not off to the side like that.

The minutes crawled by until Joelle saw the slash of headlights as they turned into her driveway. Backup, no doubt. She didn't breathe easier, though, because she needed to let the responding deputy know there was someone out there, maybe someone waiting to fire shots.

She hurried back to the front and silently cursed when she glanced out the front window and recognized the dark blue truck. Not a deputy but rather Sheriff Duncan Holder. Once, he'd been a fellow deputy but had been elected sheriff after her father's death.

Duncan was also the father of her unborn child.

As always, she got a serious jolt of conflicted feelings whenever she laid eyes on Duncan. Memories. Heat. Guilt. Grief. A bundle of raw nerves mixed with the old attraction that Joelle wished wasn't there.

Because she didn't want Duncan or anyone else to be gunned down tonight, Joelle fired off a quick text to let him know about the unfamiliar black car and the out-of-sight driver. Duncan responded just seconds later with a thumbs-up emoji, and he pulled his truck into her yard and closer to her porch. He sat there for a few moments, still on his phone, and Joelle figured he was probably running the license plate on the visitor's vehicle since he'd likely have a good view of the one on the rear of the car.

Duncan finally put his phone away and stepped from his truck, keeping cover behind the door while he fired glances around the yard. He, too, had his Glock drawn and ready.

Her heart did that stupid little flutter it always did whenever she was around him, and for the umpteenth time, Joelle wished she could make herself immune to him. Hard to do, though, with those unforgettable, heart-fluttering looks. The dark brown hair, blue eyes and a face that had no doubt gotten him plenty of lustful looks.

More seconds passed. Her heart raced. Adrenaline pumped through her. Her stomach tightened.

The gusts of wind sure didn't help, either, with her raw, edgy nerves. Those gusts kicked up, stirring seemingly everything at once, including an owl that sounded agitated by the noise. It was bad timing since the owl's hoots and squawks could conceal any sounds her visitor might make.

Duncan finally moved away from his truck, coming up the porch steps, and that was her cue to use her phone app to disarm the security system and unlock the door. He stepped in and brought the scent of the fresh night air with him. His own scent, too, one she wished wasn't so familiar to her.

"You're not on shift," she muttered, well aware that her tone wasn't exactly friendly.

"No. I couldn't sleep so I went into the office to do some paperwork. I was there when you called. Have you seen anyone around that car or the house?" he tacked onto that.

He met her gaze for just a fraction. She was betting that he was also trying to make himself immune to her.

Joelle shook her head, locked the door and reset the security system. "I heard the car door shut about fifteen minutes ago. It woke me, and when I got up and didn't see anyone, I called dispatch." She'd tried to make her voice steady, as if giving a report to her boss. Which she was. But it was hard to keep the emotion out of it.

Duncan glanced at her pale yellow gown that in no way concealed, well, anything. It was thin and snug enough to show the outline of her breasts and baby bump.

Yes, definitely hard to keep the emotion out of this.

"I ran the plates," he told her. "The vehicle belongs to Alton Martinez in San Antonio."

She repeated the name to see if it rang any bells. It didn't. "Does he have a record?"

"I'll know in the next couple of minutes." Duncan stepped around her and went to the kitchen window to look out as she'd done.

He'd been in her house before but not in a while. Not since that night her father had died. In fact, Duncan had been here in her bed while her dad was being gunned down. Joelle knew she stood no chance of forgiving herself for that.

For years, Duncan and she had resisted the scalding attraction that'd been between them. They'd believed resisting was a necessity since they were fellow deputies, working side by side in sometimes dangerous situations. They hadn't wanted to risk a failed relationship that could have interfered with them doing their jobs. They'd resisted time after time, year after year. Until that night of her father's murder.

And it'd had disastrous consequences.

One good one, though, too.

Joelle hated she hadn't been with her father to try to stop his death, but she loved the baby she was carrying, and the pregnancy was the main reason she was managing to hold her life together. Duncan had helped some with the managing, too, by making sure they were on different shifts so she wouldn't have to see him that often. That's why it'd been such a jolt to have him respond to her call for help.

"Have you gotten any recent threats that I don't know about?" Duncan asked, the question yanking her out of her thoughts and forcing her to focus on the here and now.

"No. And I haven't made any recent arrests, either," she added, even though as sheriff, he would have already known that.

Of course, it wouldn't have to be anything recent to continue to be a threat. Sometimes, when criminals got out of jail, they went looking for anyone who'd had a part in their incarceration. No one immediately came to mind, though.

Duncan's phone dinged, and he tore his attention from the window to read the text he'd just gotten. "Martinez doesn't have a record, but about four hours ago, he reported his car stolen."

Joelle's chest clenched, and another wave of adrenaline washed through her. She had steeled herself up for the worst, but she'd hoped this would turn out to be nothing. The fact it was a stolen vehicle meant it was almost certainly something bad.

Staying on the other side of the window, she peered out, searching again for whatever sort of threat this might be. Her mind was having no trouble coming up with some awful scenarios. Especially one.

"Before I went to bed, I accessed some internet newspaper articles on my father's murder and my mother's disappearance," she told him.

No need for her to explain either of those incidents. Her father had been murdered, and on the same day, her mother, Sandra, had simply vanished. Both incidents had gutted her. Both had left her in desperate need of answers.

"I read any and every article connected to my parents," Joelle added to let Duncan know that wasn't anything out of the norm. "In one of them, a journalist mentioned that she was continuing to look into the murder and would post updates. I knew it was a long shot, that she probably didn't know anything we didn't, but in the comments, I asked if she'd found anything."

Duncan looked at her, their gazes connecting, and even in the dim light, she could see the sympathy in his eyes. Could practically hear the sigh that Joelle was certain he wanted to make.

"And you think…what…that your father's killer saw the comment and believed that maybe he or she wanted to stop you from digging?" he asked. He still didn't sigh. Nor did he dismiss it. "I saw the article. Saw the comment you posted."

Joelle figured she shouldn't have been surprised. Duncan felt guilty about her father's murder, too, and he was a cop just as she was. This was a crime they both wanted solved, and that meant digging through any and all possible leads.

"It's been five months," Duncan went on a moment later. "If the killer had planned on coming after one of us, you'd think that would have happened before now." He paused. "But the car was stolen, and the driver is nowhere in sight. So, I'm not writing anything off right now."

Good. Joelle had wanted him to take this seriously because she certainly was.

"We can work this a couple of ways," Duncan explained a moment later. "We can wait for the driver to show himself, or I can go ahead and call in every available deputy. We can flood the grounds with headlights and maybe spook the person enough for him or her to come out."

Joelle knew that no one in law enforcement wanted to be woken up at this hour, but her fellow cops, including the reserve deputies, would gladly come if they thought it meant catching her father's killer. Every member of the Saddle Ridge Sheriff's Office wanted justice for their former boss.

"Bring in the deputies," she advised. She glanced down at her gown again. "I'll hurry and change and then will keep watch at the front of the house."

Duncan made a sound of agreement, and while she hurried to her bedroom, she heard him call dispatch who in turn would contact the deputies. Since a few of them lived only a mile or so away, it shouldn't take long for them to start arriving.

Joelle wanted to believe that the extra help would mean a killer could be captured tonight. A capture that'd take place when she had plenty of backup so as to lessen the risk to her unborn child. But she had to stay grounded since this might not even be related to her father's death or her mother's disappearance.

Moving as fast as she could, Joelle pulled on a pair of maternity jeans, a loose top and her boots, and she hurried back into the living room. However, she came to a quick stop when she caught a whiff of something.

"Smoke," she heard Duncan say from the kitchen.

This time, the adrenaline came as a hard slam. Because Duncan was right. There was the faint scent of smoke in the air.

Duncan came barreling out of the kitchen and toward the front. "I don't see any signs of a fire in the back," he relayed to her as they both hurried to the living room window.

Joelle's heart was thudding now, and the fear came. A fire could be a ploy to get them out of the house. Or rather to get *her* out of the house. So she could be gunned down. But she didn't see flames anywhere.

"The scent's coming from here," Duncan muttered, glancing at the east wall of the living room.

The only windows on that particular side of the house were what was called clerestory, which meant they were above eye level and had been designed to let in natural light. That didn't stop Duncan. He dragged over a chair, anchoring it against the wall and hefted himself up to look out.

He cursed.

"There's a fire right next to your house," he told her, causing her heart to race even more. "It's already at least four feet high."

The exterior was wood, and while Joelle hoped it wouldn't easily ignite, her visitor must have believed that would be the result. Either that, or he or she had wanted Duncan and her just to go running out.

Duncan made another call to dispatch, this time to alert the fire department. Something the person outside must have figured they would do. And that meant the seconds were ticking down. If Duncan and she waited until the firefighters arrived, the house could be engulfed in flames, putting them and the baby at risk. But the risk could be there if they ran, too.

"My car's in the garage," she let him know.

The vehicle wasn't bullet resistant but then neither was Duncan's truck, which was parked by her porch. Still, if they were in her car, at least they could try to drive out of there if the fire overtook the house.

Duncan made another of those sounds of agreement, and he took her keys from her when she scooped them up from the foyer table. That meant he was no doubt planning on being behind the wheel and that he would insist she get down. The cop part of her hated she had to make such concessions. However, the baby changed her priorities, and Joelle knew that both Duncan and she would do anything and everything possible to keep their child safe.

"I have to disarm the security system until we're through the garage door," she relayed to him, using her phone to do that. The moment they were inside her car, though, she reset the alarm.

In the distance, Joelle heard the welcome sound of a cruiser's siren, but her relief over the backup was short-lived.

Because the next sound she heard was a blast.

Some kind of explosion roared through the house and garage, shaking the very foundation. Paint cans and gardening tools fell from the shelves and hooks, smashing onto the concrete floor. Each crash only escalated the urgency and fear.

So did the smoke.

The scent of it got much stronger, and Joelle could see whiffs of the smoke seeking beneath the mudroom door and into the garage. Thankfully, there was no smoke around the garage door itself, and that was likely the reason Duncan started the car and hit the remote on her visor to open the door.

"Stay down," he ordered her.

Joelle did. She strapped on her seat belt and sank down as low as she could. She also kept her gun ready in case she had to return fire.

Duncan threw the car into reverse and hit the accelerator, bolting out of the garage. Because of the way she was positioned, Joelle couldn't see the person responsible for the fire, but she had no doubts that Duncan was keeping watch.

The sirens got louder, and she saw the whirl of the blue lights slashing through the darkness. That would almost certainly get their attacker running. Or so she thought.

But she was wrong.

The bullet slammed into her windshield, crashing through the safety glass on the driver's side. For a heart-stopping second, she thought that Duncan had been hit, but he pressed even harder on the accelerator and got the car out of her driveway and onto the country road that fronted her house. He stopped just as the cruiser pulled in next to them.

"It's Luca," Duncan told her, referring to Deputy Luca Vanetti. "Text him and tell him to stay put until the others arrive. We have an active shooter. Tell him to let the other deputies know."

Joelle fired off a quick text, then braced herself for another shot. Or an explosion. Her house was burning, she was sure of that, but she couldn't deal with the sickening dread of losing her home and everything she owned. For now, she just had to focus on staying alive, and then she could figure out who was doing this.

And why.

She especially wanted to know the why in case that led her to her father's killer.

There was the sound of another siren. More whirling lights. Two more vehicles arriving on scene. What didn't happen was another round of gunfire, which meant the shooter was likely already on the run. Joelle prayed, though, that someone would spot the person.

Because she was so focused on listening for their attacker, Joelle gasped when the sound shot through the car. But it wasn't a bullet. It was her phone, and Joelle saw a familiar name on the screen. Molly Radel, a former deputy who'd transferred to working as a dispatcher after she got pregnant. Even though Molly was on leave, awaiting the birth of her baby, it was possible she'd been called in to assist in some way.

"Molly," Joelle answered, and she was about to give the woman a quick explanation as to what was going on, but Molly spoke before Joelle could do that.

"You have to help me," Molly said, her voice trembling and frantic. "Someone's breaking into my house."

The words had no sooner left Molly's mouth when Joelle heard the woman scream.

Chapter Two

Even though Joelle hadn't put the call on speaker, Duncan heard the woman's scream loud and clear. Since Joelle had greeted Molly by name, he also had no trouble figuring out that something was seriously wrong.

"Put the phone on speaker," Duncan told Joelle, and the moment she'd done that, he tried to figure out what the heck was going on. "Molly?" he asked.

He could hear what he thought were the sounds of a struggle, but the dispatcher didn't answer. And that caused Duncan to curse. He had every available lawman responding to the situation here at Joelle's. A situation that might escalate even more if the attacker continued to shoot at them. But Duncan knew he had to go to Molly, and he had to do that now.

"Use my phone to let the deputies know that I'm heading to Molly's place," Duncan relayed to Joelle. "I want Luca to follow us as backup."

Of course, that meant he'd be taking Joelle with him since there wasn't time for him to get her safely into a cruiser. He got confirmation of that when he heard Molly scream again. The woman was obviously fighting for her life, and there wasn't a second to lose.

Duncan gunned the engine to get them out of there,

and he kept watch around them as he headed for the road. Thankfully, no shots came their way. That was the good news. The bad news was that could mean the shooter had stopped firing so he could go in pursuit of them.

Joelle finished a quick call to Luca to request backup and then went back to her own phone. "Molly?" she tried again.

The sounds of the struggle had stopped. No more screams. Nothing. And that tightened every muscle in Duncan's body. Hell. The sounds of her screams had been terrifying, but the silence was even worse. Because the screams meant she'd at least been alive.

He thought back to the petite, young brunette who'd been a dispatcher for about six months now. She was pregnant, and she wasn't married but had instead opted for artificial insemination to have a child. Molly's parents were dead, and since she had no siblings, she would almost certainly be alone. It was info that everyone in town knew, and it was possible that someone had used that particular info to go after her.

But why?

"This can't be a coincidence," Joelle muttered, taking the words right out of Duncan's mouth.

Yeah, Duncan was leaning that direction as well. Two pregnant women attacked on the same night in the same small town. That would, indeed, be one hell of a coincidence if the incidents weren't related. Still, it was possible that there were two forces at work here. Duncan just didn't know exactly what those two forces were right now, but he'd need to find out and fast.

When there was an attack or kidnapping involving a pregnant woman, it was usually connected to some kind of domestic dispute. In fact, the number one threat to a pregnant woman was being murdered or seriously injured by the woman's partner. But there were also those crimes that involved kidnapping or killing a pregnant woman so the baby could be taken. With Molly so close to giving birth, that was definitely a motive at the top of Duncan's list.

But that didn't explain the attack on Joelle.

She was in her fifth month of pregnancy. Still a long way from delivering their child. A kidnapper would have to hold her for months. Not exactly a comforting thought, but then none of this was anywhere near comfortable.

Duncan cranked up the speed when he reached the road and headed toward town. Since he'd known Molly his whole life, he knew where she lived and didn't have to look up her address. He just drove and tried to figure out how to make this trip as safe as possible for Joelle.

A safety she likely wouldn't want if she was thinking like a cop.

But if necessary, he'd need to remind her that she was on desk duty until the baby arrived. That wasn't a personal preference on his part simply because she was carrying his child. It was standard practice in the sheriff's office, and it was something her father would have insisted on had he still been alive.

Beside him, Joelle continued to try to get some kind of response from Molly by calling out the woman's name into her phone. Molly didn't answer. But there was a response in the form of a dead line. When she tried to call again and got the same thing, Duncan knew that someone had switched off the phone.

"I'll call dispatch to have Molly's phone tracked," Joelle told him.

He could hear the fear and nerves in every word she'd spoken. Fear that was there for a reason because they both knew that whoever was attacking Molly could have also disabled the phone, making it untraceable. Duncan hoped like the devil that hadn't happened, though, because if Molly wasn't home, the phone would be their best bet in tracking her.

Thankfully, there was no other traffic on the rural road at this hour so Duncan continued to press on the accelerator, eating up the distance between Joelle's and Molly's. Luca stayed right behind him in the cruiser.

Duncan's phone rang, and when he saw Deputy Ronnie Bishop's name on the screen, he took the call on speaker. "Is everyone all right?" Duncan immediately asked since he knew Ronnie was at Joelle's.

"So far," Ronnie quickly assured him. "No signs of the shooter, though, and there's been no gunfire since Joelle and you left. No one's attempted to get to the stolen black car, either."

If the gunman had, indeed, been coming after Joelle and him, that would mean he or she had a second vehicle. And likely a partner. Either that or the gunman had positioned a second vehicle earlier and then driven the stolen one to Joelle's. Duncan couldn't think of a good motive for a would-be killer to do that, but the reason could be a clue to who had attacked them and why.

"How many deputies are there?" Duncan asked Ronnie.

"Six, including me. The fire department is here, too, but they're holding off until they get the word from you that it's safe to try to put out the fire."

It wasn't safe. Not with a gunman, maybe two, in the area. Hell, there could be even more than that if this was some kind of coordinated attack. No way could Duncan risk the lives of his deputies and the firemen when Joelle wasn't even there. Yes, she might lose her house to the fire, but the goal was to get everyone out of this alive and then catch the SOB responsible.

"Everyone stays in their vehicles for now," Duncan instructed, "but have two of the deputies go to the end of Joelle's road and keep watch for anyone trying to sneak away from there. Two more should stay put in case the shooter isn't done. Send the other two to Molly's."

If Molly had been kidnapped, or worse, then Duncan figured he was going to need as much help as possible.

Ronnie gave a fast assurance that he'd do as Duncan asked, and they ended the call just as Duncan finally made it to the turn to Molly's. It wasn't a typical subdivision or neighborhood like in a city but rather a spattering of homes that had been built on multi-acre lots. With all the trees and natural landscape, it was more like living in the country, which made for a peaceful lifestyle.

It also meant Molly's neighbors might not have been able to see or hear what was going on.

Added to that, Duncan was well aware that her nearest neighbors were all senior citizens. That was the reason he hadn't called any of them to go check on Molly and try to stop whatever was happening. Duncan hadn't wanted to risk any of them being hurt or killed. This was definitely a situation for law enforcement.

"I want you to stay down," Duncan told Joelle, and he made sure it sounded like the order it was.

She didn't protest. Not with words, anyway. But he knew this was eating away at her. Especially since someone was threatening and maybe had already harmed someone she knew well.

Duncan sped into Molly's driveway, his gaze immediately firing all around. There were no vehicles in front of the house. Nor was there anyone in sight. Just the darkness and the milky yellow illumination coming from the porch light.

"The front door's open," Joelle murmured.

It was. Duncan had noticed that right away, but he aimed a quick scowl at Joelle to let her know if she had seen that, then it meant she wasn't staying down. Joelle muttered some profanity and slipped lower into the seat.

With Luca's cruiser squealing to a stop behind him, Duncan hurried out of the car, and while keeping watch, he ran toward the porch. He couldn't risk sitting around, waiting to see if he could figure out what was going on because at this exact moment, Molly could be inside fighting for her life.

Duncan barreled up the porch steps, taking them two at a time, and pinned his focus to the open door. If Molly's attacker was still in there, he had to be prepared in case the guy shot at him. That's why Duncan tried to listen for any sounds of a struggle or movement.

He heard nothing.

And knew that wasn't a good sign. Ditto for what he spotted on the porch just to the right side of the welcome mat.

Drops of blood.

Duncan was sure that's what it was, and cursing, he stepped around the drops and went inside. Of course, just his mere presence could contaminate the scene, but again, Molly was the priority here. He had to hold out hope that the blood belonged to her attacker, that Molly had somehow managed to fight him off and sent the SOB running.

"Molly?" he called out.

No need for him to stay quiet since there was no element of surprise here. If the attacker was still inside the house, he would have heard the car that Duncan had been driving and the cruiser. Molly would have, too, and that meant if she'd been capable of calling out for help, she likely would have already done it.

Trying to steel himself for the worst but praying for the best, Duncan went into the house, staying low and leading with his gun. His attention whipped to the right, then the left. He took in the toppled lamp on the floor, but it seemed to be the only sign of a struggle.

Room by room, he made his way through the place, recalling the time or two he'd been here with his folks when they'd visited Molly's parents. Years ago, even before Molly had been born. Duncan was thirty-seven and Molly just twenty-four so he'd been plenty old enough to recall coming here for her folks to show off their baby girl. Maybe that was one of the reasons Molly had wanted to raise her child here. Her home. A place where she'd no doubt felt safe.

That last thought twisted his gut into knots so Duncan kept moving, kept searching, all the while listening for, well, anything. In addition to being able to hear anything in the house, he also needed to make sure nothing was going on outside with Joelle and Luca. So far, he wasn't hearing or seeing anything. Nothing out of place except for that lamp.

Until he made it to one of the bedrooms.

Molly's no doubt, and there were plenty of signs of a struggle here. The bed was empty, but the covers had been dragged off, and the clock and lamp that'd almost certainly been on the nightstand were now on the floor.

"Molly?" he called out again and still got no response.

The overhead light was off, but there was a nightlight plugged in the outlet near the door to the adjoining bath. It was enough for him to see more of those blood drops.

Hell.

Duncan moved faster now, checking out the bathroom for any signs of Molly. Nothing. So he kept moving, hurrying to the other rooms. They were all empty, but he got another jolt when he saw the nursery all decked out in shades of pink. Since Joelle's and his baby was also a girl, it made the gut punch even harder.

Pushing that aside, he made his way back through the house and was careful not to touch anything. Whoever had taken Molly might have left prints or some kind of trace evidence in the struggle, and Duncan didn't want to compromise that any more than he already had.

He went back to the porch and saw that Luca was out of the cruiser and near Joelle's vehicle. The deputy immediately looked up at him, but Duncan had to shake his head.

"Molly's not here," Duncan relayed to them. "And there's blood on the porch and in the master bedroom. I want a BOLO for Molly and a CSI team in here right away."

That got Joelle coming out of the car. "There's a garden shed in the back," she said, already moving as if to head in that direction. "Molly could be in there."

Duncan cursed and went after her. "I know about the shed and was about to check it out." He was about to order her back to the car, but she spoke before he could manage to say it.

"I have to help," she insisted.

Joelle wasn't crying. She was too much of a cop for that. But her voice was shaky, and he figured that applied to the rest of her as well. Along with the mother lode of adrenaline, she was also battling the overwhelming fear that a woman they both knew had been kidnapped or killed and that the same thing had nearly happened to her.

"Stay close to me," Duncan finally agreed.

He'd make this search quick so he could get Joelle into at least some minimal cover. Then, he could take her to the sheriff's office while they regrouped and figured out their next move.

As he'd remembered, the shed was in the backyard, not far from the porch that wrapped around the entire house. Duncan made a cursory look of the area, then a quick glance into the shed just to see if by some miracle Molly was hiding there. She wasn't.

"Molly?" he called out one last time.

When he got no response, he hurried back to the car with Joelle and got her inside. "Start calling her neighbors," Duncan instructed. "I want to know if anyone saw or heard anything."

He doubted that'd been the case, though. If so, those neighbors would have already headed over. Still, it was possible that someone had heard something that would give them clues as to who had taken Molly.

There was the howl of sirens in the distance, and Duncan knew it wouldn't be long before more deputies arrived. Good. He'd have them check around the place while he got on the phone with the Texas Rangers and Highway Patrol. Both agencies would get word of the BOLO, but Duncan wanted to emphasize that Molly was pregnant and she worked for law enforcement. Molly was one of them, and that would hopefully get her the highest priority.

Duncan took out his phone, ready to get started on those calls, but he stopped when he caught some movement from the corner of his eye. He pivoted in that direction, in the same motion taking aim with his Glock. Then, he stopped when he spotted something.

The woman walking toward them.

Correction: staggering toward them.

It wasn't Molly. No, this woman was older and had graying black hair that was tangled around her face. She was barefoot and wearing a ripped shirt over stained gray yoga pants.

Duncan's first thought was this was Sandra McCullough, Joelle's mother who'd deserted her family the day her husband had been murdered. No one had seen or heard from her since. But it wasn't Sandra, and Duncan had no idea who she was.

Joelle got out of the car, taking aim as well. So did Luca, but Duncan could see both of the woman's hands, and she wasn't armed. Still, this could be some kind of ploy so he approached her with caution.

"Who are you?" Duncan demanded. "Are you hurt?" He didn't see any signs of injury, but it was possible some of the stains on her clothes were dried blood.

"I'm sorry," the woman said as she came even closer.

That put some ice in his veins. "Sorry for what?" And because it had to be asked, he added. "Are you the one who took Molly?"

She didn't answer but rather just kept walking, her feet dragging through the yard. Her eyes looked vacant. Robotic, even. As if someone had forgotten to turn on a switch. Duncan was betting she'd either been drugged or was in shock.

"This is all my fault," the woman muttered. Her voice was flat and barely a whisper. "Everything that's happening is my fault." She dropped to her knees, her gaze shifting to Joelle. "I'm so sorry, but he wants you dead."

A hoarse sob tore from her throat, and the woman collapsed into a heap on the ground.

Chapter Three

While Joelle sat in the waiting room of the emergency room of Saddle Ridge Hospital, she tried to keep her breathing level and tamp down the worry that was threatening to cloud her mind. Worry wouldn't help—not her baby, not Molly and not her. What she needed right now was for Molly to be found alive and well and for her to find answers as to what the heck was going on.

Duncan was clearly after those answers, too, and he had been on the phone nonstop since they'd arrived at the hospital with the mystery woman. The woman who'd delivered that sickening message.

I'm so sorry, but he wants you dead.

That was definitely something Joelle hadn't wanted to hear, and it'd left her with even more questions. Who was the woman and who was the *he* she'd proclaimed wanted to kill her? Was he the person who'd driven that stolen car to her house and set the fire? It was hard for her to believe that it wasn't connected, but until the woman regained consciousness, all Joelle could do was speculate and deal with her own phone calls. So far, none of those calls had given her any good news.

Plenty of bad, though.

Her house was basically in ashes now because the fire department hadn't been able to move in to try to save it since there'd been the threat of an active shooter. There were no signs of the shooter now, though. No sign of Molly, either. And the now-unconscious mystery woman had had no ID on her so they didn't even know who she was.

However, Joelle had gotten some good news, not from a call but rather the checkup she'd had shortly after Duncan and she had arrived at the hospital. Despite the traumatic situation she'd experienced, the baby was fine. The monitors had shown a strong, steady heartbeat and lots of movement—signs that had fulfilled a lot of Joelle's prayers. Her baby was okay.

Now, Joelle had to make sure she stayed that way.

The only instructions the doctor had given her was to get some rest, and Duncan had been there to hear that part. Which meant he'd soon be trying to get her off her feet. She was exhausted, no doubt about that, and exhaustion wasn't good for the baby, but neither was having shots fired at them. To make sure an attack like that didn't happen again, they needed answers fast.

Since Duncan was still on the phone, Joelle went after some of those answers by making a call to dispatch to check if there'd been any missing persons' reports in the area of someone matching their mystery woman's description. There hadn't been, but Joelle had known that was a long shot, that the woman could have come from anywhere and maybe wasn't missing at all. She could have arrived shortly before she'd staggered toward Joelle's house.

Emphasis on *staggered.*

She hadn't been steady on her feet at all and seemed dazed, perhaps even drugged. But it was also possible she had been experiencing some kind of medical emergency that had created those symptoms. If so, the woman might not have even been aware of what she was saying.

I'm so sorry, but he wants you dead.

Though she certainly hadn't seemed so dazed or drugged when she'd spoken those words. She'd seemed adamant about delivering a warning with a potential deadly outcome.

Joelle was about to text one of the deputies to see if there'd been any signs of a vehicle that the woman could have used to get to or near her place, but before she could press the number, she got an incoming call from one of her brothers, Ruston McCullough, a homicide detective with San Antonio PD.

It wasn't Ruston's first call of the morning. That initial one had come while Duncan and she were en route to the hospital. She had assured Ruston and her other brother, Slater, and their kid sister, Bree, that she hadn't been harmed, but Joelle knew they were worried about her. Knew, too, that the calls to check on her would continue until they could see her face-to-face and make sure the baby and she were, indeed, okay.

"Anything?" Ruston immediately asked. His tone was brusque as it usually was, but Joelle was aware that the question covered a lot of bases, including her own state of mind.

"No. We're still in limbo when it comes to any info that'll help." She paused, had to because of the sudden lump in her throat. "Still nothing on Molly. Someone took her, and she has to be terrified."

Joelle refused to believe it could be worse than that. She wouldn't accept that Molly could be hurt or dead. She had to cling to the hope they would somehow find her and bring her safely home.

"Any ransom demand?" Ruston questioned.

Joelle had to repeat her "no." But in a way, a ransom demand would be a positive sign. It meant she'd been taken for money and would presumably be released unharmed if the money was paid.

Ruston sighed and paused a long time. "I'm sorry about your house. You've got the keys and security code to stay at my place, but I don't want you there alone. Just hang with Duncan until I can get there. I want to keep coordinating with the Rangers to try to locate Molly."

"Keep on that," she insisted. She would have also told him she would come up with a safe place to stay, however, when Duncan ended his latest call and started her way, she put the rest of this conversation on hold. "I have to go," she told Ruston. "I'll let you know if I get any updates."

She ended the call and stood to face Duncan. He definitely didn't look to be the bearer of good news, and that caused her heart to sink again. She prayed he wasn't about to tell her Molly was dead.

"We haven't found Molly yet," Duncan immediately said, probably picking up the worst-case-scenario vibe from her expression. "Some of the reserve deputies are canvasing the area around her house to find out if anyone saw anything."

The late hour wouldn't help with that, but maybe Molly had managed to scream or something. If so, that would have already been reported, but Joelle had to hang on to the hope that they'd get a viable lead.

"The CSIs are going through Molly's house and the stolen car left at your place," Duncan continued. "They're still looking for her vehicle, too." Even though it wasn't necessary for him to identify what *her* he was referring to, he tipped his head to the exam room where the medical staff had taken the mystery woman. "She didn't have any ID on her."

"And there's no missing person's report matching her description," Joelle provided.

Duncan nodded. "Apparently, she drifted in and out of consciousness when she was in the ambulance so when we're able to speak to her, she might be able to tell us who she is. And why she issued that warning," he tacked onto that.

Yes, that was vital for the safety of their baby, and Joelle reminded herself that there were a lot of people working to get answers and make sure that *safety* happened.

"Do you think this woman and the warning are directly connected to Molly?" Joelle came out and asked.

Duncan's gaze locked with hers. Something they usually avoided because of the heat that was always there between them. Heat that came despite any and everything going on. There'd always be an intimate connection, especially now that she was carrying his child, but because she was so worried about Molly, it was easier for Joelle to shove that heat aside.

"Yes," he admitted. The sigh he added was long, heavy and weary. "That's why I made a call to the FBI. I wanted to see if they were aware of any black market baby rings or perpetrators in the area who could be targeting pregnant women. Nothing like that is on their radar, but they're checking to see if this is someone from out of state."

Joelle had tried to maintain a stoic expression, her cop face. She tried not to let the possibility of something like that give her this jolt of fear. But it did. Mercy, it did.

Duncan muttered some profanity and took hold of her arm. Probably because she looked ready to collapse. Joelle was almost certain that wouldn't happen, almost, but she allowed him to help her back into one of the chairs, and he sank down on the one beside her.

"Deep breaths," he advised her. "Count to ten. Tell me the latest names you're considering for the baby."

Part of her resented Duncan for seeing the weakness in her and knowing she needed help. Part of her also resented that such measures might be necessary to keep herself from spiraling. But the resentment was really for herself, for feeling this clawing terror all the way to the bone. Those sort of emotions didn't help. In fact, they could hurt, and she didn't want anything else that could hinder them in this investigation.

"I'll be all right," she muttered, hoping it was true.

The sound Duncan made let her know that he wasn't so sure of that at all, and she might have launched into more attempts at convincing him if her phone hadn't rang. "It's my sister again," she muttered, and even though Joelle wasn't in the mood to talk to her, she had to answer it or it would cause Bree to worry even more than she was already was.

"Bree," Joelle greeted. "I'm all right."

"So you say." Her sister's sigh was plenty loud enough for Joelle to hear. "I'll believe it when I see it. I'm coming home, but I can't get there for at least a couple of days."

Joelle groaned. Bree was a lawyer working on a special task force in Dallas, six hours away, and she knew Bree had used all her vacation time and then some when she'd come home after their father's murder and disappearance. Since Joelle figured she stood no chance whatsoever of convincing Bree she was fine and didn't need her sister to be there, she went with a different tactic.

"Everyone in the sheriff's office is tied up with the investigation," Joelle spelled out. "And right now Saddle Ridge isn't the safest place to be."

"I'm coming home," Bree insisted, and then she paused.

Sighed again. "I need to see you. There are things I want to talk to you about."

Joelle didn't like the sound of that, especially since she and her sister communicated at least weekly either by phone call or text. "Is something wrong?" Joelle came out and asked.

It was a valid question. Like her, Bree had been devastated with what had happened to their parents. Added to that, Bree had broken up with her longtime boyfriend, Luca. Then again, Luca and Bree had had an on-again, off-again thing going on since high school. Since Bree was often involved in high-profile legal cases for the state and was gone a lot, both Luca and she had had other relationships. But something had happened between Luca and Bree to make her sister pull the plug and now things were permanently off.

Or so Bree had said.

Luca wasn't offering up anything so Joelle wasn't sure what had happened. Maybe it was something similar to what had gone on between Duncan and her. Too much pain and grief. Too much guilt. Too much, period.

"I should be home by early next week," Bree added a moment later. "In the meantime, you stay safe. I love you, Joelle."

"I'll certainly try," Joelle assured her. "And I love you, too," she said, ending the call just as the door to the exam room finally opened.

It wasn't the mystery woman who came out, of course, but it was a familiar face. Dr. Chase Benton, one of the doctors who worked at Saddle Ridge General Hospital.

Dr. Benton spotted them and walked their way as Duncan and she headed to him. "Is she awake?" Duncan immediately asked.

"She is, for the moment anyway," the doctor said, but

there was caution in his voice. He stepped in front of Duncan when he started toward the exam room. "I'm well aware that you need to see her," he quickly added. "I've heard what's going on, and I understand you have to question her, but you should know that she's still unable to stay awake for more than a couple of seconds. Unable to tell me her name as well. I suspect she's been drugged, and that the drugs combined with a head injury are the reasons she's lapsing in and out of consciousness."

That wasn't a surprise to either Duncan or her, and that led them to more questions. Who'd drugged her and why? Hopefully, they'd know the answers to that soon.

"Her blood pressure is high as well," the doctor continued. "And that means when you question her, you can't push too hard. I can't give her anything right now for the blood pressure until I find out what other drugs are in her system."

Duncan groaned. "I have to push," he insisted. "Molly Radel and her baby's life could depend on it."

Dr. Benton's eyes widened. "You believe the patient had something to do with that?"

"I think the likelihood is high that there's a connection. It's possible the woman can tell us who took Molly."

Despite Duncan's use of *likelihood* and *possible*, the doctor nodded and stepped to the side. "All right, you can question her, but I have to be there. And trust me, I will pull the plug on the interview if I feel she can't handle it."

Duncan nodded, too, while he was already on the move. With Dr. Benton and Joelle right behind him, Duncan stepped into the ER room where the woman was lying on the bed. She was hooked up to a monitor and had an IV in the back of her hand. Joelle also spotted some injuries. There was a gash on the side of her head, some bruising as well and her feet were covered with cuts and scrapes.

"She obviously walked barefoot through some rough terrain," the doctor pointed out. "There was also powder on her clothes. The kind of powder you'd get from a deployed airbag."

So maybe she'd been involved in a car accident. However, that didn't explain what had happened to her shoes or why she'd ended up walking to Molly's. Or the ominous message she'd delivered.

The woman's eyes were open, and when she lifted her head, her attention went straight to them. Joelle didn't see any recognition in her expression, only wariness and confusion. Added to that, her gaze still had that dazed look she'd had when she arrived at Molly's.

"I'm Sheriff Duncan Holder," he said, stepping closer to her. He tipped his head to Joelle. "And this is Deputy Joelle McCullough. Could you tell us your name?"

The woman looked at the doctor and then shifted her attention to Joelle. "I came to see you," she muttered, her voice a ragged whisper.

That gave Joelle some hope. If the woman remembered that, then she might recall other things, too.

"You did," Joelle verified. She started to remind her of what she'd said before she collapsed but decided to press for an ID instead. "Who are you?"

She shook her head as if trying to figure that out, and then murmured. "Kate Moreland."

Duncan got out his phone as she spoke the last syllable, and he fired off a quick text, no doubt to get someone at the sheriff's office to run a background check on her.

"Kate Moreland," Joelle repeated, mentally testing out the name, but it didn't ring any bells. "You know me?"

Kate shook her head. "I know of you." Her voice broke

into a hoarse groan. She eased back onto the bed and closed her eyes. "I had to warn you."

Another positive sign that she'd remembered that. Of course, the warning she'd delivered hadn't been positive at all.

"You said someone wanted me dead," Joelle reminded her. "Who?"

She didn't open her eyes, and it was at least fifteen seconds before she answered. "My son," she finally said, and she broke down into a heaving sob. A reaction that caused the numbers on the monitor to spike.

"You need to leave," Dr. Benton insisted. "Her blood pressure's too high. Step out while I try to get her stabilized." It wasn't a request, and the doctor practically muscled them out of the room.

Duncan cursed and took out his phone. "Slater's running the background check on her. I'll see if he's got anything yet." However, Duncan's phone rang before he could call her brother.

"It's Ronnie," he relayed to her, and he put the deputy's call on speaker.

"We found a car, a dark blue Audi," Ronnie said right off. "It looks as if the driver hit the east side of the bridge and lost control. It was off the road and all the way down on the banks of the creek."

The creek was only about a half mile from Molly's, and if it did, indeed, belong to Kate, then the woman had likely been traveling from the interstate. If she'd been coming from town, then the collision would have probably happened on the west side of the bridge. Also, if she'd been coming from town, Duncan or one of the responding deputies would have spotted her on the road before she'd made it to Molly's.

"I'm running the plates now," Ronnie continued. "But

there was a purse and a phone in the vehicle. According to the driver's license, the purse's owner is Kate Moreland. She has a San Antonio address."

San Antonio was a half hour away, which meant Ruston could no doubt help with getting them any info they needed on her. And her son. Joelle wanted to know his name and why Kate had believed he might want to kill her.

"When you do a thorough search of the car," Duncan said, "check her GPS to confirm if she was heading to Molly's or Joelle's. And let me know if you find anything we can use."

Ronnie assured him that he would, and Duncan ended the call to make one to Slater. Her brother answered on the first ring.

"Kate Moreland," Slater immediately said, and he rattled off an address in San Antonio. "Age fifty-three. Divorced. No criminal record. She's a very wealthy businesswoman who owns a half dozen martial arts and workout gyms."

"You have the name of her son?" Duncan pressed.

"Yeah. Brad. Age twenty-eight, and I'm just scratching the surface on him. Why? Is he part of this?"

"Kate seems to think so," Duncan quickly verified. "She believes her son might be out to kill Joelle."

Slater cursed. "He's got a record for assault during a bar fight, but I don't see any connection to Joelle or Saddle Ridge..." His words trailed off, and he cursed again. "But his ex-wife, Shanda Cantrell, does. My dad and you arrested her nearly two years ago for reckless driving and resisting arrest. Either of you remember that?"

"I do," Duncan said.

"So do I," Joelle murmured, trying to zoom in on any info that was lingering around in her memory. The info had plenty of gaps in it so she took out her phone and started searching while she continued. "I recall Dad and Duncan bringing in a woman for those charges. They had me search her for weapons, and because she was being so combative, Dad put her in a holding cell."

"A definite yes to her being combative," Duncan agreed. "She tried to take a punch at me. And she cursed and spat at Joelle. Cursed the sheriff, too."

Slater must have pulled up the file right before she did because he was the one to add more. "She ended up pleading guilty, paid a fine and did some community service. Dad worked it out so she could do that service in San Antonio so she wouldn't miss any work at her job as a florist." Slater paused a moment. "Had she been drinking?" he asked. "Was that the reason for the reckless driving?"

"No alcohol," Joelle was able to provide. "She admitted to having been in a heated argument with someone on her phone. She was also speeding when she rammed into a mailbox, swerved and nearly hit another car." Then, she paused. Had to. Because she spotted something in the file notes. "Shanda was three months pregnant."

Both Duncan and Slater went silent, but she could hear Slater clicking away on a keyboard. "She has no children listed. Neither does Brad."

So either Shanda had miscarried or the baby had died. Either way, that might play into motive. If there was motive for Shanda, that is. Kate hadn't said a word about her ex-daughter-in-law, only her son. Maybe then, losing a child had something to do with why Kate had come here to issue that warning about Brad.

"I'll obviously want a conversation with both Shanda and Brad," Duncan insisted.

"I can arrange that," Slater volunteered. "When I call him, how much do you want him to know about his mother?"

Duncan's forehead bunched up while he gave that some

thought. Joelle definitely wanted to hear how he was going to handle this, but her phone rang, and her chest tightened when she saw Unknown Caller on the screen.

"This could be the ransom demand," Joelle muttered, answering the call on speaker and hitting the record function on her phone.

She steeled herself up to hear a snarled threat and demand from the kidnapper. But it wasn't.

"Help me," the woman said.

It was Molly.

Chapter Four

"I'll have to call you back," Duncan told Slater the moment he heard Molly's voice.

He didn't wait for Slater to respond. Duncan ended the call and went closer to Joelle.

"Where are you?" Joelle asked Molly. "Are you all right?"

Molly didn't answer, but Duncan could hear some kind of shuffling around, and several moments later, someone spoke. But this time, it wasn't Molly.

"Don't ask any questions," a man said. His voice was muffled and practically a growl. No doubt because he was trying to disguise it. Did that mean Duncan knew this person? "I made a mistake, and I'm trying to fix it."

Despite the man demanding no questions, Duncan had so many of them. Joelle no doubt did, too. But at the top of their list had to be if Molly had been harmed.

"We're listening," Duncan prompted so the man would continue.

"A big mistake," he muttered, adding some profanity. "I'll leave the woman somewhere you can find her."

Duncan jumped right on that. It wasn't the ransom demand—or any other kind of demand—he'd been expecting. "Where?"

"I'll call you once I've dropped her off, tell you where she is, and you can come and get her," the man was quick to say.

Of course, that meant the guy would probably be long gone by the time they arrived to get Molly. But this could also be a trap to draw Joelle and him out.

"Is Molly all right?" Duncan asked, hoping that Molly would be able to answer that for herself.

"She's shaken up but fine. Like I said, taking her was a mistake."

Duncan wanted to press for more. He wanted to know why kidnapping Molly had been a mistake. Had this been a case of the wrong person being taken? Had Joelle been the target? He needed answers to all of that, but he especially wanted to know whose blood was in the house and on Molly's porch. If it was Molly's, then she was more than just shaken up.

"Leave Molly somewhere now," Duncan bargained. "She and her baby need to be checked by a doctor."

Silence. For a long time. And Duncan hoped like the devil that the guy was considering that. The sooner they got Molly, the better.

"I'll call you when I call you," the man finally snarled, and he ended the conversation before Duncan could say anything else.

Duncan immediately cursed and tried to call the kidnapper back. It wasn't a surprise, though, when the guy didn't answer. Still, Duncan reminded himself that the call was a positive sign. Molly was alive, and the man who'd taken her wanted to return her.

Supposedly.

He cursed again and looked at Joelle. "He could be using Molly and her baby as bait," she muttered.

"Yeah." But Duncan didn't need to spell out the rest. He'd

have to go to Molly even if a trap was a high probability. Which it was. He'd have to go even if there was only a slim chance they'd get Molly back.

"You'll take backup," Joelle said, proving that they were thinking the same thing. "And you'll be careful."

Duncan shouldn't have felt good about her adding that last part. But he did. There'd been so many weeks of tension between Joelle and him. So much guilt. Now, though, they were on the same side again, and he realized just how much he'd missed this. He'd had a thing for her for years, that wasn't going away, but he missed working with her almost as much as he missed being with her.

Almost.

He glanced up the hall when he saw someone approaching, and his body braced. But it wasn't a threat. It was Luca who'd gone back to Joelle's after he'd escorted Duncan and her to the hospital.

"No sign of the gunman yet," Luca reported. "No other shots fired after you left the scene. How are you two? Were either of you hurt?"

"We're fine," Joelle assured him. "We just got a call from the kidnapper." She handed him her phone. "The recording of the conversation is on there, but the kidnapper claims he intends to return Molly."

That put some hope in Luca's intense brown eyes. Hope that disappeared as fast as it'd come. "You believe him?"

"Too soon to tell," Duncan muttered.

Luca's phone rang. "It's the fire department," he explained. "I'd better take this." He stepped away to do that, and Duncan turned back to Joelle.

"When the kidnapper does call back, you won't be going with me to pick up Molly," he told her.

Her mouth tightened, but she didn't argue. She had to know if this was a trap, then she was likely the intended target.

Well, maybe she was.

"You don't resemble Molly," he said, thinking out loud. "You live miles from each other. Yes, you're both pregnant, and she's a former cop, but that's about it."

Joelle nodded. "Maybe it wasn't about mistaking Molly for me but he could possibly see the kidnapping as a mistake. It's possible he didn't know she was pregnant." She paused. "Or he could have just changed his mind."

That was true, but it still didn't explain the attack on Joelle. Or maybe it did. "If someone wanted to kidnap pregnant women, there could have been two teams operating. The one that hit your place and the one that went after Molly."

Joelle made a sound of agreement but wasn't able to add anything else because the door to Kate Moreland's room opened, and Dr. Benton came out.

Benton was quick to shake his head. "You won't be able to speak to Ms. Moreland for at least a couple of hours. Maybe longer. Her blood pressure isn't stable, and she's at risk for a hypertension crisis, which could lead to a stroke or heart attack. I'll give you a call when it's safe for her to have visitors."

Duncan couldn't press to continue the interview, not when it could put the woman's life in danger. But there were also more pressing dangers than Ms. Moreland's health.

"Ms. Moreland was worried about her son, Brad," Duncan told the doctor. "She thought he might want to harm Joelle in some way. That's why she was heading to Joelle's place, but she was near Molly's when she was involved in a car crash."

A crash that might or might not have been an accident. That was yet something else Duncan would need to find out about.

"If she's right about her son, he could be dangerous," Duncan went on. "I'll keep Deputy Vanetti standing guard outside her room now," he added, motioning to Luca who was only a few feet away and still on the phone. "And I'll get a reserve deputy in to replace him." That's because Duncan needed all his best trained deputies on the investigation.

The doctor nodded and gave an uneasy glance around. "I'll alert security, too, that there could be a potential problem."

Security was basically one guard who monitored the cameras positioned in and around the hospital. Duncan didn't know who was on duty tonight, but a deputy would be the best bet to keep Kate safe.

"I'll contact a reserve deputy," Luca volunteered after the doctor had walked away, already on his phone. No doubt to call security. "And I'll get the hospital guard a photo of Brad Moreland so he can keep an eye out for him."

"Good idea," Duncan told him and added a thanks before he got Joelle moving.

"You want me to walk with you to the exit?" Luca asked.

It was tempting, but he had to shake his head. "Best to stay on Kate's door. But I will use your cruiser."

It was bullet-resistant and parked right outside the ER. A safer way to get Joelle to the sheriff's office than using her car.

Luca immediately handed over the keys, and while Joelle and Duncan started down the hall, she typed out a text. "To Slater," she explained. "I want to fill him in about what's going on."

Good idea because Slater and all the other deputies

needed to know about Kate and her son. About Shanda as well. Even though they didn't have any direct proof, the attacks on Joelle and Molly might, indeed, be related to Shanda's arrest two years ago. That was a long time to wait to act out on a grudge, and that's why they had to learn everything they could about the woman.

Duncan stopped at the ER doors and peered out into the parking lot. He didn't see any immediate threat. In fact, because of the early hour, there wasn't anyone around.

No one visible, anyway.

Of course, there was always the threat that a gunman had positioned himself to wait for them to come out. And that's why Duncan had to test the waters. Something Joelle wasn't going to like. The cruiser was close, but he wanted it as close to the ER doors as possible. That would minimize Joelle's time for being out in the open where she'd be an easy target.

"Wait here," he instructed.

Nope, she didn't like it, but she didn't voice her objection. However, she did take out her gun and started glancing around to make sure he wasn't about to be ambushed.

Duncan also took out his weapon and hurried to the cruiser. He kept an eye on Joelle as well because if she was a target, then an attacker could use this opportunity to go after her. But he held out hope that Molly's kidnapper believed her abduction to be a mistake. If so, then maybe going after Joelle had been, too, and it could mean she was no longer in danger. Duncan had to hope for the best and prepare for the worst, though, and that meant making this trip to the sheriff's office as safe as possible for her and their baby.

Thankfully, no one fired at him when he raced outside and to the cruiser, and he moved fast to bring the vehicle closer to Joelle. Duncan lifted his hand in a wait gesture, though, and didn't give her the go-ahead to move until he'd gotten back out of the cruiser first to open the passenger's side door for her and also so he could shield her as best he could.

All of these security measures had to be both a blessing and a curse for her. After all, Joelle was a good cop, as good as they came, and she was normally in the role of the protector. Added to that, it was probably especially uncomfortable for her since he was the one doing the protecting. But like him, she needed to take all available precautions for their child.

The moment Joelle was inside the cruiser, Duncan hurried back to the driver's seat, and he got them out of there fast. Again, though, he had to keep watch since it was possible for a sniper to be perched on top of one of the buildings that lined Main Street. Thankfully, they made it the six blocks without anyone trying for round two of an attack.

Duncan parked right out front, and they both hurried into the building. Which was practically empty. No surprise there since he had the deputies working the crime scenes at Molly's and Joelle's and others out looking for the gunman. The sole occupant was Carmen Gonzales, a reserve deputy who'd retired several years earlier but still made herself available for emergencies. This was definitely an emergency.

"Any word about Molly?" Carmen immediately asked.

"Nothing confirmed, but her kidnapper called and claims he'll release her," Duncan explained, and he tacked on a question of his own to that. "Are there any reports from the deputies in the field?"

Carmen shook her head. "Nothing that I didn't forward to Luca and you." She glanced down at the laptop she'd been using when Joelle and he had come in. "I'm doing the background checks on Kate Moreland, her son and his ex-wife, Shanda."

"Good. Keep on that," Duncan instructed, though he wanted to do some digging in those areas as well. "Do you have the son's contact info?"

Carmen checked the computer screen again and nodded. "I'll forward it to you. The phone number for his ex as well."

Duncan muttered a thanks and put his hand on the small of Joelle's back to get her moving first toward her desk in the bullpen where he grabbed her laptop. Then, he picked up his from his office before heading to the break room at the back of the building.

"The doctor said you should rest," he reminded her.

"I can rest and work at the same time," she was quick to respond.

Duncan had expected that and already come up with a compromise. He took her to the break room with him where there was a fairly comfortable sofa, had her sit and then handed over the laptop.

"I want you to contact the techs at the crime lab and see if they can get anything from the number Molly's kidnapper used to call us," Duncan instructed. "That's priority."

Even though both of them knew that was a long shot. The kidnapper had probably used a burner that couldn't be traced. Still, they might get lucky.

"After that, if you're not ready to get some actual sleep, I need any and all preliminary reports from the CSIs and fire department," he continued.

"I won't be ready to sleep," she assured him. "Not with the adrenaline still burning through me."

Yeah, he knew all about adrenaline overload. Hard to come down from that, and when you did, it was a crash.

Joelle would no doubt soon be exhausted. Maybe enough that she'd actually grab a nap.

He went to the small fridge in the corner and took out two bottles of water and one of Joelle's yogurt cups she kept stocked. He set one of the waters, the yogurt and a spoon on the end table next to her.

"Also, if you still have any bandwidth left after dealing with the techs and getting the reports, go through the file of Shanda's arrest. See if there are any red flags that could have predicted something like this."

It wasn't busy work, and Joelle knew that because she got started on it right away. All were necessary steps in the investigation. So was what Duncan had to do next. Despite the fact it was barely five in the morning, he used the contact info Carmen had just emailed him and called Brad Moreland. There was no answer for four rings, and just as Duncan thought the call might go to voice mail, someone finally answered.

"What?" a man snarled, and judging from the grogginess in his voice, Duncan had woken him up.

"I'm Sheriff Duncan Holder from Saddle Ridge. FYI, this call is on speaker, and I have a deputy listening. Are you Brad Moreland?"

The man cursed. "Saddle Ridge," he spat out like venom. "Yeah, this is Brad Moreland, and anything you want to say to me should go through my lawyer. We're going through with the lawsuit for what you did to my wife."

"Your ex-wife," Duncan corrected. "And what lawsuit?" He figured he'd get that out of the way before bringing up the reason for this call.

"My wife," Brad snapped. "Shanda and I are reconciling. And as for the lawsuit, you'll soon know all about that because we're filing a civil suit for my wife's unlawful arrest and detainment. An arrest and detainment that was so traumatic she ended up miscarrying."

Bingo. There it was. The motive all spelled out. Though it did seem odd that they'd file a civil suit, which would draw attention to themselves. That could mean they weren't behind the attack and Molly's kidnapping. Or else they wanted to use the civil suit as a sort of reverse psychology. Why go after them physically when they were already going the legal route?

"We're going to sue you and your department into the ground," Brad threatened. "And then we'll go after your personal assets. You and your deputies aren't above the law, Sheriff." Again, he used that venomous tone for the last word.

Since Shanda's arrest had been justified, Duncan seriously doubted there'd be a payout of any kind, but a civil suit was an annoyance since he would still have to defend the actions the former sheriff had taken. That would in turn stir up bad memories for Joelle.

One look at her face confirmed it was already doing that.

"You and the deputies are going to pay for—"

"I'm calling about your mother, Kate Moreland," Duncan interrupted.

Brad clearly hadn't expected him to say that because it stopped his tirade, and after a few seconds of silence, the man muttered, "What about her?" There was concern, but then the anger returned. "Did you come up with some reason to arrest her?"

"No." Duncan took a moment to consider what he intended, and didn't intend, to say. "She was involved in a car accident and was taken to the hospital."

Brad cursed. "Is she alive?"

"She is." And he waited to see how Brad would react to

that. If Brad did, indeed, have criminal intentions as his mother claimed, then the man might have wanted the news that the car crash had been fatal.

"I need to see her," Brad insisted. "Where is she?"

"She's in the hospital and in protective custody."

There was some more cursing. "*Your* protective custody. This from the sheriff's office that killed my child and wrecked my life—"

"It's odd that you'd mention someone being killed because that's what your mother claimed you wanted to do."

That brought on the silence. "You're lying."

"I have witnesses," Duncan pointed out.

Brad huffed. "Witnesses who you coached no doubt because you want to get ahead of the lawsuit and try to defame me."

"I didn't know about the lawsuit before I called you. Now, explain why your mother would accuse you of plotting to kill a cop." Duncan made sure that wasn't a suggestion but rather an order from a sheriff.

"I have no idea." Now there was plenty of defensiveness in Brad's voice. "You said she was in a car accident so maybe she got a head injury and was confused."

Duncan hadn't missed the fact that Brad hadn't asked about his mother's injuries right from the start. Most people did once they understood their loved one was alive. Brad had demanded to see her, but he hadn't pressed about her condition.

"Is my mother in the hospital there in Saddle Ridge?" Brad finally said after a long silence. "If so, I can be there in under an hour."

"She can't have visitors. Doctor's orders. But even if she could, I won't let you in to see her unless I'm convinced your mother was wrong about you wanting to kill one of my deputies."

"Deputy Joelle McCullough." Brad said her name like profanity. "She was one of the cops who arrested my wife. Oh, her dad was the head honcho in that, but he's dead so the lawsuit will be aimed mainly at his daughter and the other cops involved. Molly Radel and Ronnie Bishop."

Everything inside Duncan went on alert, and he mouthed for Joelle to send Ronnie a heads-up about being a possible target.

"It's interesting that out of the three people you just named," Duncan continued with Brad, "one was kidnapped and the other attacked. According to your mom, she specifically came to Saddle Ridge to warn Deputy McCullough."

Brad's next round of profanity was quick and raw. "Like I said, my mother was mistaken. Sure, I've talked about Deputy McCullough and Deputy Radel but I'll go after them in the courts for what they did. I'm not on some vendetta."

"So, you have an alibi for the past five hours?" Duncan fired back.

"I was in bed at my house. Alone," Brad tacked onto that in a mutter. "That doesn't mean I did those things."

Maybe. But it didn't look good, not with his mother accusing him and with no alibi. "I want you here at the Saddle Ridge Sheriff's Office in three hours. That'll give you time to arrange for your lawyer to come with you."

"You better believe I'll have a lawyer. And I'll expect to see my mother when I'm there."

"You can expect it, but you might not get it," Duncan snarled right back. "Be here in three hours," he repeated, and he ended the call.

Duncan immediately fixed his gaze on Joelle, prompting her to give her take on the phone call.

"Brad's angry enough to come after Molly and me. And he has plenty of money to hire someone to orchestrate the attacks," she amended and then paused. "But if he hired that gunman and the kidnapper, then why didn't he establish an alibi for himself?"

Yeah, that was the thing that stood out for Duncan, too. "Maybe Brad didn't know his mom was going to rat him out. He also might not have thought we'd connect the kidnapping and attack to what happened to his ex-wife nearly two years ago."

Still, a guilty person should have thought of those angles and covered his butt. Brad hadn't. Was that cockiness, sloppy work or was he actually innocent?

Joelle's phone dinged with a text, and she sighed when she read it. "While you were talking to Brad, I texted the tech guys with the kidnapper's phone number. They obviously took me at my word when I said it was high priority because they checked it right away. It's a burner, and it's no longer in service."

Duncan went with a sigh of his own, even though it was expected news.

"Of course, the tech guys will keep searching to see if they can link it back to anyone," she added.

That was standard operating procedure, but it was a rarity when they found those links. Still, it was all they had at the moment.

"I'm hoping the kidnapper will arrange for us to pick up Molly before Brad comes in for his interview," Duncan said, and he checked the time. "Why don't you try to get some rest—" He stopped when his phone rang. Unknown caller. And his heart raced at the possibility of this being the kidnapper who was using a different phone.

"Sheriff Holder," Duncan answered. He hit record and

put the call on speaker. But it wasn't a man's voice who greeted him.

"Sheriff," a woman said. It definitely wasn't Molly, either. "I'm Shanda Cantrell. I just got off the phone with Brad, and he was very upset."

Duncan would have preferred for this call to be about Molly and her release, but he'd intended to call Shanda so this saved him the step of having to get her number.

"A lot of people are upset right now," Duncan verified. "And by the way, I have you on speaker, and one of my deputies is listening. I'm also recording this conversation."

That brought on a couple of moments of silence. "All right," Shanda finally said. "I'm calling because Brad told me his mother was delusional and talking out of her head," Shanda went on. "Kate accused Brad of intending to commit a crime."

"Did he?" Duncan asked, figuring that was the fastest way to cut to the heart of this conversation.

Shanda didn't gasp or make a sharp sound of surprise. Instead, she sighed. "No. Not that I know of," she tacked onto that.

Interesting. Those weren't the words of a woman jumping to defend her ex-husband. "But it's possible he committed a crime," Duncan pressed.

"Not that I know of," she repeated, and this time there was an admonishment to her tone. "I can tell you that the relationship between Kate and Brad is strained right now, so if Kate sustained a head injury or something, that might have caused her to say what she did."

Duncan disregarded the last part of that and went for the meat of the remark. "Strained how? Why?"

Shanda sighed again. "It's because of me. Brad wants to get back together and Kate loathes me."

When Shanda didn't add more, Duncan went with a prompt. "Brad wants to get back together. How about you? How do you feel about that?"

"It's complicated." Shanda groaned. "I know that's a cliché, but in our case, it's true. Brad and I share a very painful past."

Duncan could relate, what with Joelle and him blaming themselves for not stopping her father's murder. So the cliché of complicated fit them, too.

"I'm not sure if Brad and I will be getting back together or not," Shanda finally admitted. "It won't happen unless he's willing to get the counseling he needs. So far, Brad hasn't shown up at any of the appointments I've scheduled for him."

Maybe because the man didn't want to forget the past but rather get revenge for it.

"Counseling has really helped me," Shanda went on. "I had a difficult childhood, and according to my therapist, that created some anger issues. Issues, too, with using people. And, yes, I used Brad. Or rather I used his money. Don't get me wrong. I loved him, and that's why I married him, but I wasn't careful with his money."

Shanda sounded a lot different than she had from the night she'd been arrested. Maybe the counseling had worked. Or maybe this was all an act.

"Why does Kate loathe you?" Duncan asked, circling back to what Shanda had said earlier.

"This is all very personal," Shanda muttered.

"You bet it is," Duncan snarled. "Someone tried to kill one of my deputies and kidnapped a former deputy who's now a dispatcher. For me, that's as personal as it gets, and if you have any information that can help me find the person responsible, then spill it."

"Yes," the woman said, her voice heavy with emotion now. "Brad told me about that, and he thinks because of what Kate said, he's now a suspect in those crimes."

"He is a suspect," Duncan verified. "And you're a person of interest. In fact, I'll need you to come into the Saddle Ridge Sheriff's Office for an official interview. When we're done talking, go ahead and arrange for that. Bring your lawyer if you want, but I expect you in this morning. The earlier, the better."

"I see," Shanda said in a whisper. "You believe the attack and the kidnapping are connected to what happened to me nearly two years ago."

"Are they?" Duncan was quick to ask.

"No, I don't think so." She paused. "Look, I understand you have a job to do, but that incident was very painful for me. I had a miscarriage, and since I couldn't deal with the grief of losing my child, I fell apart. It ruined my marriage."

Duncan listened for any signs of bitterness and rage, but he didn't pick up on anything. What was there was the pain and grief of trauma. Then again, maybe that's what Shanda wanted him to hear.

"As I said, I've gone through counseling," Shanda went on. "Lots and lots of it. It's helped, but Brad seems stalled in that deep rut of loss over our baby. You see, I'd had a hard time getting pregnant and gone through many fertility treatments. The pregnancy was a miracle, and it was snatched away."

Now there was some bitterness, but Duncan figured it was a drop in the bucket to what Brad had revealed.

"I understand Brad has filed a civil lawsuit over what happened," Shanda went on. "I'm trying to talk him out of that because I don't think that will help with his healing. He needs to heal," she emphasized.

Duncan had to wonder just how "broken" Brad was. Maybe Kate was dead-on when she'd accused her son of going after Joelle.

"Any idea why Brad would wait two years to file the lawsuit?" he pressed.

Shanda sighed. "He's talked about it for a while, months. And I know he interviewed several lawyers before he finally found one who actually encouraged him to go through with it."

So, Brad had shopped around to find someone who had told him what he wanted to hear. And once Brad had that approval, maybe he did more than just start a legal battle. Maybe he decided to get full on revenge.

"Could Brad have been responsible for the attack and kidnapping?" Duncan came out and asked.

"I don't want to believe he is," Shanda admitted. Then, she stopped and muttered something Duncan didn't catch. "I'll contact my lawyer and see if he can meet me right away so we can go to the sheriff's office together. As soon as I have a time for our arrival, I'll let you know."

"I want you in before ten o'clock," Duncan insisted.

"I'll let you know," Shanda repeated, and then she ended the call.

Duncan put his phone away and began to process everything he'd just heard. Judging from the way Joelle's forehead had bunched up, she was doing the same.

"Shanda believes Brad could be guilty," Joelle concluded. "Along with Kate's statement, maybe that's enough for us to get access to Brad's financial records to see if he hired the gunman and the kidnapper?"

"Maybe," Duncan muttered, but he could already hear Brad's lawyer putting up an argument about that. An argument he might win since Kate's own mental state couldn't be verified right now. Still, it was worth a try.

Duncan texted the assistant district attorney to put in the request. He'd have to follow that up with some paperwork, but he might be able to get enough out of Kate and Shanda to justify the warrant.

"You want to try to get some rest now?" Duncan asked her after he'd finished his text.

Joelle opened her mouth, no doubt to argue, but was cut off by the sound of footsteps. Moments later, Carmen appeared in the doorway.

"There's a PI here to see you," Carmen said. "Al Hamlin."

Duncan repeated the name, but it didn't ring any bells. Joelle shook her head to indicate she didn't recognize it, either.

"Did he say what he wants?" Duncan asked.

Carmen nodded. "He claims he knows who kidnapped Molly and tried to kill Joelle. And he says he has proof."

Chapter Five

Joelle slowly got to her feet, her attention fixed on Carmen. She immediately had a bad thought, that this was one of the gunmen using this visit as a ploy to come after Duncan and her again. The concern must have shown on her face, too, because Carmen spoke right up.

"Hamlin didn't set off the metal detector," Carmen pointed out, "but Luca's back, and he frisked him. He was armed with a Glock that he's licensed to carry, but Luca is holding onto that and keeping an eye on him." She shifted her gaze to Duncan. "Do you want to see him, or should Luca interview him?"

"Oh, I want to see him," Duncan assured her. "Take him to interview room one. Joelle and I will be in there in a minute or two."

Carmen nodded, stepped away and then backtracked. "While Luca was frisking him, I ran a quick background on Hamlin. He is a PI from San Antonio but currently living in Austin, and he's twenty-three. That's all I have on him right now, and I'll dig for more, and if anything comes up while you're talking to him, I'll let you know."

"Thanks," Duncan said. "Dig, but finding Molly is the top priority, and I want you to sit on the lab to get the results on the blood that we found at Molly's place. So, don't spend much energy on Hamlin because this visit might turn out to be nothing," he added in a mutter.

Joelle knew Duncan was right about both things. Molly being the priority and this turning out to be nothing. Crackpots surfaced all the time during investigations, and even though there hadn't been that much time between this PI showing up and the attack and Molly's kidnapping, word of it would have already gotten out. Still, Joelle felt herself clinging to the hope that this Allen Hamlin could give Duncan and her some much-needed answers.

"I won't insult you by asking if you're up for doing this interview," Duncan told her once Carmen had left. "But if you want to keep on the searches you're doing, I can handle Hamlin solo."

"I want to hear what he has to say," Joelle was quick to let him know. Oh, yes. That hope was burning bright and hot in her.

Duncan studied her a couple of seconds, not with the heat that was sometimes in his eyes when he looked at her. All right, there was some heat. Always was, but Joelle was certain he was trying to make sure she was holding up okay. She was barely holding on and now battling the dreaded adrenaline crash, but there was no way she would sit this one out.

He finally nodded and tipped his head toward the interview room just down the hall. Judging from the sounds of footsteps and voices, Carmen was already escorting the PI there.

Because Joelle was behind Duncan, she didn't get her first glimpse of Hamlin until they were in the room with him. He looked even younger than twenty-three and was wearing khakis and a white button-down shirt. His short cropped hair was a pale blond. Actually, pale described the rest of him, too, what with his light skin tone and gray eyes. He had a thick envelope tucked under his arm.

"Let me know if you need anything," Carmen muttered to Duncan before she left them.

"Sheriff Holder," the man immediately said, and he extended his hand for Duncan to shake. Duncan did, but before Hamlin had released his grip, he looked at Joelle. "Deputy McCullough. I'm Al Hamlin."

Joelle was a little uneasy that Hamlin could identify them when she was reasonably sure she'd never seen him before. "Have we met?" Joelle came out and asked.

Hamlin shook his head. "I followed news of your father's murder so that's how I knew who you were. Both of you and the other deputies were mentioned in the press a lot."

Father's murder. No way for her not to react to that, but Joelle tried to mask the quick punch of grief. But Hamlin was right about the press. No one in her family or the sheriff's office had escaped the publicity.

"Thanks for seeing me so early," Hamlin said, glancing at both Duncan and Joelle. "You're going to want to hear what I have to say."

Duncan motioned for Hamlin to take a seat, and when he did, Duncan and she sat across from him. "You told my deputy that you had information about two crimes that were committed a few hours ago."

"I do." Hamlin handed Duncan the envelope. "There's a lot of information in there so I'll try to summarize and hit the high points. Five months ago when Sheriff McCullough was murdered, he was investigating a missing pregnant teenager."

"Mandy Vernon," Duncan automatically supplied while he opened the envelope. He took out what appeared to be police reports.

"Yes," Hamlin agreed. "Some thought Mandy had just run away because she wasn't getting along with her folks or her boyfriend, but Sheriff McCullough thought she might have been kidnapped or lured into the hands of someone who wanted her for the baby she was carrying."

Joelle knew that was also true. Her father had been insistent that something bad had happened to Mandy.

"I believe Sheriff McCullough was right," Hamlin went on, and then he stopped and took a long breath as if steeling himself up. "A month ago, my own sister, Isla, went missing. She's seventeen and was seven months pregnant at the time she disappeared. I swear on my life that Isla wouldn't have just left. Like Mandy, I believe someone took her for the baby."

Joelle glanced at the reports again. "Do you have proof?"

"Circumstantial but yes, there's proof," Hamlin insisted. "Over the past year, eight pregnant teenage girls have gone missing in the state, and none has been seen or heard from since." He leaned in, putting his arms on the table, and he looked straight at Joelle. "I believe there's a black market baby ring operating, and that your father found something that could have gotten him killed."

This wasn't a total news flash. Joelle, Duncan and everyone in law enforcement in Saddle Ridge had looked at that connection since it was a case that had occupied a lot of her father's time. But if her dad had actually found anything big related to the investigation, he hadn't put it in his reports. Nor had he mentioned it to anyone. Since three of his kids were cops, Joelle thought he would have told them.

If he'd gotten the chance, that is.

It was possible he'd been murdered before he could reveal something he'd learned.

"Bottom-line this," Duncan said, holding up the one-inch

thick stack of papers he'd taken from the envelope. "Is there proof of any kind for who killed Sheriff McCullough? And for the attack on Deputy McCullough and the kidnapping of the dispatcher?"

Joelle expected the PI to hedge and repeat his *circumstantial*. But he didn't.

"Yes," Hamlin stated, and he gathered his breath again. "Since Isla went missing, I've been digging, and talking to every informant I could. One name kept popping up when people would whisper about a black market baby ring." He paused a heartbeat. "Kate Moreland."

Of all the names Joelle had thought he might say, that wasn't one of them. "Kate?" she questioned.

Hamlin gave a firm nod. "Don't ask me how I got access to her financial records, but something doesn't add up. The woman's bringing in a lot more money than her businesses."

Joelle scowled, and she was certain Duncan was doing the same. "I will ask how you got her financials," Duncan stated, "because if you obtained them illegally, then you don't have proof."

The PI muttered some profanity and shook his head. "The proof is there for someone who can get it through legal channels. I took some shortcuts because I wanted to see if there were any red flags, if this woman could possibly be the person responsible for the disappearance of my sister and other teenage girls. I believe she is," he added with what sounded to be absolute certainty.

"Spell it out for me," Duncan ordered.

Joelle figured Duncan wasn't forgetting about those short cuts that Hamlin had admitted to taking. He'd no doubt get back to those, but if Kate did have some part in Molly's kidnapping, then that was the priority here.

"I have a statement from two women who say that Kate Moreland brokered the sale of their babies," Hamlin went on.

"Their names and details are in here?" Duncan asked, motioning toward the papers again.

"They are." Now Hamlin paused, and some of his enthusiasm waned. "But those incidents happened over ten years ago. There are some more recent," he was quick to add. "However, those women wouldn't go on record."

Playing devil's advocate, Joelle tried to see how this all might have played out. "Isn't it possible that Kate didn't broker the sale of the babies but rather just put the teenagers in contact with prospective adoptive parents?"

Though, so far, Joelle hadn't come across any reference to Kate having done that sort of thing. Still, info like that didn't usually turn up in background checks unless there had been something illegal about it.

"Kate might try to say that," Hamlin answered, "but she'd be lying. The girls said Kate paid them five thousand for the babies."

"Is there any kind of concrete proof of that?" Duncan asked.

"The statements from the girls." Hamlin's voice turned hard, and he huffed. "I figure Kate's been doing this for years, and that she then sells the babies for a whole lot more than five grand." He paused, looked Joelle straight in the eyes. "I also believe when she couldn't find a readily available teenager to give up their kid, then Kate had pregnant adults kidnapped. And I think that's what your father uncovered."

Part of Joelle wanted to latch on to this since it would be a lead not only in Molly's kidnapping but also her father's murder. But as working theories went, it wasn't nearly as strong as Brad's and maybe Shanda's motive. Or what had happened to her father. Because maybe Brad or Shanda had had her dad killed because of the arrest and miscarriage.

Maybe Kate had the same motive as her son.

But then why would the woman have shown up proclaiming Brad was behind the attacks? That didn't make sense, unless…

Joelle's mind followed that through. If Kate was, indeed, guilty of everything that Hamlin was saying, she might want to set up her son to take the blame. But certainly, there'd be someone else, someone not in the woman's gene pool, to try to frame.

"Read the files," Hamlin said after another huff. "You'll see the connections, and you'll see that Kate is guilty."

Duncan made a sound that could have meant anything. He certainly didn't jump on the "Kate did this" bandwagon.

"I'll definitely read through all of this," Duncan assured him, "and I'll want to talk to the two women who gave you their statements about selling their babies to Kate."

Duncan stood, signaling an end to the meeting, and Hamlin clearly didn't approve of what he obviously thought was a brush-off.

"Kate did this," Hamlin snarled. His gaze fired to Joelle. "Arrest her if you want your father's killer behind bars."

"If Kate did it, trust me, she'll be arrested," Joelle confirmed.

That brought on another huff from Hamlin, and he stood and stormed out. They followed him to make sure he did leave the building. After all, everything Hamlin had just told them could have been done to get closer to them, to get them to let down their guard.

Because Hamlin could be one of the gunmen who'd attacked her earlier.

They went into the bullpen, and Hamlin didn't linger. He went straight past Carmen and Luca and out the door.

"Did he actually have proof of anything?" Luca immediately wanted to know.

Duncan lifted the papers. "To be determined. Until we know for sure, though, call the deputy who's guarding Kate Moreland and tell him or her to keep a very close eye on the woman. I doubt Kate's in any shape to leave, but I want to make sure she stays put." His gaze slid to Hamlin who was now on the sidewalk. "And tell the deputy to make sure that guy doesn't get into her room."

Luca glanced at Hamlin, too, and took out his phone to make the call.

Duncan shifted his attention to Carmen. "Get me anything you can find on Hamlin and Kate Moreland. Use the techs to help with that, but I need thorough background checks on both of them."

Carmen nodded and hurried back to her desk.

Joelle looked at the papers. "I can start going through those."

Duncan hesitated, and she knew why. There was probably a lot in there about her father's murder. A lot that would take jabs at some still raw, painful memories.

"It needs to be done," was all Joelle said, and Duncan handed over half the papers to her. He'd almost certainly be poring through the other half.

They went back to the break room but had barely made it inside when Joelle's phone rang. Her heart jolted when she saw *Unknown Caller* on the screen, and she nearly dropped the papers when she fumbled to answer it.

"Joelle," a woman said.

Molly.

Joelle fumbled the papers again to put the call on speaker. "Molly."

Since her voice had way too much breath and hardly any sound, Joelle repeated the woman's name. Duncan sprang into action, taking out his phone and contacting tech so they could try and trace the call.

"Are you okay?" Joelle asked Molly. "Where are you?"

Molly didn't answer right away, but Joelle could hear someone muttering in the background. Even though she couldn't make out the words, she guessed it was the kidnapper giving Molly instructions about what not to say.

"I'm not hurt," Molly finally answered. "And the baby's moving and kicking so I think she's fine, too."

Joelle had so many things she wanted to ask, but she blurted out the first thing that popped into her head. "There was blood at your house."

"It's not mine," Molly said, but then stopped when there was more muttering in the background.

Duncan's gaze flashed to Joelle, and then he fired off a text. And she knew why. If the blood wasn't Molly's, then it likely belonged to the kidnapper, and they could use it to identify him.

"I'm to tell you that he's releasing me in a couple of hours," Molly went on several moments later. "But you're to send him ten thousand dollars to this account." She read off a series of numbers, and Duncan typed them into the notes on his phone. "You can get the money from my savings. I have an inheritance from my grandmother, and once the money's in the account, he'll call you with the location where he's dropping me off."

Ten thousand. That wasn't a huge ransom so maybe the kidnapper just wanted some cash to get away. Joelle was betting that the account would be offshore and not traceable. But they still had the blood.

"He also said I was to tell you not to look for him," Molly added. "Please don't look for him," she said, her voice breaking into a sob. "I just need this to be over, and it won't be if he gets spooked. I need to come home."

"We'll get you home," Duncan promised, but he was talking to the air because the call had already ended.

Duncan took her phone and immediately tried to call Molly back. There was no answer, and Joelle suspected in a minute or two the burner phone would be disabled.

A flood of emotions slammed through Joelle. The relief, the fear, all mixed together with the adrenaline crash. It was a bad combination because she started to shake. She headed toward the sofa so she could drop down onto it, but Duncan pulled her into his arms.

"We will get her home," he repeated, and he eased her even closer to him. Until they were right against each other.

Joelle knew she should move away. But she couldn't. She needed this. Needed Duncan. Even though there'd be a high price to pay for it. This kind of closeness could lead to dangerous feelings. Ones that would drown her in guilt because Duncan was the ultimate reminder that she hadn't saved her father. That she might have been able to stop him from dying or her mother from vanishing if she hadn't been with Duncan.

"I'm okay," she managed to say.

It wasn't anywhere close to the truth, but when the heat came, swirling in with the other emotions, Joelle forced herself to move. Not far. Just one step back, and she made the mistake of looking up and into Duncan's eyes.

Yes, the heat was there. But there was so much more. He was worried about her. Heck, she was worried about herself, about what the stress of this was doing to their baby. The best way to minimize that worry, though, was to try and forget the heat and focus on getting Molly safely home.

"I can transfer the money into that account," she said. Her voice was still shaky. So was the rest of her, but Duncan must have realized, too, that the work was what they both needed now. "I can get it from my savings so we don't have to go through the bank to get it from Molly's."

"Use the sheriff's office funds and instruct the bank to delay releasing the money," Duncan told her. "The kidnapper will see the funds deposited and maybe go ahead and release Molly. Once we have her, we can try to trace the kidnapper's location when he or she attempts to withdraw or transfer the money."

Like her, he didn't seem hopeful of that happening, but they had to check and double check. Even if Molly was safely returned, a serious crime had been committed. The kidnapper, and anyone who hired him, should pay and pay hard.

Since Joelle had never done a transfer like this, it took her several minutes to work through the process of it. While she did that, Duncan called the tech who'd been trying to trace the call. They were both still busy with their tasks when Carmen appeared in the door. She had her laptop balanced in the crook of her arm and continued to read whatever was on the screen until Joelle and Duncan finished.

"The kidnapper was using another burner," Duncan said. "Couldn't be traced, and like the other, it's already been disconnected." He glanced at Joelle. "Did the transfer go through?"

Joelle nodded, and she looked at Carmen. "The kidnapper called again and had Molly tell us that he wanted ten grand."

"Is Molly okay?" Carmen immediately asked.

"She said she was," Joelle relayed. "I hope that's true."

"So do I," the other deputy muttered, and she turned her attention back to her laptop.

"Please tell me you have something on the blood that was found at Molly's," Duncan said to Carmen.

"No. Luca's calling about that now. But I got a preliminary report on Hamlin. Since his sister went missing, he's focused only on that. No other clients."

Duncan huffed and put his hands on his hips. "It's hard to earn an income when you don't have clients."

"He inherited life insurance money from his parents who died in a car accident three years ago. It was about half a million, so I'm guessing he lives off that and apparently devotes all his time to finding his sister. There's no sign of her, by the way," Carmen added. "But Austin PD believes she ran away with her then boyfriend since he went missing, too."

"Is there anything in that prelim report to indicate that Hamlin could have been behind the kidnapping and attack on Joelle?" Duncan asked.

"No criminal record or anything like that, but I'll keep digging. I should be able to get access to the background that would have been done on him to get his PI license. That would give us a bigger picture of him."

"Do that," Duncan said just as his phone rang.

Joelle immediately got to her feet, and everything inside her went tight again until she remembered the kidnapper would likely be calling her number, not Duncan's.

"It's Dr. Benton," Duncan relayed, answering the call. "I'm putting you on speaker so my deputies can hear. I hope you're about to tell me we have the green light to question Kate."

"Not yet. She's sedated, and I want her to stay that way

for at least another hour or two," the doctor explained. "I'm calling because I got back her tox results, and I thought you'd want to know."

"I do," Duncan verified. "She was drugged?"

"There were traces of a prescription sleep aid in her system. Doxepin. Traces," the doctor emphasized. "There certainly wasn't enough of it to cause unconsciousness."

Joelle frowned, and she waited for Duncan to ask the question she knew had to be on his mind. "Do you think she faked her symptoms?"

"Hard to say, but it's possible she had some kind of allergic reaction. I'll be checking for that. When I checked her online medical records, there weren't any allergies listed. Not only that, she's been prescribed this particular sleep aid for years. Still, it's possible the drug in combination with something else caused the disorientation and the unconsciousness. As I mentioned earlier, that *something else* could have caused the car accident."

Yes, that could explain it. Joelle recalled seeing the cut on the woman's head.

"How serious is that injury to the head?" Duncan wanted to know.

"We ran a CT scan, and there was no obvious signs of brain damage or even a concussion," Dr. Benton was quick to say. "Once the patient is out of sedation for her blood pressure, I'll do some neuropsychological evals since a CT scan doesn't always confirm a concussion. It's possible, too, that the trauma of the car accident is playing into her reactions."

Duncan's expression let Joelle know he was skeptical about that. But why would Kate have pretended to be drugged? The woman had literally staggered onto Molly's property and then collapsed. Why do that?

Unfortunately, Joelle immediately came up with an answer. A bad one. If Hamlin was right about Kate being a criminal, then maybe her behavior was meant to make her look innocent while also pointing the blame at Brad. But Kate could have also done this to get closer to them. So she could try to do to Joelle what was done to Molly. Still, that seemed an extreme ploy especially since the woman hadn't been on their radar before she'd shown up at Joelle's.

"I still want to talk to Kate once she's awake," Duncan stressed. "I'll also want the results of those tests you mentioned."

"Is she a suspect in the attacks?" the doctor asked.

"A person of interest, but some information has come to light that I need to question her about. It could be related to the murder of Sheriff McCullough."

"I see," the doctor muttered after a long pause. "I'll let you know the moment you can talk to her," he assured Duncan.

When the call ended, Duncan stared at his phone for a moment before his gaze shifted to Joelle. "We really need to dig into Kate's background."

She couldn't agree more. "I'll do that and check for any updates from the CSIs, techs and lab." They had a lot of cogs going in this particular investigative wheel, and any one of them could provide them with answers.

Maybe, *finally*, answers about her father.

Joelle couldn't fully process that. Couldn't deal with the emotions that would bring. She had to rely on the work not only bringing a closure to the case but to help her find the mental healing that had so far eluded her.

Of course, the healing would only be partial. She would still need to know what had happened to her mother.

"I'll get that PI background report on Hamlin," Carmen said, and she headed back toward the bullpen.

Joelle forced her hands to steady on the laptop keyboard while she checked for those updates. There was one which had come a little too late to say that the blood at Molly's hadn't been hers. That comparison had been fairly simple because her DNA was on file. Now that Molly had been ruled out, the sample would have to make its way through the database to see if there was a match.

Since Duncan was already at work on his laptop. Joelle didn't relay the blood news. She just moved on to the next task—finding out if Kate Moreland had something to hide. The basics about the woman meshed with what they had already learned. She owned a lot of businesses she had inherited from her father who'd died a decade earlier.

Joelle continued looking into the woman's personal life. Divorced, ex-husband deceased and only one child. Brad. There were plenty of social media posts about Kate's fundraisers, parties and such, but there were no recent mentions about Brad. Joelle had to go back five months to find them, and she immediately saw a pattern. Before five months ago, Kate had posted many photos of her and her son together. Then, nothing.

Joelle had to wonder about the timing since her father had been murdered five months ago.

From across the room, Duncan's phone rang, immediately getting her attention since it could be news about Molly. "It's Ruston," he said.

She automatically sighed. Her brother was no doubt checking on her again and probably thought she'd try to gloss over how she was doing. Which she would have done. No way did she want her brothers worrying about her any more than they already were.

"Ruston," Duncan greeted, and unlike the other calls he'd been getting, he didn't put this one on speaker.

Joelle couldn't hear what her brother said, but whatever it was had Duncan slowly getting to his feet. "Hell," he spat out.

That caused Joelle to stand as well, and she went to Duncan. "What's wrong? What happened?" And too many worst-case scenarios started flying through her head.

Duncan lifted his finger in a "wait a second" gesture. "You're sure it's her?" Duncan asked Ruston.

The answer he got caused Duncan to curse again, and then he added, "Yeah, call me the moment you know anything." He pressed end call, and he looked at her.

"Is it Molly?" she managed to ask, even though Joelle's throat had seemingly clamped shut.

Duncan shook his head. "It's Shanda Cantrell. She's been murdered."

Chapter Six

Duncan drank more coffee and paced with his phone anchored between his shoulder and ear while he waited for Joelle's brother, Detective Ruston McCullough, to take him off hold and give him the update on Shanda's murder.

It'd been over an hour since Ruston's initial call to deliver the shocking news that Shanda had been found dead just outside her house in San Antonio, and Ruston had only been able to provide the basics. Apparently, Shanda's lawyer had found her dead when he'd gone to her place. Cause of death had likely been a gunshot wound to the chest.

"Sorry about the wait," Ruston said when he came back on the line. "I just got another call from the CSIs out at Shanda's house, and I wanted to hear what they had to say so I could pass it along to you. And Joelle. She's there, right?"

"I am," Joelle verified. She looked too exhausted to pace, the way Duncan was in an effort to burn up some of this adrenaline and nerves. She was on the sofa, watching and waiting.

"How are you holding up?" Ruston asked, and Duncan knew that question was for Joelle.

"We need answers," she replied, clearly dodging her brother's question.

Ruston sighed because that dodge had given him the answer. His sister was exhausted and worried about everything that had gone on not just since the attack but the events of the last five months. All of this could be linked, and that was a connection that wasn't going to allow Joelle, or the rest of them, to get much rest anytime soon.

"All right," Ruston continued, "here's what I have. At approximately 6:45 this morning, Shanda's lawyer, Frank Salvetti, arrived at her residence in San Antonio. She had called him about a half hour before that and instructed him that she needed him to accompany her to Saddle Ridge right away."

Hell. A lot had gone on in these hours following Joelle's attack. It was barely six in the morning, but it felt as if they'd been at this for days.

"That's a fast, and very early, response for a lawyer," Duncan pointed out.

"Yeah," Ruston agreed. "I'm guessing it's because Shanda either pays him well or else they have a personal relationship that made him react so fast. Not lovers. I've found no proof of that but maybe just friends. Anyway, he found her lying partway inside her door and on her porch, and he called 911. The ME just confirmed that cause of death was the gunshot wound to the chest. No surprise there. I was one of the first on scene, and it was obvious that she'd been shot and bled out."

"Any witnesses?" Joelle asked.

"None, and there were no security cameras. But it's definitely not suicide. No other weapons around, and even though I don't have the report back on it yet, it'll turn out that she was shot at point-blank range. What it looked like to me was that she opened her door to someone, maybe thinking it was her lawyer or possibly because she knew the person, and then she was shot."

Duncan groaned. Ruston was a good cop so his account

was almost certainly what had happened. But with no witnesses and Shanda dead, they didn't have an ID on the shooter.

"Shanda called me about an hour before she was killed," Duncan explained. "I was going to question her about the attack on Joelle and Molly's kidnapping."

Ruston made a sound of acknowledgment. "Joelle had messaged me about that." He paused. "Shanda's arrest could be linked to Dad's murder. Who else knew that?"

"My three suspects," Duncan was quick to say. Technically, he should be using the "persons of interest" label, but in his mind, they were solid suspects. "Shanda's former mother-in-law, Kate Moreland, who's still hospitalized. Shanda's ex-husband, Brad. A hothead who blames your dad, Joelle and a few others for Shanda's miscarriage following her arrest. The third suspect is Al Hamlin, a PI who showed up out of the blue to point the finger at Kate."

Duncan paused to give Ruston some time to consider all of that.

"Who's your top suspect?" Ruston asked several moments later.

"Well, it would have been Shanda before she was murdered," Duncan admitted. "After all, she's the one who lost the baby, and she's got the funds to hire a gunman and a kidnapper." He stopped again, cursed. "And she could have done just that. Hell, maybe one of her hired thugs wasn't pleased with her and killed her. Molly's kidnapper said what he'd done was a mistake so maybe this is the way he dealt with it."

"You have a name for the kidnapper?" Ruston wanted to know.

"Working on it. We collected some of his blood from Molly's house, and it's being processed now."

If the kidnapper had a record, then they might get a quick match. Rarely did he hope someone was a criminal, but in this case, it would make getting the ID much easier.

"Kate Moreland is in the hospital with a deputy guard on her door," Duncan added to Ruston. "I've been trying to call Brad, but he's not answering."

"He's not answering my calls, either," Ruston supplied. "I've sent two uniforms out to his place to check on him. Brad didn't answer the door and didn't appear to be home. Of course, he could be on his way to see his mother before he's due to come in for his interview."

True, and he might not answer his phone if he was on the road. But it occurred to Duncan that Brad could be dead as well, and if so, he wasn't sure how that would have played out. Maybe Kate had gotten fed up with both Shanda and Brad and hired someone to kill them? Or maybe Brad was very much alive and just dodging cops. If so, that moved him to the top spot of suspects.

Duncan heard the sound of approaching footsteps, and he expected to see either Luca or Carmen step into the doorway. But it was Joelle's other brother, Slater, who was the senior deputy in the sheriff's office. He was definitely a welcome sight since there was plenty to do.

Like Ruston, Slater was the spitting image of a younger version of their late father. Tall and lanky with black hair and green eyes. Joelle had gotten the black hair, but she had her mother's misty gray eyes.

"Let me know if you get any updates," Duncan said to Ruston. "I'll do the same for you."

He ended the call and watched as Slater gave both Duncan and his sister long examining looks. Slater sighed because he could no doubt see the exhaustion on Joelle's face.

"I just did a report with the case updates," Joelle said,

maybe to cut off her brother's insistence that she get some rest. "I'll fill in what Ruston just told us and forward copies to you and the other deputies."

Slater didn't address that. He went to Joelle, eased her off the sofa and into his arms. He brushed a kiss on the top of her head and touched his hand to her baby bump. "How's my niece?"

The argument that had been in Joelle's eyes instantly faded, and she returned her brother's hug. "I think she's swimming around in there."

"Good." Slater leaned down and put his mouth to Joelle's stomach. "Hang in there, kid. I just ordered your mom a huge breakfast to be delivered from the diner. Get ready for all kinds of goodies."

"Thank you," Joelle muttered.

Duncan sent him a look of thanks, too, and wished he'd thought of it. Of course, Joelle might not eat. She hadn't touched the yogurt he'd given her earlier, but maybe Slater could give her a brotherly reminder that eating would be good for the baby.

"I managed to postpone my testimony in the trial," Slater explained, going toward Duncan now. "I figured you could use me back here."

"I can," Duncan verified. "We're hoping the kidnapper will be contacting us soon about releasing Molly, and we need a lot of research done on our suspects."

"Brad Moreland, his mother, Al Hamlin," Slater named off. "I saw the report Joelle did about Shanda's murder so she's off the list. As soon as I had Hamlin's name, I contacted a PI friend who lives in San Antonio, and I asked her about him. This particular PI is a *Girl with the Dragon Tattoo* sort of computer whiz, and she's created all these programs to mine data from old internet articles and social media posts." He paused. "And yeah, she sometimes hacks to find what she wants."

Duncan didn't approve of doing something illegal since they wouldn't be able to use the info in court. But at the moment he was for any and everything that helped them solve this so they could get Molly back.

"Did this PI find something?" Duncan prompted.

Slater nodded. "On the drive back here, she called me with what she'd dug up. Six years ago when Hamlin was seventeen, he and his then pregnant girlfriend were accused of trying to extort money from a couple who wanted to adopt the baby. They were convicted as juveniles so that's why the record didn't pop in a normal background check."

Joelle went closer to them. "Of course, Hamlin didn't mention that to us. What happened to the baby?"

"Unknown. The baby's mother, Erica Corley, was only in juvie lockup for two months, and she was released when she was eight months pregnant. She disappeared shortly thereafter, but my PI friend is trying to track her down."

"Good," Duncan muttered. "Because it'd be interesting to find out if Hamlin and she did sell the baby. It also makes me wonder if Hamlin's missing sister left because he was pressuring her to sell the child."

"Since I was wondering the same thing, the PI will be looking into that as well," Slater said. "People put all sorts of stuff on social media so she might be able to find something that'll clue us in to Isla Hamlin's disappearance."

Duncan made a quick sound of agreement just as he heard a shout coming from the bullpen. And the shout came from a voice he instantly recognized from the phone conversation he'd had with him.

"Sheriff Holder?" Brad called out.

So Brad had surfaced after all, and Duncan was a little

surprised that he'd actually come in as scheduled without being further prodded. Surprised and very much interested in what the man had to say. With Slater and Joelle following him, Duncan went into the bullpen to find the sandy-haired man struggling to get past Luca who was trying to frisk him. Carmen had stepped in to help, but Slater moved toward the trio, too.

"Settle down," Slater snapped to Brad. "You don't get past this point until we're sure you're not armed."

"I'm not armed," Brad snarled, and he aimed a venomous glare at Duncan. "Shanda's dead. Dead," he repeated, his voice breaking on the word. "You should have stopped that from happening. You shouldn't have allowed her to die."

Brad's voice didn't just break that time. He began to sob, tears spilling down his face. He also stopped struggling with the search.

"He's not armed," Luca told Duncan. "What do you want me to do with him?"

"Interview room one," Duncan said. Because one way or another, he intended to get answers from Brad.

Since Brad wasn't steady on his feet, Slater took one side of him and Luca took the other. They maneuvered him to the interview room, sat him in the chair, and Joelle got a box of tissues and a bottle of water. What none of them did was give Brad any sympathetic looks because they all knew this could be an act.

That they could be looking at a killer.

"Let me know if you need me," Luca muttered, heading back toward the bullpen.

"Same here," Slater said. "I'll do some more of that digging we were talking about."

That no doubt meant Slater was going to try to find Hamlin's old girlfriend, Erica. Duncan hoped he could manage it since Erica, who'd now be in her mid-twenties might be able to provide them with some insight into Hamlin.

Duncan and Joelle sat across from Brad and didn't say anything for several minutes. They just waited for Brad to cry it out. When he finally reached for a tissue to dry his eyes, that was Duncan's cue to get started. However, Brad beat him to it.

"Who killed Shanda?" Brad asked. The anger was back in his voice now. "Was it my mother?"

Duncan didn't respond to that. Well, not a direct answer, anyway. Instead, he read Brad his rights, and he didn't think it was his imagination that Brad became more incensed with each line of the Miranda warning.

"Do you understand your rights?" Duncan asked when he'd finished.

"Of course, I do," Brad snapped. "You're covering your butt, but there's no need. I didn't kill my wife."

"Do you understand the part about your right to have your lawyer present?"

"I do, and he'll be coming in soon, but I don't want to wait for him to get answers. I need to know now. Did my mother do this?"

"Your mother is under guard at the hospital," Duncan reminded him. Of course, that didn't mean Kate hadn't hired someone to do it. He leaned in and stared at Brad. "Did you kill Shanda?"

Outrage bloomed across his face, and his mouth dropped open. "No, I did not." Brad snapped out each word. "I loved her, and we were getting back together."

"Maybe," Duncan concluded. "I talked to Shanda right before she was killed, and she didn't confirm a reconciliation. Just the opposite."

No trace of Brad's tears remained, and his eyes narrowed. "I don't believe you. You're lying to provoke me."

"I'm repeating to you what she told me."

Duncan withheld anything else about that conversation he'd had with Shanda, and he let the silence roll through the room. In his experience, most people being interrogated or interviewed were uncomfortable enough with the silence that they started talking.

It worked.

"Shanda wanted me to see a shrink," Brad finally admitted. "She wanted me to rehash the past."

"Isn't that what you're doing with the civil suit?" Joelle asked.

Now Brad turned those narrowed eyes on her. "No. That's retribution. That's payment for a wrong that you and your father did." He stopped and visibly reined in some of the anger. "I thought the best way for Shanda and me to move on was to get back together and start that family she's always wanted."

Interesting. Not the family *we'd* always wanted. "You wanted to have a child with Shanda?" Duncan came out and asked.

"Of course." Brad had gone back to snapping. "And now that won't happen because she's dead."

Brad made the sound of a sob, but Duncan saw no fresh tears in his eyes. Being the cynic that he was, Duncan wondered if the man had tapped his supply of fake drama.

"I understand you called Shanda after you and I had our phone conversation," Duncan said, shifting the conversation a little.

Brad nodded, attempted another sob, and he must have given up on that because he pressed a tissue to his eyes. "I told her what was going on, and I said I wanted to see her.

She said we could meet for lunch after I was done with my interview." He stopped again. "If I'd gone over to her place then and there, she might not be dead. I could have stopped her from being killed."

Maybe that was true. But not the truth if Brad had been the one who'd pulled the trigger.

"Where were you from the time you got off the phone with me and Shanda's murder?" Duncan pressed.

"Home," Brad was quick to say.

Duncan was just as quick with a response. "Can anyone verify that?"

"I was alone," the man snapped. "But I tried to make some calls to my mother so it's possible those can be pinpointed to my house."

Yeah, it was possible. But it wasn't proof. Someone could have used Brad's phone to make it look as if he were home. And even if Brad had personally made the calls, it didn't mean his hired gun hadn't been doing his bidding. Still…

"I want permission to get access to your phone records," Duncan insisted. "If you don't agree, I'll assume you have something to hide, and I'll get a search warrant."

Brad didn't seem especially bothered by that. "I'll give you permission," he said, making Duncan silently groan. It meant any communication Brad might have had with hired guns had likely been done through a burner. Maybe one like the ones Molly's kidnapper had been using.

Next, Duncan went with an outright lie, something he was allowed during questioning. "We have footage from security cameras up the street from Shanda's. It's being analyzed as we speak, but I already know there was a vehicle in the area. A vehicle matching the description of one registered to you."

Brad sprang to his feet. "It wasn't mine. I wasn't anywhere near Shanda's this morning."

That might be true. Might be. But Brad could have hired someone to kill her. And that led Duncan to motive.

"Here's my theory," Duncan started. "You arranged to have Deputy McCullough killed or kidnapped. Ditto for the dispatcher who was also a deputy during Shanda's arrest two years ago. Shanda either found out what you'd done or you told her, and when she said she was going to the cops, you made sure she wouldn't be talking to anyone."

If looks could have killed, Brad would have finished off Duncan and Joelle on the spot. He sank back down into his chair. "This interview is over," he insisted, taking out his phone. "I'm not saying another word until I have my lawyer here."

Duncan didn't press, and he figured he could use the time before the lawyer arrived to assemble as much of a case as he could against Brad. What he needed was some physical evidence, something that would get him an arrest warrant so he could take Brad off the streets. Of course, if Brad was the killer, it was possible he'd already set hired guns in motion for another attack.

Joelle and Duncan stepped outside the interview room, closing the door behind them, and they looked at each other. "You believe him?" Joelle whispered, taking the question right out of Duncan's mouth.

Duncan had to shrug. Then, he groaned and scrubbed his hand over his face in frustration. "I want to believe he's the killer, but I'm not sure."

Since he didn't want Brad to overhear any part of this conversation, he motioned for Joelle to follow him back to the break room.

"Everything we have on Brad is circumstantial." He took

out his phone. "I'll have Carmen get Brad to sign the agreement to get his phone records. If he's still willing to do it, that is. And there might be something in his call history that could help us get a warrant for his financials."

Duncan fired off a quick text to Carmen, but before he got a reply, his phone rang with an incoming call from Dr. Benton. Duncan couldn't answer it fast enough.

"Kate is awake, and she's insisting on seeing Joelle and you," the doctor said without a greeting. "Obviously, I'd like for her to hold off on that for another hour or two, but she got agitated when I suggested it. Can the two of you come to the hospital now?"

"Absolutely," Duncan readily agreed. "We'll be there in about ten minutes."

Joelle and he hurried back to the bullpen, and Duncan saw the instant alarm on the three deputies' faces. "Brad decided to wait for his lawyer," Duncan explained because the deputies had obviously thought Brad had done something to provoke them. "Joelle and I need to get to the hospital to question Kate Moreland."

"I can go with you for backup," Slater immediately volunteered.

Duncan nodded and got them moving toward the door. After he'd checked to make sure there were no threats lurking around, they got into the cruiser with Joelle in the back seat, Duncan in shotgun and Slater behind the wheel.

As expected, it was not a peaceful, relaxing ride. They were all very aware that the hired guns could be nearby, ready and waiting to strike. It was the reason Duncan had considered asking Joelle to stay behind. But not only wouldn't she have agreed to that, Kate had asked specifically to see her. It was possible the woman would say something to Joelle that she wouldn't to Duncan.

When they reach the hospital, Slater parked by the ER doors so that Joelle and he could hurry inside. Slater got out as well, and Duncan knew he would stand guard, watching for any kind of danger. Simply put, if any hired guns came into the hospital after Joelle and him, Slater would be the first line of defense against that.

Also as expected, there was a reserve deputy outside Kate's room. Anita Denny. Since she obviously recognized Duncan and Joelle, she opened the door and motioned them inside.

"She's waiting for you," Anita, the reserve deputy, informed them.

They stepped into the room and saw that Anita was right. Kate was, indeed, sitting up and clearly expecting them. She didn't look drowsy but rather alert and very worried.

"A friend of mine called the hospital and left a message to tell me that Shanda had been murdered," Kate immediately said. "Is it true?"

Later, Duncan would want to know the name of that friend. For now, though, he basically did a death notification.

"I regret to inform you that Shanda was murdered earlier this morning," he told her while he carefully watched her reaction.

A reaction that included widened eyes and a shudder of her breath. Kate touched her fingers to her mouth that trembled. "I'd hoped it wasn't true. I didn't want it to be true," she amended.

Duncan didn't have time to treat this like a normal death notification. He needed to jump right into questions that had to be asked. And he had to start with the basics.

"I'm going to Mirandize you," Duncan stated. "It's to cover the legal bases and make sure you're aware of what your rights are."

Kate didn't ask why he was doing this. She merely sat and listened while he finished, and then she nodded when he asked if she understood everything he'd just spelled out.

Since Kate didn't voice any kind of objections, Duncan continued, "From what I've heard, Shanda and you didn't have a good relationship. You were at odds. In fact, when I spoke to Shanda before she died, she claimed that you loathed her."

Kate didn't show any flares of temper as Brad had done. The woman sighed and shook her head. "I did loathe her," she admitted. "I thought she didn't handle her miscarriage and divorce nearly as well as she could have, and I believe she never actually loved Brad."

Duncan lifted an eyebrow. "I didn't pick up on that last part from either Brad or Shanda."

"You wouldn't have." Kate glanced away, groaned softly. "Brad was blindly in love with her, and he couldn't see Shanda for what she was. A gold digger. That big house she lives in? That was part of her divorce settlement. She took half of Brad's money when she divorced him."

Now there was some anger, but she kept her gaze pinned downward while she picked at the sheets covering her. Duncan had to wonder if she was looking down so he wouldn't be able to see some truth that she couldn't conceal in her eyes.

Truth that she was glad Shanda was dead. And that she was the one who'd made that happen.

"I should tell you something in case it comes up later," Kate said. "I don't want you to think I'm withholding anything."

"I'm listening," Duncan assured her.

"On the night Shanda was arrested, she and I were arguing on the phone. A very heated argument," Kate emphasized. "I'd called her about some charges I saw on Brad's credit card. Shanda had gone to a high-end boutique and treated herself to the best the place had to offer. I'm talking nearly ten grand. Shanda said that Brad had given her the shopping trip as a surprise gift, and I told her that Brad wasn't paying the bills, that I was." She stopped. "Anyway, Shanda was yelling at me and that's probably why she was driving erratically."

Duncan had known about this. It'd been in the statement Shanda had given. Well, she'd given a thumbnail of it, anyway. She'd told Sheriff McCullough that she'd been having a dispute with her mother-in-law.

"You must have been very upset when you found out that Brad and Shanda were getting back together," Joelle threw out there. All sympathy. Fake, of course. But Duncan knew she was going for the "good cop" angle here. That gave Duncan the leeway to go badass.

"I was," Kate muttered. "I thought it would only lead to Brad being crushed all over again." Now she finally looked up, her attention going to Joelle. "Crushed," she emphasized. "Brad was never the same after the miscarriage and his marriage breaking up."

That was Duncan's cue to jump in. "Is that why you went to Molly's to accuse Brad of trying to kill Joelle?"

On a heavy sigh, Kate closed her eyes. But she nodded. She took in a few shallow breaths, opened her eyes and looked at Joelle again. "I'm sorry, but Brad blamed you and your father for what happened to Shanda. He should have blamed Shanda herself. She's the one who got herself arrested. Instead, Brad decided she wasn't at fault and that the cops involved needed to pay."

"Pay by killing me and kidnapping a former deputy?" Joelle supplied.

Kate nodded again and repeated her apology. "I think my son has had some kind of mental breakdown. I blame Shanda for that. She led him on, making him believe she'd get back together with him, but there were always new conditions for a reconciliation. One day, she'd say he had to go to counseling. The next, she'd tell him he had to cut me out of his life." She paused. "And he did."

Neither Brad nor Shanda had mentioned that so Duncan had no idea if it was true. However, it was something he would definitely ask Brad about.

"It must have hurt when Brad did that," Joelle murmured.

"It did." There was another flash of anger in her eyes, but Kate seemed to quickly shut that down. "It cut me to the core."

"And that cut made it easier for you to go to Joelle and tell her that Brad wanted her dead," Duncan pointed out.

Kate's mouth tightened for a couple of seconds. "Yes, it did make it easier," she confessed. "If my son hadn't basically disowned me, I might not have been willing to believe the worst about him. But I do believe it. I think Shanda convinced him to go after the people who arrested her. I think this was all her doing."

That was possible, but there was a big question mark in that theory. "Then, why is Shanda dead?"

"Maybe she hired the wrong people to do her bidding, and it backfired." Kate offered that up so quickly that it was obvious she'd given it some thought. "If you play with fire, sometimes you get burned."

"So, you don't think Brad would have killed her?" Joelle asked.

Kate stayed quiet a while. "I don't want to believe he would, but it's possible. Shanda broke him, so anything is possible."

Duncan wasn't sure about the broken part, but it was obvious that Brad had some serious issues. Obvious, too, that he could have certainly murdered his ex-wife.

"I saw your tox results," Duncan said, and he noted the flash of surprise in Kate's eyes. She hadn't been prepared for a quick shift in topics. "There didn't seem to be enough of the sleeping aid in your system for you to behave the way you did when you arrived at Molly's."

Kate stared at him and touched her fingers to the bruise on her forehead. "This must have caused the wooziness," she said. "That and maybe my blood pressure." She paused again. "But I don't recall taking any of my sleeping pills that night. In fact, I'm sure I wouldn't have since I'd planned on driving to Saddle Ridge to see Joelle."

Duncan and Joelle exchanged a glance, and it was Joelle who voiced what they were thinking. "You believe someone might have drugged you with them?"

"Yes," Kate muttered. She squeezed her eyes shut for a moment. "Brad came to see me as I was getting ready to leave. He was furious because I'd shut off his accounts and canceled his credit cards. I was paying him a hefty salary to manage some of my businesses," she added. "I figured since he'd disowned me, then he shouldn't have access to that money." Her mouth tightened again. "He'd planned on buying Shanda another big engagement ring and was enraged when his credit card was declined."

"You two argued?" Duncan prompted when Kate went quiet.

"Yes. A loud ugly argument. I poured myself a shot of scotch, and it's possible Brad could have put one of my sleeping pills in it."

Now Duncan was the one to shake his head. "Why would he have done that?"

"I don't know. To get back at me," Kate suggested. "Maybe because he realized I was going to see Joelle. I didn't tell him that, but it's possible he guessed since just the day before he'd been ranting about how much Joelle needed to pay for what'd happened to his precious Shanda."

Duncan still wasn't convinced. "If Brad wanted to drug you so you couldn't drive to Saddle Ridge, why not put more than one pill in the drink?"

"Because he might not have wanted to risk me tasting it," Kate answered without hesitation. "And I probably would have. I did notice a funny taste after I drank the scotch in a big gulp, but I didn't think anything about it. Not until later, when I was here at the hospital."

Everything the woman was saying could be true. Or it could all be lies. Duncan knew he was going to have to compare Kate's and Brad's responses side by side and try to figure how this had actually all played out.

Joelle's phone rang, the sound shooting through the silence that had fallen over the room, and he saw *Unknown Caller* when Joelle showed him the screen.

"We have to take this," Joelle said, and Duncan and she went out into the hall. They moved away from Kate's door before Joelle accepted the call.

"Thanks for wiring me the money," the man said. "I'm taking Molly to the drop off now."

It was the kidnapper, the same one who'd called earlier.

"Where?" Joelle asked.

"You'll know soon enough," the man said. "Keep your phone ready because in exactly twenty minutes, I'll be calling you back to come and get Molly."

Chapter Seven

Even though Joelle knew that Duncan still had plenty more questions for Kate, that would have to wait. Twenty minutes wasn't a lot of time to get ready for the kidnapper to drop off Molly.

Or for the kidnapper to put the finishing touches on a ploy to draw Duncan and her out.

Joelle was well aware that might be the case. So was Duncan, and he would almost certainly insist that she stay at the sheriff's office. That wasn't what Joelle wanted to do, but she figured she would end up going along with it. There was no need to put the baby at even greater risk.

"I'll have to come back to finish this interview," Duncan told Kate, and he didn't wait for the woman to respond. He motioned for Joelle to follow him, and they headed out the door.

"Keep a close watch on Kate," Duncan muttered to Anita. "And if she makes any calls, I want to know about it."

Yes, because Kate could be behind whatever was about to happen, and she might want to make a call to someone she'd hired to do her bidding.

They hurried back toward the ER doors where Slater was waiting for them. The moment they were back in the cruiser, Duncan took out his phone. "I need to assemble some backup," he muttered.

Yes, that was a must, and Joelle could see how this could play out. She'd man the sheriff's office, probably along with Luca and Carmen, and then every other available deputy would go with Duncan. Joelle prayed that would be enough protection if something went wrong.

Before Duncan could even make a call, her phone rang, and Joelle frowned when she saw the *Unknown Caller* on the screen. She showed it to Duncan, and the sudden alarm on his face no doubt mirrored hers. Joelle answered, put it on speaker, and the kidnapper's voice poured through the cruiser.

"Molly's at the former sheriff's house," the man snarled.

Oh, mercy. *There.* It would be there. The house where Joelle had been raised. But where her father had also been murdered. She hadn't been able to step inside the place since the initial investigation.

In the background, Joelle heard Molly call out, "Joelle." That was all Molly managed to say before the kidnapper issued an order for her to shut up.

"If you're not here in ten minutes, the deal is off," the man warned them.

"But you said twenty minutes," Duncan snarled right back.

"Ten," the kidnapper repeated.

Slater and Duncan both cursed. "I want proof of life," Duncan demanded.

The kidnapper cursed, too. "You already got it. You heard her yell Joelle's name."

"That could have been a recording," Duncan pointed out.

Joelle hadn't considered that, but it was possible. Likely, even, if the kidnapper had already dropped off Molly somewhere else and was putting some distance between him and her. Added to that, Duncan didn't really have any bargaining power since the money had already been transferred. They'd had no choice about that, though, since it had been the kidnapper's only demand for Molly's release. Now these new demands with the quick time restraints spelled trouble.

More cursing from the kidnapper. "Tell him you're alive," the man growled.

Seconds ticked off, and Joelle had to breathe because her lungs were starting to ache. "I'm alive," Molly finally said.

"Where are you?" Duncan asked her.

"I'm not sure. I'm blindfolded, but it's possible I'm at the McCullough ranch like he said."

Possible. But maybe the kidnapper had her elsewhere. Still, Molly was alive, and Joelle was going to latch on to that.

"Don't be late," the kidnapper added. "You wasted one of your minutes with all this yakking. Be here in nine minutes, Sheriff." He ended the call.

"This is a trap," Slater spat out, and his gaze met Joelle's in the rearview mirror.

She couldn't disagree. It had all the markings of a trap, but there was another factor here.

"He has Molly, and we have to get her back," Joelle stated. "The cruiser is bullet-resistant, and I'll stay inside. Yes, this might be a ruse so he can come after me, but he could do that at the sheriff's office, too. In fact, that might be what he has in mind. Get all of you hurrying there to the ranch while he's already right here in town."

Both Slater and Duncan knew that was true, and this was definitely a "damned if you did, dammed if you didn't" situation. Duncan seemed to be having a very short mental debate about that.

"Go to your dad's house fast," Duncan instructed, and like Slater had done to her earlier, he looked at her, the worry in his eyes. "I'm sorry," he muttered.

"Don't be. Let's go get Molly," she said. "Who should I call for backup?"

A muscle flickered in Duncan's jaw when it tightened. "Have dispatch send all available deputies to the location."

Joelle made the call, already calculating how long it would take them to arrive. Too long probably, and the kidnapper would likely know that. Would likely know, too, the emotional punch that her father's house would have for her. She hated these sick mind games. Hated the person who'd set all of it into motion.

She checked the time. They'd already burned one of those nine minutes, and she didn't know the exact time it would take them to get to the ranch. At the speed Slater was going, though, they should make it with maybe a minute or two to spare. A minute or two they wouldn't have had if Duncan had insisted on taking her back to the sheriff's office.

The question was what would they face once they were there at the ranch?

"You want me to call my ranch hands and have them meet us there?" Slater asked Duncan.

"Do that. Have them stay back, though, until they get the word we need them."

He was thinking this could turn into a gunfight. And it possibly could. Joelle tried not to think of the risk this would be to her baby. Especially since Molly and her child were in even greater danger.

While Slater threaded the cruiser around the curvy country roads, Joelle fixed the image of her family's ranch in her head. Of course, she knew every inch of the house and grounds. Knew, too, that there were plenty of places for someone to lie in wait for them. It didn't help, either, that there was no one working full-time at the ranch. Slater often sent over his own hands just to check on the place, but there likely wouldn't have been anyone around when the kidnapper had set all this up. Which could have been hours ago. Heck, he could have been holding Molly here all along, though that would have been risky since eventually, when Duncan had had the manpower, he would have sent someone out to check the place.

"The second floor of the house will be a good place for a sniper," Joelle said. "Not the roof, though, because of the steep pitch."

"There are four front-facing windows on that second floor," Slater added.

Duncan had been to the ranch many times so he no doubt knew all of this, but Joelle thought it wouldn't hurt to spell out the potential points for an attack.

"From the barn loft," she went on, "there's a direct view of the road so anyone there would be able to see the moment we arrive."

Duncan muttered a sound of agreement and took out his gun. "Try to call the kidnapper again and see if he'll give us Molly's exact location. Yeah, it's a long shot," he grumbled.

It was, but Joelle tried anyway. As expected, he didn't answer. It rang out, and she figured he was already in the process of disabling it. Not that they would have the time to trace it. No. This was coming to some kind of showdown fast.

The minutes ticked away but so did the miles as Slater drove toward the ranch. He took the curves at a higher speed than he probably should have, the tires squealing in protest, but her brother kept control of the cruiser and ate up the miles.

Joelle had to force herself to breathe again when the ranch's pastures came into view. She hadn't needed proof that things weren't the same as they had been five months ago, but she got that proof, anyway. There was no livestock in the pastures. None of the beautiful palomino horses her father had loved. Those had already been moved to Slater's ranch.

The sun was fully up now, but the morning mist was still hovering over the pasture grass, giving the place an eerie, otherworldly feel. The mist hung around the house, too, and while it wasn't dense enough to conceal a shooter, she couldn't help but think of the smoke. And the fire that had destroyed her house. It was possible the kidnapper would do that here, too.

Slater cursed again, and Joelle soon saw why. There was a man at the end of the long driveway that led to the house. He was standing next to a black truck.

Hamlin.

"What the hell is he doing here?" Duncan grumbled, taking the question right out of her mouth.

"He's armed," Slater was quick to point out.

Joelle had noticed that as well. Hamlin had a gun in his right hand, and he jerked as if about to aim it at them. He didn't, though. Nor did he relax the grip he had on the weapon.

Her first thought was he was the kidnapper, and this was that showdown they'd expected. But she was betting none of them had expected the man to be out in the open like this.

Slater pulled the cruiser to a jarring stop just a few feet away from Hamlin. "Do you see anyone else?" he asked, his gaze already combing the house and grounds.

Joelle and Duncan were doing the same thing. Looking for hired guns that Hamlin might have brought with him, but there was no one visible in any of the second-floor windows or the barn.

Duncan lowered his window a fraction. "Stay put, Hamlin," he called out when the PI began to walk toward the cruiser. "And drop your weapon."

Hamlin glanced at his gun and scowled. Then, he huffed. "What the hell is this? Did you set me up or something?"

"Drop your weapon," Duncan repeated. His voice had a bite to it, but he added even more with the repeat.

On another huff, Hamlin tossed the gun on the ground and lifted his hands in the air. "I haven't done anything wrong," the PI protested.

"Then, why are you here?" Duncan demanded.

"Because you texted me and asked me to come." Hamlin's response was quick. Maybe rehearsed.

"I didn't text you," Duncan informed him, and Joelle noticed that Duncan was continuing to look for anyone else.

Hamlin shook his head. "But you did. My phone's in my pocket. I can show you."

Duncan didn't take him up on that offer, probably because he knew the text had been sent by someone else to set this all up. But what was *this*? "We're here looking for a kidnapped woman, and the kidnapper gave us this location."

That put some alarm in Hamlin's eyes, but since Joelle was plenty skeptical when it came to the PI, she figured that, too, could have been rehearsed. "I don't know anything about that, and I haven't seen anyone else since I got here."

"He could be telling the truth," Slater whispered. "Brad, Kate or the kidnapper could have arranged for Hamlin to come here to muddy the waters. Of course, if it's Brad or Kate, then it means they know all about Hamlin."

Yes, which would mean they'd know he was investigating the sale of babies. And that he believed Kate was behind that. However, Brad could have arranged this, too, if he wanted the cops looking at someone else other than him for Shanda's murder, the kidnapping and the earlier attack.

"There's only a minute left on the kidnapper's deadline," Joelle reminded them. Though she wasn't sure if that deadline applied any longer since they were, indeed, at the ranch.

Where there was seemingly no sign of Molly.

"Yeah," Duncan muttered, and he seemed to take a breath of relief when there was the sound of sirens in the distance. Backup would be there soon. "Hamlin, get face down on the ground, and don't block the road."

Joelle looked at Duncan, but she already knew what he had in mind. He'd leave backup to deal with Hamlin, and the PI would no doubt be handcuffed so he wouldn't be a threat. Good, because Joelle had the sickening feeling they already had enough threats to deal with.

And priority was finding Molly.

"Find out who's in that cruiser and let them know what's going on," Duncan told her just as his phone dinged with a text. "Never mind. It's Woodrow Leonard and Ronnie Bishop. They were on their way back from your place."

That explained how they'd gotten there so fast. It would have put them miles closer since her house was only an eight-minute or so drive from here. And that was a reminder they were already out of time for finding Molly. Of course, the deadline might not mean anything since it could have simply been part of the ruse to get them here, but Duncan apparently wasn't going to take the risk that those ten minutes had been part of the ploy.

"Joelle, text Woodrow or Ronnie and tell them to cuff Hamlin and take his gun," Duncan instructed. "Tell them to be careful and watch for gunmen. Slater, drive closer to the house."

She typed out the text, but Joelle also continued to glance around at their surroundings. Specifically, looking for any signs they were about to be shot at. But no bullets came.

Not yet, anyway.

Slater went slow, no doubt doing his own checking, and he finally came to a stop in the circular drive in front of the house. He positioned the cruiser close to the porch steps but still had a good view of the barn. Of course, that meant any gunman would have a view of them, too.

"Woodrow and Ronnie will deal with Hamlin," Joelle relayed after she got a response from Ronnie. "They'll cuff Hamlin, put him in the back of the cruiser and drive closer to assist."

"Good," Duncan muttered, and he turned to her. "You're staying put. I'm going inside the house to look around."

Oh, that gave her a nasty jolt of fear. "You're not going in there alone."

Duncan's mouth tightened, and she saw the debate in his eyes. "I want Slater to stay here with you in case you're attacked again."

She shook her head. "You're just as likely to be attacked in the house. Slater can go with you, and I can crawl over the seat and get behind the wheel." Her baby bump wasn't so big, not yet anyway, to prevent her from doing that. "Then, I can move the cruiser if necessary."

Joelle didn't want to think of what might make that necessary, but it would almost certainly mean some kind of attack. Maybe a firebomb to the house. But if that happened, she wouldn't be driving away unless Duncan and Slater were out of harm's way and with her.

The debate in Duncan's eyes continued a moment longer, and when he cursed, she knew he'd made his decision. So did Slater. They both reached for their doors.

"Don't get out of the cruiser," Duncan warned her one last time. He looked as if he wanted to add more, so much more, but thankfully he didn't. Now wasn't the time to bring up anything about "if the worst happens."

"Find Molly," Joelle said as they exited the cruiser.

The moment the doors were shut, she climbed over the seat and got behind the wheel while she continued to keep watch. Behind her, she saw Woodrow and Ronnie's cruiser pull to a stop, and in the distance, she heard yet more sirens. More vehicles, too, and Joelle spotted Slater's ranch hands as they arrived. Good. The more, the better.

But "more" didn't help Slater and Duncan right now.

Joelle quickly lost sight of them after Slater unlocked the front door and they hurried into the house. She could imagine, though, that they would immediately start the room-to-room search. It was a big house, and that meant there were plenty of places to check.

Plenty of places for a killer to hide, too.

Added to that, the house didn't have an open floor plan so Duncan and Slater wouldn't be able to do a quick visual sweep to determine if anyone was there. It'd be a slow process, searching through all eight rooms on the bottom floor before going to the second floor and then likely the attic if there was no sign of Molly before then.

She purposely didn't watch the time because she didn't want to mark off the seconds and minutes of the search for Molly. That wouldn't help her stay focused. Just the opposite. She didn't want to think of the extreme danger Duncan and her brother were in. Molly, too.

The baby stirred, a reminder of why she had to stay safe. It was also a reminder of Duncan. For the past five months, she'd worked so hard to keep her distance from him. Worked hard not to feel anything. Because those kinds of feelings also deepened the guilt and grief. But it was impossible to keep him out of her thoughts when they were thrown together like this. The closeness and the danger were breaking down barriers she'd fought to keep in place.

She forced all of that aside for now and tried to get a glimpse of the upstairs windows, to see if Duncan and Slater had made it to the second floor. It was impossible, though, with the way Slater had parked. The eaves of the porch blocked her view.

Another cruiser pulled in behind the others, and her phone dinged with a text. From Luca. We're coming closer, he messaged.

Hamlin is cuffed in the cruiser. Woodrow, Ronnie and I are going to check the barns and the other outbuildings. David will be here any minute now to help.

Deputy David Morales who normally worked the swing shift. Obviously, he'd been called in, and he would probably have his usual partner with him, Deputy Sonya Grover. Since Sonya and Molly were also friends, the woman would have insisted on coming to help.

All possible help would be needed since in addition to the big barn adjacent to the house, there were two smaller barns farther away and four other smaller outbuildings scattered around the grounds. There was even a fishing cabin on the banks of the creek that snaked through the ranch.

Joelle responded to let Luca know that she understood the plan, and she watched as they sprang into action. Not just the two cruisers but the three ranch hands from Slater's ranch. They didn't park near her, though, but rather between the house and the barn, and soon the deputies and hands began to pour from their vehicles. That didn't make her breathe easier, though.

It just meant a gunman would have more targets.

Her phone dinged again, and the relief washed over her when she saw it was from Duncan.

First and second floors cleared. Molly's not there. Heading into the attic now.

That rid her of any relief she'd just gotten. Yes, Duncan and her brother were still safe, there was no gunfire, but Molly wasn't there. It sickened Joelle to think of where the woman could be. And if she'd been hurt or worse. Now Duncan and Slater would have to basically climb a ladder to get into the attic, and there could be a gunman waiting for them.

She caught some movement from the corner of her eye and turned to the side of the house that was on the opposite side of the barn. Joelle immediately saw the white rectangular spots on the ground. Not the lingering morning mist. These appeared to be sheets of paper.

Joelle didn't want to move too far from the front door in case Slater and Duncan had to come running out, but she backed up the cruiser, keeping close to the porch so she could have a better look. Definitely paper and not some kind of explosives. She inched the cruiser back even farther, and she looked down.

Photos.

Four of them.

And her heart skipped a beat. Because they were pictures of her father. Not crime scene photos, either. These had been taken just as the blood had started to seep out from beneath his fallen lifeless body.

Oh, mercy.

The killer had taken these. And had left them for her to see.

Joelle's gaze immediately fired around. Just as there was a blur of motion. A man came charging at the window of the cruiser. Since he was wearing jeans and a gray work shirt, at first she thought it was one of the ranch hands or a deputy.

It wasn't.

She had a split second to realize this wasn't someone she knew, and she drew her gun. Too late, though. The man had a gun rigged with a silencer, and he immediately jammed it against the window.

And he fired.

The point-blank shot blasted through the cruiser, deafening Joelle and creating a half dollar-sized hole in the bullet resistant glass. The pain shot through her head and quadrupled when he fired another shot. Then, another.

For a horrifying moment, she thought she'd been hit. But no. He wasn't aiming at her. He was tearing the glass apart so he could get to her.

He managed it, too.

She turned her gun toward him, ready to fire, but his fist came through the hole, and he knocked her gun away. In the same motion, he unlocked her door from the inside and opened it, dragging her out of the cruiser.

The pain was still ramming into her head and ears, but Joelle didn't allow that to make her forget her training. She had to protect herself. She had to protect her daughter so she tried to ram the heel of her hand into his throat.

He dodged the blow, and before she could try to deliver another one, he grabbed her hair, dragging her in front of him.

"Stay back or I'll kill her," the man snarled.

That's when she realized Luca, Woodrow and two of

the ranch hands had their weapons trained on her attacker. There was no sign of Duncan or Slater, but she figured they were racing out of the attic to the sound of that gunfire. Yes, the gunman had used a silencer, but the shots had still made some sounds that cops would have recognized. Added to that, there'd been the breaking glass. That would have alerted them, too.

"Let her go," Luca demanded.

"Not a chance," her attacker growled, and he began to walk backward with her.

He was pulling her hair hard, causing more pain to shoot through her, but Joelle was gearing up to start fighting him. He stopped her with a single sentence.

"Don't do anything stupid to get your kid hurt," he whispered right against her ear.

She didn't pivot and try to throw the punch she'd been planning. Nor did she attempt a kick. Joelle froze for a moment. Her baby. He was threatening to hurt her baby. And he could do it. That's why he'd said it, and he likely thought it was cause her to give up.

It wouldn't.

No way was she going to let her baby be at the mercy of this SOB. If he managed to get her away from the ranch, then heaven knew where he'd take her. And what he'd do to her and her precious child.

Joelle braced herself and got ready to do what she had to do.

Fight.

Chapter Eight

Everything inside Duncan went cold when he heard the shots. Three of them, one right behind the other.

He forced himself not to think, especially about Joelle and their baby. Duncan just scrambled down the attic ladder and started running. Fast. As if Joelle and the baby's lives depended on it.

Because he had the sickening feeling that it did.

Duncan took the stairs two and three at a time to reach the first floor, and he was about to barrel out the front door when something from the living room window caught his eye.

Joelle.

Hell. She wasn't in the cruiser but on the side of the house, and there was a hulking thug with one hand twisted in her hair and the other holding a gun that was pointed at her head. He was dragging her toward the back of the house. Maybe toward a vehicle he had stashed somewhere on the ranch.

Duncan turned around and headed for the back door, and he cursed when he had to waste precious seconds fumbling to get a deadbolt open. He finally managed it. Finally, got onto the back porch. But he didn't run. In fact, he tried to stay as quiet as possible when he made his way to the side and peered around it.

Duncan silently cursed. Then, he prayed.

The thug had his back to Duncan and was manhandling Joelle. The grip he had on her hair had to be excruciating, but she was alive, and Duncan couldn't see any blood. However, he could see Joelle trying to shift her feet as the would-be kidnapper maneuvered her over some kind of photos on the ground. Later, he'd see what those photos were all about, but for now he had to figure that Joelle was attempting to get into a position so she could fight back.

Duncan had to admire her grit, but this was a situation that could get her killed. Even if that wasn't the thug's intention. The fact he was dragging her somewhere meant he wanted her alive, but he might accidently shoot her if this turned into an outright scuffle.

Still, something had to be done. And it wouldn't be a shot since Duncan didn't have a clean one. The guy was big, at least a head taller than Joelle, but he was well aware of that and was hunkering down enough so that someone wouldn't put a bullet in his brain. Even Duncan couldn't risk shooting him from behind because the shot could go through him and into Joelle.

Duncan glanced over his shoulder when he sensed the movement. Not another thug but rather Slater who was quietly making his way to the end of the porch next to Duncan. Slater didn't curse when he saw what was playing out in the side yard, but Duncan suspected there was plenty of silent profanity going on. Plenty of questions, too. Well, specifically one question.

How the hell had this snake gotten Joelle out of the cruiser?

He suspected that a trio of gunshots in the same exact

spot and a hefty sized gun had something to do with that. The cruiser was bullet-resistant, but shots could still get through. Or maybe something had happened to force Joelle out of the cruiser. Later, he'd want the answers to that, but for now he focused on keeping Joelle alive.

Duncan kept his gun aimed and ready, and he watched as the thug continued to drag Joelle. Duncan had to duck back out of sight, though, when he saw the guy turn to look over his shoulder. Thankfully, Slater did the same.

Since Duncan didn't want to risk the thug seeing him, he just stood there and waited. It felt like a couple of lifetimes. Bad ones. Long grueling moments with the stakes as high as they could get.

When the thug finally came into view, Duncan could see that Joelle was still squirming, still trying to fight this snake with her bare hands. The guy turned to take another glance behind him.

And that's when Duncan knew he had to make his move.

It was a risk. Anything he did at this point would be. But he tossed his own gun aside and launched himself off the porch, right onto the guy's back.

Duncan didn't do anything to break his fall. Or the thug's. Duncan didn't care if he broke the SOB's neck. Instead, he focused on knocking away the gun that was pointed at Joelle. That was the danger now. That had to be his priority. That and making sure Joelle didn't get hurt in what was about to happen next.

The thug grunted in pain when Duncan slammed into him and then yelled when Duncan's tackle rammed him onto the ground. Duncan didn't try to break his own fall but rather Joelle's. He hooked his right arm around her, cushioning her as best he could. He wasn't sure if it worked, but she didn't cry out in pain.

He hoped that wasn't because he'd knocked her unconscious.

But he soon felt her move, scrambling away from them. Good. Though Duncan knew Joelle wouldn't be running. She would no doubt be looking for a way to help him win this fight. He didn't especially want her to do that, but this was Joelle, and there'd be no stopping her.

Cursing, the thug used his elbow and jammed it right into Duncan's jaw. He could have sworn he saw stars, but he didn't let the pain faze him. Couldn't. Duncan grabbed the guy by the throat and punched him right in the face. There was a satisfying popping sound, followed by a spray of blood that let Duncan know he'd broken the man's nose.

Duncan didn't stop there. He rammed his fist into his throat, a maneuver he knew would disable him. And it did. Sputtering out a hoarse sound that was akin to a death rattle the SOB dropped back on the ground, clutching his throat and gasping for air.

Slater was suddenly right there, with his gun aimed at the man. Joelle was, too, and Duncan guessed that she'd grabbed the thug's weapon and was now ready to use it on him. Duncan was hoping that wouldn't be necessary.

"It's best if he's alive so we can question him," Duncan managed to say.

It was a reminder that he thought Joelle needed because she had her steely gaze pinned to her attacker, and the look in her eyes told Duncan she was ready to put a bullet in the guy if he tried to attack them again. The man wouldn't be able to do that, though, because he'd need breath to manage it, and it'd be a while before he got that back. Added to that, it'd be suicide for him to try to move with two cops—no, make that five—holding him at gunpoint.

Duncan got to his feet as fast as he could. "Where's Molly?" he demanded. "Point if you can't speak."

The guy kept groaning, kept gasping, but he still somehow managed a defiant look. Added to that, he tried to mutter something, and Duncan thought it was "go to hell, Sheriff."

So, he wasn't going to bend. Not at the moment, anyway.

"Cuff him and get him to jail," Duncan told Woodrow and Ronnie. "Charge him with attempted kidnapping and murder of a police officer. No bail for that." He turned to Luca and the others. "Keep searching for Molly. She might be in the vehicle this SOB used to get here."

With those steps set in motion, Duncan took hold of Joelle's arm. She was trembling, but she wasn't in shock, and other than a few red marks on her temple and neck, she didn't appear to be injured. He sent up a whole load of thanks for that.

"It's not safe for you to be outside," Duncan reminded her. "This guy might not be alone."

She looked at him, their gazes connecting, and it seemed as if she was using him as some kind of anchor. A way to stop herself from falling apart. It was one thing for a cop to be involved in an altercation, but it was much worse when the cop was the target. And there were no doubts about that. Joelle had been the target.

Again.

Joelle managed a nod, and she lowered the thug's gun to the side of her leg. Duncan eased it from her hand and passed it to Luca.

"Bag that," Duncan told him, and he got Joelle moving.

First, up onto the porch and then into the house since it had already been searched.

The moment they were inside, he pulled Joelle into his arms. Yeah, it was unprofessional, but he'd been scared out of his mind about her getting hurt, and he needed this. Mercy, he needed it.

She dropped her weight against him, melting into his arms, and she made a hoarse sound. Not a sob. He figured she'd fight tooth and nail to stop any tears. But she couldn't totally stave off the effects of an adrenaline slam like this.

"Are you okay?" he asked. "All right, dumb question. Of course, you're not okay, but were you hurt?"

Joelle dragged in a few quick breaths. "I wasn't hurt. And the baby's fine because she's moving around."

That gave him a punch of relief that was even more powerful than the elbow slam the thug had managed into Duncan's jaw. He'd still need Joelle examined, which would mean checking the baby's heartbeat and such, but they'd come out of this a whole hell of a lot better than he'd imagined when he'd first seen the thug dragging Joelle through the yard.

"He shot out the window of the cruiser at point-blank range," Joelle said, her voice a shaky tangle of breath and nerves. "But he could have shot me. He didn't. He was going to kidnap me."

Yeah. Duncan had already gone there, and the "there" would give him some hellish memories for the rest of his life.

"With him being alive, we might be able to find out if he's a hired gun," Duncan said. "Or learn if he's actually the one who orchestrated these attacks." If so, the man wasn't on their radar. "Did you recognize him?"

Joelle shook her head, the movement causing his mouth

to brush across her forehead. And that caused her to look up at him. Their gazes connected again and held firm.

She had to be experiencing a whirl of emotions right now. He certainly was. And Duncan figured those emotions played into him lowering his head and touching his mouth to hers. Just a touch, but it packed another punch.

Man, did it.

The heat would have rolled right through him, and he wanted to take her mouth as he'd done the night they'd landed in bed. And they would both pay dearly for that lapse, too. Joelle and he already had enough regrets, and Duncan didn't want this to be one of them. He figured Joelle felt the same.

But he was wrong.

Joelle came up on her toes and kissed him. Not a touch this time. It was a whole lot more. It was hard, hungry and filled with so many of those emotions. So much heat. She seemed to be using it as an anchor, too. Or maybe something that would help her remember she was alive.

"Thank you," she said when she finally pulled back. "You saved my life. You saved the baby."

In the moment, it felt as if they'd crossed some kind of threshold, that some of the old guilt might be lessening. But Duncan figured this was literally just that—*in the moment*—and that once Joelle leveled out from this attack, then she wouldn't want to be kissing him. Well, she might still want the kiss. Might want *him*. But after a little while, that guilt would hold her back just as it had for the past five months.

Duncan didn't have time to dwell on that. Or on the heat the kiss had notched up. He heard Slater call out his name, and Duncan knew he had to make sure nothing else had gone wrong.

"Wait just inside the door," Duncan told Joelle, and he reached down into his boot and came up with his backup weapon.

Since her gun was still somewhere out in the yard, he wanted her to have a way to protect herself. Of course, he was hoping with all the hopes in the universe that she didn't have to do that. Joelle had already been through way too much.

Duncan opened the back door and stepped onto the porch. He had his own gun ready as well, but he didn't see any immediate signs of danger. However, Slater, Woodrow and Ronnie were hurrying toward an outbuilding that Duncan knew Joelle's father had used to store ATVs and other equipment. At least Duncan thought that's where they were going, but they stopped about six feet in front of the shed.

"Ronnie spotted this," Slater added, reaching down and picking up a piece of green fabric that was almost the same color as the grass.

While Joelle did as he'd asked and remained in the doorway, Duncan went down the steps to have a closer look. He couldn't be sure, but it looked like the torn sleeve of a pajama top. Since Molly had been kidnapped when she likely still would have been in bed, the fabric could belong to her.

Slater went to his knees and began pulling at something. Some kind of flat circular metal cover the size of a tire. It was obviously heavy because Slater was struggling with it, and Ronnie dropped down to help him.

Behind him, Joelle gasped, and Duncan whirled around to make sure no one had come up behind her. She was alone, but she had gone pale, and she pressed her fingers to her trembling mouth.

"It's an old well," she said. "It terrified me when I was a kid, and Dad had that cover put on it to make sure no one fell in. It weighs too much for kids to move it. But..." She stopped, groaned. "But a kidnapper could have done it. Molly could be in there."

Hell. That got Duncan hurrying out into the yard to help them.

"The cover's been moved recently," Slater said, still focusing on the task. "You can tell from the grass around it. But whoever moved it put it back in place."

Duncan growled out another "hell," aloud this time. And he hoped if Molly was in there, she was still alive. By the time Duncan reached them, Slater and Ronnie had already dragged the cover to the side.

"Molly?" Slater called out, looking down into the gaping hole in the ground.

The opening was definitely wide enough that a person could be shoved in there, but if Joelle's dad had had it capped up like this, it had to be deep. Probably deep enough to kill a person if they fell or were pushed in.

"Molly?" Slater shouted again.

No response. Not from the well, anyway. But Duncan heard something coming from the outbuilding. Not a voice but a barely audible thump. It was enough to get the three of them running toward it.

"Woodrow and Sonya, keep an eye on Joelle," Duncan told the deputies who had just come out of the barn. They'd obviously been searching it for more gunmen and Molly.

Slater reached the outbuilding first, and Ronnie and Duncan both readied their weapons while Slater threw open the door and then immediately darted to the side in case someone was about to fire at him.

But no shots came.

A sound did, though. Another of those thumps, and when Duncan looked inside, he saw Molly on the floor.

Alive.

Duncan couldn't add the "and well" part to that, though. Her eyes were wide. Her forehead, smeared with dirt and maybe even some blood. Her hair was a tangled halo around her face. But she was very much alive.

He quickly saw that Molly was gagged and tied up, and she was bumping the side of her leg against the tire of an ATV, the only movement she could have managed, considering the way she was positioned in the shed. That bumping had likely caused the sounds they'd heard. They would have no doubt found her in the search, but that had allowed them to get to her even sooner.

Slater hurried to her, easing down her gag while Ronnie got to work on the ropes around her feet. Duncan called 911 for an ambulance. The moment the gag was off her mouth, Molly cried out in pain.

"Hospital," she managed to say. "I'm in labor."

Chapter Nine

The images came at Joelle hard and fast. The blood. So much blood. And it was on those photos she had seen in the yard at the ranch. The ones she'd been forced to walk through when the kidnapper had her.

Joelle groaned and tried to yank herself away from those images. She had to climb her way out of this nightmare because she couldn't be here. She couldn't—

"Joelle," someone said.

Duncan.

And she thought that was his hands on her arms. It was enough to yank her back, and her eyes flew open. Yes, Duncan. He was right there, hovering and looking very concerned.

"I'm okay," she managed to say. "It was just a nightmare."

A nightmare she'd lived when the kidnapper had her. Oh, this was going to stay with her for a while, and she didn't need any new horrific memories to blend with the others she already had.

"No, you're not okay," Duncan said, sitting beside her. "But you soon will be. Just level your breathing. In and out," he instructed.

She tried to do that. Tried, too, to push away the lingering bits of the dream. Then, she remembered the rest of what happened. Remembered where she was as well. She was in a hospital bed. Not because she'd been injured. No, both the baby and she were fine. The doctor had told her that during the exam he'd given her after they'd arrived at the hospital.

With Molly.

Molly wasn't okay. Joelle had seen the cuts and bruises on her face, and she remembered Molly had been in labor.

"Did Molly have the baby?" she asked. "Are they all right?"

"She's okay. She's still in labor so the baby hasn't come yet." He dragged in a weary breath, and there was plenty of worry on his face. Some of that worry was no doubt for her and their own child. "The doctors have assured me that six hours isn't that long when it comes to labor."

Six hours. That's how long it'd been, and Joelle realized she'd slept nearly a full hour of that. Well, slept and dreamed anyway.

"The last update I got was that Molly was about seven centimeters dilated," Duncan explained. "So, maybe it won't be long now." He paused a moment and eased a strand of hair off Joelle's cheek. "Molly's injuries aren't serious, thank God. And the baby seems to be perfectly fine."

Joelle felt the relief shove aside some of those remnants of the nightmare. "Good." And she repeated it several times.

"Obviously, we haven't been able to ask Molly about the kidnapping," Duncan went on. "There'll be time for that later after the baby's born."

She figured he was wishing he could question Molly since the woman might be able to tell them more than they already knew. And it occurred to her that Duncan might know a whole lot more than he had when she'd fallen asleep.

"Sonya is with Molly in labor and delivery," Duncan went on before she could ask him for an update on the investigation. "Sonya went to childbirth classes with her and is Molly's coach. It's possible Sonya and Molly have been talking in between contractions." He eased off the bed and lifted a white bag. "The hospital food didn't look that good so I had this delivered from the diner. A grilled chicken sandwich, a fruit cup and milk. You should eat."

Joelle's stomach growled at the mention of food, and she realized that despite everything that'd gone on, she was in fact hungry. Duncan took out the items he'd mentioned, laying them out on the rolling table that he pulled over.

Apparently, she wasn't the only one hungry because he took out another sandwich, a bag of chips and a bottle of water for himself. He hadn't gotten his usual can of Pepsi, though, and she suspected that was because he knew it was her favorite as well but that she'd given up soda for the duration of the pregnancy.

"You've been here the whole time I've been sleeping," she commented, already knowing the answer. Duncan wouldn't risk leaving her, not when there were those two gunmen still at large. "Did you get any rest?"

He tipped his head to the chair in the corner. "Some."

Which meant maybe a catnap at most. Since there was also a laptop on the chair, it likely meant he'd spent the bulk of those six hours working. Joelle felt a little guilty about that, but then she reminded herself that her resting had been necessary. Doctor's orders. Yes, she and the baby were all right, but the doctor had said some sleep would remedy the effects of stress caused by the attack.

They ate in silence for a few moments, but she didn't miss the glances he kept giving her. Often, she could pinpoint what was on Duncan's mind just by looking at him, but there had to be plenty on his mind right now. Joelle plucked out one of the possibilities.

"Have you managed to ID the man who tried to kill me?" she asked.

"Not yet."

She hadn't thought it possible, but just admitting that tightened his jaw even more. Of course, everything about this bothered him because the attacks were aimed at her which meant they were also aimed at the baby.

"And we had to let Hamlin go," Duncan added a moment later. "I can't prove he didn't send that fake text to himself. Hell, I can't prove anything that'll land him in jail."

Yes, definitely plenty of frustration mixed with the worry and exhaustion. Not a good mix.

"Did you see the photos of my father in the yard?" she added.

Of course, she knew that he had. He wouldn't have missed something that big at a crime scene, and even though he'd left with her to follow Molly in the ambulance, Duncan had likely gotten a glimpse of them. He'd probably had more than a glimpse by now since one of the other deputies would have bagged them for processing and sent him pictures of them.

He nodded and continued to study her. "The man we have in custody won't talk about them, but I'm guessing he's the one who put them there. Is that what caused you to drive the cruiser to that part of the yard?"

It was Joelle's turn to nod. And to wince and shake her head. "It was a trap, and I fell for it. He was right there, hiding, waiting for me."

"If you hadn't driven over to them, he likely would have just come after you where you were parked," Duncan was quick to point out. "It was a risky plan, what with cops and ranch hands all over the place."

Yes, it had been risky. And it'd nearly worked.

"The man was wearing Kevlar beneath his shirt," Duncan went on, "but he could have been shot elsewhere if someone had spotted him charging at you."

That was also true. "Does that make him an idiot, cocky or desperate?" she wanted to know.

"Maybe all three." He took a bite of his sandwich, motioned for her to do the same, and she did. "His name is Willie Jay Prescott," he added after he'd washed the bite down with some of his water. "At least we think that's his name. The lab got a match on the blood found at Molly's, and it belongs to this Willie Jay. Since the guy who tried to take you had a cut on his arm, we're guessing Molly wounded him and he left some blood behind."

That made sense. Well, maybe it did. "There were at least three gunmen involved in the combined attack on me and in Molly's kidnapping," Joelle reminded him.

He made a quick sound of agreement. "When I'm able to talk to Molly, I'll show her Willie Jay's picture and ask if he was the one with her the whole time. It's possible he wore a mask around her, but she might be able to ID him."

Since Molly was a former cop, Joelle was betting the woman would be able to do it, too. Even though Molly would have been terrified during her captivity, she would have no doubt paid attention to the man holding her.

"My father's killer or his accomplice is probably the one who took those photos," she said. Again, this wouldn't be a surprise to Duncan. "That means Willie Jay could have been the one who murdered him?"

"Possibly." Duncan added a heavy sigh to that response. "But it could have been someone else. I'll try to come up with a way to get Willie Jay to open up about that. Hell, to open up about anything because right now, he's refusing to say a word."

"Has he lawyered up?" she asked.

"Not so far, but he also won't confirm he even understands his rights. That means a psych eval. I've already scheduled one to give the official determination that he's competent enough to be charged with kidnapping, forced imprisonment, attempted kidnapping of another police officer and any other charge I can tack onto that."

The attempted kidnapping charges would definitely stick since there were plenty of witnesses. A crime like that would send him to jail for a long time. But it'd be a heck of a lot longer if they could prove he'd been the one to take and hold Molly.

And if he'd killed her father.

She doubted Willie Jay was just going to confess to that.

"We could maybe build a circumstantial case for murder if we can connect Willie Jay to those photos," she said, thinking out loud. "Because only the killer or someone who had knowledge of the killer would have those."

Even if Willie Jay was only an accomplice in that particular crime, it would carry the same penalty as the murder itself. Which would put Willie Jay on death row. Joelle wanted that. She wanted her father's killer to pay.

But she also wanted answers.

Why had her father been gunned down? And had Willie Jay orchestrated that, or was he merely a hired gun? Added to that, why had he wanted her? As she'd told Duncan earlier, he could have killed her, and he hadn't. He had intended to kidnap her. It was possible that was so he could get the baby, but there had to be an easier way to get his hands on a pregnant woman.

And that circled her back to the pictures.

Then, back to their suspects.

"If Brad, Kate or Hamlin are connected to Willie Jay,"

Joelle said, hoping this idea made sense when she spelled it out, "then, maybe you can use that as a trigger to get Willie Jay to talk. Maybe let Willie Jay believe you'll let one of them get access to him. *Bad access,*" she emphasized. "As in the kind of access to have him murdered because he can link one of them to the attacks, Molly's kidnapping and my father's murder."

Of course, there was no way Duncan would actually allow a prisoner to be hurt or killed like that, but it might work if Willie Jay thought Duncan would do something that drastic. Judging from the sound Duncan made, he agreed.

"Willie Jay might tell us something that'll pinpoint who's responsible for what happened. Including your father's murder," he added. "Because I think it's highly likely that someone hired Willie Jay. There's nothing in his background to lead me to believe he's capable of putting together something like this. I could be wrong, but I don't think so."

Since Joelle hadn't had a chance to pour through what they'd learned about Willie Jay, Duncan's assessment was enough for her to believe the man was a lackey. It was his boss they wanted.

"What about Brad?" she asked as they continued to eat. "Is he still at the sheriff's office?"

Duncan shook his head. "His lawyer showed up and insisted Brad had to leave to make funeral arrangements for Shanda. Brad apparently broke down, and Carmen thought he might need to be sedated."

Joelle raised an eyebrow, and Duncan must have picked up on the question she was about to ask.

"I have no idea if Brad's grief is real," he said, "or if he's the one who killed Shanda, but since we had so much going on, I had Carmen reschedule the rest of the interview for tomorrow. Ruston arranged for some SAPD cops to tail Brad to make sure he doesn't try to flee. By the way, Ruston's on his way here to check on you."

She didn't groan, though Joelle hated that her brother was taking the time to do that. Especially since there were so many other things that needed to be done. But she also knew that talking Ruston out of a visit would be impossible. He was her big brother, and he no doubt felt an obligation to make sure she was all right.

"Kate is clamoring to get out of the hospital and go home," Duncan said a moment later, continuing the update of all three of their suspects. "She claims she's in danger." He lifted his shoulder. "She might be if Brad or Hamlin want her dead, and that's one of the reasons I'm keeping a deputy on her door."

Yes, and the other reason was to make sure Kate didn't leave before they had a chance to find out if she was the mastermind behind what was going on.

The silence came again. So did some memories. Recent ones. Or rather a recent *one*. And Joelle knew they needed to talk about it.

"I should apologize for kissing you," she said.

Duncan laughed. "Joelle, you never need to apologize for that. But I know where this is leading," he was quick to add. "Kissing me brings back a lot of bad stuff for you."

It did. But it brought back good stuff, too. Specifically, the heat. "It's a distraction neither of us need right now," she pointed out.

No way could Duncan disagree with that, but he certainly didn't jump to say she was right. "There are a lot of different distractions," he said, his gaze sliding to her stomach. "The baby's the top priority."

Joelle was thankful he'd spelled that out. Despite the bitter feelings between Duncan and her over her father's murder, she knew he was committed to this baby. That he loved her. And right now, Joelle very much needed that.

"I always figured when I had a baby, that my parents would be around to share the experience," she said. Of course, that brought on a wave of bitter memories. "They very much wanted to be grandparents."

"They did," Duncan muttered.

She heard something in his voice, some of his own bitter memories, and she thought this went beyond what'd happened in the past five months. Duncan hadn't had the loving childhood she had. Just the opposite. From the bits and pieces he'd told her, his bio-dad had never been in the picture, and when he'd been six, his junkie mother's boyfriend had killed her in a domestic dispute. Duncan ended up in foster care and bounced around from place to place until he landed with an elderly aunt who lived in Saddle Ridge. The aunt had died when Duncan was a senior in high school so he had no family to speak of.

Well, no family except this baby she was carrying.

"You'll be a good dad," she muttered.

It was the truth, but part of her wished she hadn't spelled it out like that. It broke down yet even more of the barriers between them. So did the look he gave her.

A long lingering look that started at her eyes and landed on her mouth.

Thankfully, they didn't have time to make the mistake of another kiss because there was a tap on the door, and Duncan practically came to attention. He moved away from the food, positioning himself between her and whoever opened the door a moment later. Duncan slid his hand over his gun. But it wasn't a threat.

Ruston stuck his head inside.

"Good," her brother said. "You're awake." Ruston glanced

at Duncan's stance and nodded his approval. "Glad you're here and taking precautions."

They had a suspect just up the hall and a possible missing gunman. Joelle figured there'd be a lot of precautions until they made some arrests.

Ruston went to her, helped himself to one of the grapes from her fruit cup, and then leaned down to kiss her cheek. He took hold of her chin, turning her face while he examined her. He frowned when his attention landed on the bruises on her neck and temple. The ones on the neck had happened when Willie Jay had put her in a choke hold. The other was from the barrel of his gun.

"The SOB will pay for that," Ruston snarled.

Joelle didn't huff or remind her brother that she was a cop and such things happened to those in law enforcement. Yes, she was a cop all right, but she would always be his little sister. So would Bree, even though there wasn't a wide age gap between any of them. Each of the McCullough offspring had been born two years apart with Ruston the oldest at thirty-seven. Slater, thirty-five. She was thirty-three, and Bree, the baby of the family, was thirty-one.

"I can give you something that I think will help you make the SOB pay," Ruston added to Duncan, and he took out his phone. "On the drive over here, one of the techs called me. Shanda didn't have security cameras, but there was one on the street."

Ruston pulled up something on his phone and held it out for them to see. It was the grainy image of a nondescript dark-colored car, but the graininess didn't extend to the part of the photo of the driver.

"Willie Jay," Duncan and she said in unison.

"Yep," Ruston verified. "This was taken just up the block from Shanda's house, and if you look at the time stamp, it means he was there right around the time Shanda was being murdered."

Joelle felt a welcome wave of relief. Willie Jay would end up in jail for a long time, maybe even on death row. But that wouldn't convict him of her father's murder. Not unless they found a connection.

"We have Willie Jay's gun," Duncan explained. "The lab can see if it's a match to the one used to kill Shanda."

"Good," Ruston muttered. "Since Shanda was murdered in San Antonio, SAPD will be charging Willie Jay with that, but I don't want him to go unpunished for what he did to Molly and Joelle. I'd like to see him convicted on all charges with the sentences running consecutively. That way, even if he doesn't get the death penalty, there'd be no chance that he'll ever see the outside of a jail cell."

Joelle got another wave of relief, but there was still that nagging thought running through her head. "I want to find a connection between Willie Jay and Dad's murder. He might have been the one to pull the trigger."

Since there was absolutely no surprise on Ruston's face, Joelle knew that had already occurred to him. Of course, it had. Ruston had probably read every report connected to what had happened.

"I'm working on it," Ruston assured her just as there was another knock at the door.

Like earlier, Duncan braced. So did Ruston. But it was Sonya who peered in, and the deputy was smiling.

"Molly had the baby," Sonya announced. "A perfectly healthy girl. Seven pounds, three ounces, and I can attest to the quality of her lungs because she yelled plenty when she finally came out."

Tears watered Joelle's eyes, but these were definitely of the happy variety. "How's Molly?"

"She's great." Sonya didn't seem to be lying about that, either. "She's totally in love already with her baby girl." Now she paused. "I think that'll help her get over the trauma of what happened."

"Did Molly talk about the kidnapping?" Duncan was quick to ask, but the question had also been on the tip of Joelle's tongue.

"Not much. And I didn't press her on it," Sonya admitted. "Molly mainly just wanted assurance that her kidnapper was behind bars. He still is, right?"

"He is," Duncan verified.

"Good. Because I'm sure Molly will ask when she sees you. You can see her now," Sonya added. "A really short visit, though, after the pediatrician is finished examining Annika. That's what Molly's naming her."

Joelle got up out of the bed, intending to head to see Molly right away, but Duncan's phone rang.

"It's Luca," Duncan relayed. "You're on speaker," he added to Luca when he answered. "Give me some good news."

"I might be able to do just that," Luca replied. "I've been digging into Willie Jay's background, and I found out something very interesting. Willie Jay used to work for one of our suspects."

Chapter Ten

Hamlin.

Duncan wouldn't have been surprised no matter which of their suspects Luca had named. Kate, Brad or Hamlin. At this point, Duncan considered the three to all be sharing that top spot for their number one suspect.

Too bad he couldn't eliminate two of them, and then he'd know which one of them was responsible. Well, maybe. The gut-twisting possibility was that the culprit hadn't even surfaced, that Willie Jay's boss was someone other than Hamlin.

Still, Willie Jay had worked for Hamlin so that was a start.

"Arrange to have Hamlin brought in right away," Duncan told Luca, and Luca assured him he'd do just that.

Duncan ended the call and slipped his phone back in his pocket. "Sonya, I figure you didn't get much rest, what with being called in early and Molly's birth coach, but do you have the bandwidth to stay here with the baby and her until I can get someone else to guard them?"

"I can stay as long as needed," Sonya quickly assured him. "In fact, I'd like to stay the night. Molly and I are friends, and I think she'd be more comfortable with me than with someone else."

"I agree," Duncan told her, "but if you feel yourself start to fade, then let me know."

Duncan checked the time. The hours were just racing by, and they had so much to do. But it was a priority now to see Molly. Not just because she might be able to give them answers but also because she was part of their Saddle Ridge Sheriff's Office family, and she'd been through a hellish ordeal. Then, Joelle and he could go back to the sheriff's office and wait for Hamlin. Duncan had no doubts that Luca would be able to locate the PI and get him in there fast.

"I take it you're up to this visit with Molly and the baby?" Duncan asked Joelle.

"Absolutely." Her answer was quick and resolute.

Ruston checked his watch as well, and he leaned over and brushed another kiss on Joelle's cheek. "I'll head back to San Antonio and work the arrest warrant there. I just wanted to see for myself that you were all right. Are you going to Slater's tonight or will you stay with Duncan?"

Obviously, the question threw her because she gave him a blank stare for a couple of seconds. "To be determined," she said at the same moment Duncan said, "I'll take her to my place."

"Good," Ruston concluded, but he didn't spell out why he felt that way.

"Good," Joelle murmured, not sounding nearly as pleased about staying with him as Ruston had been.

They went into the hall with Ruston heading for the exit, and Sonya, Duncan and her going in the direction of labor and delivery. Sonya must have sensed Duncan needed to have a word with Joelle about the sleeping arrangements because she walked ahead of them, giving them some privacy.

Duncan waited for Joelle to spell out that it was risky for

them to be under the same roof. Especially after the kiss and the steamy looks they'd been giving each other.

"My resistance for you is really low right now," she whispered. "You saved my life, and you're the father of a baby we both love and want to protect."

That was it. No extra line to clarify where that low resistance would lead them. Duncan's guess was to bed since he didn't have a whole lot of resistance when it came to her, either.

And that caused him to curse.

Because she'd just confessed she was vulnerable. Of course, she was. She'd nearly been kidnapped and could have been killed. So, landing in bed was totally out since it'd be taking advantage of her.

"Yes," she murmured when he cursed again, and the response confirmed she was well aware of his thought process.

His body didn't want to give up on the "landing in bed" part, but Duncan had to shove all thoughts of that aside as Sonya opened one of the hospital room doors. When Duncan looked in, he immediately saw Molly on the bed. She was smiling and cooing down at the baby she was holding.

"Isn't she beautiful?" Molly asked, her smile widening when she looked up at them.

Duncan took one of the paper surgical masks from a wall holder, put it on and went closer. "Yep, she's beautiful all right."

And she was. A perfect little face with fingers so tiny that Duncan hoped Molly didn't insist he hold her. She seemed way too fragile for that, but he got a reminder that soon, in four months or so, he'd have to get past that fear since he'd be holding his own child.

Joelle put on a mask and walked closer, peering down at the baby. Even though Duncan couldn't see her expression, he knew she was smiling. "Molly, she's adorable." Joelle gave Molly's arm a gentle squeeze. "Congratulations, Mom."

"It's all a little daunting," Molly admitted, "and a whole lot amazing." She seemed ready to go on about the joys of motherhood. She didn't, though. She looked at Duncan. "You want to ask me questions about the kidnapping."

"Are you up to that?" he offered. "Because it can wait—"

"I can tell you what happened," Molly interrupted, "and then maybe we can do a more formal statement after I've gotten some sleep."

Duncan nodded and decided to let Molly say whatever it was she clearly wanted to say. If he saw her energy levels draining, then he would put a stop to this and come back.

Molly dragged in a long breath. "I was asleep when I heard my security system go off. I picked up my phone, thinking that maybe it was some kind of malfunction, but it wasn't. I heard someone moving around in my living room so I hit the last number I'd called. Joelle's. Then, I saw two men coming into my bedroom."

"Two?" Joelle asked.

Molly nodded. "They were both wearing ski masks, dark clothes. Both were about six feet and with somewhat muscular builds."

That described Willie Jay. Hell, it described a lot of men, and while Duncan was certain they had one of the kidnappers in custody—Willie Jay—they obviously needed to look for his partner. And Joelle's attacker. Of course, it was possible the second kidnapper was also the one who'd fired those shots into the cruiser at Joelle.

"I tried to get to my gun that I keep in the drawer next to the bed, but they grabbed me before I could do that," Molly went on. "I hit one of them with my phone and then dug my nails into his arm. I guess I cut him deep enough for him to leave blood at my house."

"We've identified that blood," Duncan told her. "Willie Jay Prescott. We have him in custody."

Molly's breath hitched, maybe from relief. "And the other?"

"We'll find him," he assured her, and Duncan hoped that was the truth. They needed to find the remaining person or persons responsible for this.

Molly paused a moment, kissed her daughter's cheek and then started again. "They put a hood over my head, tied up my hands and feet, and got me into a vehicle. A truck, I think, because of the way they had to lift me to put me in it. And they drove away."

It was hell for Duncan to hear all of this. To know the terror that had to have been going through Molly's mind. She'd probably thought she would lose her precious baby as well as her own life.

"The men didn't talk when we were driving," she went on. "But we weren't in the vehicle long. Maybe ten minutes or less."

Duncan calculated that was about the time it would have taken the kidnappers to get from Molly's house to the McCullough ranch. "Did they take you to the location where we found you, or did you go somewhere else first?"

"Just that one location. Your dad's ranch," Molly muttered, looking at Joelle. "I didn't know that's where I was until the EMTs were taking me to the ambulance."

That made Duncan do more mental cursing. All those hours, Molly had been so close. But they'd had so many places to search, and Molly hadn't had any connection to the McCullough ranch. She had been taken there because the kidnappers no doubt knew it was empty.

Molly cleared her throat before she continued, "After I was in the shed, I'm sure one of them left. The one who smelled like cinnamon stayed, and the other left."

"Cinnamon?" Duncan pressed.

Molly nodded. "He was chewing some kind of gum or candy. He's the one who made the calls to Joelle." She paused. "And I honestly believed what he was saying, that he regretted kidnapping me."

Maybe he did. But obviously Willie Jay hadn't felt that.

"A couple of hours before you found me," Molly continued, "the second man came back, and they had a whispered conversation. The cinnamon guy was pleading with the other to let me go, but the second man said no. They went out of the shed, and they argued, but I couldn't make out what they were saying. Then, neither one came back in. I didn't hear anyone else until you and the deputies showed up."

Duncan could only speculate as to what'd happened. Maybe the "cinnamon guy" had stormed off. Or maybe Willie Jay had eliminated him. If so, the man's body hadn't been found on the ranch, and the CSIs and some of his deputies had been combing the place.

"If you get me a sample of Willie Jay's voice, I should be able to confirm he was one of the kidnappers," Molly offered.

"I'll do that," he said just as the baby let out a kitten-like cry. That was his cue to leave and let Molly have some time with her daughter.

Joelle gave Molly another gentle hug, ran her fingers over the baby's cheek and left with Duncan. He was about to call Slater or Luca to provide backup while they went to the sheriff's office, but Slater was already in the hall, waiting for them.

"Ruston told me about Hamlin's connection to Willie Jay," Slater explained as they headed for the exit. "He's on his way in for an interview, but he's not happy."

"Welcome to the club," Duncan muttered. But in Hamlin's case, not being happy was a good thing. Riled people often said more than they intended to.

As expected, Slater had the cruiser waiting for them right outside the ER doors, and the three of them hurried to get in. Duncan glanced at Joelle and saw that she was looking at the window next to her. And she was no doubt recalling that Willie Jay had shot through a similar window to get to her.

The bullet-resistant glass was better than nothing, but this had to be a reminder that they weren't safe, not even in the cruiser. Duncan could only hope they'd be making an arrest soon that would put an end to the danger.

Duncan kept watch as Slater drove, but he didn't see anyone he didn't recognize. If Joelle hadn't been with him and if they hadn't been in the middle of town, Duncan would have wanted to spot the missing attacker. Would have liked to have a showdown with him. But the thug apparently wasn't showing his face in broad daylight.

After Slater parked, they went into the sheriff's office. Which was nearly bare. Understandable, what with all the various components of the investigation going on and with some of the deputies needing rest after a hellishly long day. Woodrow was at his desk, working on his laptop, and Ronnie was at his. Not alone. There was a young brunette woman sitting next to him. Both Ronnie and the woman got to their feet, their attention turning to Duncan.

"This is Erica Corley," Ronnie said. "She just came in to talk to you."

The name was familiar, but Duncan thumbed through his memory to figure out if he recognized her. He didn't.

And when Joelle and Slater shook their heads, he figured they didn't know her, either.

"I'm Sheriff Holder." Duncan went closer to Erica and hitched a thumb at Joelle and Slater when he introduced them.

The woman nodded, swallowed hard. "I'm Al Hamlin's ex-girlfriend. Al and I had a baby together when we were teenagers."

Duncan was certain he looked surprised because he was. Not about the baby part but that Erica would just show up like this. Then again, it was possible the PI they'd talked to had located her and sent her to them.

"I heard about the kidnapping and attacks on the news," Erica went on. "One of the reports mentioned Al, that he was on the scene when a man was taken into custody."

Duncan silently groaned. He didn't know how the media picked up on such details, but he had to admit a story like this would make good press.

"And I thought… Well, I wondered," Erica added a moment later, "if Al was involved in some way?"

Since that was exactly what Duncan wanted to know, he motioned for Erica to go into his office. Joelle came, too, but Slater muttered something about needing to check for updates, and he headed to his desk in the bullpen.

"Can I get you some coffee or water?" Duncan asked her.

Erica shook her head and took one of the seats next to Duncan's desk. Joelle took the other.

"Was Al involved in the kidnapping and attacks?" Erica pressed.

Considering that Willie Jay had worked for Hamlin, the answer was yes, but Duncan kept that to himself and went with a question of his own. "Do you believe your ex is capable of something like that?" He'd asked Brad's ex,

Shanda, the same thing, and she'd more or less waffled on her response.

Erica didn't.

"I believe he's capable," she said after a heavy sigh. "I don't know why he'd do it, but..." She stopped. "It could be because of what happened with our baby. I suppose you know about that?"

"We do," Duncan verified.

Erica nodded. "I wanted to give the baby up for adoption, and Al wanted to, well, sell it."

There was some anger, maybe even shame, in those last few words, and Erica lowered her head, shook it.

"I was against it," Erica went on after several moments. "But Al kept pressing me. He said he'd gotten in touch with someone, and the person would pay us ten thousand dollars. I don't come from money, and that sounded like a fortune to me. So I went through with meeting with this person, even though I wasn't sure I could actually sell my child."

That meshed with what Duncan had read in the juvenile records that Slater had managed to get. The arresting officer had mentioned that Hamlin had been the one to orchestrate the sale and had also contacted the couple two more times to up the amount he wanted them to pay for the child. That's how the extortion had come into play.

The wannabe adoptive parents had been charged, too, since they had planned on paying for the baby, but no one involved in the case had pointed the finger at Erica as being the aggressor in the sale or the extortion. Still, she'd been convicted since she had gone along with meeting the couple.

"What happened at the meeting?" Joelle prompted when the woman fell silent.

Erica gave another of those long sighs. "The San Antonio cops found out what Al and I were doing because they showed up and arrested us." She shifted her attention to Joelle. "I think your late father was the one who told the cops."

Duncan didn't know who was more surprised by that, Joelle or him. "My father?" she questioned.

"I spoke to Sheriff Cliff McCullough shortly after I was arrested. He'd gotten a tip from a longtime confidential informant that a couple was trying to buy a baby, and he gave SAPD the couple's names, and that in turn put the cops on Al and me. We didn't even make it to the meeting with the couple because they in turn told the cops about us. We were convicted of attempted extortion and trying to sell the baby."

Joelle stayed quiet a moment. "Did Hamlin know about my father's involvement in this?"

"Sure," Erica was quick to say. "Your father spoke to both Al and me after the arrest. I'm not sure what he said to Al, but your dad was kind to me. He knew my folks had kicked me out, that I had no place to go and had been staying with friends just to have a roof over my head. He told me if I needed help with a legal adoption agency or if I decided to keep the baby, he could find me a place to go."

That part didn't surprise Duncan one bit. Sheriff McCullough had been a good man, and he would have done whatever possible to right a bad situation. If Erica was telling the truth, and Duncan believed she was, then her situation had definitely qualified as bad.

"I took the sheriff up on his offer," Erica explained. "I got out of juvie three months before Al did, and the sheriff helped me get into a home that had other girls like me. I had the baby, legally put her up for adoption and then the sheriff arranged for me to get my GED and a job."

Joelle and Duncan exchanged glances, and he could practically see the wheels turning in her head. "How did Hamlin take that?"

"Not well." That answer was also quick. "He didn't find me until after I'd had the baby, and he was furious. Not because he wanted the child. But because he still thought I should have gotten some money for the baby. Money that I should have shared with him." Her bottom lip trembled a little. "I told Al to leave me alone or I'd ask Sheriff McCullough to help me file a restraining order against him."

Duncan figured Hamlin wasn't happy about that, either. In fact, it could have riled him to the core. Did it rile him enough, though, to carry on a vendetta to murder the sheriff and go after Joelle? Maybe. And maybe Molly played into the plan simply because she would soon give birth to a baby that Hamlin could sell.

Erica lifted her head and met Duncan's gaze. "I think Al might have pressured his sister to sell her child. That might be why Isla disappeared."

Duncan considered that for a moment and then tried to link that to what was happening now. If Hamlin had continued to dabble in selling babies, then it's possible Isla would have run from him.

"Did Al ever mention Kate Moreland?" Duncan asked.

Erica opened her mouth to answer, but the sound of a man's voice stopped her. Speaking of the devil, Hamlin came in, pushing his way past one of the deputies, and his attention must have landed on Erica.

"What the hell is she doing here?" Hamlin demanded.

Erica sprang to her feet, and Duncan thought the woman might cower in fear at the sight of her ex, but she turned and faced him head-on. "I came because I thought you might be involved in what happened to Deputy McCullough and the woman who was kidnapped."

Hamlin cursed, and he opened his mouth as if about to unleash some rage and profanity, but he quickly bit that off.

He turned around, pacing a few steps, and when he turned back toward Erica, he scrubbed his hand over his face.

"Don't you see?" he asked her. "They'll use anything you've told them to try and pin these crimes on me. I'm just trying to find my sister and make the people who took her pay."

"I had to come," Erica fired back. There was no real anger in her voice, just that shamed reaction again. "I don't know for sure if you've had any part in what happened, but I wanted to tell the sheriff about our arrest. I didn't think it would come up in a normal search since we were underage."

"And it's irrelevant," Hamlin insisted. He snapped toward Duncan and repeated that. "Yes, I was convicted of doing something very stupid by trying to get money for our child. I was young and desperate, and I made a mistake. All of that has nothing to do with the attacks. I told you I was there on scene because I got a text from you. Or rather a text I thought was from you."

"It wasn't," Duncan verified. And that's why Duncan had had his phone records entered into the investigation log so it would be clear he hadn't been the one who'd messaged Hamlin telling him to go to the McCullough ranch. According to the techs, the message had come from a burner, which meant Hamlin could have sent it to himself.

That was a reminder of why Duncan had wanted Hamlin to be interviewed, but he wasn't sure if Erica had more to add to the investigation or not. "Thank you for coming in today," Duncan told the woman. "Deputy Slater McCullough will take your statement because there are some things I have to ask Hamlin."

And Duncan didn't want to do that in front of Erica. He needed to keep this all by the book since he soon might be charging Hamlin with a boatload of felonies.

Duncan tipped his head to the interview room. "This way," he told Hamlin, and Joelle followed in step behind them. On the short walk, Duncan repeated the Miranda warning.

Hamlin muttered throughout the warning, and he was still muttering when they were in the room and seated. "Erica shouldn't have come and stirred up things like that," he snapped. "I had nothing to do with what happened to Deputy McCullough and the dispatcher."

"Nothing to do with Sheriff Cliff McCullough, either?" Duncan threw out there.

Hamlin flinched. Then, he huffed again. "Erica told you that the sheriff is the one who ratted us out. Yes, he did. He poked his nose into something that wasn't his business, but I'm going to repeat myself again. I had nothing to do with what's been going on."

Duncan just stared at the man, and after a few seconds had crawled by, he said, "Willie Jay Prescott." And he watched Hamlin's reaction.

Joelle was no doubt watching, too, which meant she saw the flicker of recognition in Hamlin's eyes. "Want to tell us about your relationship with Willie Jay?" she suggested, though it was more of an order.

Hamlin's mouth tightened, and he belted out some more profanity. "What about him?"

Duncan huffed. "Stop playing games with us. Willie Jay is in a jail cell right here in this building, and he's had plenty to say."

Of course, that last part was a lie. Willie Jay hadn't said a word, but it was obvious that the revelation of Willie Jay's arrest put some serious concern on Hamlin's face.

Hamlin stayed quiet a moment, his gaze flickering right and then left. "Mr. Prescott briefly worked for me when I first became a PI," he finally said. "I employed him to help me track down leads on my cases. The employment didn't last because Mr. Prescott turned out to be not very reliable at showing up for work or doing his assigned tasks. So, I fired him."

Duncan continued to fix his hard stare on the man. "When was this?"

Hamlin certainly wasn't quick to answer. "I officially fired him about two months ago, but he hasn't actually worked for me in nearly a year. I just quit giving him assignments." He paused a heartbeat, and some more anger flared through his eyes. "Mr. Prescott was *not* happy about me terminating his employment so I'm sure anything he told you is to get back at me for firing him."

Duncan made a sound to indicate he was giving that some thought and he shook his head. "He didn't mention anything about you firing him." And Duncan left it at that, letting Hamlin squirm.

He squirmed all right and did more cursing. "Look, I don't know what Willie Jay said about me, but I've done nothing illegal. Nothing illegal since that incident when I was a teenager," he amended when Duncan lifted an eyebrow. "The person you should be looking at is Kate Moreland. She's behind these attacks."

"So you've said," Duncan commented. "But I'm not seeing a whole lot of proof that she's guilty. You, on the other hand, have a strong connection to a hired thug, Willie Jay, who we caught red-handed. He's going down, and he's going down hard. It'll be interesting to see who he takes with him."

The anger came again, like a burst of red-hot heat, but it faded just as quickly. "The person he should be taking down with him is Kate because I didn't hire Willie Jay to go after Deputy McCullough or your dispatcher."

Joelle leaned in. "Why are you so sure it's Kate? There has to be more to this vendetta of yours—"

"She was the one who contacted me when I was seventeen and Erica was pregnant," Hamlin blurted. "I'd been asking around, and she got in touch with me. She called herself a middleman in the process. A *facilitator* was the word she used."

Interesting. Because Kate hadn't mentioned anything about that. Then again, this might all be Hamlin blowing smoke.

"Kate contacted you personally?" Duncan asked.

Hamlin nodded. "With a phone call. I'd left my number around in case anyone was interested. I spelled out that Erica and I wanted some money to cover the expenses of her pregnancy and the upcoming delivery."

Duncan raised his eyebrow again.

"All right." Hamlin huffed. "I wanted more than expenses covered. I wanted to be able to give Erica and me a fresh start. And she had already said she was giving up the baby. It wasn't as if I pressured her to do that."

Maybe. Duncan figured some pressure was involved once Hamlin realized he could get money for the baby. Still, Duncan didn't want to muddy this line of questioning.

"So, did you actually meet with Kate when you were trying to arrange for the sale of your child?" Duncan asked.

The wording clearly riled Hamlin, but Duncan wasn't planning on sugarcoating anything. "No," Hamlin snarled.

"Then you can't know for certain it was Kate Moreland," Joelle was quick to point out. She obviously wasn't sugarcoating, either.

"It was her," Hamlin insisted, but then he paused and seemed to have a lightbulb over the head moment. "It was her voice. I've heard recordings of her speaking at various social events, and I'm positive it was Kate."

"Maybe," Duncan repeated.

"There's no maybe to it. It was Kate, and after that initial call, I dealt with one of her employees."

That got Duncan's attention. "Who?"

"A man named Arlo Dennison," Hamlin said without hesitation. "I've researched him, and he used to manage one of her gyms. He doesn't any longer. In fact, he's not officially on her payroll that I can find, but she's probably paying him under the table for more black market baby deals."

"That's possible," Duncan admitted. "But other things fall into the area of possibilities, too. For instance, you're the one doing the baby-brokering deals, and you want to toss some bad light on Kate so she'll take the heat for something you're doing."

Yeah, it was a hard push, but Duncan had wanted to see how Hamlin would react. And he saw all right. Hamlin got to his feet.

"I'm going to terminate this interview right now and come back with a lawyer," Hamlin insisted. He glared at Duncan. "Unless you plan on arresting me simply because I once employed a man you now have in custody."

Duncan wished he could arrest Hamlin. It'd take one of their prime suspects off the street. But there was no way he could get an arrest warrant much less a conviction with what he had.

"Come back first thing in the morning with your lawyer," Duncan told Hamlin. "By first thing, I mean eight o'clock. Be here or I'll send someone to bring you in."

Of course, that riled Hamlin even more, and the man stormed out. Duncan immediately took out his phone to look up this Arlo Dennison, but Joelle had already done it.

"Arlo Dennison," she relayed, "is forty-two and did, indeed, manage one of Kate's gyms. He's got a sheet, an old one for assault and extortion. That was eleven years ago, so he either learned his lesson or he's gotten better at covering up his crimes. I'm texting you his number now," she added.

The moment Duncan's phone dinged with the text, he clicked on the number to call Arlo Dennison. There was a single ring before the call went to voice mail. The greeting was automated and simply told the caller to leave a message. Duncan didn't, though if Arlo checked his phone, he'd be able to figure out that the sheriff of Saddle Ridge was calling him.

"Arlo lives in San Antonio," Joelle added. "You want me to have Ruston send someone out to pick him up and bring him in for questioning?"

Duncan thought about it for a couple of seconds and nodded. "See if Ruston or another SAPD cop can do the interview."

That would save them from having to wait around for Arlo to come in. Duncan figured Joelle was spent for the day. He certainly was, and added to that, they would need to re-interview Kate and try to get Willie Jay to talk.

Joelle nodded and immediately called her brother. She'd barely had time to convey what they wanted when Duncan's own phone rang, and he saw Luca's name on the screen.

"We have a problem," Luca said the moment Duncan answered the call on speaker.

"What?" Duncan asked after he groaned.

"Woodrow found a truck on one of the ranch trails that's near the McCullough ranch. Inside it, there were two dead bodies."

Chapter Eleven

Two dead bodies.

Hearing Luca say that had given Joelle an initial hit of adrenaline. But that had been six hours ago. Now she was just wiped out and had to force herself to stay alert and focused as Duncan read the latest update he'd just gotten from Woodrow and the CSIs.

"Two males," Duncan said. He was standing behind his desk, reading from his laptop. "Both were identified through prints since they had criminal records. Darrin Finney, forty-two, from San Antonio, has a sheet for B&E, assault and drug possession. Troy Oakley, thirty-six, from Austin, has a nearly identical sheet, minus the drugs. The deaths were set up to look like a murder-suicide with Troy being the killer."

Joelle, who was seated in the chair, looked up at Duncan. "Set up?" she questioned.

Duncan nodded. "There was a note left at the scene, but the CSIs said the angles of the kill shots were wrong for it to have gone down that way."

He turned his laptop so she could read the note that had been photographed. The handwriting was basically a scrawl so it took her a moment to make out what it said. "Too many cops after us," she read aloud. "This is better than going to prison. We were wrong to go after that deputy and the other woman."

Even without the wrong angles of the kill shots, Joelle would have suspected the murder-suicide was a ruse. Sometimes, criminals did do things like this, but the truth was the cops weren't on the trails of these two. Their names hadn't even surfaced so far during the investigation.

"Both men had GSR on them," Duncan continued. "And Darrin Finney had some cinnamon gum in his pocket."

Continuing to fight the fatigue, Joelle considered that a moment. Molly had said one of her kidnappers chewed that particular flavor of gum so that probably meant these two were the ones who'd taken her.

"The truck they were in was reported stolen earlier today," Duncan added a moment later, "and there doesn't seem to be a connection between the owner of the vehicle and either of these two dead men."

Molly had also mentioned she believed they had transported her in a truck. So that matched as well.

"These two took Molly," Joelle summarized. "Maybe they did, anyway. Since Willie Jay ended up at the ranch with Molly, he could have been one of her initial kidnappers." She paused. "And that would mean the two worked together with someone else to cover both her kidnapping and the attack aimed at me. The *someone else* could be just one person. Or two."

"Probably two," Duncan said. "Because I don't believe they'd see going after a cop as a one man job. So, with two dead and one in custody, there's almost certainly someone else out there we need to find."

"You're thinking the fourth man might be this Arlo Dennison Hamlin told us about?" she asked.

Duncan shrugged and then sighed. She wasn't exactly

sure the reason for the sigh until he closed his laptop and walked around the desk to take her by the arm.

"I'm taking you to my place," he said, lifting her from the chair.

Part of her wanted to argue, to try to continue to push through the avalanche of information they'd gotten on this investigation. But the baby moved just as she opened her mouth to insist she had another couple of hours in her. She didn't. And the baby was a reminder that she had already had too much stress on her body today and she needed rest.

Duncan let go of her arm once they got moving out of his office and into the bullpen. Slater, Woodrow and Luca were all there. All still working. And that gave Joelle some fresh guilt over leaving when they hadn't. Still, the exhaustion wasn't giving her much of a choice about this.

Slater and Woodrow were both on the phone so Duncan turned to Luca. "Could you follow Joelle and me to my place?"

Luca's nod was quick. "You want me to stay there with you tonight?"

Duncan considered that for a moment and nodded. "Three of the attackers are out of commission, but I believe there's a fourth one and their boss are still out there. Let's go in one cruiser."

Luca nodded as well, and after mouthing the plan to Slater, he grabbed his laptop and went out the door first with Joelle and Duncan right behind them. Following their recent travel patterns, Duncan rode shotgun and Joelle took the back seat.

It wasn't far to Duncan's house, only about two miles, but travel anywhere wasn't exactly a breeze because of the attacks. All three of them knew any time out in the open could lead to another one. Added to that, it was dark now so someone could be lying in wait.

While Luca drove and they kept watch, Joelle tried to recall if Duncan had more than one guest room. Even though Duncan had owned the small ranch for five years now, she hadn't been to his place that often. Mainly because they'd spent a good chunk of those five years keeping their distance from each other.

Clearly, they'd ultimately failed since she was carrying his baby.

From the handful of visits she had made to his ranch, she recalled the house being fairly large, but even without guest rooms, she figured they'd all end up getting some sleep somewhere in the house since they had all been going at this for way too many hours.

Duncan's phone dinged with a text. A sound that instantly put Joelle on alert in case it was a message about an attack being imminent. She tried to hold onto the hope, though, that it was good news.

"It's from Slater," Duncan relayed to them. "SAPD uncovered something interesting on Kate. About three months ago, she accused Brad and Shanda of drugging her. She talked to a detective about it, and he investigated, but nothing came of it since there were no drugs in her system when Kate came in to report it."

Joelle worked that through in her mind. "I can see this playing out two ways. Either Brad and/or Shanda did, indeed, drug the woman. Or else Kate was laying the groundwork to set them up for the attacks she was planning on Molly and me."

Duncan made a sound of agreement. "And that takes us back to Kate's motive. If the attacks are to set someone up, why not do that to Hamlin? That would get him off her back."

"True," Joelle admitted. "But maybe her motive is about getting revenge for what happened to Shanda. I know she hated Shanda," she quickly added, "but the arrest and miscarriage ultimately caused a rift between Kate and her son. Kate would want to get back at Molly and me for that, and in the process she could end up with two babies to sell."

The thought of that sickened Joelle. Kate could possibly want to use her baby and Molly's to settle an old score.

It didn't take long, less than five minutes, before Luca took the turn into Duncan's driveway, and Duncan used his phone to open his garage door. He also turned on some security lights. Lots of them at both the front and sides of the house.

Unlike her place, Duncan had neighbors—a small-time rancher directly across the road from him and another about two hundred yards to his right. Not exactly right next door but close enough that the lights from those two places also provided some illumination as well.

Luca pulled into the garage, and they all stayed inside the cruiser until Duncan had shut the garage door behind them. "I have a security system," he said, checking his phone. "And I would have gotten an alert had someone gone into the house. Still, I want to do a sweep of the place just in case someone hacked into the system."

That wasn't exactly a comforting thought, but Joelle was glad Duncan had even considered it. The problem with being so tired was that it could cause a loss of focus on something critical like this.

Duncan got out, and he searched the garage first before he went into the house. Luca and she sat in the cruiser, waiting and hoping that all was well. They'd already been through way too much. Ditto for Molly, but Joelle had talked to the woman about an hour ago, and the baby and the new mother seemed to be doing well.

"Have you heard from Bree?" Luca asked, drawing Joelle's attention back to him.

"Yes. She's planning on coming home soon." Though now that she'd given that some thought, Joelle would try to talk her sister out of it. Saddle Ridge just wasn't a safe place to be right now.

Luca made a sound that could have meant anything, but Joelle thought she detected some kind of undercurrent. And she knew why. At best, Bree usually managed to come home three or four times a year and then for only a week or two.

The exception to that "coming home" pattern had been five months ago when their father had been murdered and their mother had disappeared. Bree had then stayed in Saddle Ridge for just over five weeks. Joelle knew that Bree and Luca had seen each other then, but there seemed to be some kind of rift between them and then Bree left. Luca might be wondering if he could fix that rift and go back to the way things had been.

That was a reminder for Joelle that she needed to have a conversation with Bree. Maybe soon if the fourth gunman wasn't caught and his boss arrested. Willie Jay could speed up the possibility of that if he'd just start talking. Arlo Dennison might be able to do that as well if the cops managed to find him. So far, that hadn't happened, which led Joelle to believe that he, too, might be dead.

Duncan finally appeared in the doorway that led into the house and motioned for them to come in. That helped ease some of the tension in Joelle's body. So did Duncan rearming the security system the moment they were inside.

"All the doors and windows have sensors," Duncan explained. "Normally, I keep the alarms at a soft beep since I'm a light sleeper, but I'll change that to a full sound. If someone tries to get in, we'll hear it."

Good. That was one less thing to worry about, especially since Molly's kidnappers had broken into her place despite her having a security system.

"This way," Duncan instructed. He led them through a kitchen with stainless appliances and white stone countertops. "Help yourself to anything in the fridge. Sorry that it isn't better stocked, but I hadn't counted on… Well, I hadn't counted on this."

Since Duncan had been steadily feeding her throughout the day, Joelle wasn't hungry, but she figured she would be by morning.

Duncan continued to lead them through the living and dining rooms and toward the hall. He stopped outside the first door. "It's my office, but there's a sofa sleeper," he said to Luca. "Bathroom is there." He tipped his head to the room directly across from the office.

Luca muttered a thanks, one weary with fatigue, and went in while Duncan continued with her to the next room. "Guest room," he explained, walking in with her. The walls and the comforter on the queen-size bed were both pale blue. "I'll be right next door. The walls are thin enough that I'll hear you if you call out."

Joelle sighed, hoping there'd be no need for her to call out, that nothing else would go wrong tonight.

Duncan stayed put, studying her for several moments. "This is probably going to sound wrong, but we can sleep together if that'll help with the tension that I can practically see coming off you in waves. *Sleep*," he emphasized.

Even though it was the worst reaction, Joelle smiled. She should have instead given him a firm look to let him know she'd be fine in here alone. But she was out of firm looks for the night. She sighed again, then shook her head.

"Tempting, but I'll be okay," she muttered. She hoped. It was possible she was too tired and had too much firing through her head to actually sleep.

The corner of Duncan's mouth lifted. Apparently, he was going for his own *worst reaction*. He compounded that by pulling her into his arms.

Her body landed against his. Familiar territory for both of them. Bad territory, too, because it instantly spurred some memories that shouldn't be spurred right now. Their defenses were down. They were both vulnerable. Yet, neither one of them pulled away from each other.

Joelle actually moved in closer, sliding her arms around his waist and dropping her head onto his shoulder. Mercy, it felt good. Not just because of the heat but because of the comfort this gave her. She wasn't a weak woman. Definitely wasn't a coward. But it felt good to be this close to someone who had her back.

She felt Duncan brush a kiss on the top of her head. Not really any kind of foreplay per se, but anything they did at this point would qualify as foreplay. Again, that was a good reason for her to move away from him,

But she didn't.

Joelle lifted her head, came up on her tiptoes and kissed him. It wasn't an especially heated kiss, but it shouldn't have happened at all. Nothing about this could stay at the comforting level. It never would between Duncan and her. The heat that stirred between them would never allow a comfort level. It would only demand to be sated.

That didn't stop her from fully kissing him. Nor did it stop him from returning the kiss and tightening his arms around her, pulling her even closer to him. Until they were touching in all the wrong places.

Duncan used his foot to shut the bedroom door, and he was the one who deepened the kiss. Joelle didn't do anything to stop that, either. In fact, she welcomed it. Needed it. She needed him, and that made the situation even more dangerous. This kind of need wouldn't just rip down barriers, it would put a permanent end to them.

That still didn't stop her.

She slid her hand around his neck, pulling his mouth down to hers so she could deepen the kiss as well. So she could take. And burn. Oh, yes. She was burning all right, and the heat continued to skyrocket when he dropped his grip to her bottom and aligned them in just the right way.

Of course, the baby bump didn't allow for the usual direct body to body contact in their midsections, but it was plenty enough for Joelle to recall in perfect detail just how good this could be between Duncan and her. Good but with serious consequences. Remembering those consequences gave her just enough steel to ease her mouth from his.

Duncan stared down at her and blinked as if trying to clear his head, and then he muttered some profanity. "I didn't think," he said. "I didn't think of the baby."

He had created a wonderful steamy heat inside her head so it took a moment to cut through that and realize what he meant. She had to smile again.

"Pregnant women are allowed to kiss," she pointed out. "And have sex."

That last part flew right out of her mouth before she even knew she was going to say it. *Stupid, stupid, stupid.* Of course, it made Duncan smile again, and Joelle gave up and smiled right along with him.

The moment seemed to freeze. Their gazes certainly did

while they were locked with each other. And the heat came at them like an out-of-control train. Cutting through what was left of any common sense.

There was a ringing sound that cut through as well, and it had Duncan and her flying apart. For one horrifying moment, Joelle thought it was the security system alerting them that someone had broken in. But it was Duncan's phone.

"It's Slater," he said when he looked at the screen and put the call on speaker. She started to move away from him, but Duncan kept his arm around her waist.

"Hope I caught you before you crashed for the night," Slater greeted.

"You did," Duncan said. "Did you get something?"

"Yes." Slater stopped, cursed. "Shortly after you left, Willie Jay got a phone call. From Kate Moreland."

"Kate?" Duncan questioned. "What did she want?"

"She wouldn't say, but I told Willie Jay she'd called and tried to get him to tell me why she wanted to talk to him. He stayed clammed up. So, I went back to my desk to see if I could get the answer from Kate. She clammed up as well and said she had to go, that the doctor ordered her to rest."

Clearly, Duncan and she would be having a chat with Kate first thing in the morning.

"I dug deeper, looking for a connection between Willie Jay and Kate," Slater went on. Joelle could hear some chatter in the background at the sheriff's office. "When I got nothing, I went to check on Willie Jay, to see if he'd changed his mind about talking to us. He was unconscious when I found him." Her brother cursed again. "Duncan, Willie Jay's dead."

Chapter Twelve

Duncan poured himself another cup of coffee—his third of the morning—in the hope that it would help get rid of the headache that was throbbing at his temples and behind his eyes. That was a lot to ask of mere caffeine, but he needed a much clearer head than he had right now.

He heard the shower going in the guest room and figured Joelle would be out soon to join him in the kitchen. Maybe she'd gotten some sleep after he'd left her in the guest room an hour or so after Slater had called with the news about Willie Jay. Maybe. But like him, she'd obviously had to try to get that sleep while processing what the hell had happened.

Duncan was still processing that.

Luca no doubt was, too, because he had downed multiple cups of coffee since getting up and was now at the other end of the kitchen table while he worked on his laptop.

Like Duncan, the deputy was digging for anything and everything that would help them make sense of this. Joelle had almost certainly done the same. She just hadn't surfaced for coffee yet, probably because she could no longer have a morning jolt of caffeine. The pregnancy had apparently put a temporary halt to that.

"The tox report came in," Luca announced just as Duncan

saw it pop into his inbox. As promised, Slater had pressed the lab hard to get those results ASAP. No easy feat since it had taken the ME nearly two hours to arrange for the body to be removed from the jail and transported to the county morgue.

Duncan was scanning through those results when Joelle came hurrying into the kitchen. Her focus was on her phone screen, and her hair was damp, but she was dressed. She was wearing the clothes she'd washed and dried the night before after she'd borrowed one of his shirts and a pair of boxers to sleep in. Once they'd gotten the news about Willie Jay, Joelle had known she wouldn't want to be scrounging up some loaner clothes today, that she'd want to focus on the investigation.

"You saw the tox report," she said after glancing at them.

Duncan made a sound of agreement. "Cyanide in the form of a capsule." Part of the capsule had still been in his mouth. "Since Willie Jay was searched before he was locked up, that means he must have had the pill concealed somewhere on him. And that he must have intended to end his life rather than spend time in jail."

That, in turn, added slightly more credence to the murder-suicide of the other two gunmen. The angles of the shots were still off, but now Duncan had to consider that the men had been willing participants in their deaths.

Why?

That's what both Luca and he were digging to find out. Joelle likely would be doing that, too.

"We start with Kate. I want to find out why she called Willie Jay last night," Duncan said, checking the time. It was nearly eight o'clock. "I've already called Dr. Benton, and he said Kate had a rough night and requested sedation. But we'll be talking to her this morning."

That seemed to be Joelle's cue to get moving to the fridge, and she grabbed an apple, and after checking to see there was no milk or yogurt, she went with some cheese. "Did Dr. Benton say anything about what had caused Kate's rough night?"

"More or less. He told Kate that she'd be going home today. She asked if the deputy guarding her would be going with her, and the doctor said he didn't think so, but he didn't know for sure. He said she became agitated after hearing that and insisted she'd be in danger if she left the hospital. He left her for a while because he had to see another patient, and when he came back, she asked for the sedative."

"Does the timing work for when Kate would have tried to call Willie Jay?" Joelle asked.

"According to Benton, it does, and he said she was holding her phone when he came back in the room." Duncan paused. "And speaking of her phone, the request came through for us to get her records."

"They just arrived fifteen minutes ago," Luca supplied, looking up from his laptop to glance at both of them. "In the half hour before Kate tried to speak to Willie Jay, she got two phone calls. One from Brad and the other from Hamlin."

Joelle huffed. "Obviously, we'll be doing a lot of interviews today."

"They're already set up," Duncan assured her. "As soon as you're done eating, we can head to the hospital and knock out the one with Kate. Then, I can have an actual breakfast delivered for you from the diner while we wait for first Brad and then Hamlin to come in."

Duncan expected they'd have lawyers with them and would deny everything. But the pieces were there, and maybe, just maybe, those pieces would fit so one of them or Kate could be arrested today.

"I do have one bit of good news," Joelle said. "I had a text conversation with Bree before I got in the shower, and I convinced her not to come home right now."

Good. That was one less person who might get caught up in this messy investigation.

"I can eat my apple on the way to the hospital," Joelle insisted. "I'm eager to hear what Kate has to say."

So was he, but Duncan took a moment to make sure Joelle was up to this. One glance at her and he knew she was. He couldn't say she looked rested, but she was clearly raring to go. So, that's what he did.

With Luca grabbing his laptop, Duncan headed to the window—again—to make sure there wasn't anyone lurking around. When he didn't see anyone, they went to the cruiser and started the cautious drive to the hospital. Only a couple of minutes. But if the missing gunman and his boss had realized Duncan and Joelle had spent the night at his place, then they might have set some kind of booby trap on the road.

Luca and Joelle no doubt expected the worst, too, because they kept watch. Joelle did the entire five-minute drive with her hand over the butt of her weapon. Thankfully, though, they made it to their destination without anyone trying to kill them.

Despite the early hour, there were already several cars in the parking lot, but Luca parked close enough to the door that Joelle only had a short distance out in the open before she hurried in through the ER doors. Duncan was right there with her, and he did a sweeping check of the ER. No one suspicious.

With Luca staying close behind them, Joelle and Duncan made their way to Kate's door, and Duncan was pleased when he saw Clyde Granger standing guard. Clyde was in his sixties now and a retired deputy, but Duncan knew the man was still plenty sharp.

"She's whining," Clyde said, his tone indicating this wasn't the first time. "She won't leave without police protection."

"So Dr. Benton told me," Duncan verified. "I'll consider it." He was stretched thin with manpower and was surprised that Kate hadn't just hired private security. The woman certainly had enough money to do that.

Luca stayed in the hall with Clyde when they reached the room. Kate immediately sat up in bed, and she had her phone gripped as if ready to call 911. She audibly released her breath when she saw it was Joelle and Duncan.

"Dr. Benton said he's releasing me this morning," she said like a protest.

Duncan nodded. "He said you believed you were in danger."

"I am," Kate was quick to verify. She glanced away, then. "Maybe in danger from my own son. Did you arrest him?"

"I'm questioning him," Duncan supplied, and he considered that the end to him answering the woman's questions. He hadn't come here for that. "Tell me why you called the sheriff's office last night and asked to speak to a prisoner we had in custody."

Kate didn't look surprised. Probably because she would have known all calls would be logged. Especially calls made to a criminal like Willie Jay.

"That PI, Al Hamlin, phoned me," Kate snarled with plenty of venom in her voice now. "He told me you'd arrested a man named Willie Jay Prescott, and that the man was going to tell you and the deputies that I had been the one who arranged to kidnap the dispatcher and Deputy McCullough."

"Did you?" Duncan demanded.

"No." That came out as a howl of outrage, followed by a groan and a lot of head shaking. "Of course not. I wouldn't do something like that."

The jury was still out on that, but Duncan tried a different angle. "Tell me about Arlo Dennison."

No howl of outrage this time, but there was plenty of surprise. "Why do you want to know about him?"

Duncan gave her a hard look to let her know she would be answering questions, not him.

Kate's mouth tightened. "Arlo managed one of my gyms. And I know what you're going to say," she continued when Duncan's look hardened even more. "That PI told you he talked with Arlo when he and his girlfriend were giving up their baby for adoption."

"He did." And Duncan made a circling motion with his finger for her to continue.

She obeyed, after she huffed. "I was very busy with work when all of that was going on, but a friend of a friend wanted to adopt a baby. So, when I got word of Hamlin and his girlfriend, I made the initial contact. Arlo followed up with them. But you should know that I had no idea Hamlin and his girlfriend wanted money for the baby. They were convicted, you know."

"And you and Arlo were questioned," Duncan reminded her. Ruston had come across that tidbit and passed it along.

"We were," she admitted, "but nothing came of it because there was nothing to find. I was trying to do this friend of a friend a favor, and I got caught up in the middle of an ugly mess. Now Hamlin thinks I took his sister and am running some kind of baby-selling business. I can assure you, I'm not."

Kate looked ready to add more to that protest, but the sound of some loud talking in the hall stopped her. "Brad," she muttered when she obviously recognized one of those voices.

Duncan knew the other voice was Clyde's, and the deputy was clearly in an argument with Kate's son.

"I want to see my mother now," Brad demanded.

His first thought was to send Brad on his way to the sheriff's office so he could wait for the interview. But then Duncan figured it would be interesting to see how mother and son reacted to each other, especially since there were four deputies ready to intercede if Brad did try to go after Kate. Or vice versa.

Throwing open the door, Duncan silenced Brad with one of the glares he'd been doling out to Kate for the past five minutes or so. Brad froze for a moment, but then moved darn fast when Duncan motioned for him to come inside.

"I don't want him here," Kate snapped.

Duncan ignored her, but he also blocked Brad when he attempted to charge closer to Kate. "Since you clearly have something to say to your mother, say it," Duncan invited.

Brad had another momentary freeze before he speared his mother's gaze with his. "You told Hamlin I hired gunmen to go after Deputy McCullough and the dispatcher."

Kate's shoulders went stiff. "I most certainly did not." She muttered some profanity. "And I'm tired of being accused of things I didn't do," she added to Duncan.

"Hamlin said he called you and that you said I should be arrested before I tried to kill you," Brad insisted.

Kate huffed. "No." She stretched out that word. "Hamlin's the one who pointed the finger at you, and he didn't say anything to me about you trying to kill me. Hamlin, however, did warn me about that prisoner, Willie Jay Prescott. Hamlin claimed you hired him."

Silence fell over the room while they all took a moment to process that. Duncan didn't need a moment, though, since he'd already come to a conclusion.

"Hamlin could be trying to stir up trouble between you two," Duncan pointed out. "More trouble," he amended, "since it's obvious that things aren't lovey-dovey."

"They aren't," Kate muttered, and her face tightened. Duncan figured it had occurred to her that he was right, that Hamlin had called both Kate and Brad to get them at each other's throats.

And it had worked.

It made Duncan wonder if Hamlin had done that with the hopes it would get Kate to say something to incriminate herself in the illegal baby sales. Or if Brad would be the one doing the self-incriminating. If so, Hamlin could have wanted that to cover up his own guilt. In fact, all the attacks and Molly's kidnapping could be to set up either Brad or Kate so Hamlin would escape scrutiny for his pregnant sister's disappearance.

"My lawyer is on his way to Saddle Ridge," Brad muttered a moment later. "I'll talk to him about suing Hamlin for slander."

Duncan didn't tell Brad that would be a long shot and turn into a "he said, she said." Added to that, Kate probably wouldn't want all of this to be rehashed in public, which it would be if there was a lawsuit.

Brad continued to stare at Kate while his jaw muscles tightened. "Look me in the eyes, Mother, and tell me you had nothing to do with Shanda being murdered."

The anger on Kate's face had cooled a bit, but that caused

it to heat up again. "No, I did not, and I'm insulted you even asked."

"I have to ask," Brad fired back, "because you hated her."

Kate opened her mouth, and must have rethought what she was about to say. "Yes, I hated her because of the person you became once you got involved with her," she finally said, her voice surprisingly calm. "You changed after Shanda lost that baby. You became obsessed with payback."

"Obsessed with getting my family back," he quickly replied. "I wanted Shanda and a baby."

"You wanted revenge," Kate spelled out.

Brad glared at her. But he didn't disagree. However, Brad did turn and head out the door. It was still open since Luca and Clyde had both been keeping a close eye on the situation.

Duncan went after Brad so he could remind the man about the interview, but when he went into the hall, he saw that Brad was practically charging toward someone.

Hamlin.

The PI was coming straight up the hall, and the men rammed into each other. That caused them to collide with a nurse carrying a tray of meds, all of which went flying.

So did the fists.

Brad managed to punch Hamlin in the face before Duncan could get to him. Hamlin retaliated, throwing his own punch, and the hall was suddenly filled with profanity-laced tirades and the sounds of the struggle. The nurse was trapped beneath the men.

Duncan reached into the heap and pulled out the nurse, sliding her toward Joelle who had moved closer to help. Once Joelle had the nurse out of the way, Duncan went after Brad next and hauled him out of the fray by the collar of his shirt. Clyde and Luca took hold of Hamlin, who came off the floor ready to run at Brad again.

"You lying SOB," Brad yelled, and he added plenty more profanity to go along with that. Hamlin was doing the same.

Duncan glanced at Joelle who was moving the nurse back toward the nurses' station. "Call for two deputies," Duncan instructed Joelle. "I want both Brad and Hamlin taken to holding cells."

That would keep both men off the streets at least until Duncan had a chance to interview them. It was possible, likely even, that Brad and Hamlin would be filing assault charges against each other. But he'd deal with all of that later. For now, Duncan needed to establish some calm and control since a crowd had gathered to see what the ruckus was all about. There were at least a dozen medical folks and patients gawking at the two men being restrained and the now-crying nurse.

"I can get this one to the cruiser now," Luca offered, keeping a firm grip on Hamlin. "Once he's in holding, I can come back for Joelle and you."

"Do that," Duncan agreed. As long as Brad and Hamlin were around each other, there'd be the possibility of another altercation.

Luca immediately got a still-cursing Hamlin moving toward the ER doors, and when Brad tried to go after the PI, Duncan had had enough. He pulled out some plastic cuffs from his pocket and restrained Brad.

"Go back and stay with Kate," Duncan told Clyde. "I'll look for a place to stash Brad until the other deputies arrive." Duncan also wanted to check on the nurse. She didn't appear to be injured, but she had taken a hard fall.

Duncan got Brad moving toward Joelle and the nurse, but he'd only made it a couple of steps before Clyde called out to him. Duncan turned to see Clyde standing in front of Kate's still open door.

"The room's empty, Sheriff," Clyde said. "Kate's gone."

JOELLE READ THE text from Woodrow to let her know that Ronnie and he had Brad out of the hospital and in their cruiser. Thankfully, she'd already gotten a text from Luca to let them know he'd arrived safely with Hamlin, and that the PI was now in a holding cell where he'd wait until Duncan and she could get back to the sheriff's office.

Whenever that would be.

There was a full-scale search going on for Kate not only in the hospital but also the grounds. Since Duncan hadn't wanted Joelle out of his sight, they had taken the patients wing with the hopes that a frightened Kate had ducked into one of them to avoid another confrontation with her son.

So far, nothing.

And that's what Clyde and some of the orderlies were reporting as they searched the grounds. Kate had seemingly vanished, and Joelle knew that couldn't be a good thing.

In the chaos of the fight, it was possible someone had sneaked in and taken Kate. There was a good argument to be made for that since Kate's phone had been left on the bed. If the woman had fled of her own accord, she likely would have taken that. Then again, she might have left it behind since the phone could be used to pinpoint her whereabouts.

If so, Kate might have left out of fear of her own arrest.

Duncan huffed when they cleared another room and there was still no sign of Kate. At least this particular room hadn't had a patient. Some of the others had been occupied, and it had to be unsettling to have two cops show up and conduct a search. Joelle had doled out a lot of apologies. Not just to the patients but the nurse who'd been shaken up in the brawl. Thankfully, the woman hadn't been hurt other than some bruising and frayed nerves.

"Three more to go," Duncan muttered when they went back into the hall. "And supposedly none is occupied." He'd likely gotten that info from one of the nurses since Duncan's phone had been dinging every few minutes with texts.

As they'd done with the other rooms, Duncan kept his gun ready while he eased open a door and peered inside. Once he'd done the initial check of the main part of the room, Joelle stepped in to cover him so he could have a look in the bathroom.

"Empty," he said, and he stopped to read another text. "The hospital security guard is searching the roof to see if Kate went up there."

Joelle figured if the woman was going to run, it wouldn't be to the roof where she would essentially end up trapped since there was only one set of stairs leading to it. Still, Kate might not be thinking straight.

Duncan and she went back into the hall, which had thankfully been cleared of any gawkers, and they made their way to the next room. This one was easier than some of the others since the bathroom door was wide open, so all they had to do was a cursory sweep before moving on to the final room. Once they checked it, they'd be able to head to the sheriff's office where they could question Brad and Hamlin while the search for Kate continued.

They came to a quick stop outside the final room when there was a thumping sound just on the other side of the door. Duncan glanced back at her, a silent warning for her to use extra caution. She would. Because even if it was Kate in there, it didn't mean the woman wouldn't attack them. Maybe out of fear.

Maybe, though, because Kate was the killer.

Duncan motioned for Joelle to stand back, and he eased open the door. Unlike the other rooms, this one was pitch-dark, probably because someone had lowered the blinds. Joelle barely managed a glance inside when she heard another sound. One that she instantly recognized.

A stun gun.

"Duncan," she managed to call out.

But it was too late.

The gloved hand that snaked out of the darkness jammed the stun gun against Duncan's throat. He staggered back, and Joelle reached for him, trying to break his fall, but she didn't get to him in time. Duncan dropped like a stone.

Oh, God.

"Duncan," she shouted.

Joelle automatically drew her gun. But it was too late for that, too. A bulky man wearing orderly scrubs and a ski mask charged right at her, pushing her back against the wall. In the same motion, he tried to knock the gun from her hand. She held on, twisting her body to try and get away from him so she'd have a clean shot. No chance of that since this thug might deflect the gun, and the bullet could hit Duncan.

"Officer down," she yelled, hoping that someone would hear her and come running.

The thug must have thought that was a possibility, too, because he clamped his hand on hers and her gun and started muscling her toward the exit. He was not only tall but strong. A lot stronger than she was, but Joelle knew she had to fight him.

For her baby's sake.

For Duncan's.

This goon might turn and shoot Duncan before he made that final push to get her out of the building. Kidnapping her. Just as Willie Jay had tried. And the other two dead gunmen.

Joelle didn't want to mentally play out what would happen to her if he did manage to get her outside and into a vehicle. Instead, she focused on the baby and Duncan and tried not to let the terror take over.

She stomped as hard as she could on the goon's foot, and while it slowed him down and made him curse her, it didn't stop him. So Joelle twisted around and rammed her elbow into his gut. That worked better than the foot stomp because he staggered back a step, his back smacking against the wall. He still managed to keep his beefy grip on her gun.

From the corner of her eye, Joelle saw Duncan struggling to move, and he was lifting his gun. She had no idea if he had the motor control yet to pull the trigger, and like her, he didn't have anything close to a clean shot.

The goon pushed himself away from the wall, throwing himself at her and off-balancing her. Joelle had no choice but to protect her stomach, and she did that by bending forward. Not an easy task because of the baby bump, but she used her upper torso to protect her child.

Her attacker cursed her, and as Willie Jay had done, he latched onto her hair. The pain shot through her. With his other hand on her gun, he probably hoped to use that leverage and the pain to force her to move.

That failed, thank heavens.

Joelle got another slam of adrenaline. Another punch of the fight mode, and she used that strength and her training to twist his hand. And her gun. Until she had it aimed at his right leg.

She fired.

He yelled, the sound echoing along with the blast of the shot. Staggering, he let go of her hair, and the maneuver allowed her to take aim again. At his left leg. The bullet slammed into him and caused him to drop to his knees.

Joelle heard the sound of running footsteps and Slater calling out to her. Help would be here soon. But she didn't take her attention off the goon. She couldn't see his face, but she figured it had to be twisted in pain.

"Move and I'll put another bullet in you," she warned him, wrenching her hand from his grip.

The goon didn't listen. He moved, reaching out so fast that it was just a blur of motion. But before Joelle could pull the trigger, someone else did.

Duncan.

He was still on the floor, but he'd lifted his head and shooting hand enough to deliver the fatal shot. Her attacker slumped forward. *Dead.*

Chapter Thirteen

Duncan paced while he waited on hold with Slater. Paced and kept his eye on Joelle who was now seated at his kitchen table.

Since she'd been covered with their attacker's blood, he'd brought her here to his place instead of the sheriff's office so she could shower. That was after she'd had yet another exam to make sure both she and the baby were all right.

They were. By some miracle, they were.

So was he since he'd also needed to be checked to make sure the stun gun hadn't done any permanent damage. It hadn't.

Duncan figured he'd be saying a lot of thanks and prayers for that. After he'd put an end to the danger so Joelle could make it through a blasted day without someone trying to kidnap her again. Because that's what had happened. Another attempted kidnapping. If the masked thug had wanted her dead, he would have shot her the moment Duncan opened the door of that hospital room.

Even though she hadn't been shot or hurt beyond a few minor scrapes and bruises, it still twisted away at him that she'd come so close to being taken. He should have put more precautions in place to prevent that. And he would. He couldn't continue to put her in harm's way when so much was at stake.

That's why he'd brought Luca with him, and like before, the deputy was in Duncan's home office doing reports of this latest incident. *Incident*, he silently repeated, the anger rising in him again. A sterile word for something that damn sure hadn't been sterile. Joelle and he had been attacked, and Duncan had been forced to kill the SOB. He'd add more thanks and prayers for having regained enough feeling in his shooting hand to manage that. If not, Joelle would have had to do it, and Duncan didn't want her having to deal with that on top of everything else.

And *everything else* was huge.

She'd been attacked three times now, and while Molly thankfully hadn't been this time around, the dispatcher was shaken to the core. So much so that she'd asked Duncan to have not one but two reserve deputies stay with her. Duncan had complied, pulling the two off the search for Kate.

Kate was another investigative thorn in his side right now. There was no sign of her, and worse, she could have been the one who'd hired that thug to come after Joelle and him in the hospital. If Duncan hadn't allowed himself to get distracted by Brad and Hamlin's fight, then he might have seen the woman sneaking out.

Or being taken.

"Stop beating yourself up," Joelle muttered.

She was watching him and sipping some milk that Slater had had delivered, and she looked so small in the loaner clothes she'd gotten from the sheriff's office. Loose gray jogging pants and a black tee that was a couple sizes too big for her.

"I deserve to be beaten up," he was quick to remind her.

"I should have brought you to the sheriff's office before I ever started searching for Kate."

Joelle lifted her shoulder, sighed and stood, going to the fridge to refill her glass of milk. That meant walking right by him, and she brushed her arm against his. Probably not by accident. He took out the *probably* when he looked at her.

"Stop beating yourself up," she repeated. "I'm a cop, and I could have made the decision to go to the sheriff's office when Luca was transporting Hamlin. If I'd done that, then who's to say this kidnapper wouldn't have come after me in the cruiser. Willie Jay did."

He had to fight back the horrific images of that attempt and this one. There had been enough bad for a lifetime, and it wasn't over. It wouldn't be over until he had the culprit behind bars.

She reached up and touched her fingers to his forehead. Duncan didn't exactly recoil, but the touch hurt a little. When he'd fallen after being stunned, his head had smacked on the floor, and the gash had needed a couple of stitches. He'd gotten those in the ER while the doctor had been examining Joelle and the baby.

There was finally a crackle of sound on the other end of the phone, and a moment later, Duncan heard Slater's voice. He went ahead and put the call on speaker since this was an update Joelle would want to hear.

"The dead guy is Arlo Dennison," Slater provided.

Hell. That circled right back to Kate since the man had been one of her employees. It was possible Arlo had still been an employee, just in a different capacity as a hired gun.

"Four dead men," Slater emphasized. "That could mean whoever hired them has run out of muscle."

Maybe. But Duncan knew it was just as likely that Kate,

Brad or Hamlin had found yet someone else to do their dirty work.

"Still no sign of Kate," Slater went on. "The Texas Rangers you requested arrived, and they're coordinating the search."

Good. Duncan figured if the woman could be found, the Rangers were his best shot at making that happen. Especially since Kate could be anywhere right now. She hadn't taken her phone with her, but she could have arranged for someone to meet her in the parking lot and take her to heavens knew where.

"Luca just filed yours and Joelle's statements on the attack at the hospital," Slater added a moment later.

No surprise there. Luca had been the one to take those statements shortly after they'd come to his place. Both Joelle's and Duncan's primary weapons and clothes had also been taken into evidence. All standard procedure. So was counseling, but that was going to have to wait.

"Any updates on Brad and Hamlin?" Duncan said to Slater.

Duncan already knew both men had made bail and the interviews had been rescheduled for late afternoon. Not with Joelle and him doing them, either. Going with standard procedure again, neither of them would be doing interviews and such until there'd been a review of how they'd handled Arlo's attack.

"Nothing new," Slater said. "Well, nothing other than both men's lawyers are clamoring about their clients being innocent and harassed by the cops. Same ol', same ol'," he muttered. Then, paused. "How's Joelle? And, yes, I'm asking you, Duncan, because my sister might not tell me the truth."

"I'm okay," she insisted. "Okay-ish," Joelle amended

when Slater huffed and Duncan gave her a flat stare. "You should be asking about Duncan. He's the one beating himself up over what happened. I'm not. We did what we had to do to stay alive and keep our baby safe."

Duncan continued to study her, to see if she'd said that to ease her brother's mind. And his. But Joelle seemed to have processed this and just might actually be okay-ish.

"I'll keep an eye on Joelle," Duncan told Slater, not only because it was true but because he also wanted to relieve Slater's worries. It would relieve Duncan's worries about her, too.

He ended the call, and when he went to put his phone away, he saw the blood smears on the back of his hand. His own blood from the cut on his head. It was a reminder that unlike Joelle, he hadn't showered.

"Shower," he muttered when he saw that her attention, too, had landed on the blood, and Duncan decided it was time to remedy that.

Time to remedy something else, too.

Duncan pulled Joelle to him and kissed her. Really kissed her. Yeah, it was a stupid thing to do, but it was necessary. He needed to have her close, this close, if only for a moment or two.

He didn't deepen the kiss. Didn't move them body to body, even though a certain part of him immediately started urging him to do just that. Duncan just kept the kiss gentle and hopefully comforting. Because he was damn sure they both needed that right now.

When he finally eased back, he stared down into her eyes and braced himself for her to warn him they were playing with fire. Which they were. But she simply smiled.

"Shower," she muttered. "Then, we can…talk."

That idiot part of him got all excited that sex might happen. It didn't matter that it would be a bad idea.

At least, it probably would be.

Joelle likely wasn't thinking straight and didn't need to land in bed with him. But her mention of *talk* had nixed the bed thing, and unlike sex, that was probably a good thing. She no doubt had things she needed to say about the attack. Maybe things about all this kissing they'd been doing.

Duncan headed to his bedroom for that shower, but he stopped by the office to check on Luca. He was still typing up reports. "Statements from the people interviewed at the hospital," Luca muttered without taking his attention off the screen.

A necessary pain in the butt. And something might be in those statements they could use. It was a serious long shot, though.

Duncan was thankful that Joelle followed him to his bedroom. Not because of the possibility of that sex happening, but because he didn't want her too far away from him. The security system was on, and two of Slater's ranch hands were outside in a truck, watching the place—something they'd been doing since he and Joelle had arrived from the hospital. A lot of avenues had been covered, but Duncan still wanted Joelle close so he'd be able to get to her fast if there was another attack.

Joelle sat on the foot of his bed while he headed to the shower. He didn't close the bathroom door between them. Another precaution, in case she called out to him for help. He hoped like hell there wouldn't be any such need for that.

Duncan turned on the shower, and stripped while he waiting for the water to reach the right temperature. The moment it was warm enough, he stepped in so he could do this fast and minimize the time Joelle was out of his sight. He had barely gotten started on it, though, when the shower door opened, and Joelle was standing there.

Joelle, who slid her gaze down the entire length of his body.

Duncan's gaze did some sliding as well. Looking at every inch of her. Man, she was beautiful. Always had been. But the baby bump actually added to that beauty.

He went hard as stone.

"I haven't been with anyone else but you since, well, in a very long time," she said.

It took him a moment to realize why she'd volunteered that. Then, he spotted the condom that she had likely taken from the drawer of his nightstand. It was a reminder they'd used one five months ago, and she'd still gotten pregnant.

"I haven't been with anyone else, either, in a long time," he told her and could have added that she was the only woman he wanted.

"So, not necessary," she muttered, tossing the condom onto the vanity.

Without taking her attention off him, she pulled off the loose clothes, tossing them on the floor next to his.

"I'll be careful," she said when he glanced down at the wet tiled floor. "Maybe you can hold on tight to me to make sure we don't slip."

And she stepped inside under the spray of warm water. In the same motion, she looped her arm around his neck and pulled him to her.

She kissed him.

Hard, hungry and long. This was no kiss of comfort, and yet it accomplished just that. Comfort. Then, a whole mountain of heat. She kissed and kissed until the nightmarish images just slid away.

"The bathroom door is locked," she muttered. "Our phones

are right on the vanity where we'll be able to hear them. And we aren't going to think about this," she tacked onto that.

Good. Because Duncan didn't want to think. He just wanted Joelle, and he wanted her now. Apparently, she was on the same page because she added some clever touching to the deep kiss. She slid her hand between their naked bodies. Down his chest. To his stomach. Then, over his erection.

If Duncan had actually wanted to do any thinking, that would have put an end to it. The only thing on his mind right now was taking Joelle.

Joelle got that taking started by hooking her arms around his neck and pulling herself up. He gladly helped with that by putting his arm underneath her bottom and lifting her until they were facing each other.

The kiss continued, raging on, cranking up the heat even more. But that heat was a drop in the bucket compared to Joelle's wet breasts sliding against his chest and with their centers pressed right against each other.

Duncan had to fight the urge just to push into her, to give both their bodies what they were demanding. But he purposely slowed so he could savor this. He eased back on the urgency of the kiss, and he kept his touch light as he cupped her breasts and flicked his thumb over her nipple.

She gave an aroused moan, and her head lolled to the side, exposing her throat. Duncan took advantage of that and slid both his mouth and tongue down her neck. Pleasuring her. Pleasuring himself.

The angle was all wrong for him to kiss her breasts so he levered her up even more, using the shower wall to stop them from falling. Once he had her high enough, he took one of her nipples into his mouth.

This time her moan was a whole lot louder, and the kiss kicked up the urgency again. She worked her way back down, aligning their centers again, notching up Duncan's own urgency when she slid herself against him.

No way could he hold off after that so he anchored her again by holding her bottom while he pushed into her. He got an instant slam of sensations. Pleasure. So much pleasure. But more. This was right. This was exactly what he'd been waiting for these past five months. Hell, longer. Since he'd wanted Joelle for as long as he could remember.

It was a balancing act to stay on his feet, but Duncan adjusted his position, and he started the slow deep strokes inside her. All thoughts of, well, pretty much everything vanished. Everything except this. The right here, right now. Everything except Joelle.

The need clawed its way through him, driving him to move faster. Pushing him to give Joelle both the pleasure and the release from this intense heat. It happened, and it didn't take long. Not with their bodies starved for each other. Duncan only needed a few of those strokes when he felt her muscles clamp around him. When he felt the climax ripple through her.

"Duncan," she muttered, dropping her head onto his shoulder.

And that was all he needed to push him right over the edge. Duncan held Joelle close and found his own release.

Chapter Fourteen

Joelle's entire body felt slack. Sated. Incredible. But she also knew without a doubt that she wouldn't be able to stand on what she was sure would be wobbly legs.

Duncan took care of that.

Just as he'd taken care of her with that sexual release.

He turned off the shower, scooped her up in his arms and stepped with her onto the rug. He didn't stop there, either, but rather sat her on the vanity while he pulled a huge towel around her. Since he proceeded to dry her off, that meant she got an amazing view of his completely naked wet body.

Mercy, she wanted him all over again.

This had been the problem with them for years. The heat. The need. And she'd thought that once they finally ended up in bed five months ago, the need would lessen some. It hadn't. And later, she was going to consider why that was. Consider, too, if it would ever go away.

Judging from the way her body was humming, the answer to that was no.

After he dried her off, he kissed her again. One of those scorching, heart-melting post-sex kisses that held promises of more to come. Too bad her body was absolutely onboard for that. Her mind, though, was reminding her to hold back, to guard her heart. And to put up those barriers again.

Joelle didn't do any of that.

She kissed him right back in the full-throttle mode. It lasted some very long moments, and when she eased back, she saw the fresh heat in those amazing eyes of his. The corner of his mouth lifted, flashing her a smile that also fell into the amazing category.

Of course, the smile didn't last. It faded by degrees, but at least she'd gotten to enjoy it for a bit.

"I'm guessing we'll have that talk now," he muttered, not sounding the least bit enthusiastic about that.

Neither was she, but Joelle thought they should spell out that this could be temporary. That this was "no strings attached" sex. Because she didn't want Duncan to feel this had to be the start of some grand commitment. He'd already committed to the baby, both offering child support and shared custody, and that was enough.

Had to be enough.

Joelle wasn't exactly sure what her feelings were for him… She stopped, mentally regrouped. All right, she was sure. She cared deeply for Duncan. Was perhaps leaning toward being in love with him. But this was so not the right time to delve into all of that.

"Let's put the talk on hold," she suggested. "Instead, let's go over the reports Luca's done, and I'll see if he needs help with any others."

Of course, Joelle had offered to help Luca when they'd arrived at Duncan's, and he'd declined, telling her to get some rest. Sex had been an incredible substitute for rest, and now she wanted to dive back into the investigation.

Duncan didn't seem convinced. He frowned. She wasn't sure if that was because he did, indeed, want to talk. Or maybe he wanted to keep kissing her and go for round two of sex. That was tempting. Mercy, was it.

"The sooner we make an arrest, the sooner the baby will be safe," she said, knowing Duncan was already well aware of that.

However, it seemed to be the exact nudge he needed to move away from her and start drying off. He did mutter some profanity, though, under his breath that had her smiling again.

Joelle started to get dressed, and despite the reminder she'd just given him, she didn't ignore the peep show going on right in front of her. Duncan was hot, but he was even hotter when he was naked.

He pulled on his boxers, his gaze meeting hers, and she saw the heat that was still there. She felt the tug deep within her body. Not sexual. Well, not totally. This was something different. Something just as strong. And it had her going back to falling in love with him. She probably would have had a mental debate with herself about that had her phone not rang.

She got a jolt when she looked at the screen and saw *Unknown Caller*, and part of her realized she'd been waiting for another would-be kidnapper to get in touch with her. Yes, four hired guns were dead, but Joelle was pretty sure their boss was still out there somewhere.

Out there and had possibly already hired new thugs to come after her.

Duncan became all cop, and he hit the recorder on his phone a split second before he nodded for her to take the call. She did, expecting to hear some muffled threatening voice of a stranger.

She didn't.

"Joelle?" the woman asked.

She nearly dropped the phone. "It's my mother," she said, the words rushing out with her breath. She looked at Duncan to see if he'd recognized it as well. He did, and he looked just as stunned as she was.

"Mom," Joelle finally managed. "Where are you? How are you?" And she had so many other questions she wanted to add to that.

For five months, she'd been terrified for her mother. Not only for her mom's safety since Joelle considered that she, too, might be dead. But there had also been the worry that Sandra McCullough had somehow participated in her husband's murder. Or was on the run because of something she'd learned or witnessed.

"Joelle," her mom repeated, but she didn't launch right into answering those questions. "I need help."

The static crackled across the phone connection, but Joelle still heard that loud and clear. "Where are you?" she repeated. "What's wrong?"

Again, there wasn't a quick answer, and the static increased. There was also the sound of a revving car engine.

"I'm at the ranch," her mother finally said. "Please, Joelle, please, come and get me before it's too late."

JOELLE FELT AS if she'd had way too much caffeine and her mind was whirling from it. However, the jumble of thoughts wasn't from any coffee but rather from hearing her mother's voice.

Slater was hearing it now, too.

Her brother and Carmen had arrived within minutes after Joelle had phoned him to let him know about the call, and now Slater was standing in Duncan's living room, listening to the recording. It wasn't the first time Slater had played it, either. This was his third, and he seemed just as shellshocked as she had been.

Still was.

"That's Mom's voice," she muttered to Slater. That was a repeat as well.

Her brother made a soft sound of agreement, and he looked up as if yanking himself out of a trance. "Yeah. But you know this is some kind of a trap."

"She knows," Duncan was quick to say.

Joelle did, indeed, and that's what had prevented her from bolting out of Duncan's house, jumping into the cruiser and driving straight to her family's ranch. Because this could all be a ploy to draw her out into the open like that. But there was a flipside to this.

Her mother could be in grave danger.

Could be.

And that was the sticking point here. Slater obviously knew something about that *could be* because he played the recording once more. Duncan and she had done the same thing when they'd waited for Slater to arrive.

"The call was almost certainly made from a burner," Slater pointed out, and Joelle made a sound of agreement. That was being checked as they spoke. Techs were also repeatedly trying to call the number with the hopes that someone would answer. So far, nothing.

"Mom never answered any of your questions," her brother added a moment later.

Joelle nodded. "And there's the static. A lot of it," she emphasized. "It seems to be coming from maybe a TV station or radio that's offline. It's too steady for the intermittent kind of static you'd get from a bad phone connection."

Slater nodded as well, and he shifted his attention to Duncan. "So, the fact that we're not charging over to the ranch right now tells me you don't believe my mother is actually in danger."

"I wish I knew for sure," Duncan said, drawing in a long

breath. "It is Sandra's voice," he verified. "But it could have been spliced together from old recordings. Maybe interviews taken from the internet."

Her mother had certainly done some of those since she'd often campaigned for bond issues to better fund the schools and libraries. Joelle couldn't recall a specific speech or such that could have been used to piece together what she'd heard, but it was possible. There was a huge *but*, though, in all of this.

"If the killer actually has her..." Joelle started, but then she couldn't force out the rest of it. Not aloud, anyway. But inside her head, the possibility was flashing bright and nonstop.

Her mother could be murdered.

She could be being held right now. Could be hurt. And she could need their help. In fact, it was possible her father's killer had taken her mother five months ago and had been holding her all this time, planning to use her to punish Joelle for whatever the killer believed she needed to be punished for. Maybe Brad for what'd happened to Shanda. Maybe Kate because her father had been on her trail for the illegal baby sales. Or Hamlin who wanted revenge for his arrest as a juvenile.

Duncan was well aware of that, too, and that's why he'd spent the past fifteen minutes assembling a team. Or rather two of them. And even though Duncan hadn't spelled it out yet, Joelle was pretty sure she knew what he was planning.

"You'll stay here," Duncan said, his gaze spearing hers. "I would take you to the sheriff's office, but this SOB could be hoping for that. To attack us along the road and try to take you."

Joelle had already considered that as well. It was the very definition of a rock and a hard place. If she went anywhere, she was a target. Ditto for if she stayed put. Duncan couldn't stop that, but he could maybe stop her mother from being killed if she was being held at the ranch.

"Luca and Carmen will stay here with you," Duncan went on. "And the two armed ranch hands will continue to guard the grounds. They'll block the driveway to prevent anyone from using a vehicle to get to the house. Stay inside and keep the security system on."

She recalled him saying all the windows and doors were rigged so if someone did attempt to break in, they'd at least get a warning. Then, whoever tried to get inside would be facing three cops.

"Slater and I will go to the ranch," Duncan continued a moment later.

But Joelle immediately interrupted him. "And you'll have extra backup with you," she insisted. "As we learned with Molly, there are plenty of places for someone to lie in wait."

Duncan didn't argue. "Ronnie and Woodrow are already on the way to the ranch. They'll hang back and use binoculars and infrared to try and spot any threats. Try and spot your mother, too, if she's actually there." He checked the time. "The plan is to make this as quick as possible."

His gaze lingered on Joelle's for a couple of moments, and she nodded. Not because she liked the idea but because there wasn't another option. The ranch had to be checked, and Duncan was the sheriff.

He went to her, and while he didn't kiss her, not with other cops watching, Duncan took her hand and gave it a gentle squeeze. "It's only a trap if we aren't ready for it, and we are," he whispered to her. "We'll take every possible precaution, and I want you to do the same."

She nodded again. "Come back to me in one piece," she muttered.

Duncan looked as if he wanted to groan at that. Because

it seemed to be the start of some grand confession about her feelings for him. About how important he was to her.

Which he was.

But no way did she want to send him off with that kind of distraction running through his mind.

"Stay safe," she added, using her cop's voice, and Joelle purposely turned away from him and faced Luca. "I can help you type up the witness statements from the hospital."

That would give her something to focus on. Or rather something to try to focus on. Joelle didn't know how long this would take Duncan and the others, but she would be on pins and needles the entire time.

"I'll reset the security system with my phone once we're out," Duncan relayed to her as Slater and he went to the door. Both Duncan and her brother gave her one last look before they headed out. One last stomach-twisting look.

Joelle stayed put, listening, and she heard the sound of the cruiser ignition. Heard, too, when Slater and Duncan drove away.

And the waiting began.

"Luca, I can do some reports as well," Carmen said, drawing Joelle's attention back to the other deputies. "So email me the notes of the ones you want me to do," she added as she took out her laptop.

Carmen didn't sit in the kitchen though but rather moved to the front window. No doubt so she could keep watch.

Since the keeping watch was a good idea, Joelle tipped her head to the hall. "Duncan's bedroom has a good view of the backyard. I can work from there. And yes, I'll stay back from the windows."

Luca didn't make a sound of agreement until she added that last part. "The office has a view of the east side of the property, and since that side doesn't face any of Duncan's neighbors, I can keep an eye on things from there. I'll email you both some of the statement notes," he added, heading to the office.

Joelle took her laptop and went into Duncan's bedroom. Of course, it was a reminder that less than an hour ago they'd had shower sex. *Amazing shower sex*. But since that brought on images of Duncan, the worry came with it, and she said a flurry of quick prayers that Duncan, her brother, Woodrow and Ronnie would come out of this unscathed.

Her mother, too.

Part of her wanted to hope her mother was there at the ranch. Because if she was, then it meant she probably hadn't voluntarily left her family. But if that was the case, then it was unbearable to think of the hell her mother had gone through all these months.

Since that kind of thinking wasn't helping her already frayed nerves, Joelle got to work—away from the window, though, she did open the curtains enough for her to be able to see out. There was a small seating area in the corner of the bedroom, and Joelle turned the chair so it was facing the window. That would keep her in the shadows and hopefully out of the line of sight of any shooters.

While she booted up her computer, she glanced out in the backyard. Unlike her place, this area wasn't thick with trees. Just the opposite. There was a small barn and some white wood pasture fence. A shooter wouldn't be able to use the fence to hide or sneak up closer to the house.

But the barn was a different matter.

The door was closed, and if a determined shooter belly-crawled through the pasture, they could slip behind the barn and try to fire into the house. With that unsettling thought, Joelle wasn't sure how much work she would get done, but she opened the file that Luca sent her, anyway.

There had apparently been thirty-one statements taken from patients, medical staff and anyone who happened to be in the parking lot at the time Arlo launched his attack and Kate went missing. Luca had sent Joelle six, nowhere near the one-third he should have given her. When she got through these, she would ask for more.

The statements were basically notes taken by the questioning officers, and they needed to be cleaned up and put in an official file that would then have to be verified and signed by those interviewers. Normally, cops did their own reports, but with so many aspects to the investigation, they all needed to chip in. Especially since she wasn't the one out there looking for Kate.

Joelle made it through the first one when she heard a soft thumping sound coming from the large walk-in closet/dressing area that was on the other side of the bathroom. The closet door was closed, and there wasn't a window in there that someone could use to break in.

She waited, her fingers poised on the keyboard while she continued to listen. Nothing.

And she was ready to dismiss it when she heard it again.

Joelle quietly set her laptop aside and got to her feet. She drew her weapon and inched to the closet door while also keeping watch of the window in the bedroom. It occurred to her that someone could be tossing something against the exterior wall to distract her so they could make sure no one was watching them if they sneaked up to the barn.

She stopped to send a text to Frankie Mendoza, one of Slater's ranch hands who was out front watching the road.

Do you see anyone on the right side of the house toward the back?

Joelle's heartbeat kicked up a few notches while she waited the couple of seconds it took him to answer. No one's there, Frankie replied.

That settled her down some, but Joelle remembered Duncan whispering to her about taking every possible precaution so she decided to get some help, especially since she was only a couple of feet away from the closet door. Even though it should have set off the security alarms, maybe someone had managed to get into the house.

"Luca?" she called out, keeping her voice calm and level. "Could you come here a second?" If it turned out to be nothing, then she would owe him an apology for interrupting him.

But it was something.

Before Joelle even heard Luca's footsteps, there were two loud thumps as if something heavy had fallen onto the floor of the closet. Her gaze whipped to the closet door as it flew open.

The two men were wearing ski masks, and they charged right at her.

DUNCAN'S STOMACH KNOTTED when he saw the McCullough ranch come into view on the horizon. Considering the godawful things that'd happened here, the place had an eerie feel to it. The approaching storm didn't help, either. The thick clouds were an angry-looking slate gray and shut out so much of the light that it looked more like twilight than daytime.

He stopped the cruiser at the end of the road and fired glances all around while Slater sent off a text to Woodrow. According to the two messages they'd already received from Woodrow while Slater and he had been en route, Woodrow and Ronnie had arrived at the ranch about seven minutes earlier, and they had done an immediate check with the binoculars.

They'd seen no one.

So they'd driven slightly closer to accommodate the short range of the infrared, and they were about to scan for heat sources. Since the deputies should have had time to at least start that, Duncan needed an update.

"Nothing so far," Slater relayed when he got a response from Woodrow. "They're moving closer now that we're here."

Ahead of them, he saw the deputies' cruiser start inching toward the house. Duncan did the same, driving slightly faster than Woodrow since he wanted to be right there with them in case someone opened fire.

It'd been less than ten minutes since he'd left Joelle at his place. Ten minutes of constant worry and doubts. And now Duncan hoped he could do this search as fast as possible so he could get back to her. He had a bad feeling about this whole situation, but he didn't know if the feeling was because he and his deputies were in immediate danger.

Or if Joelle was.

Possibly all of them were.

So far, their attacker had used guns and the fire at Joelle's to attempt to kidnap her, but it was possible they had something much bigger in their arsenal now. Then again, they wouldn't need bigger if they had Joelle's mom. If Sandra was truly here, she would be a damn good bargaining tool. One no doubt designed to draw out Joelle.

Slater's phone dinged again. "Woodrow spotted a heat source in the center of the barn," he told Duncan as he read the text. "If it's a person, he or she is lying down."

Hell. Lying down because she could be tied up. Like proverbial bait.

"No other heat sources," Slater finished.

Of course, that didn't mean no one was around. If the hired guns or their boss figured infrared would be used, they could be staying just out of range.

"Tell Woodrow that I'm going to pull ahead of them," Duncan instructed Slater. "I'll have to knock down a fence, but I'll drive to the barn." Maybe even into the barn itself since the person wasn't near the entrance. That would keep Slater and him protected for a while longer.

While Slater dealt with sending the text, Duncan maneuvered around the other cruiser and drove through the yard. He accelerated when he got to the fence, and the reinforced cruiser bashed right through it. Wood went flying, some of it thumping against the cruiser, but Duncan didn't think there'd be any real damage to the vehicle. He'd owe the McCulloughs a fence, though.

"Heat source hasn't moved," Slater said, giving Duncan the latest update from Woodrow.

That added some weight to the possibility of the person being tied up. Or maybe unconscious. Hell, perhaps even dead, because a body could continue to register as a heat source for minutes after dying.

Duncan was about to rev up to bash the front end of the cruiser into the barn door, but his phone rang. His heart went to his knees when he saw Luca's name on the screen.

"What's wrong?" Duncan immediately asked.

But he didn't get an immediate answer. And no answer at all from Luca. "It's me," Carmen said, and her trembling voice confirmed something was wrong.

"What happened?" Duncan snarled.

"Luca was hit with a stun gun," Carmen muttered. There was both urgency and pain in her voice. "And someone clubbed me on the head. I didn't see the man in time, Duncan. He just charged right at me."

Duncan had to fight the fear that was clawing its way through his throat. "Who charged at you? And where's Joelle?" he couldn't ask fast enough.

"A man wearing a ski mask." Carmen moaned. "There's a hole in the ceiling of your closet, and I think that's how they got in. Through the roof."

Hell. The roof wasn't rigged with the security sensors so an intruder wouldn't have set off the alarms. No one in the house would have known they were about to be attacked.

Duncan hit the accelerator, not heading into the barn but turning around. The tires kicked up clumps of dirt and grass as he sped away.

"God, Duncan," Carmen said. "They took her. They took Joelle."

Chapter Fifteen

Joelle's heart was pounding in her chest. Her breath was gusting. And the fear was right there, clawing away at her.

So much fear for her precious baby.

But she wasn't fighting as the two thugs manhandled her out of the house, down the porch and into the backyard. Not fighting. She had to get away from them, but she couldn't do that now.

Not with one of them holding a stun gun directly against her stomach.

She had no idea what a stun gun would do to the baby, but it couldn't be good. No. She had to wait for a safer way to try to escape, and she had to pray that opportunity would happen soon. Especially since they had gotten her out of Duncan's house and were taking her heavens knew where.

At least they hadn't killed her on sight, and she didn't think they'd killed Carmen or Luca, either. While one of the goons had used her as a human shield—after he'd knocked away her gun—he had held her at bay with the stunner. The other one had used a stun gun on Luca, and Joelle had seen him drop to the floor. Hard. Maybe hard enough to crack his skull.

Carmen had come at the hulking attacker, and she'd had her gun drawn, but she hadn't got off a shot before the thug hit her with a billy club. Carmen went down, too, and then the men had dragged Joelle toward the back of the house.

Now she had to pray they didn't shoot the ranch hands.

Since the hands were at the front of the house, they didn't have the best angle to see what was going on, but if they did, hopefully they'd take cover and call—

She mentally stopped right there.

Someone would call Duncan. If not the hands, eventually Carmen or Luca would do that when they were able. And Duncan would come for her.

Which was possibly what these thugs wanted.

The chance to have her while also forcing Duncan to put his own life in danger to save her and the baby. Was that the thugs' intention? Or would they try to get as far away from Duncan and the other cops as possible? She just didn't know, but she had to be ready for either of those things to happen.

"Was that really my mother who called me?" she asked. Not that she especially wanted to know the answer, not at the moment anyway, but if one of them spoke, she might recognize the voice and then she could know who was doing this.

Not Kate.

She was the only one of their suspects who couldn't be dragging her past Duncan's barn. Of course, Kate could have hired the pair, but it was possible one of the men was either Hamlin or Brad. The smaller goon was the right size to be one of them. But neither of them spoke. They just kept moving.

Joelle tried to tamp down the panic that was threatening to consume her. Hard to do, though, when everything was at risk. Her breathing didn't help. Way too fast. Way too shallow, and it didn't help that the air felt so heavy, like wet wool.

Soon, those heavy clouds would unleash a bad storm, and

she figured that wouldn't help matters. It'd mean Duncan would be driving through that to get to her.

The manhandling continued toward the back of the barn, and Joelle heard someone shout. Carmen. The deputy was calling out to the ranch hands for help. That caused both alarm and relief for Joelle. Carmen was alive, but Joelle also didn't want the ranch hands gunned down if they charged at them. Hopefully, the hands would use caution if they figured out where she was.

Once her attackers were behind the barn, they kept moving. Kept dragging her, and just ahead she spotted an old ranch trail. They were commonplace in the area, and this one had a spattering of trees flanking it. A car was there, tucked in between the shadows of those trees. Definitely not visible from the house.

"Where are you taking me?" Joelle asked, trying to make that sound like a demand.

Of course, they didn't answer, which meant they either had orders not to speak to her or there was the real possibility that she would be able to ID one of them from his voice. The men just kept moving until they reached the car, and they shoved her into the back seat.

Since the maneuver caused the stun gun to shift away from her stomach, Joelle tried to pivot so she could do something to escape. But the bulkier man pointed at her with the billy club. The threat was clear. He'd hit her if she tried anything.

She stayed put.

The big guy got in the back seat with her, and the other man jumped behind the wheel. He drove out of there fast. Not heading toward the house, of course, but rather using the trail. She had no idea where it led. They obviously did, though, since they had driven it to get to Duncan's.

She glanced around for anything she could use as a weapon. And she froze. Not because there was something that could help her defend herself but because of the photos.

Dozens of them scattered on the floor of the car.

The pictures of her father. Bleeding. Dying. The same ones that'd been left on the side of the ranch house.

Her gaze fired to the big thug, and while she could see his eyes, there was nothing. No concern that he had just kidnapped a pregnant cop. No worry that she'd just seen photos that could link him to her previous attack.

And to her father's murder.

She hadn't needed any further proof that this was a hired gun. A person capable of cold-blooded murder.

"Did you kill him?" she had to ask.

Still no reaction, though, she heard the driver. He growled out a "shut up." Maybe meant for her. Maybe meant for the big guy as a reminder not to say anything. Either way, the two words had been so low that she hadn't been able to tell if this was Hamlin or Brad who were both out on bail. It was possibly neither of them since the driver could be a hired gun as well. This way, their boss took no risks and kept their hands clean.

Her body shifted and leaned as the driver threaded the car around the ranch trail, and Joelle pushed all thoughts of their suspects aside. Instead, she tried to focus on the shifting and leaning. If she timed it right, she might be able to shove herself against the big guy. Might be able to ram her elbow into his gut and strip him of that billy club and stun gun. But any hopes of that vanished when the driver came off the trail and onto the road.

Joelle glanced around again to get her bearings, and she recognized where she was. It was, indeed, the road that led to Saddle Ridge, and to the interstate, but they weren't heading in that direction. Just the opposite.

The driver didn't stay on the road for long, though. He took another turn onto another ranch trail. The car bobbled over the uneven surface, and Joelle knew even if she managed to somehow jump from the vehicle, she could be killed since there were thick trees on both sides of this trail.

The minutes crawled by before the car exited out onto another road. She recognized this one as well. And her heart dropped when she realized where they were going.

"You're taking me to my family's ranch," she muttered.

Neither man responded, but Joelle didn't need their confirmation. This wasn't the main route to get to the ranch. This was a much less traveled farm road, one she'd used as a teenager to learn to drive.

They were taking her to Duncan at her family's ranch.

But she immediately rethought that. Duncan would almost certainly be on his way back to his place. And he would be driving the usual faster route. He wouldn't see her. In fact, maybe these goons were taking her there to hand her off to someone. To their boss. Though Joelle couldn't figure out why they'd choose her family ranch for the exchange, she knew she had to be ready to try to escape.

The goon behind the wheel took the turn onto the ranch grounds. Again, not the usual front driveway but rather the back trail that led from the road to the pasture. It was dirt and gravel, not paved like the other, but it was in decent enough shape since it's how her father had often had hay and feed delivered to the barn.

Even though it was hard for her to see the front driveway, Joelle did her best to look around and tried to spot Duncan. Or Woodrow and Ronnie since they were backup. She couldn't see any of them so it was entirely possible that the two deputies had followed Slater and him back to Duncan's place.

And that could be what the goons had counted on.

Maybe that's why they'd left Luca and Carmen alive. It would have ensured one of them would be able to call for help, and Duncan would come running. Once he arrived at his place, though, Duncan would see she wasn't there.

Would he think to come back here?

It was possible, but it was just as likely he'd be frantically trying to shut down the interstate exits and roads to try and stop the goons from getting her out of the area.

The driver pulled to a stop at the end of the road. Directly in front of the back door of the barn. The loading door was wide enough to accommodate a vehicle, but he didn't open it and park inside where the vehicle would be out of sight. However, he did park, and he immediately got out, throwing open the door on her side and pulling her out. He put the stun gun to her stomach again.

Goon number two made a fast exit, too, and he hurried to his partner so he could hook his arm around Joelle's waist and get her moving. Again, not into the barn but across the backyard.

And that's when Joelle realized where they were taking her.

They were dragging her straight toward the well.

DUNCAN WANTED TO smash his fist into the steering wheel. But that wouldn't help him get to Joelle. Still, the smashing would give him a hard jolt of pain that might rid him of some of the anger, fear and frustration bubbling up inside him. Then again, nothing would help that.

Nothing but finding Joelle and making sure she was safe.

Slater was on the phone to Carmen, and since the call

was on speaker, Duncan was hearing what a hellish situation was waiting for him at his place. The ambulance was on the way to get Luca who apparently had a head injury. Carmen had one as well and was bleeding from being hit. And while all of that was important, it wasn't at the top of his worry list.

Joelle was.

And she hadn't been seen since two masked SOBs took her. The ranch hands hadn't spotted anyone. Hadn't seen a vehicle. That could mean the kidnappers had taken Joelle into the barn and were waiting for some kind of showdown. But it was just as likely they'd had a vehicle on one of the ranch trails and used that to escape with her. If so, she could be anywhere by now.

Duncan couldn't let that thought linger in his head. Like bashing his fist on the steering wheel, it wouldn't help, and right now, he just had to focus.

Where would they take her?

And why?

For the baby? So they could wait until she delivered and then try to sell the child? Maybe. But like the other times he'd considered that, it just didn't feel right. Four months was a long time to hold a woman, and if it was the baby they wanted, then why not wait to take her until closer to her due date?

Because this was about revenge.

Of course, that didn't rule out any of their suspects. Hamlin had been riled at Joelle's father for alerting the authorities about the sale of his baby. Hamlin could have decided to aim that anger at Joelle. But Brad hated Sheriff McCullough, too, and he had a beef with everyone in the sheriff's department over Shanda's arrest.

That left Kate.

Joelle's father had been investigating the sale of babies. Had his investigation led him to Kate, and had she silenced the sheriff before he could arrest her? If so, maybe Kate believed that Joelle would follow the same trail as her father and that trail would eventually lead her to Kate.

Of course, none of those theories addressed the baby. And maybe their child didn't directly play into this. It was possible the person doing this didn't want to kill a pregnant woman.

In the background of Slater's phone call, Duncan could hear the wail of sirens approaching his place. He also heard something else, the dinging sound that Slater had an incoming call.

"It's Woodrow," Slater said. "Carmen, I'll call you right back," he added, and he switched to the incoming.

Duncan immediately thought of the heat source they'd seen on infrared in the barn. Possibly Joelle's mother. Or another hostage. And that's why Duncan had had Slater call Woodrow and Ronnie and tell them to stay at the McCullough ranch. Not by the barn, either, in case the person inside turned out to be a gunman. But rather Duncan had wanted them to pull the cruiser out of sight and keep watch of the barn. Hopefully, things hadn't gone to hell in a handbasket there.

"Slater," Woodrow said the moment he was on the line, and Duncan could hear the urgency in the deputy's voice. "A dark blue car just approached the barn from the pasture side of the property."

It took Duncan a second to realize that Woodrow was talking about the McCullough ranch and not Duncan's place. "Is Joelle in the car?" Duncan couldn't ask fast enough.

"I'm pretty sure she is," Woodrow was equally quick to answer. "There's a woman in the back seat that I believe is Joelle. There are two people with her, both wearing ski masks."

Hell. They had taken her there and that made Duncan even more suspicious of that heat source. The killer could be inside the barn.

Duncan slammed on the brakes, and even though the road was narrow, he executed a U-turn to get them headed back to his place. He only hoped he was in time to stop whatever was about to happen.

"We're on our way back there," Slater explained to Woodrow. He glanced at Duncan. "You want Woodrow and Ronnie to move in or wait for us to get there?"

This might turn out to be a "damned if he did, damned if he didn't" situation, and it could put Woodrow and Ronnie at extreme risk. Still, Duncan didn't have a lot of options here.

"Woodrow, move in if they get Joelle out of the car," Duncan instructed the deputy. "Do as quiet of an approach as you can manage. I want you to try to sneak up on them and see if you can get her away from them. We'll be there as fast as we can."

Slater ended the call so that Woodrow could get started on that, and then Slater phoned Carmen back to fill her in on what was happening. Or rather what they thought was happening. Duncan wasn't sure what the hell was going on, but if these SOBs hurt Joelle, he was going to rip them to pieces.

Duncan drove too fast and had to fight to keep the cruiser on the road when he took one of the many curves. He had to push. Had to get to Joelle. Because he could be wrong about the boss not wanting to kill a pregnant woman. This could be a sick attempt to use her to replay her father's murder.

Duncan had to stop thinking like that.

"We'll get to her in time," Slater muttered under his breath when he finished his call with Carmen.

Duncan prayed he was right, and he kept up the speed, eating up the distance to the ranch. He was still a good two minutes out when Slater's phone rang again.

"It's Woodrow," Slater said, taking the call on speaker.

"Ronnie and I are out of the cruiser and are approaching the barn on foot," Woodrow said in a whisper. "They just took Joelle out of the car, and one of them has a stun gun pointed at her belly."

That gave Duncan a nasty punch of fear and adrenaline. "Is she injured?" he managed to ask.

"I don't think so." Woodrow paused a heartbeat. "I don't have a clean shot," he added. "They're holding her close."

Duncan got another of those nasty punches. They were using Joelle to protect their sorry butts. "Are they taking her to the house?" Specifically, to the front door so they could recreate the murder.

Woodrow wasn't so quick to answer this time. "No. They're taking her to the well."

Duncan went stiff with surprise. Then, dread. Pure, sick dread.

They were planning to toss her in.

"If we don't get there in time," Duncan said, his voice strangled now from the tight muscles in his throat, "move in to save her. Save her, Woodrow. Don't let her die."

"I won't," Woodrow assured him.

And Woodrow would try. Even if it meant giving up his own life, both Woodrow and Ronnie would attempt to save her. That could get them all killed. But Duncan had to hold on to the hope that all of them would make it out of this alive.

Had to.

Because he couldn't imagine a life without Joelle.

Woodrow ended the call, no doubt so he could focus on

getting to Joelle. Duncan focused, too, and he decided not to go with a quiet approach. That would eat up precious time since he would have to park at the end of the driveway and run to the well. Instead, he turned on the sirens, hoping it would distract the two men and cover up any sounds from Woodrow and Ronnie's approach.

Duncan took the turn into the ranch, the cruiser practically flying when he slammed on the accelerator again. Everything inside him was yelling for him to get to Joelle.

He spotted the car in the pasture by the barn. Then, he spotted Joelle. She was, indeed, being used as a shield for two masked men. But she was alive. For now, anyway. She was also right next to the well, and one of the snakes holding her stooped down to shove the cover of the well aside.

Duncan couldn't be sure, but he figured both men were looking at his cruiser now. Joelle certainly was, and he saw the mix of emotions on her face. The fear. The hope. The extreme sense of dread that their baby wasn't safe.

That none of them were.

He fired some glances around, to see if there were any other gunmen lying in wait. No sign of them, but Duncan did spot Woodrow and Ronnie. They were skulking toward the barn, staying on the side where the two thugs hopefully wouldn't be able to see them.

Duncan drove through the yard until one of the thugs motioned for him to stop. That wouldn't have caused him to hit the brakes, but then the thug's partner yanked back Joelle's head, using the choke hold he now had on her. Duncan stopped about thirty feet away, drew his gun and threw open his door. He used the door as a shield and took aim, even though he had nowhere near a clean shot. On the other side of the cruiser, Slater did the same.

Neither man spoke, but the bigger one of the two continued to hold Joelle while the other looped a rope around her. Not in the usual way someone would tie up a person. This was more like a harness that they looped around her bottom.

When the two goons started to move Joelle, Duncan's heart slammed against his chest. They were going to put her in the well. Duncan tried not to look at Joelle's face since he knew that would be too much of a distraction. Instead, he focused on the men, waiting for one of them to move so he could take the shot.

But that didn't happen.

He could only watch as Joelle clutched the rope, and the goons began to lower her into the well.

"Shoot me or my hired help, and we drop her," the smaller man said.

And that's when Duncan knew who was behind this. Because he instantly recognized the voice.

Brad.

JOELLE CURSED WHEN she heard Brad's voice. Everyone in the sheriff's office had searched nonstop to find out the identity of their attacker, and now they had confirmation of who it was with just that handful of words.

Shoot one of us, and we drop her.

And they would. They already had her over the opening of the well, but she had no idea why. If they wanted her dead, why not just kill her...

That thought immediately stopped because she knew why. A moment later Brad confirmed that, too.

"We're going to play a game, Sheriff Holder," he said, his voice dripping with venom. Brad yanked off his ski mask. "You and Slater McCullough are going to die. No way around that," he added in a snarl. "Joelle, too, but you can make her death painless or a nightmare."

It was already a nightmare. She was literally hovering over a well that was at least a hundred feet deep. The sides were narrow so it was possible she could try to hold on, but she wouldn't be able to do that for long. Brad had a grip on the end of the rope, but there were no guarantees whatsoever that he wouldn't just let her drop.

"What the hell do you want?" Duncan snarled.

"Revenge," Brad spat out just as the first drops of rain started to fall. "For ruining my life. For bringing me to this."

"You brought yourself to this," Joelle muttered.

Brad apparently heard her because he made a feral sound of outrage. "You and your fellow cops arrested Shanda. You caused her to miscarry," he shouted.

"And you killed her," Joelle said. Yes, it was a risk to agitate him like this, but the agitation might distract him so that Duncan and Slater could shoot him.

No feral sound this time. Brad made more of a hoarse sob. "That was an accident. She was going to the cops because she thought I'd killed Sheriff McCullough, and I had to stop her." He sounded genuinely sorry about that. And maybe he was.

"You had to stop her," Joelle repeated, and she managed to keep her voice calm. "But you couldn't reason with her."

From the corner of her eye, she saw Woodrow peer around the side of the barn, and she felt another surge of hope. If Duncan and her brother didn't get a shot, then maybe Woodrow could.

"Yes," Brad muttered, and it seemed for a few moments, he was lost in some memories with Shanda. "The hired guns, too, since they chickened out after taking the dispatcher who helped arrest Shanda. Not Arlo, though. He tried and tried hard. So did Willie Jay, and he knew to do the right thing after he was caught."

"I'm guessing Willie Jay knew he was a dead man once he was in custody so he ended things," Duncan said.

"He did the right thing," Brad emphasized. "Not my mother, though. She was going to rat me out, just like Shanda," he added in a mutter that was coated with pain.

"Is your mother alive?" Duncan asked.

"Of course." The pain in his eyes evaporated, and Brad's gaze flicked to the barn. "She's, uh, waiting her turn. I've already planted some records for the withdrawals from the bank to point to that idiot Hamlin hiring some muscle to carry out the kidnappings and such, and now I'll walk away," he said.

Oh, mercy. If Kate was in the barn, Brad probably didn't have plans for her to come out. He would likely kill her and pin that on Hamlin, too.

Then, Joelle had a sickening thought. What if Brad had managed to get his hands on Molly? She could be in the barn right now, gagged, unable to call out for help.

"You waited a long time to come after us," Duncan said, his gaze fixed on Brad. "It's been five months since you murdered Sheriff McCullough."

"I didn't kill him," Brad snapped, and the grip tightened on the rope, yanking Joelle back and nearly causing her to fall in the well. "Shanda thought I did, and I was afraid she'd be able to convince you that I had. Convince you enough to arrest me. But I didn't kill him. Someone beat me to it."

Joelle hadn't thought anything else could add to her grief, but that did it. From the moment Brad had revealed himself, she'd thought they had found her father's killer. Of course, Brad could be lying.

But why would he?

He'd just confessed to killing Shanda and orchestrating

a plot to get revenge for her arrest. Why not just own up to her father's murder if he'd done it?

Because he hadn't, that's why.

Now it was Joelle who had to choke back a sob, and later—sweet heaven, there would be a later—she'd deal with that. For now, though, she had to stay alive and make sure Duncan, Slater, Woodrow and Ronnie did, too.

"Do you have Sandra McCullough?" Duncan asked. "Or was it a recording you spliced together?"

Brad's brief smile gave away his answer, but Brad confirmed it anyway. "Easy to fake a recording when she's blabbed on and on during interviews. I had a lot to work with to create a lure."

Part of her was relieved that Brad didn't have her mother. Joelle had to hope that meant she was alive and would be found.

"So, what now?" Duncan demanded.

"Now, you step away from your cruiser," Brad said, his voice eerily calm. He was blinking hard because the rain was getting in his eyes. "Slater, too."

"Step away so you can gun them down," Joelle spelled out. She saw Woodrow again, and he was on his belly inching closer.

"Of course." Again, Brad's voice stayed calm. "This was the best way I knew to draw them out into the open, and I'll deal with Molly later. She's the only one left, and then all the loose ends will be tied up."

"My baby is not a loose end." In contrast, there was plenty of anger in Joelle's voice. "She's an innocent victim in all of this."

"I know. And I'm sorry about that. I am," Brad repeated when she glared at him. "But I'll make this fast. Once Duncan and Slater are dead, then I can finish you fast. You won't feel a thing."

Joelle doubted that, and when Brad started to glance around, she knew she had to do something to pull his attention back to her. "Slater had nothing to do with Shanda's arrest."

Fresh rage flared in Brad's eyes. "He's his father's son, and if he'd been on duty, he would have taken part in it." He shifted those anger-filled eyes to Duncan. "You've got five seconds to step away from the cruiser." And he started the countdown. "One, two, three—"

Before he could get to four, Joelle caught onto the rope and gave it a quick hard jerk. It did what she wanted. It off-balanced Brad. But it did the same to her, and Joelle had to struggle to catch hold of the sides of the well so she wouldn't fall and plunge to the bottom. She scrambled onto the ground, clutching at the grass to make sure she didn't slip back into the gaping hole.

Brad cursed, calling her a vile name, but the sound of the gunshot stopped his profanity tirade. A split second later, there was another blast. Then, a third.

Behind her, the big thug fell. The headshot had made sure of that. Brad, however, stayed on his feet. Frozen with his face pale with shock. He dropped the rope, clutching his left hand to his chest.

Where the blood was spreading fast.

"I'm not sorry," Brad muttered, his gaze fixed on Joelle. "I wish I could have killed you." He pressed something in his pocket before he slumped lifelessly to the ground.

Behind them, fire erupted around the barn.

Chapter Sixteen

Duncan had already started running toward Joelle before he even saw Brad press whatever he'd had in his pocket. Some kind of detonation device no doubt.

The last ditch act of a dying man to kill the person in the barn.

Joelle moved fast, too, hurrying toward the barn. "Molly or Kate could be in there."

Yeah, the heat source they'd seen on infrared could definitely be one of them, but it was equally possible this was another hired gun, lying in wait to finish what his boss had started. That's why Duncan raced ahead of Joelle.

Slater hurried in to help, too. "Joelle, make sure Brad and his hired help aren't anywhere near weapons," Slater told her.

That accomplished two things. Joelle would no longer be close to the barn, and Duncan definitely didn't want Brad or the thug to try any retaliation if they'd managed to survive the gunshots. He was pretty sure they hadn't, but it was too big of a risk to take.

Woodrow hurried to help Joelle, and Ronnie stood guard, making sure no one else was about to launch an attack. Duncan reached the barn first and was thankful that most of the flames were on the sides of the building. Not for long, though. Brad had obviously used some kind of accelerant because the fire was quickly eating its way to the door.

Duncan threw open the barn door and immediately stepped to the side in case he was about to be gunned down. But no shots came his way. Smoke did, though, thick billowing clouds of it. Something that had no doubt been part of Brad's sick plan. The rain would help, some, with the flames, but if the fire didn't kill the person inside, smoke inhalation might.

Even though the storm had blocked out so much of the light, Duncan still spotted the figure on the ground in the center of the barn. "Kate," he muttered. She was trussed up and gagged, but she was conscious and trying to move.

Duncan didn't take the time to untie her. He scooped her up and started toward the door. Not a second too soon. The fire must have triggered some kind of secondary device because the back wall of the barn burst into flames. That got Duncan moving even faster, and in that short distance, the smoke was already clogging his throat and lungs.

The rain was definitely welcome when he darted out into it, and he continued to run, continued to get Kate and himself as far away from the barn as possible. Because there could be another device, one meant to bring the whole barn down, and he didn't want Kate or anyone else hit with fiery debris.

"I just called for an ambulance," Joelle said, hurrying to help him with Kate when Duncan placed the woman on the ground. He got to work on removing the ropes while Joelle tackled the gag.

"Brad's going to kill all of you and set me up for it," Kate blurted the moment she could speak. "He bragged to me about, egging on that PI so he'd look guilty of these attacks."

"Yes," Duncan confirmed. "Brad admitted to planting some evidence that would point to Hamlin."

"Did he also tell you he drugged me?" Kate asked, and Duncan shook his head, though he'd suspected that's what had happened. "He said he drugged my tea, and then he cursed because I apparently didn't drink enough of it. He wanted me unconscious so he could kill me. But I managed to get out of the house and go to Saddle Ridge."

Duncan nodded since that worked with his theory, too. Brad would have eliminated his mother so she wouldn't tell the cops about him, and then he could have chalked up her death to Hamlin.

"Brad spooked me into leaving the hospital," Kate murmured. "I thought he was going to sneak in and kill me. That's why I ran." She squeezed her eyes shut a moment and shook her head. "At least I tried to run, but one of Brad's hired thugs caught me."

Duncan hated to question the woman, but while they were waiting on that ambulance, she might be able to provide him with more answers. A big one in case any other lives were at stake. "Did Brad say anything about the PI's sister?"

"Isla," Kate was quick to say. "Yes. Brad did more bragging about her, too. He took her a month ago when he started setting all this up. He said she was insurance. That if the cops didn't arrest Hamlin for murder, he would use Isla to force Hamlin to do it. And that if the cops did arrest him, then he could still sell the baby when she had it and then get rid of Isla."

Duncan cursed. "Where was Brad holding Isla?"

Kate shook her head again. "He didn't say. Maybe at his house in San Antonio? It's a big place, and he told me he'd closed off the second floor because he never used it."

Before Duncan could even ask, Slater was taking out his phone. "I'll get SAPD out there right now to do a search."

Good. He prayed she was there and safe. He didn't want Brad to add any more victims to his list.

"My son was a very sick, very disturbed man." Kate's gaze slid to the bodies, and a hoarse sob tore from her throat.

"One of them is Brad," Duncan told her. Not the best way to do a death notification, but she had to know. "I stopped him."

Kate looked up at him, and a mix of both tears and rain slid down her cheeks. "You did what you had to do," she muttered.

He had, and while Duncan didn't need Kate's validation about that, he was glad she didn't appear to be on the verge of being hysterical with grief. But there would be grief. He was sure of that, and somehow Kate would have to try to come to terms with what her son had done.

And what Brad had done was create a nightmare.

Five dead hired guns. Duncan wouldn't mourn that. But he was desperately sorry for the hellish memories Brad had given Joelle, Molly and Kate. Hell, had given him, too, because he doubted he'd ever be able to forget the terror of Brad coming so close to putting Joelle in that well.

One thing that Duncan was certain of was that Kate had had no part in her son's plan. That was good for tying up the loose ends of the investigation, but again, Kate would have to deal with her son pulling her into all of this.

Duncan looked at Joelle, their gazes connecting, and he didn't care who was watching. He pulled her into his arms and kissed her. There was both relief and hope in that kiss. Relief that she and their baby were alive. Hope that nothing like this would ever happen to them again.

"SAPD already had officers in the area of Brad's house,

and they're going in right now," Duncan heard Slater say, and he looked up to see Joelle's brother watching them. Well, watching as much as the rain would allow. It was coming down hard now.

Woodrow was heading to the back of the ranch house, and Ronnie was near the bodies. The chaos of a crime scene had already gotten started.

"Woodrow's getting some umbrellas from the house," Slater explained. "We won't move Kate any more than necessary until the EMTs give us the okay, but why don't Joelle and you go wait on the porch? No need for all of us to get soaked."

Duncan didn't care about the "getting soaked" part, but he wanted Joelle off her feet. Of course, she'd need another exam at the hospital, but he wanted to check for himself to make sure she hadn't physically been harmed.

Even though he figured it wasn't necessary, Duncan scooped her up in his arms and carried her to the porch. She didn't balk. In fact, she sighed and buried her face against his neck. He held her that way for several moments until they were beneath the porch roof. Then, he eased her back to her feet so he could kiss her.

It was another of those comfort kisses, and she didn't balk about that, either. Just the opposite. She returned the kiss, making it long, hard and deep.

"I thought Brad was going to shoot you," she said when she finally pulled back. She looked at him, examining him as he was doing to her.

Duncan didn't voice his fears about what he thought Brad would do to her. No need. They both knew how close they'd all come to dying.

"I think Brad was telling the truth when he said he didn't kill my father," Joelle muttered.

He nodded. And wished it weren't true. Because if Brad had killed Sheriff McCullough, then that would have given them all some closure. It would have closed the case, and they could have started the process of moving on. From that, anyway. In other ways, Duncan felt as if Joelle and he had, indeed, moved on.

In the best possible direction.

He hoped he wasn't wrong.

"I'm in love with you, Joelle," he said, "and I'm sorry I didn't tell you that sooner. I'm sorry that it took us almost dying for me to realize that I love you and I want a life with you and our baby."

Duncan braced for her reaction, which he knew could be a shake of her head and a reminder that the timing was all wrong for this. That the timing might never be right.

But that didn't happen.

Joelle smiled. Actually, smiled. And like the kiss, Duncan felt as if it lifted a whole mountain of weight off his shoulders. He would have kissed her again to taste that smile, but Slater called out to them.

"The cops found Isla," Slater said, adding a fist pump of celebration. "She's alive and as well as she can be. They're transporting her to the hospital as soon as the ambulance arrives."

"Did she have the baby?" Joelle asked.

Slater shook his head. "She's due in a couple of weeks." He motioned toward his phone. "Should I call Hamlin and let him know?"

"Call him," Duncan verified. From everything that Kate and Brad had said, Hamlin hadn't been responsible for any of this mess.

Slater moved away to do that, and Duncan turned back to Joelle to give her that kiss. But she beat him to it and kissed him first. She seemed to pour everything into it. Especially her heart. It turned way too hot, considering they were on a porch with a yard full of cops and the approaching sirens from an ambulance and more cruisers.

Joelle didn't break the kiss until there was a risk of passing out from lack of oxygen, and when she finally did pull back, she laughed.

"I'm in love with you, too, Duncan," she said, pinning her gaze to his. They were eye to eye. Mouth to mouth. Breath to breath. "And, no, that's not the adrenaline crash talking. Or the effects of that kiss. Though it was pretty potent," she added in a mutter.

Now he laughed, and he let the heat and the joy of the moment wash over him. Duncan knew it would be the start of more moments just like this one. With the woman he loved and their baby.

* * * * *

SMOKY MOUNTAINS MYSTERY

LENA DIAZ

Chapter One

Keira Sloane two-handed her service weapon, elbows bent, pistol pointing up toward the ceiling as she flattened her back against the wall outside the motel room. The dim lights from the dark parking lot one story below glinted off the rusty railing across from her. Chuck Breamer, one of two fellow officers with her, mirrored her stance on the other side of the door. In front of him, Gabe Wilson held his gun pointed down. He glanced at Chuck, then Keira. After receiving their nods, he rapped loudly on the door again before jerking back to avoid potential gunfire.

"Maple Falls Police. Last chance. Open the door." As with the first knock, there was no response.

Gabe held up three fingers, silently counting down. *Three, two, one.* He delivered a vicious kick to the doorknob. The frame splintered. The ruined door flew open and crashed against the wall, making the large window beside the door rattle.

All three ran inside, sweeping their guns back and forth.

The metallic smell of blood struck Keira immediately. A wounded or dead man lay on the bed closest to the window. She quickly checked behind the chair in the corner for any hidden suspects while her fellow officers checked under both beds.

"Main room clear," she announced.

Chuck jogged to the doorway on the back left. Gabe checked the one on the back right.

"Bathroom's clear," Chuck said.

"Closet clear," Gabe echoed. "No one else is here." He motioned toward an indentation in the cheap floral comforter covering the empty bed where it appeared that someone had sat at one time. "At least, not anymore."

Keira holstered her pistol and rushed to the side of the victim's bed, grimacing in sympathy at the extent of his injuries. Dressed only in navy blue boxers, the approximately thirty-year-old Black man was mottled with bruises and cuts on all of his extremities, with most of the damage to his chest.

Beneath him, the formerly white sheet was turning red. Blood dripped down, adding to a growing wet tangle of carpet. When she pressed her fingers against the side of his neck, to her surprise it was warm. There was a weak, thready pulse.

"He's alive. Get a bus out here."

Chuck radioed for an ambulance.

Keira grabbed the edge of the comforter and used it to apply pressure to what appeared to be bullet entrance wounds on his chest. Someone had beaten and tortured this man before shooting him. He'd lost so much blood it was a miracle that he was still alive, even more of a miracle if he made it to the hospital.

A hand grabbed her wrist, making her jump. She was shocked that it was the man on the bed. He stared up at her with pain-glazed dark brown eyes, his hand clutching hers. But whatever strength he had immediately drained away. His hand fell back to the mattress.

"Hold on," she told him. "Don't go into the light, buddy. Help's on the way."

His face turned ashen as his lips moved. But she couldn't make out what he said.

She leaned close. "Say it again," she encouraged him.

"L… Lance," the faint whisper sounded.

"Lance," she echoed. "Hang on, Lance. I'm Keira. I'm a cop. We're here to help you and—"

"Move." Chuck roughly pushed her out of the way.

"He's bleeding," she said. "His chest—"

"I've got it." His prior experience as an EMT kicked in as he maintained pressure on the victim's chest with one hand and checked his airway with the other.

Keira watched with a growing feeling of helplessness as Chuck assessed the victim. She wanted to help. But of the three of them, Chuck had the best chance of keeping him alive until the ambulance arrived.

She turned to check on Gabe and saw him reaching for the top drawer of the cheap particle-board dresser opposite the two beds.

"We need a warrant," she reminded him. "Exigent circumstances are over." Even though the motel manager was the one who'd called 911, he hadn't formally given them permission to search once they'd responded to the report of "shots fired."

Gabe shrugged and dropped his hand. "The lieutenant's on his way. Knowing him, he'll already have the warrant anyway."

She smiled at his statement. They both knew no one, not even their scarily efficient supervisor, Owen Jackson, could have gotten a warrant that fast.

Chuck straightened and stepped back from the bed. "He's gone. On top of being treated like a punching bag and sliced with a knife, he was shot at least three times. There's nothing anyone could have done to save this guy."

Keira blew out a shaky breath. Her wrist tingled as if the man were still holding it. He'd wanted her help. But she hadn't been able to do anything to change his fate. "Lance. His name is Lance."

Chuck frowned. "You know this guy?"

"No. He whispered it. Lance. Might have been Vance or Vince. But I think it was Lance."

"Did he say it was *his* name? Maybe it was the killer's name."

She winced. "I hope not. I called him Lance."

"We'll know soon enough, once we get a warrant to search for his wallet. Assuming it wasn't stolen." He started typing a text, no doubt updating their boss on the current status.

She glanced around the small room. Even the blood spatter on the wall behind the victim didn't mask the years of grime. But, aside from the twisted, bloody covers on the bed, everything else was neat and orderly. The dresser and nightstand drawers were closed. No belongings had been dumped onto the floor and rifled through. The second bed was made with the pillows and comforter in place.

"The room doesn't look tossed," she said. "His business suit's lying over there on that chair, as if he'd planned on wearing it tomorrow. It's rumpled, so the killer may have checked the pockets. But if this was a robbery, you'd think they'd take the suit. It's not cheap. Could fetch a few hundred at a consignment shop."

Gabe joined them. "I doubt a robber in this part of town would recognize the value of a suit or want to bother with it. But they'd definitely have taken the fancy Mercedes out front that the manager said belongs to this guy. Why would a man who can afford a car like that stay in a nasty, cheap motel?"

Keira glanced at the man on the bed, wishing he could answer those questions, that he'd wake up in the morning and call his family, his friends. Tell them who'd attacked him and why. "Maybe he was hiding out from someone who'd never expect him to stay in a place like this." She shrugged. "That's one of many things we'll have to figure out."

Gabe gave her a doubtful look. "What makes you think Owen is finally going to let you play detective?"

She stiffened. "I can play whodunit as well as anyone else. I'm ready."

He held his hands up in a placating gesture. "No argument here. It's the LT you have to convince."

Chuck slid his cell phone back in his pocket. "We need to identify potential witnesses before they scatter like ants in a thunderstorm. Gabe, you take the rooms to the right. I'll go left. Names and addresses, verified with ID. We can't force them to hang around. But at least we can follow up with them once we have more manpower."

"Or woman power," Keira said. "I'll help."

Chuck frowned. "You're on guard duty. If the EMTs get here before we're back, try to keep them from destroying evidence. Once they verify our victim is DOA, get them out of our crime scene."

Gabe sent her an apologetic glance as he closed the door behind him and Chuck.

Chapter Two

Keira swore. How was she ever going to advance in the tiny town of Maple Falls, Tennessee, if her fellow officers kept coddling her and never gave her a chance? She knew exactly why they'd told her to wait here for the EMTs. In spite of them all being sworn law enforcement officers, her male counterparts couldn't set aside their Southern manners to treat a woman like one of the guys.

Even though she had a uniform on, they saw the woman first, the cop second. They didn't want her doing knock-and-talks and putting herself at risk in this part of town. Three years. She'd been working with them for three years, and she was still the lowest one on the food chain, the last to be given real opportunities to make a difference.

A quick glance at the shooting victim had guilt riding her hard. Here she was worrying about her career, her future. At least she *had* a future. This man, who was in his prime, had no future. His life had ended in violence and pain. What mattered right now was getting justice for him.

She edged closer to the bed, careful to avoid the bloodiest section of the carpet. He was a handsome man, with closely shaved black hair, his skin a medium brown color. The absence of a gold band on his ring finger meant he likely wasn't married. But he still might have a child, or children, perhaps an ex-wife or girlfriend. If he had siblings or parents still alive, people who loved him, they'd be devastated by his loss.

This was why she wanted to become a detective.

It was too depressing being bombarded on a daily basis by the awful things that human beings did to each other without some ray of hope or happiness. She craved the good parts of the job. She wanted to be the one to give a family the answers they desperately needed, the why and the who behind whatever had happened to their loved one. That would be the ultimate reward. Putting a name with the face of tonight's victim was the first step toward getting him, and his family, justice.

She glanced at the closed door. Would it really hurt to look for his wallet? Just to check his driver's license so she'd be sure about his name? If she was careful, if she wore gloves, she wouldn't destroy potential evidence or muck it up with her own DNA and fingerprints. She could already hear faint, distant sirens. The ambulance would be here soon, a few minutes out at most. If she was going to cross a line and not get caught, she had to do it now.

Always prepared, she had a pair of latex gloves in her pocket. She quickly pulled them on and went on the hunt for a wallet. It wasn't in the pockets of the suit jacket or in the dresser drawer. Instead, it was neatly sitting in the top drawer of the vanity in the bathroom, along with a ring of keys and his car's key fob.

Her heart seemed to squeeze in her chest when she flipped open the wallet and saw a photograph in a plastic sleeve. A little girl, probably no more than two, was in his arms, pressing a kiss against his cheek. He'd been a father after all. Or maybe an uncle or family friend. He was clearly loved and would be missed. She swallowed against the tightness in her throat and pulled his driver's license out. When she saw his name, her stomach sank. Rick. His name was Rick Cameron. The name he'd given her wasn't his.

Forgive me, Rick. I'm so sorry that I called you Lance, especially if he's the killer.

The victim's address was in Baton Rouge, Louisiana. She snapped a quick picture with her cell phone camera. Then she risked a precious few more seconds to check the rest of the wallet.

There were more pictures, a couple of credit cards and two one-hundred dollar bills. This definitely hadn't been a robbery. She started to set the wallet back in the drawer when a flash of white stopped her. Tucked into a credit card sleeve was a small piece of paper. She took it out and carefully unfolded it. There were two words written in a neat cursive script.

unfinished business

Voices sounded in the hallway outside the room. Keira quickly snapped a picture, then hurriedly refolded the note and put everything back the way she'd found it.

The squeak of the exterior door told her that someone had just entered the motel room.

"Keira? You in here?"

Chuck. Dang it. "In the bathroom. Give me a sec." She flushed the toilet and then flipped on the faucet as if she were washing her hands and hurriedly shoved her gloves into her pocket. When she stepped out, Chuck was standing with his hands on his hips while Gabe directed the EMTs toward the bed with the victim.

"You couldn't wait and use the bathroom in the motel office?" Chuck's voice was frigid.

Her face flushed warm as the EMTs glanced curiously at her. She knew the rules, knew not to disturb the scene. Heck, she'd warned Gabe not to open a drawer earlier. But she'd rather Chuck think she'd forgotten or had gotten sloppy than to tell him the truth—that she'd rummaged through the dead man's belongings knowing full well she shouldn't have.

"Sorry. It hit me all of a sudden." She gave him a pained smile as she strode toward him. "How did you two finish your knock-and-talks so fast?"

Gabe joined them near the dresser, giving the EMTs space to confirm the victim was beyond help. "Most of the rooms were empty, curtains open, beds made. We could tell there wasn't anyone inside refusing to come to the door. Lots of vacancies in this place." He wrinkled his nose as he glanced around. "Go figure, huh?"

"Not exactly the Ritz."

Gabe smiled.

Chuck didn't. He stared at her, his disapproval thick in the air, before turning to respond to a question from one of the EMTs.

Gabe gave her a sympathetic look before joining Chuck.

Keira blew out a frustrated breath. *Stupid.* She should have waited for the official investigation to find out the victim's name. No doubt she'd hurt her chances to be included on the case. If it had only been Gabe who'd caught her, he'd have kept it quiet. But by-the-book Chuck Breamer would no doubt tell their supervisor what she'd done at the first opportunity.

Sure enough, when the LT arrived, Chuck's summary of everything the three of them had done included her trip to the bathroom. Their boss's words fell on her like a death knell as he barked his orders.

"Wilson, secure the crime scene until we can borrow a

CSI tech from the DeKalb County Sheriff's Office to assist out here. Breamer, interview the motel manager. Get their surveillance video, assuming the cameras outside even work. Sloane—" his flinty gaze zeroed in on her "—let's see if you can manage to return to the station and write up your report without touching anything on the way out."

Gabe winced. Chuck didn't even look her way as he headed outside, presumably to speak to the manager.

Keira straightened her shoulders and took the walk of shame past her supervisor without comment.

BY THE TIME Keira finished her report, she wanted to kick herself for screwing up.

Gabe, upon his return to the station, had reluctantly admitted that Owen had said he'd planned on letting her help on the investigation—until he'd heard about what she'd done. Now she'd likely have to spend several more months trying to earn another chance.

Murders rarely happened in Maple Falls. So even if she was given a chance, it probably wouldn't be on a case this important. It would likely be on a stolen property investigation or a domestic violence situation that she could wrap up in less than a day. Her original plan in leaving Nashville PD to join a small police department because there'd be less competition definitely wasn't going the way she'd expected. She was beginning to think it was the worst mistake she'd ever made.

Gabe, her only true friend around here, kept sending her looks of pity from across the squad room. Unable to take it anymore, she locked up her desk and left the station ten minutes early. If that was enough for Owen to write her up, so be it. At this point, she was too depressed to even care.

Later at home, in a calmer frame of mind, she reluctantly

admitted that Owen wasn't petty enough to worry about ten minutes unless it was habitual. She was almost never late and rarely left early. But she had no doubt she'd still be written up for not following policy at a crime scene. And he was right to do it. She hadn't followed the rules. In fact, she'd broken them far worse than anyone knew.

She thumbed through the pictures on her cell phone that she'd taken in the motel bathroom. Technically, she should log them into evidence and then erase them from her personal device. The fact that she had no intention of doing either of those things could mean that her boss was right in thinking that she wasn't cut out to be a detective.

Forget that. She'd make a great detective. The only reason she occasionally broke the rules was because it was the only way to be let in on the action.

She studied Rick Cameron's driver's license photograph and the picture of his note. *Unfinished business* was cop slang for a cold case. But that didn't make sense in this context, especially since there wasn't anything in Rick Cameron's wallet to suggest he was a police officer working a case. Then again, if he was truly undercover, she wouldn't expect him to carry official police ID.

But that theory seemed weak. What kind of cold case would lead a detective from Louisiana to DeKalb County and the tiny Middle Tennessee town of Maple Falls? With a population just over two thousand, it wasn't exactly a sprawling metropolis where criminals fled to from big cities around the country to escape justice. Rick Cameron had to be passing through. To where? There was only one way to find out. She'd conduct her own investigation. And she'd do whatever it took to solve it, get justice for Rick and his loved ones, and prove herself.

When she presented her findings to the lieutenant, he'd

be forced to recognize her as worthy enough to be allowed to work as a detective when warranted. Their ten-person police force didn't have any full-time detectives. Maple Falls was too small to justify that. And only a select few were allowed to act as detective when needed—like Chuck.

She grabbed her laptop computer from the end table and opened up an internet search.

THREE WEEKS LATER, Keira had little to show for her secret investigation into the motel murder. But neither did anyone else. As she sat at her desk in the squad room snooping through the latest printed copies she'd made from the official case files, her stomach sank at the lack of progress.

The name Lance had led nowhere. There weren't any local thugs on their radar with Lance as either their first or last name. A brief bio stated that the victim worked in the computer tech industry, remotely from home. He was a contract programmer currently in between contracts. That explained why an employer hadn't reported him missing.

He lived alone. No one in his neighborhood had ever noticed any family members visiting him, in spite of those pictures in his wallet. They hadn't noticed friends visiting either. Keira had no idea who the little girl was in the photo in Rick's wallet. All she could figure was that it was a friend's child and that she'd read far too much into it. After all, if he was close to that friend, or that little girl was part of his life, wouldn't someone in that circle have contacted the police by now, asking where he was? Baton Rouge law enforcement was supposed to let Maple Falls know if someone inquired about him. So far, that hadn't happened. With no friends, family or loved ones to advocate for him, no one was pushing the Maple Falls Police to keep digging and figure out who'd killed Rick Cameron.

None of the potential eyewitnesses at the motel had offered much of value either. The last person to make any notes in the case file was Chuck. And that had been four days ago. The case was already cold. Soon it would go into a deep freeze.

Gabe stopped by her desk and balanced a hip on the corner. "Two weeks off starting tomorrow, huh? Bet you're looking forward to it. Where you going?"

She shuffled the papers on her desk, mainly to hide her copies of reports from the Cameron case. "Probably what I do every vacation. Sit at home and watch TV, take naps. Lots of naps."

He clucked his tongue. "That's a waste, especially for a cute little brunette like you. Go do something fun. Pick up a guy. Trust me. For someone with your looks, it would be easy." At her eye roll, he laughed. "Okay, okay. Maybe you should pay a visit back home. Nashville, right? You must have some family or friends back there who'd love to see you."

Her only response was to stare at him. Although they were friends, she refused to discuss her family with him or anyone. The situation was…complicated. Going to see them during her two weeks off definitely wasn't on her itinerary.

When he gave up with his less than subtle interrogation, he wandered off to someone else's desk. Keira stuffed the papers she'd hidden into her purse and headed out. Her suitcase was already in her car. Let the so-called vacation begin.

Ten minutes later, she was at the town cemetery standing at the back corner where those without money or with no one to claim their bodies were buried. Pauper's graves. That felt so wrong for Rick Cameron.

His suit was expensive. The car he'd driven to the motel was a late-model Mercedes. He could afford a better burial.

But he'd left no will, and his estate was tied up in the courts. For now, at least, he was here.

Keira placed the white silk roses she'd purchased earlier in the little vase beside the grave marker. It was a small slab of marble with only his name and dates. Normally a grave the city dug would only have a cheap metal marker with numbers on it. But Keira had scrabbled together enough money to buy the little marble headstone and vase. The man had used his last bit of strength to clutch her arm and whisper his dying word. How could she not give him a headstone after that?

Unfinished business. That note from his wallet was what had set her on her current path. It had cemented where she was going during her time off. After performing hundreds of internet searches on that phrase over the past few weeks, resulting in millions of useless hits, this morning she'd had better luck. She'd keyed in a ridiculously long string of additional search terms and the top result that popped up had her staring at the screen for a long time.

Unfinished Business, with both words capitalized, was the name of a private company in Gatlinburg, Tennessee, about four hours from Maple Falls. The purpose of the company? They investigated cold cases for law enforcement throughout the East Tennessee region. Since Maple Falls was in Middle Tennessee, they didn't officially support her county, which was why she'd never heard of them before. But here was the kicker. One of the investigators listed on their website had a name she'd rarely heard, until a few weeks ago.

Lance.

The odds were astronomical against UB's Lance Cabrera being the Lance that the victim had whispered with his final breath. Or even that UB was the same unfinished business listed on the note, especially since Rick hadn't capitalized either word. But the two things together seemed like a sign, a good omen that going there might help. Somehow.

Best scenario, UB and this Lance guy might actually know Rick Cameron and could lead to a resolution of the case. Worst scenario, they knew nothing about the victim. But as cold-case professionals they might give her some expert advice on how to proceed. Either way, it was a win.

She touched a hand to the cold marble. "Chances are a million to one against this being a real lead, Mr. Cameron. Or that this Lance guy I've found is *your* Lance. But it's all I have. Hopefully something will come out of this that will put your killer or killers in prison. I'm off to Gatlinburg to take care of your *unfinished business*."

A crunching sound had her whirling around. No one was there. The cemetery was empty. Her silver Camry was about fifty yards away, the only vehicle in the parking lot. She scanned the tree line behind the chain-link fence. Nothing. It was probably just the light breeze blowing through the trees, making some branches click together. Or an animal rooting around in the woods, stepping on dried leaves that were everywhere, with it being the middle of autumn. But that didn't stop the unease that settled in her gut. After one last scan, she hurried toward her car, pistol out and at the ready.

Chapter Three

Lance Cabrera had always known his days were numbered. That the past would catch up to him sooner or later. But he'd really been hoping for later. Much later.

He kept his expression bland as the pretty young officer from Maple Falls told her story to him and his fellow cold-case investigators. She sat across the table from him in one of the glass-walled conference rooms of Unfinished Business, perched near the top of Prescott Mountain overlooking Gatlinburg, Tennessee, far below.

In the past, someone bringing UB a case who wasn't from the Tennessee Bureau of Investigation or an East Tennessee law enforcement agency wouldn't have gotten past the front door. But that rule had been eased after one of their own was abducted because they'd turned away the wrong person.

Now, when they could spare a few moments, they'd at least listen to people lobbying for their help outside of their contracted area. That help usually took the form of advice or referrals to other agencies. But their main goal was to determine whether the person was a potential threat.

This petite, brown-eyed, dark-haired wannabe detective—Keira Sloane—probably didn't concern the other UB investigators in the room. But in the twenty minutes that she'd been speaking and answering questions, he'd recognized the enormous threat she offered not only to him but to everyone in this room—including herself.

She tapped the pile of pictures she'd set on top of the table—crime scene photos she'd admittedly copied from the official case file. She was painfully honest, not even attempting to pretend that she wasn't supposed to be working on this case.

"There's one more thing," she said.

Her dark gaze locked with his. He could almost feel the nails pounding into his coffin as he waited for her next words.

"I told you the note in the victim's wallet said 'unfinished business,' which led me here. But he also *said* something to me right before he died."

Grayson Prescott, the genius businessman billionaire and former Army Ranger who'd created UB, leaned forward at the head of the long conference room table. "Don't keep us in suspense, Officer Sloane. What did Mr. Cameron tell you?"

"It was one word, a name. With his dying breath, he whispered, 'Lance.'"

Lance couldn't help wincing, thinking of Rick whispering his name as he lay dying in a motel room. At least he hadn't died alone. Lance would be forever grateful that Officer Sloane's kind face was the last one Rick saw, not the face of his killer.

"Hell of a coincidence," Ryland Beck, their lead investigator, said.

"It is," Lance agreed, careful to keep his grief from his voice, his expression. He had to play this carefully. A lot was on the line. "But I wouldn't call it compelling. There's no obvious connection between the note and what he said. The words *unfinished business* weren't capitalized like they would be if it was our company's name. It was likely just a reminder that this Cameron guy needed to take care of something."

"That's one theory," Sloane allowed. "Another is that he knew someone was after him, so he wrote that note in lowercase letters on purpose to throw them off if they found it."

"Why even have the note if he was worried that someone might find it?"

"I've asked myself that same question. The only thing that rings true to me is that he specifically hoped someone *would* find the note if something happened to him. To the killer, it meant nothing. But to law enforcement, well, we dig. We don't stop until we make sense of the evidence. That phrase is a clue, a breadcrumb left by a murdered man who whispered your name as a second breadcrumb. He anticipated that an investigator would follow that trail here. The question is, Why? And what does it have to do with you, Mr. Cabrera?"

He chuckled as if amused. "There's no way he could have known there'd be someone with him when he died and that he'd be able to give them a name."

"That occurred to me as well."

"And?"

She shrugged. "If I had everything figured out, I wouldn't be here asking for help."

"Fair enough. How certain are you that he said 'Lance'? Could it have been Vance? Vince? Something else? You said he bled out. I doubt his mind was firing on all cylinders. He probably wasn't even aware of what he said. It was random."

Her face reddened slightly, whether from embarrassment or anger, he wasn't sure. "He was lucid, his eyes clear as he looked at me. Could I have heard him wrong? Possibly. But I truly believe he said Lance."

"You truly believe?" he scoffed, trying to make light of her rather impressive conclusions that were likely spot on. "Let's assume you're correct. Why link that name to his murder? Maybe it was the name of a family member or friend, and he wanted them to know he was thinking about them at the end."

"My team explored those possibilities. He has no family that we've been able to discover. No friends that we know of. The name Lance had to hold some kind of significance for him to use his last breath to give me that information."

Lance's fists were clenched so hard beneath the table that his hands were going numb. He forced himself to relax his grip.

"If he truly said 'Lance,' and was lucid, how does that help you? It's not a common name. But it's not exactly rare either. It could be someone's first name or their last name. I'm sure if you run an internet search, you'll come up with thousands of hits in Tennessee alone. Did you? Run a search?"

Her eyes narrowed. She didn't appreciate him challenging her investigative skills and wasn't doing well at hiding her resentment. Good. Her defensiveness would help cast doubt on her conclusions.

She crossed her arms over her ample chest, making her appear even more defensive. "I searched our local law enforcement databases, as well as some national ones for known criminals with that name. Nothing of significance came up for our area. And you're correct that my internet searches yielded a large number of hits. But the name Lance linked to a company called Unfinished Business? That combination only came up once and led me to you."

A ripple of unease seemed to eddy through the room. Lance sighed heavily and sat back. "I don't buy that for a second. You'd have gotten thousands of hits on that phrase, tens of thousands. There's no way you hunted all of those down and then determined only one hit was connected to the name Lance in any way. You're reaching. I totally get that. I've been there, many times. But jumping from point A to point Z without anything in between isn't how you find the *right* answers. Please tell me you have something else—facts, some actual evidence—for you to have come all this way and taken up our valuable time with your theories."

An elbow jabbed his ribs.

Frowning at Faith sitting to his left, he rubbed his side. "What was that for?"

"Manners," she said. "Remember those? Our team doesn't belittle people who come to us for assistance."

He glanced around the table. Pretty much everyone was looking at him with disapproval. He felt a flush creeping up his neck. Belittling someone, as Faith had put it, wasn't how he typically treated anyone, especially a woman. Apparently he was coming across as a bully and Sloane the sympathetic victim.

If the stakes weren't so high, he'd apologize profusely and shut up. And he'd do everything he could to make it up to Sloane for how he'd been acting. But the stakes *were* high, and this wasn't just about him. If he couldn't discredit Sloane's theories, both her and anyone in this room who might decide to assist her with the case was in jeopardy.

"All right, all right." He held up his hands in a placating gesture. "I might have been overzealous in playing the devil's advocate, looking for holes in your conclusions. It wasn't my intention to be offensive, to come across as a—"

"Jerk?" Faith offered.

Several of those around the table laughed.

Officer Sloane's brows rose, apparently unsure whether they were teasing or not.

Lance waited for the laughter to die down. Time for a more direct approach, to go for the jugular.

"I won't argue that particular conclusion," he allowed. "I've behaved badly. And although I don't excuse how I've acted, I hope everyone can at least understand it. After all, it's not every day that someone comes to my place of employment and essentially accuses me of being involved in a murder. That is why you're here, isn't it, Officer Sloane? Because you think that I may have killed Mr. Cameron?"

She arched a brow in challenge. "Did you?"

Grayson rapped his knuckles on the table. "Enough." His hard tone cracked through the room. "Accusing one of my investigators of murder won't be tolerated."

Her eyes widened. "I…ah… I didn't mean to… I mean, I did, but I didn't—"

"Wait," Lance said, ready to play his trump card. "Now that I understand Officer Sloane's…intentions, I can easily put her concerns at rest by offering up an important fact to go along with her misplaced theories."

She stiffened, her expression wary. "What *fact*?"

"My alibi of course."

She blinked in surprise.

He motioned to Faith and her husband beside her, fellow investigator Asher. "Where was I on the night that Mr. Cameron was killed?"

Faith frowned. "I don't—"

"At the beginning of this meeting, Officer Sloane said the victim was killed on September 22. In the early evening. Isn't that correct, Officer?"

"Around eight thirty, yes."

"Oh," Faith said. "Of course." She gave Sloane a pained

smile. "Lance definitely couldn't have been involved." She motioned to Asher. "My husband and I had a housewarming party for UB's investigators that night. We were celebrating buying our first home together as a married couple. And before you ask, no, there isn't any possibility that Lance could have left without someone realizing he was gone. Although UB has administrative staff, an IT department and a forensics lab, the actual investigative team is small, less than a dozen of us. We're all close, more like family than friends. His absence would have been noticed."

Grayson gave Lance a subtle nod of approval and relaxed back in his chair. He'd been at the party too and no doubt was relieved that this could be put to rest so easily.

"Faith took an obscene amount of pictures," Lance teased, chuckling when she tried to elbow him again. "I'm sure I'm in more than a few of them. The metadata on the camera cards can prove the date and time each photo was taken. You mentioned that Maple Falls is in DeKalb County. Can't say I've ever been there. But I know my geography. That county is a good three and a half hours from here."

"Four, actually." Sloane sounded defeated, as if she were finally accepting that she was wrong. "More if you hit traffic."

Lance smiled apologetically. "I'm truly sorry to have been so hard on you. But I hope you can see now that the two clues you've put so much credence in have nothing to do with me or this company. They probably have nothing to do with your case at all."

She nodded, looking defeated.

Lance regretted being the one who'd made her feel that way. But he was enormously grateful that they'd all managed to dodge a bullet.

She offered a sheepish smile to Lance and Grayson. "I'm

sorry that things went sideways. Diplomacy and tact have never been my strong points. And now I really am back at square one. I'll have to reexamine the entire case file and figure out another starting point, the true reason for that note and for why Rick Cameron whispered the name Lance. Honestly, I'm at a loss."

Lance stared at her in dismay. "You're not dropping the investigation? Letting the detectives in Maple Falls handle the case?"

"Detectives?" She shook her head. "We don't have any, not really. There's no lab, no IT department like you have here. Mr. Cameron's murder was investigated by a couple of our officers who are deemed qualified to be detectives when needed. In an emergency type of situation, our chief will ask the county sheriff for assistance. But he hates to do that and hasn't with this case aside from using their crime scene techs to gather forensic evidence. At this point, it's as cold as a case can get, even though it's less than a month old. That's why I'm working it on my own time. My vacation ends in less than two weeks. If I haven't solved the case by then, it might never be solved. To that end, if someone here has any tips or suggestions, I sure would appreciate it."

Grayson motioned around the table. "Everyone here, except me, used to be a detective in law enforcement. I recruited Ryland to help me recruit the others to work in the private sector when I started this company. These investigators represent decades of experience solving crimes. And you already know their current specialty is cold cases. I'm sure they can offer you some pointers."

The look of desperate eagerness on Sloane's face as the team began offering tips shot a feeling of dread through Lance. All of his arguments had been for nothing. This determined police officer wasn't going to stop digging after all. But at least Grayson and the team lead, Ryland, hadn't offered to pull any of the investigators off their current cases to officially work with her. That might be the only good thing to come out of today's meeting. Him playing his alibi card had taken away the need for them to work the case to prove his innocence. As long as it stayed that way, his friends were safe. But Sloane might not be, not if she'd done something to attract the killer's attention.

That's what Lance needed to know, what exactly she'd done so far, in detail. Maybe it wasn't too late for her. As long as the killer didn't consider her to be a threat, she was safe. But for him, everything had changed. The past had reared its ugly head again. He couldn't ignore it without risking anyone associated with him becoming collateral damage. Finding Rick's killer, and keeping the lid on their shared past, was paramount.

While Sloane furiously typed notes on her computer tablet, Lance took the opportunity to briefly study each of his friends.

Grayson Prescott—their leader, a military hero who'd come home to a murdered wife and a missing daughter. Instead of buckling beneath his grief and ensuing frustration over a case that went cold for years, he'd formed Unfinished Business. After UB solved Grayson's cold case, he'd dedicated the company to helping other families dealing with similar situations.

Next to Grayson was Willow, his current wife, a former Gatlinburg detective who'd helped him solve his first wife's murder and find his missing daughter alive and well.

Ryland Beck, their team lead.

Trent. His full name was Adam Trent. But no one ever called him Adam. He'd gone through hell and back to save a woman who'd been on the run for years against unknown enemies determined to kill her.

He smiled at Callum Wright, who'd spent his life hating his last name because of all the jokes about him being Mr. Right. Callum had once despised lawyers. Now he was married to one.

Asher and Faith Whitfield. When they'd ended up together, the only people who were surprised were Asher and Faith.

A few members of the team weren't here. Rowan Knight, their liaison with the TBI. Other fellow investigators, Brice Galloway and Ivy Shaw.

Lance cared deeply about each and every one of them.

When he happened to glance at the end of the table again, he was dismayed to see Grayson intently watching him. There were questions in Grayson's eyes. No doubt he'd noticed Lance studying his fellow investigators and wondered why. Hoping to turn Grayson's attention, Lance pretended interest in what Ryland was currently discussing with Sloane.

To Lance's relief, a few moments later, Grayson stood, signaling the end of the meeting. "Best of luck with your investigation, Officer. I wish we could have done more."

She began sliding her photographs and computer tablet into her leather satchel. "Everyone's been exceedingly generous with their time and advice. I really appreciate it."

The team slowly filed out of the glass-walled conference room and down the stairs to the war room below. It was a large open area with lofty two-story high ceilings so that anyone in the conference rooms could look down and potentially signal to other investigators to join them. Or anyone below could see who was upstairs, including Grayson's office beside the largest conference room.

Lance waited for the others to leave so he could time his exit with their guest's. He held the door open. "Officer Sloane—"

She paused in the opening. "Call me Keira, please. I think after practically coming to blows, we should be on a first-name basis, don't you?"

He laughed, genuinely amused. "Keira. If any of us come up with more ideas for your investigation, where can we reach you? Are you staying in Gatlinburg for a while?"

Her eyes widened. "I appreciate you asking. Although I admit to being—"

"Surprised?"

She nodded.

"My apologies again. I really didn't mean to come across so rudely. Your visit, what you said, caught me off guard." Understatement of the decade. "But that's no excuse for the way I treated you. Forgive me?"

The smile she gifted him with completely transformed her. Where before she'd been pretty, now she was…stunning. In another lifetime, maybe they could have been friends. Or more. In addition to being incredibly attractive, she had qualities he greatly admired: honesty, integrity and a quick mind. Normally he'd appreciate her stubbornness and refusal to give up on an investigation too. But right now those qualities were extremely inconvenient.

"You're forgiven." She handed him a business card. "I'm booked in a chalet for a couple of days, up Skyline Road. It's a small A-frame hanging off the side of the mountain with a driveway sloping so steeply down toward the cabin that I refuse to use it." She shivered for effect.

"I think I know the place. People make bets about whether a tourist will slide down that driveway one day and barrel through the house and off the mountain." At her horrified look, he grinned. "I'm teasing."

She blinked. "Oh, well, I'm still not using the driveway. I park on the street out front."

"Four-wheel drive, I hope. It's not cold enough to snow yet, but sometimes you need that extra power to get up these mountains."

"My Camry's got all-wheel drive. So far, it's been great at hugging the curves and holding the roads. I think I'll be okay."

"I'm sure you will." He slid the business card into an inside pocket of his suit jacket.

She started to leave, then stopped. "If anyone needs to call me, be sure to use the personal cell number on that card. Not my office number. Because, well—"

"You're not there. And your coworkers don't know you're playing detective." At the light flush on her face, he smiled again. "Your secret's safe with us. Have a good day, Officer Sloane."

She gave him a grateful smile. "Keira."

"Keira."

As she headed down the stairs, Lance paused at the top landing to watch her. The two-story windows of the war room looked out at the parking lot. True to her word, she got into a silver late-model Camry. He couldn't see the license plate to take down and potentially track her. But he didn't need to.

He knew exactly where she was going.

A few moments later, he reached his desk and grabbed his laptop computer.

"Hey, Lance." Asher motioned to him from his desk two aisles over. "Can you take a look at this?"

"Sorry, buddy. I've got something I need to take care of." He headed toward the exit.

"Catch me later, all right?" Asher called out.

"Will do." The lie was bitter on his tongue, especially when he turned in the doorway for one last look at his team and noticed Grayson and Ryland watching from Grayson's second-floor office. Lance nodded, then turned away, knowing he'd never see them again. Because, contrary to what he'd just told Asher, he was never coming back.

Chapter Four

Keira looked up from her computer tablet, surprised to hear a knock on the cabin's door. She'd gotten back from Unfinished Business a few minutes ago and had only just now settled in front of the coffee table to review her notes from the meeting.

Although she wasn't expecting trouble, someone stopping at this remote rental cabin deep in the mountains had her grabbing her service pistol from an end table. When she looked through the security peephole in the front door, no one was there. Even more surprising was that a black SUV with dark-tinted windows was turning down her steep driveway.

When the SUV's door opened, a familiar broad-shouldered figure stepped out. She blinked in surprise. As he pulled his shades off and slid them into one of the pockets of his charcoal-gray suit jacket, she shook her head. What in the world was Lance Cabrera doing here? And good grief, was he this handsome, and tall, when she'd seen him earlier? She'd been so pumped with adrenaline and nervous energy when she'd presented her information to the room full of investigators that she hadn't really paid attention to how ruggedly good-looking he was.

She set her pistol on a decorative table against the wall before opening the door.

"Mr. Cabrera," she said as he climbed the steps of the front porch. "What happened? Did I leave my favorite pen at UB and you rushed over to return it?"

His deep blue eyes crinkled at the corners with amusement. "I didn't notice any wayward writing instruments in the conference room when I left."

"Then I confess to being confused about why you'd show up here. I couldn't have made a good impression by essentially accusing you of murder. So I'm guessing you're not here to ask me out on a date."

He grinned. "If I thought you'd be amenable, and the stars aligned, it would be my honor to ask exactly that." His smile faded. "Unfortunately, this isn't a social call. We need to talk." He motioned toward the opening. "Mind if I come in?"

"Oh, of course." She moved to the side and pulled open the door the rest of the way. "You're probably cold, and here I am running my mouth. I can get you a hot chocolate or a…" She stared at him in surprise when he immediately shut the door behind him and flipped the dead bolt.

A prickle of unease ran down her spine. "Okay, that's weird. First, a knock on the door with no one there. Then you show up and lock the door as if the devil's on your heels." She laughed awkwardly. "Is there an axe murderer on the loose in the Smoky Mountains that I should be on guard against?"

His intense gaze zeroed in on her. "Someone knocked on your door? Then hid?"

"Yes, I suppose, I mean…it sounded like knocking. But it could have been a bird or an animal making noise outside. I was just checking the peephole when you drove up."

His pistol was suddenly out, pointed down by his side. "Are all your windows and doors locked?"

"I, ah, I guess so. I mean, I haven't opened any of them since I got here. But—"

"Lock the door behind me. Wait here. Don't go outside." He was out the door, turning left and running toward the side of the cabin before she could stop him.

She shut the door harder than necessary and locked it as he'd told her. But when she started toward the couch, she stopped. "The heck with this. I didn't drive four hours to be treated like a helpless little woman. I get enough of that at work." She grabbed her pistol and headed outside.

Since Lance had gone left, she went right, hoping that if there was someone out here, she and Lance would corner them. It seemed a bit ridiculous having her pistol out, looking for what likely amounted to some teenager playing a game of doorbell ditch. Although there weren't any other cabins immediately nearby, there were some farther down this road. Definitely within walking distance if some kids wanted to play a prank on a tourist. But if Lance was concerned enough to pull his gun, she was going to follow his lead, at least until she found out why he was so worried.

As she continued around the side of the house, she didn't encounter any juvenile delinquents or anyone else. She didn't hear anyone either, or really much of anything. Other than a light cool breeze blowing through the branches overhead, making her long for her jacket, the woods were eerily silent. No squirrels chattering. No birds chirping. No rustling in the undergrowth as a raccoon or other small creature searched for food. She hesitated. Had it ever been like this since her arrival? It seemed as if there was always something making noise. Why was it so quiet now?

On high alert, she raised her pistol out in front of her,

sweeping it back and forth as she checked the bushes near the cabin's foundation. To her left, she studied the thick undergrowth of the woods, looking for something that didn't quite belong. Listening for a potential threat.

Stopping at the back corner of the cabin, she ducked down. Keeping her head low, she peered around the corner through the maze of timbers driven deep into the slope of the mountain, anchoring the house to bedrock. Nothing. No rebellious teenagers. No bad guy hanging off a stilt, aiming a gun at her. But Lance wasn't there either. Shouldn't he have reached the other corner a few seconds before her?

Her stomach sank. Maybe he'd run into some trouble. And she was his only backup. She whirled around and jogged toward the front of the house.

It nearly killed her to stop at the corner. But running full tilt into the open without looking first was a newbie maneuver. With only six years in law enforcement, she didn't come close to matching the experience of those at UB. But she sure as heck wasn't a rookie.

Crouching down low again to make herself less of a target, she peered around the edge of the cabin toward the raised front porch. Empty. So where had Lance—

Crunching leaves sounded behind her. She jerked around. A man dressed in black dove at her from the trees. Before she could even react, he slammed against her, crushing her against the log wall of the cabin. Her gun flew from her grip, skittering across the ground. She twisted and clawed at his arms around her waist, furiously trying to break free.

He cursed in her ear and jerked her up in the air.

She raked her nails across both of his arms, but couldn't reach any skin through his long-sleeved black shirt. Clawing at his hands didn't work either. They were covered with leather gloves. Grabbing one of his gloved fingers, she yanked back, hard. A loud pop was followed by his shout of rage and pain.

He threw her against the cabin wall as if she were a rag doll. She slammed hard against it, letting out a yelp of pain as she fell to her knees. Her ribs hurt with every gasping breath. Her ears rang from the impact. But she couldn't just curl up in the fetal position. She had to push through the pain, defend herself. Where was her gun? Where?

He stood a few feet away, chest heaving from exertion, his injured hand clutched to his chest. Dressed completely in black, with a cloth covering the lower part of his face, all that showed were his dark brown eyes, staring at her with the promise of retribution.

Using his uninjured hand, he drew a long jagged knife from beneath his shirt.

"What do you want?" she demanded, desperately looking around. There, her pistol. It was about three feet away, half buried in some dried leaves.

He rushed toward her, knife raised high.

She rolled to the side, barely avoiding the swipe of his deadly blade. Then she dove for the pistol. His guttural yell sounded behind her. She let out a panicked whimper as she grabbed her gun and flipped onto her back.

Lance was suddenly there, tackling the man with the knife. They both fell onto the ground, locked together in a deadly embrace.

Keira leaped to her feet, her protesting ribs making her breath catch. Stumbling, she pushed through the pain, bringing her gun up. But she couldn't get a clear shot.

She didn't need one.

The fight was over as quickly as it had begun. The man with the knife grunted and collapsed onto the ground, his own blade protruding from his neck. Blood quickly saturated his collar as he made a sickening gurgling sound.

Lance jerked his head up, eyes widening in alarm. "Keira, hit the deck!"

She threw herself to the ground.

Bam! Bam! Bam!

She gasped in shock as another man dressed in black fell to the ground a few yards from where she'd been standing. A gun skipped across the dirt from his lifeless hands. Lance had saved her. But why did she even need saving?

"What the heck is going on, Lance? Why did these men follow you here?"

"They didn't follow *me*. They followed *you*." He grabbed her hand. "Come on. We have to get out of here." He tugged her toward his SUV.

"What do you mean they followed me? The only people I've met around here are you and the others at UB."

"We'll figure it out later." He motioned toward the passenger side as he aimed his key fob at the vehicle. "Get in."

Gunshots echoed through the trees. Bullets shattered the rear window, raining glass across the concrete like pennies pinging against a metal pan.

He jerked back and fired toward the trees on the incline across the street. More bullets slammed into the back of the SUV.

Keira returned fire, aiming where she'd seen the flash of muzzle fire in the trees.

"Get in the cabin," Lance yelled. "I'll cover you."

"We'll cover each other."

He frowned, but didn't argue. They both fired their pistols toward the trees as they raced up the steps and charged into the house. This time, she was the one who slammed the door shut and flipped the lock. Lance pulled her to the floor beneath the front windows a few feet from the entryway. He covered her body with his as bullets slammed into the front door.

Keira shoved at him, her lungs straining for air beneath his tight hold even as her sore ribs screamed in pain. "You know I'm a cop, right?" she forced out, then dragged in another painful breath. "I can defend myself. Get off me."

"And you know I'm a man, right? And a former cop myself? I'm not going to cower while a woman takes a bullet for me."

She shoved at him, cursing.

He laughed. "Maybe you should have been a sailor. Those are some salty words coming out of that pretty mouth."

"You think this is funny?" She coughed, then dragged in another painful breath. "People are trying to kill us."

"Not the first time. Won't be the last." He cocked his head, listening, his weight still crushing her ribs. "The shooting has stopped."

She shoved against him again. "Good. Maybe they gave up."

"Don't count on it. Lucky for us that solid door and the log walls stopped the bullets. They're obviously not using high-powered rifles. Must be using handguns."

"And knives."

He grimaced. "And knives. I'm guessing we have a couple of minutes while they regroup and plan their entry."

"Then you really need to get off me. Now, before I faint from lack of oxygen."

He looked down, a wry grin on his face. "Sorry about that." He rolled off her but stayed on the floor beside her. "Don't stand up until we're clear of the windows."

"No kidding." She drew her first deep breath and immediately regretted it, grimacing in pain.

"What's wrong?" He slid a hand across her abdomen, then up toward her chest as if searching for wounds. "Did he cut you? Were you hit?"

She grabbed his hand before things got embarrassing. "No cuts. No bullet wounds. The guy outside threw me against the side of the cabin." She shoved his hand away. "I don't think anything's broken. Just bruised." She drew some quick, shallow breaths, relieved that the pain was much more bearable that way. Rolling slightly to her side, she slid her cell phone out of her jeans pocket.

He frowned. "What are you doing?"

"Calling 911."

"I'd rather not involve the police."

She gave him an incredulous look. "Seriously? I *am* the police. We're *already* involved."

He grinned. "Well, there is that. I don't suppose we really have an alternative at this point. I didn't expect them to move on you so fast."

She paused with her phone in her hand. "Move on me? That's the second time you've essentially said that I'm the target. Maybe it's you they're after."

"Oh, they are. No question. But they didn't know where I was until you led them to Gatlinburg, to Unfinished Business."

"You're blaming all of this on me?"

"Of course not. I was just explaining—"

A thumping sound came from above. They both looked up.

"They're on the roof," he said. "They're probably leery of trying the front windows, guessing we'll shoot if they do. Please tell me this place doesn't have a skylight."

"Kitchen, back left corner." She tapped the phone's screen, dialing 911. But when she put the phone to her ear, there was only static. She checked the phone to see if it had been damaged. It was pristine, not a single scratch. And there were four bars. Excellent reception. So why wasn't the call going through?

Lance grabbed the phone and held it to his ear. "Cell service is jammed."

"Jammed? What the—who *are* these people? What do they want?"

"At the moment? Both of us dead. Or, more likely, you dead and me alive long enough to be tortured for information. Then they'll kill me."

She stared at him in horror. "What did you do? Sleep with a mafia boss's daughter?"

He let out a bark of laughter. "I wish. At least then all of this might have been worth it."

"You're joking at a time like this?"

"I'm multitasking, trying to come up with a plan that involves both of us staying alive, minus the torture part."

"What's the plan?"

"Did you miss the *trying to come up with one* part?"

She rolled her eyes. "We need to get out of here. Hide somewhere."

"On that we agree. It's the how that I haven't figured out. Cabin layout?"

"Kitchen on the left, this family room, bedroom and bathroom through that door on the far right."

"What about the door beside the bedroom door? Closet?"

"Basement. The rec room. But there's no exit. No windows or doors. Solid concrete walls. We'd be trapped if we went down there."

"Those concrete walls will offer protection, with only one entrance to guard—the stairs. That's more than we have on this level."

"I don't like it," she said.

A loud bang sounded from the kitchen, followed by the sound of shattering glass.

Lance tightened his grip on his pistol. "Time to make our stand, General Custer. Outside, where the bullets were flying earlier? Or the basement without windows?"

"I'll take my chances outside." She jumped up to open the front door.

He tackled her back to the floor just before a barrage of gunfire shattered the window where she'd been standing, raining glass down on top of them.

She swore, grabbing the edge of a blanket from the back of a nearby chair and tossing it on the floor over the glass. Then she scrambled across it toward the front door.

He quickly followed, blocking her way so she wouldn't try to open the door. "About that plan—"

"I know, I know. As much as I hate it, the basement's our only viable option."

"Smart lady. *Go.*" He pushed her ahead of him. They both crawled as fast as they could, knees bumping against the hard wood floors, staying low to avoid becoming a target through any of the windows.

They were almost to the basement door when shouts sounded behind them.

"Hurry," Lance yelled.

Keira jumped up and shoved the basement door open. The dark, constricted space below had her hesitating and drawing a painful, bracing breath to try to tamp down her fears. At Lance's questioning look, she straightened her shoulders, then forced herself to hurry down the stairs. At the bottom, she anxiously whirled around, expecting Lance to be right behind her. Instead, he stood silhouetted in the doorway above.

"Lock the door," he yelled, then slammed it shut. Something thumped against it.

She stood there, stunned. What the heck? She whipped out her pistol and raced back up the stairs. But when she pushed the door, it barely moved. She strained against it, only managing to open the door a few millimeters. That thump she'd heard. Lance must have shoved a chair or something else under the doorknob to keep her in the basement.

The fears from her past battered at her, narrowing her vision with darkness. She had to get out. She yelled some choice phrases at him and slammed her shoulder against the door. Her ribs protested the abuse, making her double over in pain. She drew small shaky breaths until she could straighten. Then she beat her fist against the wood, over and over, her whole body shaking. "Lance! Let me out!"

Gunshots sounded from the main room. Grunts. Shouts. More breaking glass. How many of those lunatics were out there? She shoved at the door over and over, fighting through the pain, desperate to get out to help Lance. And desperate to escape this dungeon before she curled into a fetal position like the terrified young girl she'd once been. Out. She had to get out!

A few agonizing minutes later, the sudden silence shook her even more than the shouts and gunshots had. Was this the calm before the storm, like earlier when the birds had stopped chirping? What was going on?

The door yanked open.

She stumbled back, grabbing the railing to keep from falling as she swung her pistol toward the man looming there. He immediately raised his hands. Recognition slammed into her. She jerked her gun down.

"Mr. Prescott?"

"Officer Sloane." He dropped his hands, sounding slightly

out of breath. There was a fresh cut on his jaw. His business suit was torn in several places. And his formerly white shirt was now dotted with blood. "At the risk of sounding cliché, the coast is clear."

Lance appeared beside him, looking far worse than his boss. Blood was smeared on his clothes, his neck, his hair. Bruises were already darkening along his jaw.

She rushed up the last few steps to the doorway. "Lance. Are you hurt? What—"

"We don't have much time," he said. "It's taken them twelve years to find me. Now that they have, they'll come at me with everything they've got. Anyone here when their reinforcements arrive is in danger." He held his hand out to Keira. "We're leaving. Now."

She shoved her pistol into the waistband of her pants and brushed past him into the main room. Her eyes widened when she saw the destruction and death around her. Several men dressed in black lay crumpled on the floor in various locations, clearly beyond help. Asher, Ryland, Faith and two other UB investigators stood near the stone fireplace at the back of the family room, looking as disheveled as their boss, several of them bleeding from various cuts.

"What happened?" she asked. "Have any of you been seriously hurt?"

Lance shoved a fresh magazine into his pistol as he peered out the back windows looking up at the mountains.

Grayson stopped beside Keira. "Thankfully, everyone's okay. Lance got the worst of it. He was fighting two men at once when we got here."

Lance turned from the windows. "I had it under control. You shouldn't have come."

"You're welcome." Grayson rolled his eyes.

Lance let out a deep breath and glanced at his teammates,

offering a quick nod of thanks. As he stepped over to Keira and Grayson, he flipped back his suit jacket and shoved his pistol into the holster on his belt. "I don't mean to sound ungrateful. But I'd really hoped to not involve any of you in this. How did you know where I was? Or that Keira might be in trouble?"

Asher motioned to the destruction around them. "We all got to talking after you left. You were really defensive during the meeting, trying far too hard to discredit Officer Sloane's investigation. It was obvious there was something going on and that it involved both of you. Figuring out what cabin she'd rented only took a few calls. We'd planned on coming over to talk to her first, then we were going to your place. We didn't expect to get caught at the O.K. Corral."

Keira put her hands on her hips. "What's going on, Lance? You said these men have been after you for years but that they followed me. Did it occur to you that you could have warned me earlier in the safety of UB's conference room?"

His dark brooding gaze locked on hers. "Nothing you told me in the meeting made me think you'd attracted the attention of these guys. I came here to talk, to make absolutely sure you hadn't done anything to put yourself at risk. And then I was going to try to convince you to drop the case, to *keep* you out of danger. If I'd known they'd followed you, that they were in Gatlinburg, I sure as hell wouldn't have let you walk into an ambush. I'd have taken you with me when I left UB and protected you."

"Hold it," Faith said. "Do I have this right? Someone's been trying to find you and kill you for *years*. Rick Cameron is somehow involved. And you were worried that Keira may have led these enemies to you. Yet, instead of telling us about it and asking us to help, you risked your life, and hers, by trying to handle this alone?"

Lance winced. "It sounds way worse when you put it like that."

Asher stepped closer to him. "You had an odd look on your face in the war room when you told me you'd see me later. You were lying, weren't you? When you left UB, you were leaving for good, not planning on ever coming back. Tell me I'm wrong, Lance. Please, for God's sake, tell me I'm wrong."

Lance looked away.

Asher swore.

Keira pulled out her cell phone.

"Don't tell me you're trying to call the police again." Lance sounded alarmed.

"Assuming the cell signal isn't still jammed, dang straight I'm calling the police."

He grabbed her phone. *"No."*

Grayson motioned toward the others. Suddenly Keira and Lance were surrounded by the UB investigators, a wall of men and one woman—Faith—blocking them from leaving.

"The police are already on their way," Grayson told him. "And you're not going anywhere without telling your teammates, your friends, what exactly is going on."

Lance looked like he wanted to argue, but the sound of sirens coming up the mountain had him fisting his hands by his sides.

Grayson put his hand on Lance's shoulder. "I can practically see the wheels spinning in your mind, trying to weave some kind of story to make us leave you alone. You're trying to figure out how to keep all of us safe while you, and potentially Officer Sloane too, face something incredibly dangerous on your own. These obviously aren't your run-of-the-mill criminals out to settle a score. They appear to be highly organized, trained and well funded. You need our help, whether you want it or not."

Lance's jaw tightened. "I don't want any of you hurt." He glanced around at them, then let out a shaky breath. "Any more hurt than you already are."

Grayson dropped his hand from Lance's shoulder. "I don't want that either. Which is why you need to level with us, give us information so we know who we're fighting against. Then we'll fight them together." He looked at the others. "Am I right?"

"Damn straight," Faith said, her words echoed by the team.

Keira arched a brow at Lance and raised her voice to be heard over the approaching sirens. "I'm already in this. And I'm not letting you leave without me."

Grayson motioned toward the front windows, or what was left of them after being shattered by bullets. "Gatlinburg PD is going to pull up out front any minute now. Lance, give me your word that you're going to work with us, that you'll explain everything, and we'll come up with a plan together. No playing this solo."

He gave all of them a pained look, then nodded. "All right. I'll tell you everything. But not in front of the police."

"The police can help us," Grayson argued.

"Not with this. Trust me."

He stared at Lance a few moments, then nodded. "All right. I'll accept that, for now. But we've got to come up with a cover story. Fast."

"Sticking close to the truth works best," Keira said. "Less chance of our stories not matching. That should be easy since Lance is the only one in this room who knows what's going on and who is after him."

He gave her an odd look, as if he were going to correct something she'd said. Instead, he shrugged and remained silent.

"Sirens have stopped." Faith motioned toward the jagged openings where the front windows used to be. "I don't see the police, so they've likely parked down the street in case there are active gunmen. But they're probably running through the woods toward the cabin as we speak. Keira's right. We should stick to the truth where we can. We can honestly say that we all came here to see Keira and were surprised that Lance was here too and that these ninja guys were trying to kill them. But how do we explain Keira being here in Gatlinburg? Why we were coming to see her? Or you, Lance, coming to see her, without us bringing up Rick Cameron's case and whatever it has to do with your mysterious past?"

"That part's easy." Lance gave Keira a half smile and put his arm around her shoulders. "You and I are dating. My friends found out this morning when I told them at UB. After I left, they came over to see you, to push for information about our relationship. I, of course, was already here, you being my girlfriend and all."

Her cheeks flushed and she pushed his arm off her shoulder. "Try to kiss me and I'll punch you."

His grin widened. "Noted."

Movement caught their attention out front. Police in flak jackets emerged from the cover of the trees, boots thumping as they raced up the porch stairs and aimed long guns through the openings.

Lance swore.

"Gatlinburg PD," one of them yelled. "Drop any weapons you have. Come out with your hands up."

Grayson straightened his suit jacket, frowning at the drops of blood and rips in the expensive fabric. "Everyone say as little as possible." He spoke low so those out front wouldn't hear him. "Stick to the story Lance just made up. Don't offer any extra information." He shook his head as if in disgust. "May God help us all. We're about to lie to the chief of police."

Chapter Five

In all her twenty-eight years, other than the awful things that had happened during her teen years, Keira couldn't think of a single day that was crazier, scarier, more frustrating, painful or confusing than today had been. And it wasn't close to being over. The sun was only just now beginning to set. But instead of being warm and cozy in her cabin as she'd planned when she first woke up, she was back at Unfinished Business.

One of the differences between this morning and now was that instead of being in a conference room, she was sitting in a chair in the middle of the so-called war room. Chairs had been arranged in a large circle. But few of them were occupied. The UB investigators were standing around in small groups talking, drinking and eating sandwiches their boss had ordered for their dinner.

The biggest difference from this morning was her reason for being here. She wasn't just looking into a cold case now. She was trying to find out why she'd been shot at, beaten, almost stabbed, locked in a dark basement and, perhaps worst of all, been forced to lie to fellow police officers. Rather than tell them she was here to investigate a murder, she'd told them she was Lance's girlfriend.

As if something like that could ever happen. She couldn't

imagine the stars ever aligning between them, not after their inauspicious start.

Making everything worse was that she'd been blackmailed at the cabin by Gatlinburg's police chief Russo to go to the hospital. She'd argued that she knew her ribs were only bruised, not broken. *After all, she'd had broken ribs before.* Of course, she hadn't shared that information with him. Still, it was only because Russo threatened to call her boss to order her to the hospital that she'd finally given in.

Now here she was, with bruised, not broken, ribs—as she'd predicted. And instead of being happy and grateful to have some tips and suggestions from a group of experienced investigators like she had been earlier, she was now desperate to find out how she could avoid the same fate as Rick Cameron.

She glanced around the room. Everyone who'd been at the cabin sported bandages or stitches on their various cuts and scrapes. Lance by far had the most injuries, with stitches on both forearms, his left calf and his scalp. Keira considered herself lucky that she'd only sustained a few minor abrasions. And that it only hurt when she breathed. Okay, maybe that wasn't something to exactly be thankful for. But considering how much worse it could have been, she wasn't complaining. Especially since none of her cuts had required stitches.

She hated needles.

And doctors.

And hospitals.

All they did was bring up bad memories.

Chief Russo had no way of knowing that. But it didn't keep him from being added to her list of people she'd rather avoid in the future. After all, it was only because of him that flashbacks of her childhood kept parading like a horror movie in her mind's eye. She didn't need that added stress on top of everything else, not today.

Impatient for everyone to join the circle so they could start the discussion, she looked past them through the two-story windows that overlooked the front parking lot.

Where the asphalt ended, the scary, twisty two-lane road up and down the mountain began. Just past that, the mountain rose steeply, its peak one of the tallest in the Smokies. From what she'd been told, the road ended at the very top of this particular mountain, at Grayson Prescott's estate. And since the mountain was called Prescott Mountain, she could only assume he owned the whole darn thing. How incredible was that?

Even if she ever had the money to afford it, she wouldn't want a mountain. Her multitude of fears from claustrophobia to heights and a ridiculously long list of other things would keep her from wanting to travel up and down a winding road every day. But, man oh man, could she appreciate the natural beauty around here.

Even in the fading sunlight, the scenery was so surreal that it made her want to stare out the windows and forget everything else around her. Tall, spindly oaks devoid of leaves marched up the steep slope beside thick, dark evergreens. Jagged rocks in varying shapes and sizes jutted out at odd angles, catching the light and forming a tapestry of colors that would make an artist weep. It was so much more picturesque than flat Maple Falls. But what struck her the most were the little puffs of white mist that gave the mountains their name—the Smokies.

When she'd first visited the Great Smoky Mountains National Park as a small child, she'd been terrified at the white puffs, convinced that the woods were on fire. Thankfully, her mom knew otherwise and had reassured her. Those were the good times, when her family had been a real family. Before her father had turned to alcohol and painkillers to drown his guilt. Before everything had gone so horribly wrong.

"Never seen a mountain before?" Lance sat beside her. The teasing note in his voice was tempered by the lines of worry on his forehead.

"Not in a very long time."

His gaze sharpened, the lines of worry deepening. "That sounded ominous. What's wrong?"

"Other than someone wanting to kill me?"

"Don't."

"Don't what?"

"Lie to me. Don't pretend that you were thinking about the mess we're in. Something else was on your mind, something that put haunting shadows in your eyes. What is it? Something from your past? You seemed so lost, a million miles away." He gently took one of her hands in his and turned it over, revealing the ugly scars. "Is this part of it? The reason for the shadows?"

Her breath caught and she snatched her hand back, curling her fingers against her palms to cover the angry red welts. She forced a laugh. "Haunting shadows? Really? When did you become a poet?"

He didn't crack a smile. Instead, he simply waited, as if he expected her to confess her deepest, darkest secrets.

That was never going to happen.

"If by something in my past you mean being attacked by ninjas," she scoffed, "then you're right on target. Yes, my past...my *recent* past is bothering me. When do we get to hear the truth about what's going on? The truth about *your* past?"

He studied her, his expression turning sad. Or was it more that he was…disappointed?

Finally, he shrugged and motioned to the others. "As soon as everyone's settled—" his voice was raised so the team could hear him "—I'll start."

The little groups broke apart. The newest arrivals grabbed their laptops or computer tablets and hurried to take their seats. Faith and her husband, Asher, were already sitting across from Lance and Keira. Ryland, the team lead, was next to Faith. The other two men from the cabin sat close by. They had been reintroduced to Keira as Trent and Callum since she had forgotten their names from the earlier meeting.

The remaining members of the UB investigative team were here too, with the exception of their boss, Grayson, and his wife, Willow. They were both at the police station, where Grayson was trying to placate the chief. There'd been no way to hide what had happened from the media with so many gunshots and the destruction at the cabin. Not to mention the body bags being carried out to coroner's vans. The chief wasn't letting this go with a simple "home invasion" explanation.

Apparently he was a close friend of Grayson's, and he was also Willow's former boss. Their history together was the only reason the rest of them were allowed to leave the hospital after being treated without enduring lengthy police interviews. But they'd had to agree to go to the station later for more questioning if Grayson wasn't able to satisfy Russo with his answers.

Once everyone was seated and quiet descended upon the room, every eye turned to Lance. This man whom Keira viewed as the epitome of confidence and decisiveness now seemed uncertain, hesitant. After briefly glancing around the circle at his fellow investigators and Keira, he drew a deep breath and began to speak.

"Officer Sloane, I mean Keira, and all of my friends here at Unfinished Business, everything you think you know about me is a lie."

Chapter Six

Lance would rather face a roomful of gunmen with only a pistol and one magazine of ammo to defend himself than the people sitting around this circle. He cared deeply for them, and even felt a deep connection to Keira. After all, she'd been through hell because his past had followed her to Gatlinburg. His biggest regret was that he was responsible for putting both her and his work family in danger. Because of his actions, or inaction, he was about to lose the friendship of everyone in this room.

On the opposite side of the circle of chairs, Faith gave him an encouraging smile. "Come on, Lance. We know you. You can't fake the stuff that really matters, the kind of person you are. That comes out in actions, not words. So whatever it is that you've been hiding, don't be afraid to share. We're all friends here, family really." She smiled at Keira. "And future friends. We can't fix this unless we know what's going on."

He grimaced. "Some things aren't fixable."

Keira surprised him by briefly squeezing his hand. "We can at least try."

He smiled, but he already knew this meeting wasn't going to help. And he still wasn't committed to fully disclosing everything in spite of his promise to Grayson. It was too dangerous.

"As I said, everything you think you know about me is a lie, starting with my name. Lance Cabrera is the alias I took on twelve years ago. My birth name is Lance Mitchell." When the huge outcry he'd expected didn't happen, he hesitated, frowning. "I don't come from out west like I've led you all to believe. My hometown is in central Florida, a city called Gainesville. My résumé that I used to join Unfinished Business is a fabrication."

Ryland shook his head, his gaze locked on Lance. "No. It isn't. I recruited you. You were working as a detective in Nashville. I visited you there at your job. Spoke to your peers, your boss. He gave you a glowing recommendation, said you were the best detective he'd worked with in his forty-year career. Are you saying he made all that up? That he allowed a civilian to pretend to be a detective the day I was there?"

"Well, no, of course not. He told the truth as he saw it. I worked for Nashville PD for over eight years."

"As Lance Cabrera."

"Yes."

"Then if you're expecting shock or recriminations from us because you changed your name prior to that, you'll be disappointed. People change their names for all kinds of reasons. Heck, Faith changed her last name from Lancaster to Whitfield when she married Asher. We still consider her to be a friend, more or less."

Faith made a rude gesture.

Ryland grinned. "My point, Lance, is that we already know from what happened this morning and what little you've told us so far, that something bad in your past has caught up to you. If I felt that changing my name would help me get a much-needed fresh start, I wouldn't hesitate. What we need to know is who these people are and why they're after you." He motioned toward Keira. "And why they went after Officer Sloane. Stop worrying about how we'll feel and give us the facts. Tell us what we're up against. Then we'll all deal with the fallout. All right, brother?"

Lance was shocked at the nods of agreement from everyone in the room, including Keira. He hadn't expected that. He offered up one last warning. "I appreciate the support, more than you know. But if we continue, if I tell you everything, it puts all of you in danger. As it is, it will be difficult to put a slant on whatever stories the media is already spinning, to placate the bad guys. We need to make it convincing that UB being at the cabin truly has nothing to do with my past. Doing that should keep you all safe. Keira and I can leave and deal with this alone. My primary concern for her is to figure out how she got involved in this and find a way to get her out of it. The rest is on me to handle."

Ryland shook his head again. "No way. You aren't facing this alone. You've saved my life on numerous occasions, plus a few more of us. You were part of the team that helped save Asher on his last big case. We owe you for that."

"You've saved my life too," Lance argued. "You owe me nothing."

"Then consider this," Ryland said. "As far as I'm concerned, we're family. Family doesn't run when one of theirs is in trouble. Not this family anyway. Am I right guys?"

"And gals," Faith and Ivy chimed in, laughing because they'd both said the same thing.

Faith smiled. "We are family, Lance. And Keira is too, because her fate is apparently tied with yours, at least right now. None of us is running away from this, no matter how hard you try to convince us."

Everyone voiced their agreement.

Lance let out a shuddering breath, his throat tight. He'd never met a group of better people. And while he didn't want to involve them any more than they already were, it was clear they weren't going to give him that choice. All he could do now was prepare them.

He nodded his thanks, and when he'd composed himself enough to speak again, he began his story.

"To understand what's happening, I have to start where this began for me, my senior year in college. My on-again, off-again girlfriend, Ileana Sanchez, was off-again. Thankfully she was majoring in IT, computer programming, and I was following the criminology track. With radically different majors, the only times we crossed each other's paths was at sporting events or the restaurants on campus. I was just a few months shy of graduation.

"Most of my classmates were applying for jobs with police departments, hoping to move up the ladder from beat cop to detective eventually. I was determined to start out right away doing what I loved, solving mysteries, figuring out whodunit. I didn't want to spend years earning my stripes and paying my dues. My naive, overinflated ego had me applying for jobs with the big dogs—FBI, CIA, Homeland Security, you name it. If it was an agency with a glitzy reputation, I tried to get in."

Trent chuckled. "Ambition with a capital A. Those places prefer their candidates to have real-world experience in other careers or agencies before signing on with them. I imagine you got turned down flat."

"You'd be right," Lance said, "with one exception. A man I'd never met—Ian Murphy—working for an agency I'd never heard of contacted me. He said he had been given my name from one of those other agencies. But who he got it from exactly, and how, was vague. He never quite explained that part."

"Red flags, buddy," Trent said.

"Where were you when I was naive and twenty-two, Trent?"

Trent laughed. "Just as young and naive as you, I'm guessing."

Lance smiled. "The sales pitch was incredible. The agency was brand-new, super secret and flush with money. They wanted young, energetic, smart people who would bridge the gap between the rules the law enforcement entities were forced to abide by versus what civilians could get away with. An example he gave me was that the FBI might not be able to secure a warrant they need in order to conduct some kind of surveillance because a judge doesn't agree that they have probable cause. But there's nothing stopping a civilian from performing his own surveillance and passing along any evidence he obtains. It provides the FBI with something tangible to convince a judge to give them a warrant. But it doesn't quite cross the line that would get the evidence thrown out. It's a legal loophole. Murphy was tasked with exploiting that loophole to help ensure the safety and security of the American people and our country. I was practically foaming at the mouth to sign up."

Keira nodded. "They appealed to your patriotism and the idealism a young man would have, not being jaded yet from the real world."

"They definitely knew which buttons to push. But, honestly, I was more excited about the prospect of getting to be a detective right out of the gate. The money he offered wasn't anything to sneeze at either. And once my ex-girlfriend got wind of the job offer I was considering, she was suddenly flirting with me again. I was too stupid to realize it was the money, not me, that she wanted."

Ryland shook his head in commiseration. "She must have been really hot."

Lance laughed. "She wasn't bad to look at, that's for sure. And I was still young enough and shallow enough that I liked having a beautiful woman on my arm, regardless of whether we got along well or not."

Keira rolled her eyes. "Was she blonde?"

"Ouch," Faith complained, pointing to her long blond hair.

"Sorry." Keira's face reddened.

"No, she wasn't blonde," Lance answered, smiling. "She had Spanish heritage and used that to her advantage. She'd never have dreamed of coloring her dark hair. It was her pride and joy." He shook his head. "Anyway, my point is, you can see the allure of the job offer on many levels, and I jumped at it.

"We took huge risks every day, putting our lives on the line with the bad guys we were after. And there was a risk that if we crossed a line too far, we might end up getting arrested. If that ever happened, we were sworn to secrecy. If we said it was part of our job, our employer would deny even knowing us. The agency's cover was that it was a private-eye service. And that's what they'd stick to, denying we even worked for them. We'd be completely on our own. Since I never expected to get caught, I wasn't worried. And since I made more money in one month than most police detectives make in a year, I had no intention of heeding the little warning bells that kept going off in the back of my mind. The money was a powerful incentive to someone fresh out of school. I paid off my student loans in the first six months of the job."

Asher whistled. "It took me a decade to pay mine off. I can see the appeal of working for this place. What was it called? Are they still in operation?"

"It was a nondescript front in a strip mall in a tiny central Florida town called Ocala. The official name is Ocala Private Investigations, or OPI. If there was an official government name for the agency, we never knew about it. Everything was on a need-to-know basis. Each of us knew a different piece of the overall puzzle. But no one knew it all, except our boss. As to your second question, OPI went out of business years ago."

Keira motioned for his attention. "Since you're focusing on this OPI, can you confirm they're the ones behind what happened this morning? That's where you're heading, isn't it?"

"Yes and no. OPI was the catalyst for everything that went wrong. But I don't have any proof that they're the ones behind what happened."

"What *did* happen?" Keira asked.

"After a handful of years working there, I was the team lead over eight other people—seven men, one woman. We were given a complicated mission that required the whole team. Each of us was supposed to develop dossiers on people whose names we were given. They weren't ordinary, everyday people with their lives plastered on social media. It was tough getting any information on them and took a lot of surveillance work. But we did it and gave the files to our boss. From there, he handed them off to his contact at the appropriate alphabet agency. Job done. Move on to the next assignment. Only, that's not exactly what happened."

He rested his forearms on his thighs and clasped his hands together, forming a fist as he thought back. "The very next day, I was surfing the internet and stumbled onto a routine story about some person getting mugged and killed that morning. The police were asking for any witnesses to come forward. When I saw the name of the victim, it sent ice-cold chills down my spine. It was one of the people whom I'd investigated. I'd given his file to my boss the night before."

Keira's eyes widened "Are you sure it was the same person? Maybe someone else had the same name?"

"I'd hoped that very thing. But it didn't take long to confirm it was the same person. I told my boss. He assured me it had to be a coincidence and to not worry about it. But it kept niggling at me. I couldn't let it go. I created some automated searches on the internet to alert me if more coincidences happened. A week later, I got a hit."

"Another person on the list was killed?" Keira asked.

Lance nodded, clasping his hands so tightly his knuckles ached. "Not just one." He glanced at his team. "All of them. There were nine people we'd investigated in that most recent assignment. In the span of one week, every single one of them was dead. Each alone didn't seem suspicious—random accidents, common health ailments like a heart attack, nothing particularly concerning. But together, it was a pattern. An incredibly disturbing pattern. One that I reported to Murphy. He glossed it over again, seemed uninterested. But I couldn't ignore it."

Asher leaned forward in his chair. "You dug into your other cases, didn't you? To see if anything like that had happened before."

Lance nodded grimly. "As you might guess, it had. Nothing recent. In fact, most of our cases were proven to be on the up and up. We found where cases we'd worked ended up going to trial and the guilty parties went to prison. The evidence we'd collected, things like recordings of people in bars or other public places spilling their secrets, most of it went to a good cause. Or so we told ourselves. We rarely did anything outrageous enough to truly cross any lines, at least, not any lines on the civilian side of things."

He shook his head and sat back, stretching his legs out in front of him. "But as we dug back over the years, we found a disturbing number of people that we'd investigated had turned up dead within days of us turning in our information. Needless to say, we were stunned. All of us had spent years thinking we were helping people and getting rich in the process. But in reality, we were being used to hurt people. It didn't take much of a leap to realize other information we'd passed along probably wasn't used for legit purposes either. We were devastated."

Trent shook his head. "Man. That sucks."

"That's putting it mildly," Lance said.

"What did you do?" Keira asked, caught up in the story. "Did you go to your boss again?"

"We did. The whole team so he couldn't blow it off this time. We'd gathered all of our data on the suspicious cases and presented it in a meeting with him one morning. He couldn't deny it in front of him in black and white. And, honestly, he didn't try to. He seemed as shocked and disgusted as we were. He told us to give him twenty-four hours to contact the right people and get the ball rolling on figuring out who was behind this abuse of power. The assumption was that one of his liaisons was a mole, a dirty agent. Three hours later, Ian Murphy was dead. He was killed in a drive-by shooting in a restaurant parking lot. The police theory was that it was a gang member who mistook him for someone else. The actual shooter was never caught."

Asher scoffed. "Sounds fishy, to say the least."

Keira nodded.

"I'll cut to the point," Lance said. "In the next few weeks, one of our teammates, Allen Stanford, was also killed. Single car accident. Ran his car into a tree. No witnesses. His blood alcohol level was twice the legal limit. But here's the catch. Allen didn't drink. Ever. Someone staged his murder to look like an accident, not realizing he'd sworn off alcohol for personal reasons. A few weeks later, another team member, Brett Foster, was framed for a crime he didn't commit. While he was in jail waiting for bail to be set, he was shanked by another prisoner. He didn't die. But it was close."

"Let me guess," Ryland said, "the prisoner who shanked him was later shanked himself."

"Close enough," Lance said. "He was found hanging in his cell. Apparently, he committed suicide even though he was slated to be released the following week."

Ryland swore. "This is crazy scary. Your team was falling like dominoes."

"It doesn't stop there either. Now we get to Rick Cameron."

"We already know what happened to him," Keira said. "He was beaten and shot in his motel room."

Lance nodded. "But there's more. Before that, when OPI was falling apart, he too was framed for a crime he didn't commit. That's when we all agreed we were on someone's hit list and needed to do something drastic if we were going to survive. We bailed Rick out of jail, picked up our other friend from the hospital where he was recovering from being stabbed, and disappeared. We took on new identities, which in this post-9/11 world was no easy feat. And we went our separate ways. Rick's birth name was Rick Parker. Cameron was his new identity."

"What about your families?" Keira asked. "And your girlfriend? Did you leave them behind?"

"We did. Breaking up with Ileana was the best part of

it for me, for both of us really. We were never healthy for each other, fought more often than not. I'd broken up with her many times. But she was gone for a few weeks, sometimes longer, then she always came back and managed to convince me to try again. This time, after I explained that I'd quit my job and that my massive paycheck was no longer going to be coming in, she didn't argue. She left. And since I went underground, I haven't seen her since. Though even if I hadn't gone on the run, I doubt she'd have tried to rekindle our relationship. She loved the money far more than she'd ever cared about me." He shrugged. "And I obviously didn't care for her the way I should have, considering how long we'd been together. Rather than pine for her, I was relieved the drama was finally over."

"Good riddance," Keira murmured.

"A hundred percent," Lance said. "The part that was really difficult was leaving our families. We considered it our duty, like joining the Witness Security Program, WitSec. We were forced to let go of our past so that we could protect the ones we loved." He gave her a baleful look. "I haven't seen or spoken to my parents, sister or brother since."

Keira swallowed, her eyes looking suspiciously bright. "From your expression, you must have really loved them."

The wonder in her tone confused him. It was as if she couldn't fathom actually loving your family. Didn't she have a family who loved her?

"What about your team?" Keira asked. "The OPI team. Have you kept in touch with them? Is that what happened to Rick? Someone traced an email or phone call from an OPI teammate back to him?"

He locked away the questions she'd raised in his mind about her family and focused on their current, dire situation. "I can't imagine Rick being that careless. The story

I've given all of you is a pared down version of everything that went on. There were other close calls. We didn't know who to trust. Every time we tried to pursue this so-called mole, to find out who was behind everything, an attempt would be made on one of our lives. The only reason more of us weren't killed was because we were hypervigilant, fully aware that someone very powerful with a lot to lose was after us. Believe me, if we could have outed them and put a stop to what they were doing, we would have. But we didn't have the resources, the ability. Going underground was our only choice. We all agreed we wouldn't call, email or contact each other in any way. That's how it's been ever since."

Faith frowned at him. "Rick was far closer to Gatlinburg when he was murdered than to his home in Louisiana. It's only logical that he found out you were in danger and was trying to reach you when he was killed. He must have given them your name and location. That's why the bad guys went after you, after Keira."

Lance was shaking his head before she finished. "We never shared our aliases or locations. We each kept our first name, but not our last. And we all moved away from Florida, not telling each other where we'd gone. Even if Rick was tortured for current information on his OPI team, he couldn't have told them what he doesn't know."

Keira stared at him, her eyes narrowed. "There's more to it. There has to be. You said they followed me to Gatlinburg, then to you. But I came here because Rick left that note and mentioned your name. He must have been in Maple Falls because he'd figured out where you were, thus the note. And he was on his way here to see you, maybe to warn you that the past was catching up."

Lance shrugged. "I believe you're partially right. Rick must have figured out where I was and felt he needed to come warn me. But he didn't want to put me in danger by trying to contact me in any way that could be traced."

"But he must have done something for them to know where you were."

"They didn't know where I was until they followed you to Gatlinburg, then to UB. Otherwise, when they'd killed Rick weeks ago, they'd have come straight here. Something else happened in Maple Falls, something you uncovered or did without even realizing it. That's why they followed you here. Was there any time when you told someone else about the words 'unfinished business' and my name? Maybe someone was watching you and the others involved in the investigation and saw, read or heard something substantive about the case."

"No way. We didn't know anything to tell. And I'm the only one who connected you to the note. The only one I told about that was Rick." She gave him a half smile. "I visited his grave on my way out of town, told him that I was trying to..." Her eyes widened. "Oh no."

"Go ahead," Lance urged her. "What are you remembering?"

She clutched her hands against her middle as if she were feeling sick. "I spoke out loud to him, mentioned that I was going to find his killer and get him justice. I said I'd take care of his unfinished business and see if this Lance guy was his Lance guy."

"Were you alone?"

"I thought I was. But literally right after I said that out loud, I heard something in the woods. I thought it was an animal rooting around in the dried leaves. But I was spooked enough to take out my pistol until I was in my car."

"That's it," he said. "Must be. Someone was watching you and heard enough to think you knew where I was."

She put her hand on his forearm. "I'm so sorry. I had no idea."

He gently took her hand in his. "Of course you didn't. I'm grateful you figured out where I was. At least now I know someone is actively hunting my team again." When he would have let go, she held on for another moment.

"I really am sorry I put you in danger, Lance."

He gently squeezed her hand. "You did me a favor. Now that I know they're here, I can do what I need to do to protect myself. And you. We have to figure out how to extricate you from all this so you can return to Maple Falls without living in fear that they'll go after you."

This time, it was Keira who let go, pulling her hand back to clasp it tightly with the other, her face pale.

Lance was about to try to reassure her when Ryland spoke.

"The key to this seems to be in figuring out how Rick knew where you were. Any ideas on that?"

"I have a few, one in particular. It goes back to three months ago, when yet another one of my old teammates from OPI was murdered."

"Oh no," Keira said. "I'm so sorry."

He nodded his thanks.

"How did you find that out?" Ryland said, continuing to press for information.

"As you might imagine, being a team lead yourself, I've always felt responsible for my old team. I couldn't figure out the identity of whoever killed our boss and has tried to pick off each of us. So the least I could do was try to look out for them, in some way, without endangering them."

The pained look in Ryland's eyes confirmed that he well understood the feeling of responsibility and the guilt whenever any of them ran into trouble.

"One of the ways I've tried to do that is to set up automated searches of the internet. Every story that goes through the major news outlets, like Associated Press, gets fed into my searches. The first names of my team go through an algorithm I set up, something we used at OPI actually. It compares known details about my team with the news stories and uses a decision tree to determine whether to alert me via email. One of the most accurate parts of the decision tree that produces alerts is when pictures are involved. The algorithm uses facial recognition software. Three months ago, one of the searches found a picture of one of my old team members, Levi, with a reported last name of Alexander. Not his original birth name of course, but it was definitely him. He'd been killed in a mugging in New York. Most people aren't killed during muggings, so it wasn't typical. But there wasn't anything obvious to link it to our time at OPI either. But since then, I've been more aware and careful, keeping a lookout for signs that I'm being watched, followed."

"Man, that's a lot of baggage and stress to live with for so long," Asher said.

Lance shrugged, not feeling particularly worthy of any commiseration. Not when two of his teammates had been murdered in the past few months and he'd been unable to prevent their deaths.

"It's smart to keep tabs on your team as best you can," Ryland said. "But if you can use that kind of technology, especially the facial recognition searches, so can your enemies."

"Which is one of the reasons we've all agreed to steer clear of the media in any way so our photos aren't plastered on the internet. It's why I typically avoid photo ops on our cases, if you haven't noticed."

Faith nodded. "We've noticed. We figured you were one of those people who was camera shy."

He arched a brow. "*Shy* isn't in my vocabulary."

She laughed. "Okay, okay. We assumed you had your reasons. But now that you've explained it, that makes sense. You can't possibly avoid cameras all the time though. Airports alone will have you on their video systems from the moment you drive onto their property."

"It's a risk, for sure. Luckily, that post-9/11 security I mentioned earlier is top-notch on airport online systems, if not their physical security. I've flown many times and haven't found any photos of me from the security scans leaked to the internet. My algorithm searches for stories about me too, just in case something pops up, so I can try to take it down. So far, I haven't been targeted. Until today of course. But I also haven't done anything to stir up trouble. None of us has. So maybe that's the bigger reason why we haven't been found."

"Until three months ago," Keira said.

He winced. "Until three months ago. I've wondered if maybe Rick has done the same thing as me over the years. He could have been running his own searches and saw that story about Levi. If he decided to go to New York to look into what happened, he could have been spotted, assuming the mole had seen the story and went there to see if any old OPI team members showed up. Rick could have been on the run since then, maybe after a close call. And he started digging, trying to find me, as the old team lead, so we could figure out what to do. And how to warn our other teammates. But they found him before he got to me."

Lance looked around, making sure that everyone was paying attention. "All of you who were at the cabin today saw the manpower the mole sent after Keira and me. There were a couple of guys outside, a few more who got into the cabin—"

"Eight total," Asher said.

Lance winced. "All heavily armed, trained and wearing identical outfits to conceal their features from any potential witnesses. From what I heard of the police talking to each other as they checked everything out, none of the bodies had ID. Ryland, I assume that you've been communicating with Grayson off and on today. Heard anything about any of the bad guys being identified?"

He shook his head. "Nothing at all. None of their fingerprints have come up as a match in any databases so far. AFIS will take a while. The FBI database checks always take longer than our local ones. Gatlinburg PD will check DNA too. But that'll take a while unless Grayson can convince them to use our lab, which isn't snowed under with queued up requests. But from everything you've said, I don't expect any matches on any criminal DNA databases, certainly not CODIS. No way would this mole hire someone with past arrests or convictions that would mean their DNA has been logged. He's got too much at stake for that."

"Agreed," Lance said. "This guy, or gal, running this operation has access to significant resources. And I don't have any clue as to his or her identity. That was the problem twelve years ago, and it's still the problem today."

The atmosphere in the room had gone somber and tense. Everyone appeared to be trying to absorb everything that Lance had said. It was finally sinking in that this was far more serious, and deadly, than anything they'd ever faced.

He rested his forearms on his knees again. "My OPI boss and three members of my old team have been murdered. It's possible more of them have been killed and I don't know about it. Assuming that hasn't happened, I have five teammates left. And I need to find every one of them to warn them. All of us from OPI need to change our aliases again, start over, again. On top of that, I need to figure out how to get Keira off the mole's radar so this doesn't destroy her life and force her to go underground too."

Lance gave her a weak smile. "I'm so sorry about all of this. But I swear to you that I'll do everything in my power to keep you safe, and get your life back."

She gave him a weak smile but was clearly upset.

"What's your plan?" Ryland asked. "It sounds as if you've made some decisions."

"My first priority is to get Keira somewhere safe where she can lay low. After that, I'll work on finding my team and warning them. Then I'm going to figure out once and for all who this mole is. I'm going to end this."

"No." Keira's brows were drawn down in a frown. "For one thing, you can't do this by yourself. It's impossible. And I'm not hiding out while you face this alone."

"Keira, with all due respect for your experience and abilities as a police officer, you're not ready for this sort of thing. And more importantly, this isn't your fight."

"It became my fight the moment those maniacs tried to kill me. I want to bring them down as much as you. I made a promise to a dying man who entrusted your safety into my hands by telling me your name. That's sacred. I'm not running. I'm sticking with you. And I won't be a liability. I'll be your wingman or woman or whatever. Besides—" she gave him a saucy look "—you're not dumping your new girlfriend that easily."

Faith burst out laughing.

Lance frowned at her before turning back to Keira. "This isn't a laughing matter."

"I'm not the one laughing."

"Sorry," Faith called out. "I'll stop." She chuckled again, then grinned.

Asher smiled at his wife, then winked at Keira. "I agree that Lance shouldn't dump you so soon in your relationship." He arched a brow at Lance. "And you're not dumping your work family either. We're in this with you."

"Agreed," Faith added.

"When one of us is in trouble, we all are," Ryland said.

The others joined in, voicing their agreement. Every one of them.

"The time for debate is over," Ryland warned. "From now on, this case, your case, is the only one that Unfinished Business is working. And we're damn well going to solve it."

Lance hadn't been this frustrated, or touched, in a long time. Part of him wanted to shout at them to stop being so selfless, to just let him walk out the door. But the other part was so moved by their determination to help him that he was having difficulty forming words.

Keira seemed to sense his turmoil when she yet again took his hand in hers. "All for one and one for all. Is that the Unfinished Business motto?"

He cleared his throat, threading his fingers with hers. "Apparently so. Though I imagine the Three Musketeers might disagree."

Ryland stood. "We need to clear our schedules, make plans, hand out assignments. Lance, you'll have to go far more in-depth about OPI than the overview you just gave us. We need information on the cases you worked, dates, the names of anyone and everyone you had contact with while you worked there, no matter how unimportant it might seem. Let's get some coffee going and get comfortable. We'll likely be here most of the night. And many more after that."

Lance held up a hand to stop everyone. "One more thing,

not that we need any added stress at this point. We don't think any other gunmen were still alive after this morning's attack, but we should all consider that someone may have remained in the woods watching. They could be watching all of us now, maybe even outside of this building. Everyone needs to be hypervigilant about your safety, and your loved ones' safety, until this is over."

Chapter Seven

Keira yawned in the back seat of UB investigator Adam Trent's truck, keeping her gaze averted from the steep drops down the side of the mountain road as they bumped along in the dark. Lance was in the passenger seat in front of her, talking to Trent. The night had been much longer than any of them had expected. Sunrise was only minutes away. And none of them had gotten any sleep yet.

Turned out, Grayson and Willow's influence with Police Chief Russo hadn't gone as they'd hoped. Eight dead bodies was just too much to explain away without a proper investigation. Russo had insisted on interviewing everyone again who'd been at the cabin and wouldn't back down. The only concession he made was to conduct the interviews at Unfinished Business because of Grayson's insistence on wanting to keep his team out of the media spotlight.

The interviews had gone well, considering. The roughest part for Keira was trying to pretend that she and Lance were a couple. Not knowing exactly what he was saying about her in his interview, she'd vaguely glossed over their relationship details and kept her answers brief. They must have both satisfied the detectives, because they were told they could go.

After a seemingly endless trip along winding narrow

roads they finally turned onto a relatively straight and flat one. The sun's first rays revealed that they were in a valley. The Smokies formed a misty white backdrop to a sparkling pond with a fountain in the middle. White three-rail wooden fences lined the road, only falling away when the truck turned once more and approached an ultramodern take on a traditional farmhouse.

Two stories of black siding were trimmed in crisp white. Charcoal-gray stone framed the bottom of the home. And a slate chimney rose up the left end. Instead of a wraparound porch, there was a stone-wrapped portico in front, held up by thick cedar posts. A three-car garage flanked the large house on the right side.

This was Lance's home, the horse ranch he'd told her about when he'd arranged for them to get a ride with Trent. They certainly couldn't return to her rental cabin. And both of their vehicles had been shot up and were still being held as part of the ongoing crime scene investigation.

Lance had assured her and Trent that it would be safe to go to his home for a short time. The property deed wasn't registered under his name. It was listed under a tangle of shell companies that would take someone a long time to unravel. Still, they didn't plan on staying. He was retrieving his OPI files for Trent to take back to UB. And he had another vehicle in the garage for him and Keira to use.

Packing a suitcase was another item he'd said was on his to-do list, along with arranging for the care of his handful of horses while he and Keira left town. For her part, she already had her suitcase. That was yet another concession made by Chief Russo. He'd had a police woman pack her things at the rental cabin and take it to Unfinished Business for her.

"Do you prefer to wait in the truck?"

She blinked and realized that Lance was standing beside the truck, holding her door open.

"Oh, sorry. Was just…admiring your house. It's beautiful."

He smiled. "It's home. Wish we had more time and I could give you the grand tour. You're welcome to explore inside on your own while I get what I need."

"I just might." She hopped out of the truck, and the three of them headed inside.

Just like the outside, the interior of the house was a study in masculinity, blacks and browns with lots of dark stone accents. The ceilings were unusually high on the first level for a two-story home. She wouldn't have even realized there was a second level if she hadn't known from the outside. This open, expansive house was something she could breathe in. Her discomfort with tight spaces wouldn't be a problem here at all.

Lance motioned toward a massive cedar-and-granite island on the left side of the room. "Help yourself to something to eat if you're hungry. Otherwise, we can grab breakfast on our way out of town."

She would have thanked him, but he and Trent had already turned away and were heading toward a door on the far right side of the room, presumably to Lance's office. She heard their deep voices in conversation as they disappeared inside. With all the stress of the long day and night behind her, she was more inclined to want to sleep than eat. But if she lay down on one of the two groupings of black leather couches, she'd probably never get back up. They looked far too comfortable for her weary body. Instead, she meandered around, learning about Lance from the way this bachelor had chosen to furnish and decorate his home.

Dark colors were definitely his thing. There were no

pinks or pastels, no feminine touches anywhere, except perhaps for a few pillows and blankets thrown over a chair and one of the couches. But she imagined those were more for comfort and warmth than to soften up the place.

He was a reader, something they both had in common. She practically drooled over the chunky floor-to-ceiling bookshelves she could see through an archway by the kitchen area. A ladder attached to a brass rail declared it to be his home library. And as she got closer, she could see there was nothing techie to interfere with the ambience. There were only books here, comfortable reading chairs and a gas fireplace on one end. She would have preferred the coziness of a wood-burning fireplace. But she could see the advantage of gas in this particular room. There wouldn't be any concern about smoke or soot damaging the books.

Part of her wanted to check the rest of this gorgeous house out, give herself that grand tour. But the reader in her couldn't pull herself away from this room. She scanned the bookshelves, delighted and in awe of his collection. There was one whole section of classics, many leather bound. Several appeared to be first editions. But she didn't want to risk damaging them by touching them, so she couldn't be sure.

Other shelves held all kinds of nonfiction, with a heavy emphasis on autobiographies and biographies of people all throughout history. Those were the most worn books, reflecting his love of knowledge rather than a desire to lose himself in a good story. Her preference was fiction, tales of every kind, from thrillers to fantasy, and her personal favorite, historical romance. Unfortunately, she didn't find any romance on his shelves. But there was a thick fantasy novel she'd love to sink her literary teeth into. Perhaps it wouldn't be too much to ask to borrow it.

The pleasing timbre of male voices again had her turning around, clasping the novel to her chest. Trent and Lance stood at the end of the foyer talking. Two large boxes were on the floor beside them, presumably the promised OPI files.

She headed over, relieved to see Lance smile at her holding the book, nodding as if to let her know he approved of her choice. She waited beside him as Trent summarized the plans they'd made earlier, as if to double-check that they were all on the same page.

"Asher and Faith are tasked with finding former OPI team member Melissa Temple. Ivy and I will search for Sam McIntosh. Callum and Brice are in charge of locating Jack Scanlon. You and Keira will look for Brett Foster. That leaves…" He thumbed through some texts on his phone.

"Mick Thompson," Lance told him.

"Right. Thompson. As soon as one of the teams I just mentioned frees up, they'll look for him. Grayson, Willow, Ryland and our TBI liaison, Rowan, will provide support from UB for all of us. They'll also run interference with Chief Russo. And they'll get started right away on these OPI files to help us locate your former teammates and to take a fresh look at what happened. Hopefully they'll find a thread to pull, something that will lead us to the mole sooner than later. Sound good?"

"Sounds real good. Thanks, Trent."

Trent responded by clasping Lance on the shoulder and nodding at Keira. "Both of you, please, keep in contact. If anything concerning pops up, let us know. We'll do the same."

Keira smiled her agreement.

Lance motioned toward the boxes. "Let me help you with those."

They each carried a box out to Trent's truck. When Trent

was driving away, Lance rejoined Keira in the main room. He motioned toward the book in her hand. "One of my favorite epic fantasies. You read Rebecca Yarros?"

"Not yet. I've heard great things about this book and have been wanting to try it. Do you mind?"

"Of course not. Although I don't know how much reading time we'll get in the next few days, or however long this takes. If nothing else, you can take it back to Maple Falls once we've secured your safety and ability to return." He gave her an apologetic look. "I really am sorry you've been caught up in all this."

On impulse, she set the book on an end table and took one of his hands in both of hers. The warmth of his skin sent a shiver of delight up her spine and had her face flushing hot, especially when his eyes widened in surprise. But he didn't pull away, and she didn't let go.

"I don't think I've ever heard a man apologize as much as you have to everyone over the past—what?—twenty-four hours? I wish you'd stop. None of this is your fault. Seems to me that you've spent the past decade, even longer, fighting just to stay alive while keeping track of your team to try to keep them safe too. You didn't choose this path. But you darn well have the integrity to see it through and protect others, including me. That's not something to apologize for or feel bad about. It's admirable, honorable. Can we stop with the apologies?"

Ever so slowly, he lifted his other hand toward her face as if to give her time to stop him.

She didn't.

He feathered his fingers lightly across her cheek, then through her hair, gently pushing it back before dropping his hand. "You're something else, you know that?"

She drew a shaky breath, more affected by that light

touch than she could have imagined. "Is being 'something else' good or bad?"

His lips curved in a sexy smile that had her hot and cold all over. Mostly hot.

"Definitely good," he said. "Maybe after this is all…resolved, I should take my chances about asking you out."

"Maybe you should."

He grinned. "Don't think for a second I'll forget you said that."

She would have made another sassy retort, but her brain cells seemed to have drowned in the rush of hormones flooding her system.

"Keira?" His deep tone was laced with humor.

"Um, yes?"

"I need to check on the horses before we leave."

"Right. Okay."

He glanced down at his other hand tightly clutched in hers.

"Oh!" She immediately let go, her face flushing hot. "Sorry."

He leaned down and pressed the lightest, barest kiss against her cheek, then winked. "I'm not. Wait here and I'll just step out back—"

"No. I'm going with you."

At his raised brows, her face flushed again. "I'd rather go with you to back you up if something happens." She tapped the holster concealed beneath her jacket, where she had her pistol. "Cop. Remember?"

"I remember. I used to be one too, you know."

"For eight years. In Nashville. Heck of a coincidence."

"Coincidence?"

"Nashville. My hometown."

"Right. Where your...complicated family lives, I assume?"

She stiffened. "Out back you said? That door off the kitchen?"

His smile widened. "Your excellent detecting skills are showing again." He held out his hand. "Come on. I'll show you my horses."

"That pickup line needs work," she teased, ignoring his hand as she headed toward the back door.

He chuckled and followed behind. Once outside, however, his amusement evaporated. Instead, he was fully alert, scanning the property and the outbuilding they were heading toward.

Feeling silly for flirting with him when both their lives were potentially in danger, she went on high alert too, in full police mode. She kept her right hand down near the holster she'd donned from her suitcase earlier and scanned for any hint of trouble.

When they reached the building, she expected him to pull out a key to unlock the doors to the stables. Instead, there was an electronic keypad beside it. But he didn't press the buttons. He pressed his hand against a black square beneath it. The doors clicked and a barely audible motor hummed, making the doors slide open.

Inside was no less modern and masculine than his house had been. Black metal rafters supported the roof instead of wooden beams. Pristine stone floors that gently sloped to rectangular drains on either side of the aisle no doubt made cleaning much easier than the dirt floors she'd expected. Sturdy cedar formed the stalls on either side.

"There are only four horses here right now," he said as she followed him down the aisle. "But it can hold up to eight. I figure one day, if I'm lucky enough to turn old and gray and still have this place, I'll fill the other stalls with little fillies and colts for my children and grandchildren."

"That sounds wonderful," she breathed, picturing it in her mind.

He stopped and looked at her over his shoulder. "You like horses?"

She laughed. "Honestly, I don't know. I've never seen one up close. Our family couldn't afford things like that when I was growing up."

He slowly nodded. "I forget sometimes just how blessed I am. We always had horses. Now I suppose I'm carrying on the family tradition. I just wish my dad could see this place."

She looked up at him, the sadness in his voice making her throat tight. "Maybe when this is over, when we stop the person behind what happened at OPI, you can see him again."

His jaw tightened, but he didn't say anything.

She stopped at the next stall, shaking her head in wonder at the beautiful animal poking its graceful head over the top of the stall door. "I can't imagine any father not approving of this. The house, the land, this place and, oh my goodness, these beautiful babies. They're amazing." She laughed when the reddish-brown horse closest to her snuffled at her shirt.

When she reached up to touch its muzzle, Lance grabbed her hand.

"Careful," he said. "She's looking for something to eat. I'd rather you kept your fingers."

Keira blinked and took a quick step back.

"I didn't mean to scare you. She's not mean. But she might bite on accident if you stick your fingers out like that. Here." He opened a metal bin in the wall behind her and pulled out a carrot. "Do it like this. Flatten your palm."

He broke the carrot in half and put one piece on his palm

and held it up toward the horse. She snuffled his hand, grasping the carrot and pulling it into her mouth.

"Want to try?" He handed Keira the other half of the carrot.

"Definitely." She did what he'd shown her, laughing when the horse's velvety lips tickled her hand and took the carrot. "Oh my goodness. She's so sweet. And so very beautiful."

His dark eyes captured hers as he responded. "She most definitely is."

The wink that followed told her he definitely wasn't talking about the horse. She tried to respond and again couldn't seem to find her voice.

He took mercy on her, taking her hand in his. "Come on. We need to hurry. I don't think anyone will figure out about this place. But I'd rather not risk it. I need to get something from this last stall over here, the empty one on the left."

When they reached the stall, he let her hand go and crossed to the far wall.

"You mentioned the horses were hungry. Should I feed them?" she asked.

"If we had time, I'd love to show you how to do exactly that. They need oats, fresh hay, water. The carrots are treats, not a meal. I called a friend from my home office earlier to take care of that. He'll be here soon to get them." He reached above his head toward a piece of cedar trim.

"Get them? He's taking the horses away?"

Lance half turned, all serious again without a hint of his earlier lightheartedness. "If the wrong people figure out this is my place, I don't expect it to be standing when I return. The horses will be at my neighbor's stable, someone I trust." He turned back to the wall.

The idea that someone would destroy his beautiful home and this stable brought tears to her eyes. But whatever she might have been about to say was forgotten when the back stall wall slid open to reveal a narrow hidden room.

He headed inside, and by the time she followed, lights had flipped on, and he was pressing on another panel. It too slid open, but instead of another room, it revealed a metal safe built into the wall. There was a small desk and chair beside it, but nothing else. He crouched in front of the safe.

"Lance? What is this place? What are we doing here?"

"Saving my team. Hopefully."

"Saving your…which one? OPI? Or UB?"

He glanced back at her. "Both." He quickly pressed a sequence of buttons. The door on the safe popped open. A small leather duffel bag sat on the bottom shelf. Above it was a dark brown accordion folder about three inches thick.

"Lance, please. What are you…?" Again she stopped, this time in shock. He'd pulled out the duffel bag and opened it on top of the desk. Even from a few feet away, she could easily see what was inside.

Money.

A *lot* of money, bills of various denominations banded together.

"My goodness. That has to be thousands of dollars."

"It's enough."

"Enough for what?"

"To ensure our safety." After double-checking the contents, he zipped it closed and set it onto the floor. "We can't use credit cards, ATMs, anything traceable. We'll pay for everything we need in cash. I've also got IDs in the bag under various aliases, extra pistols and magazines of ammunition."

"I've heard of people having go bags to grab in an emergency, but normally they have clothes and toiletry items in them."

"I always figured I could buy those things wherever I ended up, if I didn't have a chance to pack a suitcase of clothes before I left. ID, cash, weapons—those are harder to get when traveling."

"Makes sense, I suppose. I've never felt the need for a go bag. Until now. I wish I'd packed extra ammunition before coming here."

"You've got a nine-mil right?"

She nodded, patting her jacket, hiding the bulge of her holster. "A Glock seventeen."

"My primary weapon is a Sig Sauer P320, nine millimeter. We can share ammunition. I'll pack extra."

"Thanks. I'll pay you back if we end up needing that ammo."

"Let's hope we don't." He sat at the desk. It barely surprised her this time when he slid more panels back and suddenly had a computer monitor in front of him with a keyboard on top of the desk.

She stepped to his side, glancing down at the bag of money, IDs and weaponry. "Lance. It's fine for you to use your money for your own protection. But I don't want you using it for mine. It had to have taken you years to save all that. We can make one stop at a local bank, and I can pull out my savings."

He'd been typing on the keyboard but stopped and looked at her. "It didn't take any time at all. I had terrible judgment when I first started out in joining OPI. But the one thing it did was give me more money than I could ever spend. And Grayson Prescott, my current boss? He's a billionaire, Keira. He pays us enough that we'll never have to worry about financial security. So don't worry about using that cash. There's plenty more."

She swallowed, then nodded. "Thank you. For helping to

protect me. You're exceedingly generous with your money, your time. I just hope it doesn't end up costing you your life." She motioned to the room around them, the safe, the computer. "For you to have gone to all this trouble, the people we're up against must be far more dangerous than I'd even suspected."

"They're dangerous, yes. But only because they hide in the shadows. The mole, even with all the resources at his disposal, is still just a person, Keira. He's not superhuman, no more powerful than anyone else. All we have to do is bring him out of those shadows and into the light. We're going to survive this. Together. Trust me. And trust yourself. I've seen your courage. You ran out of the cabin when you could have stayed inside and been safe. But you didn't. You ran outside thinking I needed help."

She rolled her eyes. "Fat lot of good I did. You didn't need help. I did. I almost got you killed."

Again her hand somehow found its way into his. He threaded their fingers together, his large, strong hand engulfing hers, but gentle. So gentle her heart seemed to shift in her chest.

"You ran toward possible danger, Keira. For me. You didn't know what or who might be out there. You still went outside. You're a good cop and a good person. And stronger than you know. Rely on your training. Trust yourself."

She offered him a tremulous smile. "Whatever happens, don't forget to ask me out on that date, okay?"

He pulled her hand to his mouth and kissed the back of it, just like the heroes in those historical romance novels she loved to read.

"I won't forget," he whispered against her hand, his warm breath making her shiver. He gently squeezed, then let go. "Just one more thing before we leave."

She pressed her hands together, covering the warm spot where his mouth had been. But the warm feelings flooding through her began to cool and freeze as she saw what he was doing. And began to understand.

The first call he placed through the computer was to someone the computer screen listed as Melissa. As soon as a voice answered, the computer voice spoke. “It was the best of times, it was the worst of times.”

The call ended.

Lance pressed a few buttons and a second call went out. To Sam.

The computer announced the same phrase. “It was the best of times, it was the worst of times.”

Another call. This one to Mick. The next was to Jack. Then, finally, Brett.

After Lance made the computer disappear and closed the wall over the safe, he straightened and stood directly in front of her.

She didn’t meet his gaze.

His hand gently but firmly pressed her chin up until she was looking at him, his gaze locked with hers. “Ask me,” he said. “Say it.”

She stared at him for a long moment. Finally she said, “I’m surprised you chose Charles Dickens as your safe phrase to warn your old team.”

He stared at her for an equally long moment. “What would you have chosen?”

She clenched her fists at her sides. “Nothing at all. Because I wouldn’t have lied to my current team. I wouldn’t send the UB investigators on a useless mission to try to find the OPI team members when you’ve known all along where they are. You knew Rick was in Maple Falls too, didn’t you? Before you answer, think very carefully. Because I’m mad as hell. Don't lie to me. Did you or did you not know that Rick Cameron was in Maple Falls coming here to see you?"

The skin along his jaw whitened. "Do you honestly think that if I knew my friend was in trouble that I wouldn't have gone to help him? That I'd just let him die?"

She leaned toward him. "Isn't that what you're doing right now? Or at least risking the lives of your current friends when there's no reason to risk them at all? You can simply pick up the phone and call Trent, call the others and tell them there's no need to look for anyone. What kind of game are you playing?"

He swore, then scrubbed his face with his hands. "This isn't a game. You think I'm risking my UB friends' lives by sending them on a wild-goose chase? Just the opposite. The information in those files that I gave Trent is ancient history. It won't lead them to danger. It will keep them away while I take care of this damned mole once and for all."

She stared at him, blinking in surprise. "What the…? Everything you told them was a lie?"

He arched a brow. "Actually, my very first statement was the truth, that everything they know about me is a lie. I just continued the charade. Not because I'm some sadistic jerk but because I care about them. They're married, have girlfriends, families. Grayson has a little girl from his first wife who was murdered. He only recently found her after she'd been missing for years. I don't want to be the reason she loses her father after only just meeting him.

"Today, with everyone confronting me, I was trapped. Trapped by my own team trying to force me to involve them in my own mistakes. Well, that's not going to happen. When I left UB this morning, heck, yesterday morning now, to go see you, I wasn't going to return. Ever. If things don't go the way I hope they do, that will still be my plan."

"Wow. I can't believe this. Did you not hear anything they said? It makes sense for them to help you. To help us. What makes you think that you can fight this mole on your own when you haven't been able to figure out who he is in over a decade?"

His jaw worked again. "Do you honestly think I haven't been searching for the mole ever since I left OPI? He forced me to give up my own family, forced all of us to do that, to keep them safe. I'm close, Keira. I've got all kinds of information, evidence, showing this mole's movements over the years. His electronic trail. And I've eliminated dozens of people through my investigation."

He let out a deep breath. "There are only a handful of people left who could be the mole, people who were in a position of power back when we were at OPI. People who hid behind the scenes and who I've discovered and focused on. I'm ready to end this, once and for all. I just need to find that one crumb, that one more piece of the puzzle that makes the whole picture come into focus. Then I can bring him to justice. I can end this."

She stared at him, stunned. "You think you're close to solving it?"

"I know I am. The death of Levi was a huge clue. Something he did put the mole on his trail. But I didn't take it as a clue or realize the significance until you came here and told me that Rick had been murdered. Their deaths, so close together, can't be a coincidence. All I have to do is find the link between them. That will be the key to narrowing my list of suspects down to one."

"That's a lot of speculation and uncertainty to be betting our lives on being able to take this mole down without help from Unfinished Business. Are you forgetting what happened at my cabin? We were almost killed."

"Don't you think I know that? It's all I can think about, how close you came to being killed."

She stared at him in surprise, then cleared her throat. "Okay. Then it's clear that I should have a say in this too. My fate is tied up in the results of this new search, finding this guy and stopping him. Because of that, I get input into what we do. And I want UB working with us. I don't think we can win this without them."

He stared at her a long moment, then swore beneath his breath. "I'm not going to change your mind on this, am I?"

"No."

"Good to know. If you're scared and don't have confidence that we can handle this on our own, then you shouldn't come with me."

"I shouldn't…wait. No. That's not what I meant."

A thumping noise sounded from somewhere inside the stables. "Lance? I'm here, like you asked. Where are you?"

Keira frowned and looked over her shoulder.

"In here," Lance called out. "Last stall on the left."

There was a sudden yank at her waist, and then something cold snapped around her left wrist. She whirled around, shocked to see Lance tossing her pistol onto the desk. He must have grabbed it from her holster. And there was a silver circle of metal shining around her wrist.

"Handcuffs? What the…?" Lance tugged her forward and snapped the other cuff around a metal ring on the wall that she hadn't noticed earlier. "What are you doing? Take these off."

A tall, imposing-looking man in his mid to late forties peered in through the opening, seemingly unsurprised to find the secret room. But his eyebrows rose when he saw Keira with her arm cuffed to the wall. "Hey, Lance. If you two are in the middle of something kinky, I can come back later."

"Shut up, Duncan."

Duncan laughed.

Keira rattled the cuffs. "This isn't funny. Lance, take these off."

"Duncan, can you give us a minute?"

"I can give you a whole lot of minutes while I load the horses. I'll come back after." He disappeared back into the stables.

Keira yanked on the cuffs again.

Lance swore and grabbed her arm. "Stop. You're going to hurt yourself."

"*You're* hurting me. You did this. You're responsible. Take them off now and I won't press charges."

He sighed heavily and let her go. "I'm sorry about this. I really am. I'll have Duncan take those off as soon as I'm gone. Have him take you to Unfinished Business. You can tell everyone the truth. It won't matter once I leave. They won't know where I'm going."

He turned away.

"Wait," she called out, panic making her voice shake.

"What now?"

"Please. Please let me go with you. I can help. I'll watch your back."

"No." He started to turn away again.

"Lance!"

His answering sigh could have knocked over one of the cypress timbers on the other side of the door. "One more question," he said, "then I'm out of here."

She licked her dry lips. "Why are you doing this? Why are you cutting me out of the investigation? It's not just about UB, keeping them out of it. There has to be more to it. You don't actually believe what you said earlier, about me being smart or courageous or that I could be an asset in your search. You think what, that I'd be a hindrance?"

His gaze locked on hers, and he was suddenly standing right in front of her. "I never lied about my belief in your abilities, Keira." He slowly shook his head as he stared down at her. "You're just as smart and courageous as I said, probably more. And you would definitely be an asset in any investigation."

"Then why? Why don't you want me to go with you?"

He flattened the palms of his hands on the wall on either side of her, his body so close they were almost touching. "I was going to. But when you were so adamant about not wanting to do this without my UB team, it made me rethink why I'd involve you when the whole reason I'm not involving them is to protect them. God knows I don't want anything bad to happen to you either. So why risk it? As impossible as it sounds, you're the best thing that's happened to me in a long time. We barely know each other, but I know this. I *want* to know you, learn everything about you. I want to take you out on a date, two dates, a dozen. But most of all, I want—I need for you to be safe."

Her whole body seemed to catch fire with his words. "Lance, are…are you saying you want to be my boyfriend?"

He choked on his laughter, coughed, then grinned. "Yeah. I guess that's what I'm saying."

"Prove it. Kiss me."

The sound of horses' hooves clopping through the stables had him stepping back. "I have to—"

"Lance. *Kiss* me."

His eyes darkened to a stormy blue. His gaze dipped to her mouth.

She closed the short distance between them, her breasts

crushed against his chest as she angled her lips up toward his. "Lance?"

"I'm going to hell for this."

"Worth it."

He groaned deep in his throat. Then she was in his arms, and his mouth was doing all kinds of incredible things to hers. Good grief, this man could kiss. She wanted to wrap herself around him and hold on and never let go, give him back as good as he was giving her. And at first, she allowed herself to respond, to enjoy. After all, a piece of heaven was being dangled in front of her. And she was too weak not to take it. But as amazing as being in his arms felt, the awkwardness of her left arm being cuffed to the wall was enough to help her keep her wits about her and remember why she'd initiated this embrace in the first place.

She suddenly twisted against him and yanked his pistol out of his holster.

His eyes flew open as she pressed the gun's muzzle against his flat belly.

Ever so slowly, he pulled back and looked down between them at his gun, and her finger on the trigger.

"You've got two choices, Lance."

He slowly raised his head and waited.

"You can unlock these handcuffs and promise that you'll take me with you to find the mole."

His jaw worked, anger darkening his eyes even more. "Or?"

She shoved the gun against him. "Or you can bet your life that you know me well enough, after only a day, to be sure that a trained police officer isn't going to shoot a man who kidnapped her and chained her to a wall."

Their standoff went on for nearly a minute. Finally, Lance pulled the handcuff keys out of his pocket.

Chapter Eight

"You wouldn't really have shot me, would you?"

Keira sat beside Lance in the dark blue SUV he'd had in his garage, once again bumping down mountain roads. But this time, thankfully, they were heading out of Gatlinburg. Soon they'd be on wider, safer roads without the constant drop-offs beside them.

"I guess we'll never know for sure," she said.

He frowned and glanced at her, then focused on the road in front of them. "Regardless, you earned the right to be a part of this hunt for the mole. But once this is done, we're done. Before we ever got a chance to get started."

His words caused an ache in her chest that was hard to hide. But she did her best to pretend they didn't bother her. "You really know how to hold a grudge."

"A grudge? You had your finger on the trigger, not the gun frame. The trigger."

"I had to. Otherwise you'd have made some kind of move, tried to grab the gun away from me."

He glanced at her again. "Fair enough. Still, your finger could have accidentally jerked or squeezed just enough on that trigger to kill me even without meaning to. That's not something I'll forget."

"I guess that first date is no longer on the table then."

"We both know the answer to that."

She smiled, but inside she was raw, hurt, tired and so angry she wanted to hit something. To shatter some glass. Bust a chair into little pieces like they did in those action movies. All she'd wanted when she came here was to get justice for a murdered man. And now her entire world had been yanked out from under her. This…thing, this bond or whatever the two of them felt for each other, shouldn't even matter with everything else that was going on. But, dang it, it did. And every time he looked at her in derision or anger or said something like he'd just said, it was another dagger to her heart.

It would be comical if it wasn't so painful. In spite of all those romance novels she enjoyed, she didn't believe in instant love. But she did believe in instant connections, in feeling powerfully drawn to someone even before knowing them all that well. After all, she'd felt that with Lance. She *still* felt that way in spite of her heart being battered and bruised. And the hopeless romantic in her would probably always wonder *What if?* when it came to Lance Cabrera.

LANCE'S GRIP RELAXED on the steering wheel at the sound of Keira's deep, even breathing. She'd fallen asleep against the passenger door, looking as miserable as he felt.

How had everything gone so wrong?

All he'd wanted was to protect the people in his life who'd had no part of his bad decisions at OPI. They were innocent, both his friends at UB and Keira. It wasn't right to drag any of them into the danger that he'd brought to their door. Instead, he'd likely alienated his UB family, once they found out he'd tricked them. And he'd certainly ended any chance he'd had with Keira.

Was he angry with her? Hell yes. But that anger was

already beginning to fade, and regret was digging its talons into him. Could he have taken his pistol away from her without getting shot? Maybe. Probably. But he hadn't tried because of one element to the situation that she hadn't thought through.

Duncan.

He was one of the few people Lance trusted completely outside of Unfinished Business. He wasn't just a guy Lance hired when he needed someone to look after his animals. He was a close friend. If Keira had shot Lance, Duncan would have shot her. And that wasn't something Lance could risk. So he'd gone along with her threat, letting her believe it was only because he was concerned for himself, when he was more concerned for her. And rather than go back on his word to let her accompany him on the search for the mole, he'd stood by his promise.

Lying to her again and not letting her come with him wasn't something he could stomach. But he still would have, in a heartbeat, if he thought she'd be safer that way. However, having seen firsthand how obsessed she was with finding the mole, he'd finally realized that nothing was going to keep her from pursuing this. It made more sense to keep her with him so he could look after her than to constantly wonder when and where she'd show up. He couldn't bear being the cause of her getting hurt, or worse. So the lesser of two evils seemed to be to keep his word and treat her as his partner in this hunt.

As for this crazy obsession he had for her, well, he'd just have to get over it. There was no way she'd ever forgive him for what he'd done. And he wasn't sure he could forgive her either. She could so easily have killed him. All because he'd cared enough to try to protect her. That whole stupid incident had destroyed their trust in each other. Without trust, a relationship was impossible.

He silently swore. He hadn't been this mixed up in the head since Ileana. She'd twisted him inside and out, leaving him, coming back, over and over until he didn't know what he felt anymore. With her out of his life once and for all, he'd finally been on an even keel again. And now here he was letting another woman tilt his world. Not in a good way either.

Maybe the disaster at the stable was fate's way of waking him up, of keeping him from potentially making another mistake. But he hated that it had taken well over a decade for him to finally meet someone he could immediately see himself with long-term. And then for all of that to come crashing down.

Sleep deprivation. That's what all of this had to be. He wasn't normally this quick to anger, this confused. He'd matured since his days of being so easily manipulated by his ex. Now he approached life with logic, not his hormones. All he needed was a good night's sleep. He'd been up for well over twenty-four hours now. Heck, it was edging closer to thirty.

Lucky for both of them, the next exit had a decent hotel with a vacancy—a two-bedroom suite with two king-size beds. And the cash bribe he gave the night clerk was enough to get her to look past the fact that he didn't have a credit card to secure the room. His false ID and a wad of cash was all she'd needed in order to hand over the room key.

A bleary-eyed, exhausted Keira mumbled good-night without meeting his gaze, then clicked her bedroom door shut with him still standing in front of it.

His shoulders slumped in defeat. He so wished that he

could have a complete redo of the past day and a half. But life didn't come with a rewind button. And as he'd told his team earlier, some things couldn't be fixed.

Chapter Nine

When Keira stepped out of the hotel bedroom, freshly showered, in clean clothes and wearing enough makeup to hide the dark circles under her eyes, she stopped in surprise. The kitchenette had a pot of coffee made with a mug and packets of sweeteners beside it. Next to that was a box of delicious-looking breakfast pastries in varying types from apple to cinnamon to cream cheese and a handful of others. And just in case that wasn't what she fancied, there was a large bowl of sliced fruit and a loaf of bread sitting beside the toaster. But Lance was nowhere to be found.

His bedroom door was open, the bed visible through the doorway neatly made. The folder he'd had in his safe yesterday was open on the coffee table in front of the couch. Papers and pictures were spread out as if he'd been studying them earlier this morning. But the suite itself was sadly empty.

A slight movement to her left had her turning. Through a slit in the curtains she could see a man in a dark leather jacket standing at the balcony railing, a cup of coffee in his hands as he looked out at the Smoky Mountains. Lance.

The guilt that had her tossing and turning last night rode

her hard. It was an uncomfortable feeling, one she wasn't used to.

She fixed herself a cup of coffee. One packet of sugar, none of that fake sweetener for her. And some creamer she'd been unsurprised to find in the refrigerator. After all, he'd thought of everything else she might want or need.

After returning to the bedroom to put on her long jacket against the chilly fall air, she grabbed her mug of coffee and headed outside. When she stepped onto the balcony, Lance smiled. But it was a shadow of his usual ones.

"Morning," he said.

"Morning. I come unarmed."

He lifted the edge of his jacket to show his pistol holstered to the belt of his jeans. "Can't say the same."

She wanted to joke about that, to say something to cut the tension. But nothing clever came to mind, so she didn't try.

They stood silently beside each other for several minutes, sipping their respective cups of coffee and staring out at the beautiful vista in front of them. This time of year, the Smokies were dressed in fading golds and oranges. Not the full-on brilliant colors that would have attracted leaf peepers a month earlier. But still colorful enough to steal her breath.

In spite of all those winding, narrow, terrifying roads without guardrails all over these mountains, she couldn't deny how amazing and awe-inspiring it would be to see this kind of scenery out her windows every day. But she'd prefer to see it from a valley looking up at the mountains rather than actually driving through them.

As she watched, thin white clouds moved over the peaks, dressing them in mist and dipping down into the higher elevations. A few minutes later, the mist rose, revealing the peaks again. But shadows from other clouds passed across the sun, emphasizing the deep variations of color dancing up and down the slopes.

"It really is beautiful here," she murmured, mostly to herself.

He set his coffee mug on the railing. "I've lived in this area for over three years and have never tired of the scenery. It's ever-changing. One minute, you can see for miles. The next, the mist settles in and you can barely see anything. In the summer, it's every shade of green you can imagine. Once the last of these autumn leaves drop, it will be gray and barren-looking to the casual observer. But if you pay close attention, you'll see things you couldn't see before. Bald spots and clearings between groves of trees. Evergreens interspersed between the spindly, naked birch and oak."

When he went silent, she prodded, "And in the spring? What's it like then?"

He smiled, as if at something only he could see. "Everything comes to life. Wildflowers dot the ranges. Trees leaf out, fill out, new branches climbing toward the bright blue sky. Baby rabbits, squirrels and chipmunks can be spotted hiding in the bushes, climbing trees, chattering at you when you encroach on their domain. At sunset the deer come out, mothers watching over their spotted fawns. Bucks scratching their antlers on the trees. Black bears are all around these parts. Mostly they stay hidden, but that time of year they wake up hungry from hibernation and eat everything they can. You'll spot some in the mountains or in town trying to score an easy meal from a careless tourist who tosses out their food without realizing it will attract wildlife."

She was mesmerized by the emotion in his voice, the wonder in his expression.

"You really do love it here, don't you?"

His smile faded as he faced her, resting his hip against the railing. "How could I not?"

"Well, for one thing, there are those narrow death-defying curvy roads up and down the mountains. I don't see how anyone could love those."

His mouth quirked up at one corner. "Believe it or not, you get used to them, barely think about it once it's part of your daily routine."

"I suppose. But it's hard to imagine. If I lived here, I'd rather stay in a low-lying area with some gently rolling hills. The mountains could form a gorgeous backdrop, in the distance."

"Sounds like my ranch."

She blinked. "Exactly like your ranch. It's beautiful."

They were both quiet for a minute, then…

"I'm sorry—" he said.

"I'm sorry—" she said at the same time.

They both laughed.

She stepped closer and put her hand on his, which was resting on top of the railing. "I mean it, Lance. I'm so very sorry for yesterday. I was shocked, angry, when you put those handcuffs on me. Even more angry that you were going to leave to pursue this investigation without me when my fate is involved as much as yours. But that's no excuse for what I did. I never should have put my finger on that trigger. You're right, one shake of my hand and I could have shot you." She swallowed against her tight throat. "I could have killed you. I'm so, so sorry."

He looked down at her hand on his, then slowly turned it so that they were holding hands. "I appreciate that. I'm sorry too, more than you can imagine. We both made mistakes. But it was my poor decision that started it all. Truce?"

She tightened her grip. "Truce."

He studied her, seeming uncertain. But then, as if he couldn't help himself, he gently pulled her toward him. He cradled her against his chest, his arms around her, hugging her close. When a brisk breeze made her shiver, he opened his coat and wrapped it around both of them, forming a warm cocoon.

Like a weary traveler finally coming home, her body relaxed against his. It felt unbelievably right being in his arms. And, man oh man, did he smell good, a mixture of coffee, soap, leather and the clean outdoors. The hard planes of his sculpted body fit against her curves as if he'd been made for her. It seemed silly even thinking that way, as if she were writing one of those romance novels. But it was true. She could have stood there forever, held by him. And dang if she didn't want to. But the world intruded all too soon. His cell phone buzzed in his coat pocket.

He murmured an apology as he extricated himself and stepped back to check his phone. When he saw the number, he grimaced and took the call.

"Hey, Trent."

She watched in surprise as he held the phone slightly away from his ear. Even from a few feet away, she could hear Trent's raised voice. He definitely wasn't happy.

Lance pressed the phone back to his ear. "I know, I know. I shouldn't have—" He winced again, then shook his head at Keira, his mouth quirking in that half grin she was beginning to become so familiar with.

"That's not going to happen." He sighed heavily as he listened to Trent's response. He stepped to the end of the balcony, leaning back against it, speaking on occasion but not really saying much.

When the call ended, he held the phone in his hand rather than slide it into his jacket pocket. "That was fun."

"What happened?" she asked. "He sounded angry."

"Yeah, well, he wasn't happy when Duncan told him I'd contacted my old team already and he and the others didn't need to try to find them."

She drew in a surprised breath. "You had Duncan tell them the truth?"

"Someone I know made me feel guilty." He winked. "At least now everything's in the open. He wants us to come back so we can work on this together since there's no reason to go searching for my old team now."

"Is that what we're doing? Going back?"

"We? No. But if you've changed your mind and don't want to go with me, I can have Duncan pick you up here and take you to UB."

"We haven't spoken about your plan. I'm guessing you're heading to New York City to look into Levi's death." She winced. "Long drive but I guess there's no other option or you wouldn't be able to bring your duffel full of weapons with you. From there, you'll try to find out whether Rick was there and whether it cost him his life too. At some point you'll head to Maple Falls to see the scene of the crime firsthand, the motel where Rick was murdered. Am I right?"

"I guess my answer depends on whether you've changed your mind about wanting to go with me. And yes, we'd be driving. Shouldn't be too rough with two drivers to switch off."

"We're in this together. Nothing's changing my mind. And I'm fine helping with the driving."

He smiled. "All right then. Heading to Maple Falls isn't in the equation. It's likely too dangerous."

"You think the mole's people are still there, watching for one of us to show up?"

"It's what I'd do. Besides, you're a walking, talking treasure trove of information about that investigation. And your copy of the case file has the crime scene photographs. We can review those together. But the first order of business is to look into Levi's death, as you said. It makes sense with everything that's happened that his murder was the catalyst to stir things up again. I want to try to figure out why he was killed and what put a target on his back. But he wasn't killed in New York City. He was killed in a small town in upstate New York called Newtown. When I mentioned New York in the UB meeting, I purposely implied that it was NYC to keep my team away from the actual location where Levi was killed."

She gave him a doubtful look. "If you found Levi's mugging story on the internet, so can your UB friends."

"I'm sure they will. But it will take time. It was a small article in an obscure paper. It's not going to come up high on any internet search engines. By the time they figure out the location, I'll have finished my investigation there and moved on to the next step."

"The next step?"

His jaw tightened. "I'm going to end this."

A feeling of dread snaked up her spine. "What, exactly, does that mean?"

Rather than answer, he checked his watch. "Trent's had all of three minutes to trace my phone. Even jumping through hoops with the phone carrier, I imagine he can bribe or threaten someone into helping him rather quickly. We probably have another five minutes, at best, before he has our location. It should take the team a good forty-five minutes to reach this hotel. But I wouldn't put it past them to call in help from Chief Russo and send a police car over here to cut that response time. We'll have to pack our breakfast to go." He winked, then picked up his phone and hurtled it deep into the woods beyond the balcony.

Keira stared at the trees where his phone had disappeared. "I sure hope that was a burner phone."

"Unfortunately, no. It was my personal phone. From here on out, we use burners so that my well-intentioned UB friends can't trace us. I do have another smartphone under my alias. It's never been used. No one will have any history of it to find us, so it's safe for internet searches or whatever else we may need. There are cheap burner phones in my go bag too. Untraceable, only good for phone calls. I'm happy to share." He held out his hand. "I will of course reimburse you for your loss."

She stared at him. "Please tell me you're kidding."

"Afraid not."

She swore and handed him her phone, cringing as he sent it hurtling into the trees.

Chapter Ten

Keira sat on the foot of the second of two queen-size beds in her and Lance's second-floor room in the only bed-and-breakfast in Newtown, New York. Lance stood a short distance away peering out the window down at Main Street.

"What do you see out there?"

He dropped the frilly curtain back into place. "Questions without answers. We walked the whole length of that street and back in, what, ten minutes? Fifteen? Newtown is even smaller than I thought it would be. There's absolutely nothing here to attract someone like Levi."

"He wasn't a nature lover? Hiker? Antique store aficionado?"

He scoffed. "Not even close. He hated living in Ocala, Florida, during our OPI days. He complained that there were more horses per capita than people." He smiled. "He might have been right. He was only there because the financial company his father worked for had transferred the family there when Levi was still in high school. He craved excitement, neon lights, plays, opera—the finer things in life. He was only biding his time in horse country until he felt he had enough money to quit and move somewhere like, well, New York City."

"Which is a good four hours from here," she said. "If he's a city-slicker type, why settle in Newtown?"

"That's what we need to find out."

"We should make a list of our to-do items," she said. "Divide and conquer. We can meet at the little café on the corner in a couple of hours and share what we've found."

He immediately shook his head no. "As small as this place is, I don't see any reason for us to split up. Without knowing whether the mole has people in town, watching for anyone asking about Levi's death, I'd rather not risk us each being on our own."

She shook her head in frustration. "You don't trust me to take care of myself. Still."

"Of course I do. I just don't see the need for it."

"The quicker we look into things here, the quicker we can move on to something else. Splitting up is the best way to do that."

He cocked his head. "Is it just me?"

"Just you…what?"

"That makes you defensive every time I suggest we do things a certain way."

"I'm not defensive. I'm just… I don't want to be coddled, that's all."

"Is it coddling to want to work together as partners, backing each other up rather than working separately?"

"Splitting up makes more sense," she insisted.

"No. It doesn't. It's far more dangerous, and you know it. So why are you getting your hackles up?"

She stiffened. "My *hackles*?"

"Poor choice of words. Come on, Keira. What is it? What am I doing wrong here?"

She blew out a deep breath, then shoved her hair back from her face. "Nothing."

He waited a moment. When she didn't say anything else, he asked, "Nothing meaning what exactly?"

"It's not you, okay? It's…men in general. The guys I work with in Maple Falls. The ones who ordered me around at my Nashville job. My father who…who…smothered me. Who wouldn't let me out of his sight. The man who…who…" She shook her head, squeezing her eyes shut. "It's not you. I'm sorry. It's just… I don't like being told what to do. Or protected. I don't… I don't—"

He sat beside her and pulled her onto his lap and into his arms. She stiffened, ready to push him away.

"Keira," he whispered against the top of her head. "Please, let me hold you. I'm asking. Not telling. I'm not coddling or protecting or telling you what to do. I'm here for you. You're in control. Please, let me be here for you. You're the one in control. It's okay."

You're the one in control.

And just like that, the floodgates opened. Instead of pushing his arms away, she held on tight, sobbing against his chest.

"It's okay," he whispered, his arms tightening around her. "It's okay. Let it out. You're in control."

His intuitive words had her sobbing harder, holding on to him so tightly it probably hurt. But she couldn't seem to let go or stop crying.

He rocked her back and forth, whispering over and over against the top of her head. "It's okay. It's okay. You're in control."

When she finally stopped crying and straightened, she gasped in embarrassment at his shirt. "I'm so sorry. Your shirt is soaked."

He smiled. "You can soak it any time you need to. I have other shirts."

She should have immediately gotten off his lap. But somehow, she couldn't seem to make herself even want to. Instead, she stared into his eyes, just inches away. "How did you know that's what I needed to hear? I didn't even know I needed it."

Ever so gently, he feathered her hair back from her face. "Every time I make a decision for both of us, you push back. I thought maybe it was just me, that you didn't want to feel as if I was trying to force you into anything. But then, what you said…before you started crying… I realized it's not just me. It's something that happened to you, isn't it?"

She squeezed her eyes shut a moment, then let out a shaky breath. "Yes."

He waited. When she didn't say anything else, he asked, "Do you want to talk about it?"

For the first time in a very long time…no. For the first time *ever*, the idea of sharing what had happened instead of being forced to felt…right. As if she could somehow lighten the burden on her soul by sharing that burden with him. But when she opened her mouth to tell him, the words wouldn't come. She shook her head. "I…can't."

He gently kissed her forehead. "If you ever want to tell me, I'm here."

"Thank you," she whispered. "And… I really am sorry. For everything. You're right that I get prickly when someone tells me what to do. But I've been doing the same thing to you. I've been forcing you to let me come with you. That's not right either. I'm sorry, Lance. Truly."

He cocked his head. "You think you've been forcing me?"

"Well, yes. Like back in the stables, when I…" She squeezed her eyes shut for a moment. "When I made you promise, at gunpoint, to take me with you. That was wrong on so many levels."

"Kind of like me handcuffing you in the first place?"

She laughed. "Well, that was somewhat outrageous. I guess we both messed up."

"To a point."

She frowned. "What do you mean?"

He gently set her on her feet beside the bed and pulled out his pistol.

"Um, Lance? What are you doing?"

"Letting you know that you don't have to apologize." He dropped the magazine out of the pistol onto the bed, then ratcheted out the bullet in the chamber. Then he stood in front of her and handed the gun to her, pointing it at his belly just as she'd done back in the stables.

She swallowed and lowered the pistol. "Why are you doing this?"

"Trust me. It's not loaded, so it's safe. Hold the gun exactly as you did at my ranch."

When she hesitated, he said, "Please."

Hating what she was doing, and feeling worse than ever for having pointed it at him before, she held it in her right hand. Mimicking the way her left hand had been handcuffed to the wall, she raised her left arm.

"Now what?"

"Put your finger on the trigger."

"Lance, I don't..."

"Please."

She sighed heavily and did what he'd asked. "Okay, now—"

He moved with blinding speed. One moment the gun was in her hand. The next it was in his but aimed at the floor.

She blinked in shock, then looked up at him. "Oh my gosh. I never really had a chance, did I? At the stables."

He reloaded the pistol and holstered it at his waist. "I'd

like to think not and that I could have taken it away just as easily. But there's always a possibility I couldn't have. Regardless, I think it's safe to say that you don't need to feel guilty for forcing me into anything I didn't want to do."

She nodded, humbled by his skills and reminded again that her few years in law enforcement didn't come close to his experience. "You need to teach me that trick sometime."

"After we bring the bad guy down, absolutely. Anytime. Maybe I'll show you how to ride a horse too, if you're game."

She smiled. "It's a date."

He grinned. "I knew I'd get you to say yes at some point."

"Overconfident," she chided.

"Highly motivated." He looked her up and down, then let out a slow sexy whistle.

She burst out laughing.

He laughed too, then crossed to the closet and pulled out a fresh shirt. She was about to tease him but whatever she was going to say flew out of her mind when he shrugged out of his wet shirt. His golden tanned skin rippled over his back muscles as he reached into the closet. His jeans hugged his narrow hips and cupped his perfectly proportioned backside. When he turned around, she had to bite back the low moan of desire that caught her by surprise. There wasn't an ounce of flab on his golden muscular abdomen. His chest and biceps would have made an artist weep at the chance to paint him. Heck, they made her want to weep with the urge to reach out and touch.

As he buttoned up and began tucking his shirt into his jeans, it did nothing to cover up the picture of him now firmly branded in her mind. How was she supposed to work with him now after having seen what was hiding underneath his clothes? Her gaze dipped to his jeans and her belly tightened.

He took some small photographs from his OPI folder and slid them into his shirt pocket. She took advantage of his inattention to hurry into the adjoining bathroom to compose herself.

"Let me fix my makeup and I'll be right out," she said as she closed the door.

"Take your time. Want me to wait downstairs?"

She blinked in horror at the dark tracks of mascara on her face from all her crying. "If you don't mind, that would be great."

"The key's on top of the dresser. I'll chat up the innkeeper for any information I can get about Levi and Rick."

"Good idea."

At the sound of the door closing, she let out a pent-up breath. His reminder about his teammates had her wanting to kick herself. She'd been on an emotional roller coaster, thinking about her past. That must have been why she'd gotten in such a dither over Lance's drool-worthy body. She shook her head. Yes, he was gorgeous. But that wasn't important right now. She had to focus on what really mattered.

Staying alive.

Chapter Eleven

Lance stood across the street from the police station thinking through possible scenarios of how he and Keira could get a copy of the case file and coroner's report on Levi's death.

Keira put her hands on her hips. "I can't imagine they'd tell me no after I explain that I'm in law enforcement. I've got my badge. I don't have to mention Rick's case. We can tell part of the truth—that Levi was a friend of yours and we'd like to find out more about what happened to him."

"The chief probably would let us look through the file. But we have to weigh the advantages versus the disadvantages. Although the innkeeper this morning didn't recognize Levi's picture when I showed it to him, he did recognize Rick's. So we've verified our theory that Rick was in town shortly after Levi's death notice was placed in the paper. We've already asked nearly every store owner on Main Street about Levi and Rick. The more we do that, the more we risk attracting the wrong kind of attention."

"You're not worried the mole will find out we're here, are you? We're registered at the B-and-B under your alias. Paying cash everywhere we go. Are you thinking the local police are in league with the mole and would tell him we're here in Newtown? That seems far-fetched."

"It does. But it also seems far-fetched that the mole would

discover and murder two of my teammates a few months apart over a decade after we went on the run. Something has happened to stir things up. Without knowing what that was, we have to do everything we can to not broadcast our location. I'd rather find him before he finds us.

"To answer your question, though," he continued, "I have no reason to suspect the local police are involved in any of this. However, if you show your badge to the police chief, he's likely to want to call your boss to talk it out with him before providing access to the files. We already know the bad guys were in Maple Falls, that they followed you to Gatlinburg. They could still have the Maple Falls Police Station under surveillance. Maybe they've even got a wiretap to see if you check in with your boss. A call from here to your boss could be exactly what the mole needs to find us."

She shook her head. "Either you're ridiculously paranoid about this mole's reach and capabilities, or you're right and I need to get paranoid."

He smiled. "Maybe a little of both. We do have another option to get the files. It would be illegal. And risky."

She held her hands up. "We're not breaking into the police station or hacking into their computer system. I draw the line there."

"You wouldn't have to go with me. I could take care of it late at night when they have a skeleton staff. In and out."

"Are you serious?"

He sighed and scrubbed his jaw. "I'm serious that it's an option. I haven't made any decisions yet."

"You can't honestly believe that risking getting caught and going to jail is better than me going the legal route and simply asking for a copy of the file."

He arched a brow. "I wouldn't get caught."

She rolled her eyes. “Someone needs to help you with this confidence problem of yours.”

He laughed and checked the time on his phone. “I vote we grab an early dinner at the café and think all of this through.”

“On that we can agree. Maybe that’s why you’re coming up with crazy ideas. We skipped lunch and your brain is running on empty.”

He grinned. “Maybe that’s it.”

A few minutes later, they were sitting across from each other in a large booth at the back of the Corner Café. With it being between the traditional lunch and dinner hours, there weren’t that many customers. And Lance had purposely asked to sit in that booth so he could have his back to the wall and keep an eye out for anyone coming close enough to overhear anything he and Keira talked about.

No sooner had their food arrived than the little bell over the entrance announced someone was coming in. Lance looked up, then swore.

Keira glanced at him in question, but before she could turn around, Trent and Asher were sliding into the booth beside them.

“What the hell are you doing here, Trent?” Lance demanded as Trent grabbed a french fry off his plate and set a file folder on the table. “And scoot over, Asher. You’re crowding Keira.”

Asher smiled at Keira and moved over. “Nice to see you again.”

She slid closer to the wall, giving him more room. “Um, nice to see you too.”

“No,” Lance said. “It’s not. What are you two doing here?”

Trent’s shoulder brushed against him. Lance reluctantly

moved over and shoved his plate with a cheeseburger and fries out of the way.

"Aren't you going to ask how we found you?" Trent asked.

"I'm sure it wasn't difficult. All you had to do was trace Levi to this town and then you called the only hotel here, gave them our descriptions, and the innkeeper ratted us out."

Asher laughed. "He totally did."

Lance shook his head. "I thought after I had Duncan give you the information I'd been accumulating about the mole and the people on my short list, you'd focus on that. Why interfere with Keira and me looking into my team member's deaths?"

Trent motioned toward Keira. "Knowing that the mole tracked Keira from Maple Falls to Gatlinburg suggests that he may still be watching for Keira and you. Which means you couldn't formally ask the police chief here in Newtown to give you the information that you need about Levi's death without risking having your names entered online and possibly triggering a notification to the mole." He tapped the folder. "So Asher and I got it for you."

Lance stared at him, afraid to hope. He flipped open the folder. Sure enough, the first few pages were the police reports about the mugging. After that were the hospital ER reports. And underneath that, even more notes on the investigation.

Trent motioned toward the folder. "That last group of pages is the coroner's report."

Lance started to pull that section out, then decided against it. Levi was his friend. He wasn't mentally prepared to view autopsy photos and records of his injuries just yet. He'd wait and review them later at the B-and-B. He closed the folder. "I'm not sure what to say."

"You don't have to say anything." Trent clasped his shoulder. "We told you that you and Keira aren't in this alone. Whatever help you want or need from us, just let us know. We respect your decision to work this angle by yourselves. We'll continue looking into the higher-ups in the agencies you pointed out in your research. When you're ready to regroup and share information, let us know."

Trent slid out of the booth and stood.

Asher did the same but paused to place another folder on top of the first. "We're working in shifts at Unfinished Business so that we've got someone moving your investigation forward at all hours. That's the summary of what we've pulled together already. Of the five men you believe could be the head bad guy, we've eliminated two of them."

Lance looked up in surprise. "You're sure?"

"Positive. At the time various events you pointed out back at OPI transpired, those two wouldn't have had the opportunity, or the power, to pull them off. The others would. We're focusing on those remaining three now."

Asher nodded at Keira, who smiled back. She turned the full wattage of her smile on Lance, who was still reeling from everything that had just happened. When he was finally able to break free from her beautiful smile, he realized his friends were almost to the door of the café. He slid out of the booth and strode after them.

"Trent, Asher." They stopped at the door. Lance held out his hand. "Thank you. I mean it. I've been an ass. And it's taken me too dang long to realize it. I'll keep you both posted on any progress that Keira and I make. Please thank the team for us."

Trent clasped his shoulder again. "We're only a phone call away, buddy." He stepped outside.

Asher shook Lance's hand, but his earlier amusement seemed to evaporate as he held on tight.

"You and I went through hell together when Faith was almost killed a few months ago. You were there for both of us. We're both here for you now. Don't forget that. And whatever you do, don't let your thirst for justice, or revenge, get you or Keira killed."

With that, he stepped out the door.

Lance watched as Trent and Asher crossed the street to Trent's car, more affected by Asher's words than he would have expected.

Don't let your thirst for justice, or revenge, get you or Keira killed.

"Lance? Everything okay?"

He turned at the sound of Keira's voice. *No. Nothing is okay.* He forced a smile and joined her at the table. "We can discuss the investigation later. Let's eat before our dinner gets cold."

"Late lunch, not dinner. Depending on how late we're up working, I may still require additional sustenance."

"I consider myself warned that I may have to raid the B-and-B kitchen at midnight."

"Count on it." She laughed and they sat down to their respective burgers and fries.

At the end of their meal, Lance picked up the folders to leave.

"Wait," she said. "At every place we've been today, we showed Levi and Rick's photographs. Might as well do that here too." She held out her hand. "I'll ask the staff. You can wait here."

He nodded his thanks and handed her the pictures from his shirt pocket.

A few minutes later, she returned and gave him back the photos. "No memories of Rick having been here. But Levi definitely ate here often. He was somewhat of a regular.

One of the waitresses remembers him meeting a woman here maybe once a week."

"A woman. As in a friend?"

"More than friends, according to the waitress who remembers them best. Before you ask, no, she never heard their names. And since they paid in cash, there aren't any credit card receipts to look through. I asked her if she could describe the woman with Levi, and she said she was very pretty, with long dark hair and light brown skin. She was tall too, about the same height as Levi."

His stomach dropped, as if he'd just jumped off a cliff. "She's just shy of six feet tall then. A couple of inches shorter than me."

Keira's brow wrinkled with concern. "Lance? You don't sound right. What's going on now?"

"I need to ask the waitress something. Which one is she?"

"Alice, the same waitress who took our orders. The young blonde woman on the right by the drink machine."

He pulled out the smart burner phone that had internet capabilities and pulled up a picture. When he reached the waitress and tried to show her the picture, she kept smiling and blinking her obviously false eyelashes. It took several attempts to get the information he needed. And several more minutes to extricate himself from her groping hands without providing his phone number that she'd asked for.

Keira wasn't at their table anymore. Instead, she was standing by the door, watching through the glass as she clutched the folders against her chest.

"Thanks for getting the folders." Lance stopped beside her. "Ready?"

"That depends. Did you get what you wanted from that Dolly Parton wannabe?"

He blinked. "Our waitress? Alice?"

"Oh. Was that her name? I forgot." She pushed the door open and stepped outside.

He caught up to her and stopped her with a gentle hand on her shoulder. "Keira? Did I do something to upset you?"

She let out a deep breath, her cheeks flushing a light pink. "No. No, you didn't. I'm being…just forget it. Sorry. I'm not myself." She drew a steadying breath and he began to wonder if she could actually be jealous. Of groping Alice. The very idea was ludicrous. And interesting too if Keira was upset that Alice had been so clingy. Very interesting.

"Was Alice able to provide more information about Levi? Or his apparent girlfriend?"

He scrubbed his jaw, forcing himself to focus on the case. Not his attraction to the beautiful woman working the case with him.

"I showed her a picture from many years ago that my old roommate in college posted on our fraternity's website. It was a frat party. The picture was of me and some of my buddies with some women we were dating at the time. In spite of the years that have passed, Alice recognized one of the women in the photo as being the one she'd seen at the café. It was Ileana Sanchez."

Her eyes widened. "Your ex?"

He nodded, his throat tight. He still couldn't believe she'd turned up in the middle of this investigation.

"Yikes. How incredibly awkward for her to have dated your friend all these years later."

He slowly shook his head. "Ileana and Levi never would have dated. Levi Alexander was gay."

Chapter Twelve

Keira sat on her bed, thumbing through one of the stacks of papers that Trent and Asher had given them. On the other bed, Lance was doing the same.

She motioned toward the notes she'd been taking on a legal pad. "I've been thinking about Ileana and Levi acting lovey-dovey in the café. With him being gay, I can't figure out any reason for them to do that."

"The only one who can explain is Ileana."

"I'm guessing you have no clue where she lives these days, other than close to this place, in theory, if she was coming here on weekly visits."

"She wasn't part of OPI in any capacity. I had no reason to keep up with her after we all went underground. That might be something Trent and Asher can look into for us."

"You're going to take them up on their offer to help?"

He looked up from the page he was reading. "I've finally given in. I'm waving the white flag. I surrender to my team's good intentions in spite of my own intentions to keep them out of this."

She gave him a suspicious look. "And none of this sudden willingness for them to help has anything to do with you wanting to avoid your ex?"

He grinned. "It's a definite side benefit."

She laughed. "Want me to give Trent the good news?"

"If you don't mind. Take a burner phone. We'll only use it for contacting Trent. Make sure he knows that and not to pass the number around and only to call if or when absolutely necessary. We'll toss that phone in a couple of days."

As she got the burner from his duffel bag, she asked, "You don't really think the people looking for us would set up a massive trace for all of the UB investigators' phones do you?"

"No. I don't. But I'm still not willing to risk it." He told her Trent's number and she punched it in.

After she made the call, she went back to the reports on top of her comforter. The room went silent while they both read through the information they'd divvied up between the two of them. It was probably an hour later when she stiffly slid off the tall bed and stretched her aching back.

"I'm too young to feel this sore."

"We've been at this for hours. Take a break. Go downstairs and get that snack you talked about earlier."

"I remember you agreeing to pilfer from the kitchen when I'm ready for a snack. But you can relax. I'm not hungry yet. And I'm not ready for a break, not a long one at least. I just need to stretch and walk it off until I'm ready to bend over those papers again." She motioned toward his bed. "Find anything interesting yet? Any leads for us to follow?"

"Not much. Mainly I'm looking through the data that made UB conclude they could mark two people off my suspect list."

She stretched up toward the ceiling, then leaned over and touched her toes, her long hair falling over her face and sweeping the floor. When she straightened, and stretched toward the ceiling again, she asked, "Do you not agree with their conclusions?"

When he didn't respond, she lowered her arms and looked at him.

He was staring at her, his eyes darker than usual, tension in every line of his body.

"Lance? Is something wrong?"

He looked away, his jaw working. A moment later, he let out a long, deep breath. "Maybe we shouldn't have agreed to sleep in the same room."

She waited, but when he didn't say anything else, she asked, "Why not? There was only one room available. If we didn't stay here, we'd have had to drive an hour out of town to the next hotel."

She stretched again, trying to relieve the pressure in her shoulders.

"Keira?"

"Um?" She touched her toes again, reveling in how much better her back was starting to feel.

"That hotel might be safer."

She turned to face him, hands on her hips. "Safer? You think our location has been compromised?"

"It's not our enemies that are at issue. It's me. If you stretch one more time, pulling that T-shirt tight across those luscious breasts of yours or tightening your pants across that curvy little ass, I may have to handcuff myself so I'll keep my hands off you."

She blinked, then swallowed, understanding now why he was so tense, his eyes so dark. His hunger for her was palpable, his hands fisting in the comforter as his gaze slowly traveled over her face, her breasts, down, down, down. His Adam's apple bobbed in his throat. When a small bead of sweat rolled down the side of his face, she licked her suddenly dry lips.

Lance groaned and started gathering up the papers on

his bed. "You can stay here tonight. No need for both of us to leave. I'll grab a change of clothes and get a hotel room down the highway. In the morning I'll meet you downstairs and—"

She climbed up onto the bed and tugged the papers out of his hands. His gaze flew to hers.

"Keira, what are you—"

She tossed the stack of papers onto the floor and straddled his lap.

His eyes widened. "I wasn't kidding, Keira." His deep voice was raspy, sending shivers of desire straight to her belly. "You're playing with fire." He grabbed her by the waist as if to lift her off him.

She grabbed his wrists. "I'm a big girl, Lance. I know what I want. The question is, what do you want?"

His nostrils flared. "What I *don't* want is for you to have any regrets. We're both under stress, tired. We've been through a lot together in a really short time." His hands shook as he gently set her to his side and scooted back.

Her face flamed with embarrassment. "Okay, guess I totally misread the situation. No harm. No foul." She gathered herself to slide off the bed.

He stopped her and pulled her back across his lap, sitting sideways instead of straddling him. Even so, the evidence of his desire for her pressed thick and hard against her bottom. He stared down at her, and slowly, so very slowly, ran his thumb across her lower lip. She shuddered and closed her eyes. He rested his forehead against hers, his warm breath fanning across her face, making her shiver with longing.

"Keira, my desire for you isn't something I can hide."

"I'll say," she teased, slightly shifting on his lap.

He sucked in a sharp breath, then laughed. "You're killing me here."

"You're killing me. Mixed signals much?"

He groaned, then slid his hands around her and twisted to the side, setting her on the bed between his outstretched legs instead of on his lap. Then he gently pulled her back against his chest and loosely looped his arms around her waist.

"When this is over," he whispered next to her ear, "when I know you're safe, you're going back to your life in Maple Falls."

She stiffened and started to push away.

"Let me finish." His arms tightened around her. "Please."

She huffed out a breath, then leaned back against him. "What? Just say it."

"Don't be angry." He feathered his hands across her arms, massaging her taut muscles. "You're a breath of fresh air, Keira. You're smart, courageous, gorgeous, funny and honest. But this, us, it happened so fast, under extraordinary circumstances. Our emotions are running high. At any other time, I'd gladly accept the precious gift you just offered me. I'd be honored. But you're special. This…thing between us is special. It should be treasured, not rushed. We need to be sure it's as real as it feels right now. Making love is a line that, once crossed, changes everything. If we act without taking our time to get to know each other, we may later find that what feels real right now causes regrets later. Do you understand? Does that make sense?"

She pushed out of his arms and turned on her knees to face him. "You're saying you don't want me to wish we hadn't made love weeks down the road."

"Yes."

"There is no planet on which that could possibly happen."

He laughed. "Well, I appreciate that. And I wish I could be as sure as you that you'll still feel that way weeks from now. But I'd rather risk you being upset with me than to do anything that can't be undone later. I want us both thinking clearly and to be sure before we take a step like this."

She shook her head. "Wow. I didn't think guys like you existed in the real world."

He frowned. "What do you mean?"

"Just that… I didn't know there were…any gentlemen left out there. Men who value a woman for her mind, her personality, more than they want to jump her bones."

He choked on a laugh. "I'm not the saint you're painting me to be. The line I'm drawing in the sand is shaky at best. And the only reason I'm drawing it, to be clear, is because I care about you. I don't want you for just one night. I want it all."

She stared at him, afraid to ask what "want it all" meant. To her, it meant white picket fences and churches and babies. It meant forever. The thought of forever with him, with anyone, was the bucket of ice water she'd needed. It cleared her mind like nothing else would have. Because it scared her. He was right. They needed to take a step back, a huge step back. And explore a relationship at normal speed, not warp speed.

As impossible as it seemed, he might be right that in a week, two, more, when things were back to normal—whatever normal was—they might not feel the way they did right now. And, holy moly, neither of them had any protection. What had she been thinking? The repercussions of that could link them forever, even if they decided forever wasn't in their cards.

She slid off the bed and straightened her shirt. "Well. I'm glad one of us had the strength to stop things before they got out of hand."

He gave her a doubtful look. "Are we okay? Can we still

work together as a team and this not cause problems between us?"

"Absolutely. Of course. We're both professionals." She cleared her throat. "I've decided to get a snack after all. I'm going to raid the kitchen. Want anything?"

He arched a brow. "I thought it was my job to ransack the kitchen."

"Yes, well. I'm not sure what I'll want until I take a look. If I see something really yummy down there, I'll bring you some. Deal?"

"Deal."

She slid her feet into her slippers and practically ran out the door.

LANCE STARED AT the closed door for a long moment. His heart was racing so fast he was surprised he wasn't having a heart attack. And his erection was so hard it was painful. Keira had no clue how difficult it had been for him to turn down her invitation. And while the reasons he'd given her for waiting to take that step were true, he hadn't told her everything.

Like that he didn't want to risk jumping into a relationship this quickly because he'd been burned so badly by Ileana.

He knew Keira wouldn't appreciate being compared to his ex. And he wouldn't blame her. But he'd fallen fast and hard before. And that had ended in disaster. He'd waited too many years for someone as special as Keira to come along to rush into things and possibly make another mistake. He was a different person now, a man instead of a boy. Mature instead of ruled by his hormones.

Or at least, he'd thought that, until he'd very nearly pounced on Keira when she'd straddled his lap.

Realizing he was so close to losing his control had scared

him. It had him thinking about Ileana and the mistakes he'd made. Keira deserved better. She deserved a man who respected and loved her, not a man ruled by physical desire who didn't know his own mind. The two of them needed time. And they didn't have that luxury right now. They had a killer to catch and stop before he hurt or killed someone else, most especially Keira.

Ever so slowly, he slid off the bed and stood. He winced and adjusted himself, then headed into the bathroom for a long cold shower.

MORE THAN AN hour passed before Keira mustered the courage to return to the room that she and Lance were sharing. She hesitated in the hallway, her hand on the doorknob. She hadn't ended up getting anything to eat. Instead, she'd sat in the front room that the innkeeper called a library even though there weren't any books in it. She hadn't needed anything to read anyway. Her jumbled thoughts were enough to keep her occupied.

What had happened, and almost happened, between her and Lance had her confused and restless. But mostly, it had her frustrated that she'd allowed her wants and desires for him to get tangled up in what they were trying to do—find and stop a killer. All the times that the lieutenant back home had chided her for not staying focused or for being impulsive, she'd chalked up to him not taking her seriously because she was a woman. But just a few days into investigating this so-called mole, she'd let personal things cloud and distract her from the case.

Maybe the LT was right, and she wasn't ready to be a detective just yet. Surprisingly, that thought didn't make her angry. Instead, it had her thinking hard about those dues she'd wanted to avoid paying as she zipped up the ladder to get a coveted detective spot. Maybe she really did need more experience first. She needed to hone her skills and truly be ready before taking that next step.

As soon as she'd come to that conclusion, her mind cleared. A sense of relief swept through her, and much of the tension and pressure she'd been under for so long lifted. She wasn't sure what that meant for her future in law enforcement. Did she want to keep going along as she had been? Or was there something else out there she was more suited for?

Whatever the eventual answers to those questions might be, for now she was eager to get back on the current case and help Lance in any way that she could. Then, well, she'd see where things went, both professionally and personally. She just hoped she could handle the embarrassment of facing him again after practically jumping his bones earlier.

Straightening her shoulders, she drew a bracing breath and opened the door to their room. When she saw Lance standing by the bed looking at some pictures on top of the comforter, she hesitated again. He hadn't even looked up when she'd opened the door. He was dressed in some soft-looking plaid pajama pants and a dark-colored T-shirt. His short dark hair was damp and curling at the ends, indicating that he'd recently had a shower. But it was the angry look on his face that had her concerned.

She closed the door. The loud click had him looking up. He gave her a brief nod, then looked down again as if still lost in thought.

When she reached the bed and saw what he was looking at, she winced. Although she'd been to a few autopsies, they'd always been a struggle for her to endure. These photos of Levi Alexander were no different. No wonder Lance was upset. Seeing his teammate and friend laid out on a metal table brought the loss home on a completely different level. It made it painfully real.

Thankfully, the black-and-white outline of a human body on the opposite page that indicated the wounds didn't show many. He'd been stabbed twice. In the abdomen. The other cuts and bruises were relatively minor, no other true stab wounds. And the cause of death was listed as exsanguination. He'd bled out.

She motioned toward the report. "Hopefully the speed and shock of the attack meant he didn't feel much pain."

He was frowning, staring down at the report. "It says he had stage four prostate cancer, which had spread to his liver and brain."

"That's awful," she said. "I'm so sorry about your friend. This all has to be such a shock. I can't imagine your pain, seeing Levi this way. He's a pale shadow of the vibrant man in that other picture you have of him. Maybe the cancer helps explain why he looks so different."

He gave her a strange look, then selected the photograph she was talking about and set it beside the autopsy photo. "You mean this one?"

"Well, yes. That's the picture we used all day when asking if anyone had met him."

He took another picture from the stack and set it beside the first. "What do you see when you look at this photo?"

"Happier, healthier times, I guess. In this one, Levi is smiling. His face is fuller and his skin color looks much better."

His jaw worked. "That second photo isn't Levi. It's another teammate of ours, Sam McIntosh. And this—" he pointed to the autopsy photo "—isn't Levi. It's Sam." He looked up from the pictures, his eyes dark with anger. "Now

I know why Levi was flirting with Ileana. It wasn't Levi at the café. It was Sam."

She drew a sharp breath and looked at the pictures again. Now, knowing they were two different men, she could see the small differences. But someone who didn't know either of them would likely do what she and others had done, including the waitress. They'd confused the two and thought they were one and the same.

"For Sam's body to have had Levi's ID on it, Levi had to have been involved and switched their identification," Lance continued. "I believe that Levi took advantage of how much he and Sam looked alike to fake his own death. Then, when Rick read about Levi's death, he must have come here and spoken to the police. When they showed him a picture from the autopsy report, Rick would have known it was Sam. Levi was either watching for any OPI teammates to show up, or he was hanging around town for some other reason. Either way, he knew that Rick knew the truth. So he kept tabs on him, made plans, then likely lured him to that motel in Maple Falls and tortured him, looking for information on the rest of the team. Then he killed him." His jaw worked again. "My old teammate and friend Levi Alexander is the mole."

Chapter Thirteen

Since Trent and Asher had told Lance that the team was working the case 24-7, and it was already late, Lance decided to call the main line to Unfinished Business rather than wake anyone. When the line finally clicked, a woman's voice came on.

"Unfinished Business, Ivy Shaw speaking."

"Hey, Ivy. How'd you get stuck with the night shift?"

"Lance! It's great to hear from you. How are things going? Is there an emergency? I can send someone to you and—"

"No, no. Sorry. Didn't mean to worry you. No emergency, thankfully. Trent told me you all were taking turns keeping the investigation going. Is anyone else there with you?"

"Callum will be back in a few minutes. He headed down the mountain to grab us some food."

"Let me guess. Pepperoni pizza and beer."

She laughed. "You know Callum well. For me, he's grabbing a salad. And breadsticks of course, with marinara sauce for dipping. A woman can't live on salad alone."

"You're currently trying to track down the OPI mole, right?" he asked.

"Yep. Making good progress too. We're down to two of the men on your list—Eli Pratt and Chris Landrew. Both are higher-ups in Homeland Security and held positions of power even back when you worked at OPI. It's looking promising that one of them at least had the potential to be involved, with the authority and opportunity to order or do the things you pointed out in your research."

"Homeland Security." Lance looked at Keira standing by his bed, watching him intently as he spoke to Ivy. "HS fits. They'd have the power, as you said. But more than that, back in the agency's early days, they'd have the reach and vaguely defined guidelines that were the rule more than the exception. I can see them having interests in many of the cases we worked that I later found out went south—for all the wrong reasons. Have you gotten any idea of the motive behind the breach? Money, revenge or power all work in this situation, I'd imagine."

"My vote is on money," she said. "It would be pathetically easy, as you said, during the inception of HS, to hide expenditures, mislabel and channel money to other items or people. But that's speculation at this point. As to deciding whether Pratt or Landrew is our mole, it's a toss-up right now. Maybe they worked together. We'll figure it out. Shouldn't take much longer. The information you amassed over the years was incredibly detailed. You'd have eventually figured it all out on your own. But I'm glad you trusted us to help you wrap it up more quickly. Is that why you called? For a status update?"

"Actually, I called to update you and the others. Keira and I have been digging into the deaths of my teammates, Levi Alexander and Rick Cameron. We've found out that there was mistaken identity that seems to have been intentional. Levi Alexander isn't the one in New York who was killed. It was another teammate, Sam McIntosh. He and Levi look a lot alike. We used to tease them that they could be brothers. I believe that Levi capitalized on that resemblance to kill Sam and take over his identity. Although, as to why he'd do that, I really don't know yet."

"Oh no. I'm so sorry, Lance. That's a heavy thing to deal with, grieving for one friend only to find out he's double-crossed your team and you have yet another teammate dead. Wow."

"It's been a surprise, for sure. Although it's nothing I ever considered before, having both a mole inside and outside of OPI helps fit a lot of the pieces together that I had trouble with while investigating everything that happened. Our missions came from multiple alphabet agencies and were vetted through our boss, Ian Murphy. What never made sense was that the murders of people we investigated were happening regardless of whether the mission was for the CIA, the FBI, Homeland Security or other agencies. I was trying to find someone with enough power that they could tap into the other agencies, maybe in conference calls with the higher-ups. If Levi was a mole inside OPI, he'd have the information on all the cases regardless of which agency it was for. He could then give that info to the agency mole, such as Homeland Security."

He shook his head, disgusted with himself. "I should have seen that years ago. But I trusted my team. I was blind to any of them being involved."

"Don't beat yourself up over it," Ivy said. "It's hard to be objective about friends, especially when they're your team that you rely on to watch your back and help you in dangerous situations. That objectivity problem is why we've been doing a deep dive into the backgrounds on each of your teammates. We'll switch gears now that we know Sam is gone and Levi is still around. With him stealing Sam's identity, he's definitely moving to the top of our priority list. I'll pass along anything we find out."

"Thanks, Ivy. Thank everyone for me. Keira was right to push me from the beginning to trust my UB family to help with this. Just be alert. Stay safe, all right?"

"You bet. Callum's pulling up in the parking lot out front. Want to talk to him about this?"

"I'll leave you to relay it," he said.

"No problem. Are you and Keira staying where you are or heading somewhere else to continue hiding out until we know it's safe for you to return to Gatlinburg?"

He held Keira's gaze as he answered Ivy. "I'll discuss it with Keira and we'll decide together. We'll keep you posted."

Keira smiled, no doubt appreciating that he was consulting with her now, rather than telling her what they were doing as he'd done at first. She sat on the foot of the bed, waiting for him to update her about the call.

"Lance," Ivy said, "you and Keira be really careful. I don't want to have to help train a newbie around here."

"Well, thanks for the concern."

Ivy laughed. "You know we love you. Later."

Lance ended the call and tossed the burner onto the bed. After he updated Keira on what Ivy had told him, she shook her head.

"It's beyond disappointing to think that someone high up in Homeland Security would use their power to have people killed to further their own greed or other objectives," she said. "My fear is that someone like that could no doubt spin a story to cover their tracks, even now. The guys who came after us were probably hired mercenaries without any traceable links to him. If he finds out that you've discovered Levi is his contact, he'll do everything he can to take us out.

We're in a perilous situation, more now than before. I don't think we should stay here in Newtown any longer. We've been asking lots of questions. And Trent and Asher, even though the police and autopsy information they provided is helpful, it could also have put us on someone's radar."

He smiled. "On that we agree."

She arched a brow. "Which part?"

"All of it."

"Oh. Good. So, we're leaving?"

"As soon as possible." He pulled each of their suitcases out of the closet and set them on their respective beds.

Keira grabbed her clothes from the top dresser drawer. "Sounds like UB is well on its way with the investigation into Homeland Security. Are they trying to figure out where Levi might be too?"

He set his duffel bag of money, IDs and weaponry into his suitcase. Then he tucked his socks and underwear beside it. "Ivy said he's now at the top of their priority list."

When he turned around, she was watching him, concern evident in her expression. "You don't sound very confident. You don't think they'll find him?"

He shrugged. "I know they can and they will. Eventually. I just think I might have a better chance of finding him than them, now that I know specifically who to look for. UB can chase after HS. Our boss and our company have the type of connections to make the inquiries that I wasn't able to make when I worked this on my own. What I want to focus on is Levi. Something is off there. If he's the OPI mole, why would he trade identity with Sam and make it look as if he's the one who died? The only answer that makes sense to me is that he's on the run, hiding."

She checked the drawers, apparently making sure that

she hadn't missed anything, her back to him. "You think he's fallen out with the HS mole?"

"That would explain why he's on the run." Lance took the few shirts and jeans he'd brought and quickly folded them. He and Keira had assumed they'd be here several days or he wouldn't have unpacked at all. "The mole probably knows everything about Levi, including where he lives. But Sam's identity ends here, in Newtown. As long as Levi doesn't go back to his own home or places he normally frequents, he has a chance at getting away."

"Right," she said. "As Sam, he's fresh, brand-new. It's a dead end for the mole to look for him as Sam anywhere other than in Newtown." She shut the dresser drawers and turned to face him. "But if HS doesn't know where to look for him, how will we know where to look for him? And something else is bugging me about all of this too. Why would your ex, Ileana, show up around here with Sam? Do you think she could be involved with what happened at OPI?"

"All good questions, Detective Sloane. Questions for which we need to get the answers."

She smiled at his use of the detective title. "Guess we'd better get busy, then, and find those answers."

When they were in his SUV, Keira fastened her seat belt and took a cautious look around, as if watching for a slew of mercenaries to come running at them. Her right hand was poised near where her gun was holstered beneath her jacket.

He hated that she had to be worried about her safety. She still felt guilty about coming to Gatlinburg and leading his enemy there. But none of this was her fault. It was his, for making the decision to run and hide all those years ago. If he could have a redo, he'd have dedicated himself to finding the mole, or moles, in the beginning. Then Sam and

Rick wouldn't have been murdered. And Keira wouldn't be caught up in all of this, with her life in danger. Meanwhile, an incredibly selfish part of him was thankful that things had gone the way they had. Otherwise, he might never have met her.

"Since we don't know yet where to search for Levi," she said, "I'm thinking we should head to Tennessee, maybe the western region so we're close enough to UB for assistance if we need it but far enough away from Gatlinburg and Maple Falls that our enemies won't stumble across us."

He started the SUV. "Ever been to Kentucky?"

She blinked. "Kentucky? No. What's in Kentucky?"

"In the southwestern corner, there's a tiny one-light farm town called Wingo, population a little over five hundred."

"That's a really small town. I'm guessing they don't even have a motel. Why would we hide out there?" Her eyes widened. "Wait, I'll bet Levi grew up there. You think he might have returned to his roots? Wouldn't that be dangerous if the HS mole knows all about him?"

"It would be. Agreed. But Levi's roots are in the bright lights of LA. He wouldn't dream of living in a rural area like Wingo. He'd be worried he'd get horse or cow manure on his wing tips."

"Oh." She sounded disappointed.

"Sam, now, he's a different story," Lance continued. "He was born and raised in Wingo on a large farm. His parents grew corn, tobacco, soybeans. But it was their small stable of thoroughbreds that they raised for the sheer love of horses that he was so proud of. He took me there on vacation many times to go riding and show me the hundred-acre property that he loved."

"Wait, so you're thinking Levi—pretending he's Sam now—would go to that farm?"

"If he's desperate, it could be a first stop until he gathers his resources and figures out his next move."

"No, it would be foolish," she insisted. "Anyone could look up Sam's birth records and trace him to Wingo. The HS mole would think of that and check it out."

"I disagree. It goes against all logic and common sense to go to Wingo, which is why the HS mole wouldn't bother. He wouldn't think Levi was that foolish. Instead, he'll focus on trying to find Levi through other means. The more I think about it, the more I think Levi would hide out there."

"I'm not sure I agree," she said. "But if we do decide to go there, at least for a quick look, what about Sam's parents? Do they still live on the farm?"

"They passed away years ago. But Sam kept the property. I checked on it a while back as part of looking into finding the mole and doing what I could to ensure the team was still safe. Sam didn't live there, of course. He'd gone underground, new identity and all that like the rest of us. But he kept the land under a web of shell corporation names. He was too sentimental to give it up. It's rental property now, a farm that a management company leases out. With no one knowing Sam is actually dead, that likely hasn't changed. If Levi did decide to go there, he would have told the management company to clear out any renters so he could stay there. With enough cash, I imagine it would have been easy to make that happen." He glanced at her, his hands on the steering wheel. "It's all conjecture. But since we need to get out of Newtown—"

"Why not head to Wingo?" She smiled. "Let's do it. Let's go find Levi."

Chapter Fourteen

The drive from Newtown to Wingo took almost twelve hours. Keira was grateful that Lance had agreed with her that driving straight through without any sleep wasn't safe. They'd stopped at a hotel just before dawn, separate rooms this time. Keira fell asleep the moment her head hit her pillow. Lance had told her he'd pretty much done the same, except for a call first to Trent to update him on their plans.

With the sun beginning to sink on the horizon, they'd finally arrived at their destination—Wingo, Kentucky. When Lance told her that Wingo was small, she'd pictured a quaint Southern town with a square anchored by a historical-looking city hall sporting a clock tower on top. Surrounding the square would be little mom-and-pop restaurants, old-fashioned dime stores and antique shops. Instead, the "town" part of Wingo consisted of one street that was probably no more than a city block long.

At the top of the hill at the beginning of the street was a funeral home. The bottom of the hill boasted a handful of abandoned boarded-up stores, rusty railroad tracks and what appeared to be a clothing factory that might have been in use during the last world war. At the top of the other side of the hill was a church.

That was it.

Wingo, the town, had apparently died long ago. Wingo, the surrounding community, wasn't much to look at either. Or, at least, at first glance it wasn't. As Lance drove slowly down potholed gravel streets out to the paved rural two-lane highway, Keira was astonished at how friendly and outgoing the people were that they passed. And how *not* stressed everyone seemed to be.

No doubt, they all struggled like anyone else to go to work each day or work their farms, pay their bills, buy groceries. But they came home every night to a place where neighbors sat on front porches and called out to each other. Children tossed footballs beneath hundred-year-old oak trees in enormous unfenced backyards. Everyone they passed waved and smiled at them, as if they were lifelong friends. And the farms, they were nothing like she'd pictured in her mind either.

These weren't corporate-run monstrosities with miles of corn waving in the fading twilight. These were family farms, with thriving gardens up by the homes to provide fresh vegetables and spices. Chickens ran free across the yards, no doubt providing delicious eggs to their owners. And fences were used to keep the chickens and other animals safe from predators, not to keep the neighbors away.

She drew a deep breath of cool, fresh air through the open window, watching the quaint little homes as they drove past. And green plants that Lance had told her were soybeans, dotting the hills in neat rows.

"It's so beautiful here," she said. "Peaceful. No one honking horns or jostling past each other in a rush to go someplace else. I could get used to this."

He chuckled. "You say that now. But you may change your mind when you realize the only shopping around here is that mom-and-pop grocery store we stopped at a few miles down the road. Real shopping is a good forty-five minutes away. If you have a medical emergency, God help you. The closest hospital is even farther away. And I'm sure you noticed the lack of movie theaters and fancy corner coffee shops around here. They don't even have a bowling alley."

"Bowling? You don't have the potbelly to convince me you like to bowl."

"Ouch. I have a lot of friends who would resent that remark. No potbelly required. It's fun, especially if there's a pool hall attached."

"Ah, there we have it. The real reason you'd go to a bowling alley—so you can play some pool and down some beers."

He grinned, not denying her assumption.

"Enough with trying to ruin my fairy-tale impression of this charming town," she told him. "Okay, maybe you're right, and I couldn't live here full-time. But to unplug, disconnect and relax for a few weeks? Absolutely. It's really not much different than you living on your ranch, right? It's pretty far out of town. Isolated."

"The nearest Wally World is only fifteen minutes from my place."

"Ah. Walmart. The epitome of civilization. Twenty self-checkout lines and not a cashier in sight."

"Exactly."

She shook her head, smiling. "How much farther to the short-term rental you got us?"

"Another mile, maybe less. But Sam's place is down that next turn on the left. We could do a quick drive-by to see if anyone's home. It'll be dark soon. This is our only chance to get a look before morning light."

She straightened in her seat. "Let's do it."

"Windows up. The dark tint should help disguise who we are if Levi's there and sees us in the SUV."

They closed their windows. When Lance turned down the driveway to Sam's farm, instead of the gravel she'd expected it was paved and wider than the rural highway they'd just left. Maybe that was to make it easier on the horses when they had to be moved in or out of the property. She knew next to nothing about horses but didn't imagine a bumpy road would be good for them while keeping their balance in horse trailers.

With the sun setting, Lance turned off the headlights to avoid anyone seeing them from the house as it came into view. He stopped, and they both took in the lay of the land. Like everything else out here in the true country, Keira thought it was absolutely beautiful. The road continued for a good quarter mile across rich green fields to the one-story white farmhouse with a black shingle roof.

A porch with white railings and four brown rocking chairs ran the entire front of the home. White three-rail fences, like those at Lance's place, lined the long driveway and split the fields into smaller sections.

"Those are the stables over there to the back left side of the house," Lance said. "I remember some large wooden outbuildings directly behind the house for storing tractors and other equipment, including the horse trailer. I imagine they're all still there."

"Why would they need tractors? The fields are all grass, not soybeans, or whatever else they grow around here."

"A riding mower would take weeks to cut these fields. You can do it on a tractor in a few hours."

Her face warmed. "Mowing the grass. Right. City slicker here. Guilty."

He squeezed her hand. "You're coming around though. Before long, you'll want your own chickens and a little garden to raise tomatoes."

She wrinkled her nose. "No chickens. And I prefer spinach to tomatoes, thank you."

He shook his head. "We'll have to work on that. No self-respecting horse rancher prefers spinach over tomatoes."

"Maybe you can train me in the ways of ranchers."

His mouth curved in a slow, sexy grin. "I can teach you a lot of things."

"Promises, promises." She winked, her face warming at her audacity to do so.

He laughed, and she looked out the windshield toward the house, her face flushing hotter. She'd never been one to flirt or tease like she did with him. Something about Lance brought her out of her shell and made everything fun. Here they were, essentially on the run for their lives, and he could make her forget the danger and actually laugh. That was a rare gift. But also dangerous. They both needed to focus right now. Playing could happen later. If she was lucky.

Her fingers dug into her palms. She *really* hoped playing happened at some point between them. She craved Lance like a drunk craved his next drink. And she wanted to find out what it was like to move past that one amazing kiss they'd shared. She had a feeling that being with him would be spectacular.

"I don't see any lights on in the house," he said. "No sign of a car or truck either, although he might have parked around back."

They both watched the place for several more minutes, but even though it was getting almost too dark to see, no lights came on.

"We'll conduct some surveillance tomorrow," he said. "Let's get out of here before I can't see the road without headlights."

He backed the truck up until they reached a wide enough spot beside the driveway to allow him to turn around. Then he flipped the headlights on and sped to the main road.

A few minutes later, he pulled into another driveway, this one short and filled with gravel. It ended in front of a small white house with a front porch only large enough to accommodate two small cane-backed chairs, one on each side of the door. It wasn't all that different from the other little cottages they'd passed. But it was just similar enough to another cottage in her memories that it sent a chill up her spine.

A few minutes later, they were inside, their suitcases sitting in their respective bedrooms. They'd have to share the only bathroom, but it was a Jack and Jill. They each had their own sink and toilet. The only shared amenity was the shower.

Just like the other cottage.

She waited inside the eat-in kitchen as Lance carried in the few bags of groceries that they'd grabbed at the mom-and-pop grocery mart just outside of town. Normally, Keira would have helped. But the queasiness and panic that had been building ever since they'd pulled up outside finally won. She pressed a hand over her mouth and ran for the bathroom.

Her misery as she threw up her lunch was compounded by embarrassment when Lance was suddenly kneeling beside her, gently pulling back her hair. She would have pushed him away, but her stomach wouldn't stop heaving.

A cool damp cloth pressed against her forehead, her cheeks, her neck. It felt so good that her embarrassment was forgotten. He held the cloth against her forehead, whispering sympathetic words. When her stomach finally settled, he started to wipe her mouth. Her face flaming hot again, she grabbed the cloth from him and took care of it herself.

He stood and helped her up. Without looking at him, she flushed the toilet and moved to the sink to wash her hands. When he again made no move to leave, she finally drew a bracing breath and glanced at him in the mirror. "I need some privacy now. Please."

"Of course. Call out if you need me."

When he closed the door behind him, she almost called out for him to come back. The intimacy of him seeing her in such a vulnerable and awful way was embarrassing. But being shut in the bathroom alone in this house was so much worse.

Desperately longing for some toothpaste and a toothbrush, she gargled warm water over and over until her mouth felt clean again. Then she was out the door, running through the house.

"Keira. What's wrong?" Lance called out somewhere behind her.

"Can't. Breathe. Air. I need air." She didn't even slow down. She threw the front door open and ran onto the porch, her shoes catching on the threshold. Pitching forward, she threw her arms up to try to catch herself. Lance managed to grab her around the waist and jerk her back, saving her from tumbling face-first down the stairs.

He turned her and clasped her tightly against him. "My God. Keira. You almost...my God." His hands shook as he held her, rubbing her back and resting his cheek against the top of her head.

His kindness, his strength, his obvious concern, had her fighting back tears. Again. But she absolutely refused to cry all over him as she had at the bed-and-breakfast. Mortified on so many levels, she pushed out of his arms.

"What is it?" he asked. "Are you sick? Do we need to—"

"Drive forty-five minutes to a doctor?" She forced a wobbly smile, still fighting the urge to curl into a ball and cry like the young girl she'd once been before she'd been forced to grow up far too fast so very long ago. "I'm not sick. I'm..." She squeezed her eyes shut, drew a deep breath, then another. Feeling more in control, she opened her eyes. "I'll explain later, but...can we...can we please go somewhere else? To stay? I can't... I can't go back in there. I'm so sorry. I know it must have cost a lot to get this place on short notice. And you might not get your deposit back and—"

"Shh. It's okay." His smile was so sweet, so compassionate, it had her heart squeezing in her chest. "I'm blessed that I don't have to worry about money. And I should have consulted you about the rental to make sure you were okay with it before I reserved it anyway."

"What? No. I knew you were calling to reserve something for us. If I wanted to provide input, I would have. I just... it never dawned on me that the place we got would remind me...would look like..." She shook her head and wrapped her arms around her middle. "Just please take us to a different house, one that's nothing like this one. Okay?"

He pressed the sweetest kiss against her lips. "If my marching orders are to get us a place nothing like this one, then that's what I'll do. No worries. Come on." He took her hand in his and led her to the truck, helping her inside and buckling her seat belt as if she were a precious gift, not the burden she knew she'd become.

"Give me a couple of minutes to call the rental agency again and grab our suitcases and groceries. I'll be right back."

She gave him a shaky smile and nodded her thanks. After

he shut the passenger door, she immediately pressed the lock, not even caring that he must have heard it and thought she'd lost her mind. He jogged up the porch steps, and a moment later the porch lights came on. But they weren't bright enough to reach much beyond the porch itself.

As she waited, she huddled against the seat, her hand on her holster. She'd forgotten how dark it could be out in the middle of nowhere, without streetlights or the so-called light pollution of a city close by. And she'd forgotten just how oppressive that darkness could be.

When she realized she was sliding down in her seat, huddled like a child, she swore and forced herself to sit straight. She wasn't that miserable young girl anymore. And there was no reason to be afraid of an empty house. There were far scarier things to be afraid of right now, like Levi Alexander and whoever he might be working for to try to kill Lance and her.

Funny how so many years had gone by and it was still her past that had the power to frighten her far more than her present. Facing gunmen as an adult, using her police training and excellent marksmanship to protect herself and potentially Lance, was something she was prepared for. She could control her reactions, and how she approached the situation. It was the nightmares of her childhood that she still didn't know how to control.

A few minutes later, Lance jogged down the steps with their two suitcases. He stowed them in the back of the SUV. One more trip into the house and he had the grocery bags. The porch light clicked off, and he hurriedly set the bags in the rear seats.

"Everything's set," he assured her, with an encouraging smile. "The next place is a bit farther, about five miles down the highway. We'll be there in a few minutes."

She watched in relief as the eerie cottage faded into the darkness. When the new rental house came into view, the tension in her shoulders began to ease. But the guilt inside her flared to life. This was definitely not a cottage. One of the more prosperous families in the area must own this one. Or a city slicker had it built as their summer vacation home. It was as modern as the other house was historical. Two stories of glass and steel were softened by gray ledge stone and cedar posts holding up the overhang above the double front door. Landscape lighting chased away the darkness.

Lance cut the engine and gave her an inquiring look. "Better?"

She unfastened her seat belt and impulsively kissed his cheek. "Much."

He grinned. "I can find a bigger house if it will get me a kiss on the lips."

Without missing a beat, she raised on her knees and pressed her lips to his. He groaned and picked her up, lifting her over the middle console and onto his lap as if she weighed nothing. Their first kiss had been full of heat and wonder. This one was scorching. She answered his every touch with her own, their bodies deliciously in sync with each other. He slid a hand around her back and one in her hair and deepened the kiss.

The honk of the horn as her back pressed it had both of them jerking apart. They burst out laughing.

"Talk about a mood killer," he teased. He popped open the door, lifting her in his arms and hopping down from the SUV. When she was standing in front of him, he leaned down and gave her another quick kiss. "The lock code for the front door is 4371. Let's check it out and make sure you're okay with everything before I bring our things inside."

"No. It's fine. Really. You did great. It's nothing like the other place. I'll grab the groceries if you don't mind getting the suitcases."

"All right, but if you change your mind about the house, I can—"

"It's perfect. Let's hurry. It's cold out here."

"Personally, I'm burning up." He winked.

Her face flamed as it did so often around him, and he laughed in response.

The house was everything the outside promised it to be. Clean, bright, open and modern. There was absolutely nothing to make her feel claustrophobic or remind her of her past. But since those dark images had already been resurrected, they were fighting to consume her. She doubted she'd get much sleep at all tonight.

While Lance put their suitcases in two of the bedrooms upstairs, she put away their groceries. There were snacks, peanut butter and jelly, crackers, bread, soup, beer, bottled water. And coffee of course, along with powdered creamer and sugar. Things that didn't need refrigeration. Neither of them planned on being in town long. A few days at most, less if they found Levi right away.

When she finished and turned around, Lance was a few yards away leaning against the massive dark quartz island. "Are you hungry? I can make us some soup and sandwiches."

"I'm starving, actually. I'll heat the soup and—"

"I'll make the ribbon sandwiches."

"Ribbon sandwiches? Fancy name for a PB&J. Did you learn that in home economics class at school?"

"Actually, Mamaw, my grandmother on my father's side, showed me. You'd be amazed at my culinary skills. I can boil water too."

She laughed, and soon they'd both wolfed down their

small hastily thrown together meal. Once the kitchen was clean again, they dried their hands on a kitchen towel.

"Seems rude to eat and run," she said. "But I'm practically asleep on my feet. Which bedroom is mine?"

"Top of the stairs, first room on the right."

"Thanks. For everything." She started past him, but he tugged her hand, pulling her back toward him. She looked up in question.

"Do you want to talk about it?" His voice was gentle, soothing, his expression one of concern.

She'd managed to avoid a discussion about why she'd panicked at the cottage. Dinner had consisted of small talk and plans for tomorrow's surveillance. But it was only fair to explain. She opened her mouth to do exactly that, but the shadows swirled in her mind, stealing the words.

"Just know that I'm here if you ever need to talk." He kissed the top of her head. "I'm not quite ready to call it a night. I'm going to log in to UB to check on their progress with the investigation, maybe catch a football game rerun. Sleep well." He headed into the main room with its U-shaped arrangement of black leather couches facing an enormous television on the far wall.

She flipped off the lights in the kitchen, leaving the dimmed canned lights in the main room as the only lights on downstairs. "Lance?"

He'd just picked up the laptop that he must have set on the coffee table after taking their luggage upstairs. He arched a brow in question.

"Thank you. For everything."

He smiled. "Anytime, Keira. Anytime at all."

Chapter Fifteen

A slight movement had Lance opening his eyes and sitting up, surprised to find that he'd dozed off in the family room. He was even more surprised to see Keira sitting beside him, facing him with her legs crossed in her lap. Her hair was mussed, giving her a sexy just-got-out-of-bed appearance. But the pink pajama tank top and shorts with cartoon cats all over them had him grinning.

"Nice pj's."

She didn't even crack a smile. It was then that he realized how pale she looked.

He glanced up the stairs, his hand automatically going to the gun still holstered on his hip. "Did you hear something? See someone through the windows?"

"What? No. No, I haven't heard or seen anyone. No one real anyway. Or, at least, not anymore." She threaded her fingers through her hair, mussing it even more. "Sorry. I know I'm not making sense. I just, well, I couldn't sleep. Or when I did, the nightmares came again." She drew a shaky breath. "I can't remember the last time that happened. Years, I suppose."

"I'm a little lost here."

She sighed heavily, her hands nervously clenching and

unclenching each other. "I owe you an explanation about earlier. The cottage."

He shook his head. "No, Keira. You don't. Everyone has demons they deal with, something from their past or some kind of phobia. That's for you to tell or not. Completely up to you."

"Okay, well. I need to tell you. I don't want you thinking I'm losing my mind. I want you to understand."

"All right. Take your time. Whatever you need."

She twisted her hands together, then turned, sitting close beside him, her right thigh snuggled up against his left one, warming him through his jeans. He swallowed, his entire body heating as she tentatively clasped his hand with hers and rested their joined hands on her thigh. She obviously had no idea how much he wanted her, how the simple feel of her pressed against him had blood flowing to all the wrong parts. Hating himself for even thinking about sex when she was obviously struggling to gather her thoughts and tell him something important, he used his free hand to pull a light blanket off the back of the couch.

Lifting their joined hands, he settled the blanket over both their laps and then set their hands back on top.

"Thank you," she murmured, no doubt thinking he was just worried about her being cold.

He tried to relax against the back of the couch, a bead of sweat running down his temple. But at least she couldn't see his painful erection straining against the front of his jeans with the blanket covering him.

When she still didn't say anything, he was about to remind her that she didn't have to and they could just sit quietly until she was ready to go to bed again. But her soft, hesitant voice broke the silence first.

"I was fifteen," she whispered.

And just like that, those three little words killed the desire flooding through his veins. Instead, he was now filled with dread, hoping, praying that she wasn't going to say what he feared she would say—that someone had hurt her when she was little more than a child.

Please, don't let it be that.

She rested her head against him. He automatically pulled his hand free from hers and settled his arm around her shoulders, drawing her close. She didn't pull back. Instead, she nestled into the crook of his arm. He wanted nothing more than to protect her, to keep her safe. But he knew that whatever she was about to tell him wasn't something he could save her from. It had already happened.

"I'd stayed a few minutes late with my algebra teacher, getting help with a homework problem. Missed the bus. Home was only a couple of miles away. At the time I was on the cross-country team, so I didn't bother calling my parents for a ride. I changed into my running shoes and took off jogging down the road. I can't tell you how many times my dad warned me not to run with earphones in both ears. He said it was dangerous, that I couldn't hear if a car was getting too close, that I should always keep one ear uncovered. Of course, I ignored his advice. Music was jamming. I never heard the van."

His stomach tightened. "Did it hit you?"

"I wish that's all that had happened. No. The driver parked on the side of the road, then came up from behind and grabbed me. I kicked and scratched for all of about fifteen seconds. He shoved a needle in my neck and everything went black. When I woke up, I was tied up in the back bedroom of a little cottage like the one we went to earlier tonight."

He swore softly and rubbed his hand up and down her arm.

"I won't… I won't go into the particulars. I did that in court, and it was like being violated all over again. I never want to relive it like I did those three days on the witness stand."

"You don't need to," he whispered against the top of her head. "You don't have to."

She nodded against his chest. "I know. But I wanted you to understand. He held me captive for fifty-six days. Tied up most of the time. Kept in a darkened, tiny room. Only let out to shower when I stank too much for him to be able to stand me."

"Good grief," he said. "He was a monster."

"Yes. He was. And it was only through luck that I was eventually rescued. He was pulled over in town for a traffic violation when he was picking up supplies. An observant policeman remembered a witness's description of the van and a girl jogging on the side of the road the day I went missing. They'd driven by, not thinking anything of it until they saw the missing-person posters a few days later. If they hadn't reported it, and the policeman hadn't been suspicious, and my abductor hadn't been dumb enough to have kept my purse in his van, I wouldn't have made it."

She slid her arms around him, holding tight. "I wasn't the first girl he'd taken. But I was the last. And the only one who survived."

His hands shook as he lifted her onto his lap and held her like the precious gift that she was. Barely contained fury roared through his veins. The need to feel the monster's bones crunching beneath his fists was palpable. "What happened to him?"

"He was convicted and sentenced to life, without the possibility of parole. But he never served a day in an actual prison. He took the coward's way out, hung himself in the county jail."

"Good. I don't like the idea of you both sharing the same planet together."

She pulled back and smiled up at him. "Here I am thinking about the most horrific period of my life, and you have the power to make me want to laugh. You're an amazing man, Lance Cabrera."

He softly kissed her but couldn't dredge up a smile of his own. "You're an amazing woman. To have gone through what you did and have gone on to be a functioning, contributing member of society is an achievement of its own. To become a police officer, to face the evil others do day in and day out after experiencing the worst of the worst, is awe-inspiring." He pulled her close again. If she didn't need a hug right now, he sure as heck did. He wished he could take away all the hurt. But all he could do was be there for her. For now, hopefully it was enough.

"That's why you didn't want to go into the basement at the cabin," he said, his cheek pressed against the top of her head. "I imagine you're not a fan of dark, tight spaces."

"And being trapped. No windows or doors."

He winced and pulled back. "I was being stubborn, thinking I knew what was better for you than you knew yourself. I never should have locked you in that basement."

She smiled again, the color slowly coming back into her cheeks and the light returning to her brown eyes. "Apology accepted. You're a strong man used to being the protector. I get that. And I appreciate it. But as you said, I'm a cop. I've been trained and I can shoot pretty darn well, top of my class for marksmanship at the academy. We need to trust each other. As a team, we're much more capable than on our own."

He shook his head in wonder. "I've been on two significant teams over the years, and you're teaching me more about teamwork than I've learned in all that time."

"Slow learner, I guess."

He laughed. "Maybe so. I know I'm pushing my luck in asking any personal questions after what you just shared. But I'm curious about something else."

"I can't imagine anything more personal than what I've already shared. Go ahead."

"Your family. You're estranged from them, right? Is that because of what happened to you? Or something else?"

Her smile dimmed but didn't go away completely. "The ordeal as I've come to think of it happened in Memphis. Everyone in town knew about it. I couldn't escape the cruel comments of other kids at school or the looks and whispers whenever I went anywhere else. My parents tried to protect me by uprooting the family and moving us to Nashville. My younger brother and sister blamed me for them losing their Memphis friends. My parents were overprotective and practically smothered me. Dad turned to alcohol, trying to drown his guilt for not having been able to protect me when I was abducted. I was miserable. We fought constantly and I rebelled, got into trouble. When I turned eighteen, my mother gave me an ultimatum. Straighten up or move out. I was gone that same day, never went back."

"That has to be hard, not having the support of your family anymore."

"No harder than you being forced to give up yours."

"We're both orphans, in a way. Maybe one day we'll both be able to move forward, overcome our pasts and reunite with our loved ones."

"Maybe," she said, sounding doubtful. "Or maybe we move forward by creating a new family. Or, ah, families."

Her face flushed a delightful pink, letting him know he hadn't misunderstood what was probably a Freudian slip. The thought of the two of them starting a family, together, having a real future as a couple, should have scared him. His last serious relationship, Ileana, had been so awful it had soured him on the idea of ever getting married or having children. And yet, that kind of future with Keira didn't sound like a life sentence. Instead, it sounded more like winning a lottery.

She carefully stood, suddenly seeming shy as she adjusted her pajama shorts and then crossed her arms over her chest. "Seems like I'm always thanking you. But I really do appreciate everything you've done, how protective, strong and kind you've always been to me. And for listening. It helped. Talking to a therapist, a stranger, never seemed to work. But telling you just a little about what happened feels…like a weight dragging me down has been lightened considerably."

"I'll always be here for you, Keira. I mean that. Always."

Her eyes widened. Had he frightened her? Or was she surprised—in a good way? Before he could try to reassure her, she called out a hurried good-night and rushed up the stairs.

Chapter Sixteen

Keira was feeling raw and off-kilter the next morning. Her emotions were far too close to the surface, and it was difficult to concentrate. She was frightened of the situation that she and Lance were in, worried about some as yet unknown enemy wanting to kill them. Concern for Lance, in particular, weighed heavily on her. He'd become so important in such a short amount of time that she was more worried about his safety than her own. Part of that was because she felt that she was in over her head, both personally and professionally.

Her law enforcement experience was nothing compared to Lance's. She was good with a gun. And she'd always had a knack for setting witnesses at ease when talking to them as part of her beat-cop duties. But her detective skills were nowhere near what she'd once falsely believed them to be. The tips and suggestions that the UB investigators had given her seemed obvious—after they pointed them out. And Lance's suggestions did as well. But their ideas had never been her ideas. They'd never even occurred to her.

The longer she worked this case, the more she was beginning to accept that maybe being a detective, or even a cop, wasn't the right fit for her. And she was finally starting to understand why. After giving Lance a watered-down version of the trauma she'd endured as a young teenager, it had dawned on her, a real light-bulb moment, that maybe the whole idea of being a cop was just her response to that trauma. Being in control and making her own decisions were crucial to her feeling calm, to staving off the panic that was never far from the surface. Maybe working in law enforcement was just her way of maintaining that sense of control. It helped her feel stronger, less vulnerable. But did it make her happy? Fulfilled? Maybe she'd been wanting the detective title as just another way to try to search for whatever would fill the empty void inside her.

It was something to think about.

As to her personal dilemma that circled around Lance and her feelings for him, they obviously were attracted to each other. But in spite of the teasing and flirting they did so often, one or both of them always seemed to find an excuse or a reason to stop before they crossed a physical line they couldn't uncross. Was it because they really weren't meant for each other? Or was it simply because each of them was unsure of what their own future might look like once this current crisis with Levi and the other mole was over?

It was all so confusing. And it made it hard to focus and do a good job backing up Lance when her thoughts were such a jumble. But at least after pouring her heart out to him last night, she'd been able to get some much-needed sleep. For the first time since the attack at her Gatlinburg cabin, she felt rested and ready to face whatever obstacles were in their way. She just had to lock up the distracting thoughts about her career and Lance, and focus on their mutual goal of stopping the mole, or moles, and reclaiming their lives. The sooner they could do that, the sooner she could make some decisions about her future.

In spite of her worries that things might be awkward

between them when she finally came downstairs freshly showered and ready for the day, things weren't awkward at all. After a quick, light breakfast and easy conversation, they headed out to Sam's farm to spy on it and see whether there were any signs that Levi was there.

They parked at the back of the property this time, using a road that Lance knew about from his many times visiting with Sam. From the way the tree branches and bushes encroached on the road, it was obvious that the most recent occupants of the farm didn't use the back entrance. So it was easy to drive up fairly close to the outbuildings in the woods behind the house and not worry about being seen. From there, it was a long boring day of watching and waiting for signs of life from the house, with just a couple of breaks to head out for something to eat and much-needed bathroom trips. Once back at the rental that evening, they'd used their respective laptops to look for clues about the fiasco that OPI had become.

The only thing of note that happened both days was that a man arrived at the stables in the mornings to feed the horses and turn them out into a pasture. Around the dinner hour, he showed up again and bedded the horses down in the stables for the night. But he never approached the house or any other outbuildings. And there were never any signs of life from the house itself.

The surveillance lasted two days. Both were essentially carbon copies of each other. No lights came on in the house. The blinds on the windows stayed closed. No one drove up the driveway toward it and no one came outside.

At the end of the second day, Keira and Lance sat down at the kitchen table to eat dinner. Keira had slow-cooked a Crock-Pot of roast with potatoes and carrots, thanks to a trip to the little market for more supplies the day before.

They'd both realized that living on peanut butter and jelly sandwiches wasn't going to cut it, even for a short stay.

Lance set his napkin on his plate and leaned back in his chair. "Either I was starving, or you're one fine cook, Ms. Sloane."

"Probably a little of both. I can steer my way around a kitchen when I want to. And we're both tired of junk food." She reached for his empty plate to rinse and wash, but he stopped her.

"I'll clean the kitchen," he said. "It's the least I can do after you cooked this delicious meal. But let's get our daily call to Trent out of the way first. I'm hopeful he's found something. We're coming up with zero on our end."

"Works for me." She moved their plates out of the way and sat beside him.

Lance got Trent on the phone and put it on speaker mode while they gave him their updates—which was basically that they'd made no progress.

Lance added, "I also tried tracing both Sam and Levi's phones that I had programmed into my computer. But regardless of which phone Levi was using when I sent the warning to my team to go underground, he's not using it now. It's either turned off or has been destroyed."

"We tried the same thing here," Trent said. "Even went through the phone carriers for their official records, courtesy of a subpoena secured by Chief Russo. Your team is well trained to ditch phones and switch to burners, is all I can say. We came up empty. This Levi character has gone completely off the radar. He hasn't returned anywhere that we've been able to trace him to in his past. And from what you've said, he hasn't gone to Sam's one hold-out property from his early life either. As much as I hate to say it, we're at a dead end on finding him unless something happens to expose his location. Are you going to perform surveillance tomorrow or switch gears?"

Lance motioned toward Keira. "What do you think?"

She shrugged. "Without another lead to chase on Levi, I'm inclined to give it one more day."

"One more day it is then," he agreed. "After that, we'll need to find a new location to keep ourselves off the radar. Even though we're using alias internet accounts, cash and burner phones, we're still leaving an electronic trail. That makes me nervous. I'd rather head out sooner than later. But I agree with Keira that one more day feels right. I really thought Levi would show up here. And I don't have any more ideas on where to look for him at the moment. Any updates on the Homeland Security link?"

"Good and bad news on that front. The good news is that we finished our investigation into both of the HS guys we'd zeroed in on. The bad news is that neither of them are the mole. We're going to have to look at everything again, see if we missed something. One thing that has come out of this is that we did deep dives into the cases you'd researched where people were killed, the ones you and your team provided intel about. Although it's not obvious at first, when you peel back the layers, you'll find that many of the people who were killed had alleged links to organized crime. If that's the common thread, then a mole in the Justice Department makes far more sense than someone in Homeland Security. He could be in the FBI or even the US Marshals, turning over locations of witnesses to a mob boss to take them out. Making this entirely about money for the moles. They get rich, the mob protects its own people, who would have gone to prison if the witnesses had been around to testify."

"FBI," Lance said. "I looked at them but found nothing."

"Like I said, we had to go deep. We've used Chief Russo's

influence, our TBI liaison and his connections to the Florida Department of Law Enforcement, as well as our boss's considerable influence on governors and other politicians. It's only through their hard work that we've gotten the subpoenas we needed, in record time I might add. And because of that we got access to information you and I would never have gotten otherwise. You wouldn't have found that link on your own. Trust me."

"I still hate that I didn't. I'll look at my FBI interactions in my OPI files again and see if I can pull any threads."

"Sounds good."

Lance motioned to Keira. "Anything you want to add? Suggestions on how to move forward?"

She cleared her throat, nervous about bringing this particular item up.

Lance smiled. "Whatever you've found, don't worry about sharing it. You might have figured out a clue that will put all the pieces together."

"Doubtful, but okay. I do have one thing I wanted to mention. And the only reason I'm bringing it up is because of Trent mentioning the Justice Department. That could mean any link to the FBI is important for the case, so—" she drew a deep breath "—something I was looking into last night, or rather someone, is, um, your ex-girlfriend, Ileana Sanchez. Or her married name now, Ileana Vale." At Lance's doubtful look, she rushed to explain. "I figured you might have had difficulty being objective about her, so I wanted to take a look just to make sure she's not the one who spied on the OPI missions. You haven't mentioned her when talking about who might have been double-crossing your team, so I—"

He held up his hand to stop her. "It's okay, Keira. You don't have to explain why you researched her. It makes sense to cover all our bases. The reason I haven't brought her up is because she didn't have any access to OPI case files. I didn't share my ID or password at any time. And I never discussed our cases with her."

"I would expect nothing less," she assured him. "But it's not you I was thinking could have had their access to OPI's computer system compromised, not on purpose anyway. She was with you for several years. She would have attended social functions with your team and their significant others, right? She knew them? Was friends with them?"

He was silent for a moment, then slowly nodded. "Yes. She was friends with them. But everyone knew the rules. No discussing our cases with anyone not on our team."

Trent chimed in on the phone. "Rules are made to be broken, Lance. You admitted you've kept up with your team as best you could in spite of agreeing that everyone would go their separate ways and not ever try to contact each other again. Maybe someone on your team stretched the rules too. Especially in the early days, before you realized someone was taking the information and using it to target people for execution."

Lance scrubbed his jaw. "Even if you're right, and she somehow managed to get someone on my team to talk about their cases, she wouldn't have had the power or connections to do anything with the information."

Keira cleared her throat again. "She got married shortly after OPI broke up. The man she married is Hudson Vale. He currently runs the FBI field office in New York City."

Trent whistled. "If Vale is our guy, the mole, that just might be the connection we're looking for."

"I've never heard of Hudson Vale," Lance said, still sounding unconvinced. "Did you look into him too?"

She nodded. "He was an assistant in the same office as

the FBI managers you looked into early on. While he wasn't at the top, he did have access, at least locationwise, to the offices of the big fish. If he's dirty, if he has relationships with those in organized crime, he might be someone we should look at more closely. Maybe Trent and the UB team can dig in and see if it pans out."

"Lance?" Trent asked. "If you feel strongly about this, I won't look into it."

He frowned. "Of course you should look into it. Keira did an excellent job discovering a potential link to someone in the FBI who could be passing information along. But I'm still not convinced that Ileana would have the access to even get the information. There's only so much my team would have shared, even over a few pints of beer at a team gathering."

Keira twisted her hands together on top of the table.

Lance arched his brows. "There's more?"

"Just one more thing I wanted to mention that goes along with what you just said. Back at UB headquarters, when you were telling all of us about how you got started with OPI, you mentioned that you were following the criminology track in college. You also said that Ileana was majoring in information technology, computer programming specifically. I just wondered how good she was and whether she may have been swayed to put her skills into, well, hacking. If so, she could have hacked into your OPI computer system. Did you two, um, live together at some point? Where she'd have access to your computer when you were gone or sleeping?"

His jaw worked, and the skin along it turned white as if he were clenching his teeth. Finally, he nodded. "We shared an apartment my senior year. And once I bought a house, she moved in and out depending on how our relationship was going at the time. I have no idea if she's skilled enough to have hacked into OPI's system. But she definitely would have had plenty of opportunities."

Trent filled in the awkward silence that had fallen over the meeting. "We'll jump on this and look into what Keira found. Should have at least an initial status update for tomorrow's call. Anything else?"

Lance looked at Keira. She shook her head. "No. That's it. Thanks, Trent." He ended the call and shoved the phone into his pocket. But instead of getting up, he remained seated, staring off into space.

Keira wasn't sure what to do. She could sense his anger, the tension in his body. It pained her that she'd done that, upset him. No doubt he was remembering his old girlfriend, both the good and bad times. Maybe the best thing to do was just let him be. Give him some space.

She stood and quietly took their plates to the sink. After quickly rinsing them, she loaded them in the dishwasher. She'd clean the rest later, once he left the kitchen. When she turned around, she jumped in surprise to see him standing directly in front of her. His face seemed drawn, his eyes a darker blue than usual. And his brows were drawn down in a frown.

She cleared her throat. "I'm sorry if I overstepped. I was trying to cover everything, make sure we hadn't missed a clue. But I probably should have asked you first—"

He ever so gently pulled her against his chest and rested his cheek on the top of her head. She was so surprised that she didn't even hug him back. She just stood frozen, not sure what to think.

"No, Keira," he murmured, stroking her back. "You didn't need to ask me first or apologize. You did exactly what I should have done and I'm glad that you did." He let her go and stepped back. "Any feelings I once had for Ileana died years ago. I'm not upset that you dredged her memory up. I'm upset that you felt you had to because I hadn't done my own due diligence. Not enough, anyway. I should have…"

He shook his head. "My point is that my ego wouldn't consider that I'd made any mistakes, or that my team had, to allow her—or anyone else—access to our files through any of us. I always assumed someone we did work for in the agencies, or their boss, would have used their meetings with my boss to obtain knowledge about the cases we were working. Making assumptions appears to be my downfall. None of the people I thought could be the mole have panned out. And now you've offered an entirely new avenue to explore as to how the information may have been leaked."

He finally smiled. "If you ever need a recommendation to help you with advancement to detective, I'll be happy to provide you one. You're proving to be a better detective than me."

She almost choked, then coughed. "Uh, no. I'm not. But I appreciate the compliment and offer."

He cocked his head. "There seems to be some hesitation there."

"I just, well, honestly I've been thinking that law enforcement may not be the right fit for me. The more I think about it, the more right it feels not to return to my old job. It was a way for me to heal, to feel I was in control after having that stolen from me so long ago. But I don't get the satisfaction at my job that I always expected."

"You have the skill set, Keira. Don't let anyone tell you otherwise. Maybe Maple Falls just isn't the right place to exercise it. Whatever you do, I hope you don't make a quick decision. Think long and hard before giving up a career that might end up providing far more satisfaction—in the right place, working for the right boss—than you might expect."

"I appreciate the advice."

"Or you're secretly thinking it's none of my business."

Her face warmed.

He laughed. "Now that all of that is out of the way, let's get to work."

"Right. Dishes." She started to turn and he tugged her hand, keeping her where she was.

"I already told you that I'm doing the dishes, cleaning up the kitchen. But that can wait. The work I was talking about is finding Levi. Even if Ileana is the true leak at OPI, I'm not convinced that Levi isn't involved too, or responsible for Sam's murder."

"Because he stole Sam's identity."

"Exactly. Watching the farm for two days hasn't gotten us any new leads. Rather than spend another day doing the same, I'm suggesting that we do some nighttime surveillance. Maybe he's somewhere else during the day and coming back at night. We haven't seen evidence of any vehicles coming in or out, other than the man taking care of the horses. But what if he's doing what we've been doing, coming in the back way? And only coming at night? It's something to check out. We can park somewhere outside of the property and walk in through the woods this time. And see if he shows up."

She glanced at the darkness beyond the kitchen window.

His warm hand urged her face back toward him. "If you don't feel comfortable outside at night, I can do this on my own. I totally get why you're afraid of the dark."

She shivered. "It's not the dark that worries me. It's the people who hide there. Plus it's extra cold tonight. Have you seen the weather reports? It might even snow in the early morning hours."

"Like I said. I'm fine doing it by myself—"

She lightly punched his arm.

"What was that for?" He mockingly rubbed his arm as if she'd hit him really hard.

She rolled her eyes. "You're not going by yourself. I'm your backup. We'll dress in layers and bring blankets. But if my feet start to lose feeling from the cold, we're leaving."

"Deal. Wheels up in ten minutes."

She laughed and they both headed for the stairs.

THE MOON WAS bright enough that they could see fairly well outside. That helped make up for the lack of lights on Sam's property. But two hours of being there, sitting on the cold ground in the woods behind the house, had Keira shivering. Lance swore and shifted around behind her, stretching his long legs out on either side of her thighs to form a warm cocoon around her. He pulled her back against his chest and wrapped both of them in the blankets they'd brought.

His warm breath fanned her cheek as he leaned down next to her ear. "Better?"

Oh boy, was it. The heat of his body warmed her all over, turning her hormones into a flood of lava in her veins. All she had to do was ease back, unzip her jeans, turn around and they could—

"Keira? If you're still too cold, we can leave."

"What? Oh, no. I'm...much better now. Thanks."

He bent down again, giving her a doubtful look. "If you shiver again we've leaving."

"I won't. I'm warm now." *Scorching.*

He watched her for a moment, as if waiting for another

shiver. When she didn't, he straightened and wrapped his arms around her waist.

They sat that way so long she really was getting toasty. In spite of the pleasure in being held so intimately by him, she was about to ask him to move back a little before she started to sweat. But then a sound interrupted the night. It was a mechanical sound, a familiar sound but one that they hadn't heard since beginning their surveillance.

She turned and looked at him. "The condenser unit just kicked on."

He nodded, hurriedly pulling the blankets off both of them. "Someone turned on the heat. Let's see who's home."

A few minutes later, they were at the back door, one on each side, pistols drawn. Keira couldn't help comparing it to the same type of situation when she and her fellow deputies were outside Rick's motel room in Maple Falls. She desperately hoped they weren't about to discover the same kind of horrific scene.

Lance silently counted down, holding up his hand. *Three. Two. One.* He stepped back and delivered a vicious kick to the doorknob. The frame split and the door crashed open. They ran inside, pistols sweeping out in front of them. A dark-haired pale man was standing in front of a couch in the main room. Moonlight coming through the ruined back door illuminated the terrified look on his face as he stared at them in shock.

Lance aimed his gun at the man's head. "Make one move, Levi, and I'll kill you just like you killed Sam."

Chapter Seventeen

Levi didn't move, not even to raise his hands as Lance pointed the gun at him. Keira wasn't even sure if he was breathing.

"Light switch?" she asked.

Levi didn't say anything. He simply stared at Lance.

"Behind me," Lance said. "To the left. Unless the place has been renovated since I was here last."

The switch was right where he'd said. She flipped it on, and overhead pot lights lit up the main room and small eat-in kitchen area off to her left.

"Cover me," Lance said, holstering his gun.

"You got it." She aimed her pistol in Levi's direction, careful not to get Lance in her sights as he pulled the other man to his feet and searched him.

Lance took a pistol from Levi's front pocket and a knife from a sheath on his ankle. After putting them in his own jacket pockets, he ordered, "Sit down."

Levi slowly sat, his gaze flitting from Lance to Keira and back again. "If this is about Sam, I swear to the good Lord above, I didn't kill him."

"Right," Lance said, his voice angry, clipped. "You just happened to be in Newtown at the same time as him, saw him get killed, then switched IDs."

Levi's eyes widened. "That's exactly what happened! Except that I didn't just happen to be there. We were friends. I was visiting. We were walking down a side street, and a car with dark-tinted windows pulled up. The passenger window rolled down and—*bam bam*—Sam fell. I ran behind a building. As soon as the shooter drove off, I rushed to Sam. But there was nothing I could do. He was…he was gone." Levi's eyes glistened with unshed tears.

"I didn't have a clue who'd shot him or why," Levi continued, "so I switched IDs in case they were going to come after me too. Sam lives, or lived, in Newtown. So there was nowhere else to look for him. But I lived in Rochester. There were plenty of places connected to me if someone was trying to find me. I hadn't exactly been living off the grid. So I figured if I pretended to be Sam, they wouldn't know where to find me as long as I didn't go anywhere I'd normally go. I had to act as if I really was dead."

"They. Who is 'they'?"

"I don't know. I assume it's whoever was after us from our OPI days. I'd honestly thought we'd left all that behind. But since I didn't know anyone else who'd want to kill Sam, I assumed our past—OPI—had caught up to us. And without knowing how they found Sam, I didn't know if they'd know how to find me. That's why I went on the run, came here to hide out until the heat died down and I could figure out my next steps."

Lance watched him intently, as if weighing his words for signs of deceit. Keira didn't know Levi or what reactions were typical for him. But every word he'd said bore a ring of truth to her. She didn't think he had anything to do with his friend's murder, which meant he likely wasn't involved in the attempted murders of her and Lance in Gatlinburg.

"What about Rick?" Lance asked. "Did you kill him too?"

Levi shot up from the couch.

Lance pulled his gun out of his holster so fast it was a blur. "Sit. Down."

The tears that had been threatening rolled down Levi's cheeks as he sat. "Rick's dead? What happened?"

"You tell me."

"I don't know. I swear."

Levi was sweating and looking down as if ashamed. He was hiding something. But Keira still couldn't picture him having killed Rick. He seemed too devastated.

As if reading her mind, Lance said, "You're hiding something, Levi. If you want to survive the night, tell the truth. All of it."

Levi swore, anger darkening his eyes. "Enough, Lance. Okay? If you don't believe me and you want to kill me, just do it. I'm tired of being accused of killing my friends."

"What are you hiding?" Lance showed no reaction to Levi's anger and cut him no slack.

Levi swore again. "Rick was religious about staying underground, using aliases, burner phones. He was more careful over the years than Sam and I have been. But he showed up in Newtown after the news reported that I'd been killed in a mugging. And before you ask, yes, I hung around a few weeks after the shooting, and that's why I know Rick was in town asking questions. I was watching for that car again, the shooter. If he'd shown up I'd have taken him out. But he didn't. And Rick left soon after checking around town. I never saw him after that and I don't think he ever saw me. I don't know where he went. And I certainly didn't know he was dead. What happened?"

Lance stood in silence.

Keira took mercy on the frustrated-looking man on the couch. "He was shot. Much like Sam was."

He squeezed his eyes shut, in obvious pain. When he opened them again, his eyes were bloodshot. "Did he suffer?"

Lance slowly holstered his gun, signaling to Keira that he'd finally accepted Sam's story.

"I was there," she told Levi, "with Rick when he died. He went…peacefully." The lie was heavy on her conscience, but she didn't want to hurt this man any more than they already had.

Lance gave her a subtle nod, letting her know he appreciated her compassion.

He sat beside Levi and put his hand on his shoulder. "I'm sorry, man. When I found out that Sam was the one who'd been killed and his ID was switched with yours, I thought you must have been the mole inside OPI."

Levi frowned. "Mole *inside* OPI? I always thought one of the higher-ups in the alphabet agencies we worked with was the one who went after us. You think it was an inside job?"

"It's a long story. But Officer Sloane and I—"

"Keira," she corrected, smiling at Levi.

Levi nodded but didn't return her smile. He seemed shell-shocked by the knowledge that yet another friend of his had been murdered. She certainly couldn't blame him.

"Keira and I," Lance said, "along with some people I work with, have been looking into why our past has come back to haunt us all again."

"Us? Did someone go after you too?"

Lance nodded. "After Keira and me. She worked Rick's case. As I said, long story. But we believe someone in the FBI, and someone either in OPI or close to someone in OPI, worked together to pass information to some organized crime bosses. My team is probably a few days from getting the evidence together to prove it."

"This is absurd. I mean, good that you think you're close to solving this puzzle after all these years. But crazy, and scary as hell, that someone in OPI is working against us. And coming after us again." He raked his hands through his shaggy hair, which badly needed a cut. "First Murphy, then Allen, Sam, Rick. Mick too, of course."

"Mick? He's dead?"

Levi nodded. "Just a few days ago, from what I heard. Cancer. Sam had cancer too. He wouldn't have lasted much longer, a couple of months at most. That's part of why he wanted to enjoy life, quit hiding. And it's why he reached out to Ileana. He was tired and wanted to spend the rest of his days with friends. He wanted to return to Wingo too, back to his horses." He shook his head. "Now he never will." He looked up at Lance. "You didn't know about Mick? Seems like you know everything else."

Lance shook his head, no doubt hearing the bitterness in Levi's voice but choosing to let it go. "I didn't know. There aren't that many of us left. Most of the team is gone."

Levi smiled for the first time. "Guess that makes it easier to figure out who in OPI was spying on us. But for the life of me, I can't imagine any of them—Brett, Melissa, Jack—leaking information to someone to murder people." Levi cast a bleary look at Lance. "I certainly didn't spy on us and pass along information."

Lance pulled the confiscated gun and knife out of his jacket pocket and held them out to Levi. "I know you didn't. And I'm sorry I put you through hell tonight. I needed to be sure."

Levi stared at him a long moment, then nodded and took his weapons. After he sheathed the knife and slid the pistol into his pants pocket, he asked, "You said you expected to have proof soon about who's behind this. Who's your money on at OPI? Brett, Melissa or Jack?"

"Actually, Keira has a theory about that, a solid one. We've been toying with the idea that it might be—"

Headlights flashed onto the front window blinds.

Lance leaned over the couch and peered between some slats in the blinds. "A car's coming up the driveway, fast."

"Only one?" Keira asked.

He nodded. "Just one." He watched while the lights flashed away from the blinds.

A few moments later, the sound of an engine indicated that the car must have pulled up right in front of the house. Then the engine cut off, leaving nothing but eerie silence.

Chapter Eighteen

A loud knock sounded on the front door of the farmhouse. Lance motioned for everyone to be quiet. He knew exactly who it was. What he didn't know yet was whether they were the mole or just another unpleasantry from his past coming back to haunt him.

He mouthed the words *Stay here* to Keira. Then, aiming his pistol toward the floor, he jogged to the ruined back door and slipped out into the night. He carefully circled the left side of the house to the front corner, using it to shield him from their visitor's view until he assessed the situation.

Headlights no longer shone from down the long driveway. The stillness of the night wasn't broken by the sound of idling engines from hidden vehicles. Moonlight didn't reveal any dark figures skulking through the pastures. The only sound at all was repeated knocking, pounding really, on the front door. And the sound of a voice Lance had hoped never to hear again in his lifetime.

"Levi, you're in there, right? Come on. It's me, Ileana. Open up. I need to talk to you."

Lance used her distraction to run behind the car, a dark-colored Mercedes. He peered through the back windows, then the front, although it was difficult to see much because they were tinted. No movement caught his attention.

And no one shot at him. So the car was likely empty. Unless someone was hiding in the trunk, she'd come alone. Or there were more people hiding in the woods somewhere, unseen and unheard.

"Levi, please. Open the door!" Ileana pounded on it again.

Hoping he was right, that she truly had come alone, Lance crept up behind her. Going with his instincts, that she was the one who'd betrayed them all, he pressed the muzzle of his gun against the back of her head.

She froze, her hand in the air, ready to knock again.

"What do you want, Ileana?" he demanded.

She stiffened, then slowly turned around, eyes wide as she backed up a step. "Lance?" She looked past him, then left and right, as if expecting others to be with him. "What are you doing here?" She frowned. "And for goodness sakes, put the gun down. I'm not a burglar or robber or whatever you're thinking."

"You have no idea what I'm thinking. What do you want?"

She frowned at the gun he had aimed at her midsection now. "Can I at least lower my hands?"

"No."

She swore, calling him several unsavory names. It certainly wasn't the first time he'd heard them from her.

"I'm not going to ask you again," he warned.

"Oh for the love of… I'm here to see Levi. Is he here or not?"

The door behind her opened. Levi stood on the threshold. "I'm here," he said.

She whirled around. "Oh my goodness. You're okay? I was so worried. I thought he'd killed you too." She smiled and held out her arms as if to hug him.

He held up a hand to stop her. "Wait."

Her arms slowly lowered. “What’s going on? Why are you both treating me as if I’m a stranger?”

“Keira,” Lance called out.

“Right behind you.”

He glanced over his shoulder, surprised to see her emerge from a crouch behind the car, her pistol down toward the ground. “You followed me?”

“I’m your backup. One day you’re going to learn to stop telling me to wait while you run into danger. It’s never going to work.”

“It appears that I’m a slow learner.”

“You certainly are.” She winked.

He chuckled. “I was going to ask if you would pat Ileana down.”

“Pat me down?” Ileana practically shrieked the words. “What the heck does that mean? Who are you anyway? Lancelot’s future ex-girlfriend?” She smirked.

“Officer Keira Sloane,” she said, as she moved past him. “I need to check you for any weapons.”

“What? No way. Don’t you touch me, you little—”

Keira grabbed Ileana’s arms and whipped her around, then thoroughly searched her. All the while, Ileana called her even more colorful names than she’d tossed at Lance. Keira straightened and held out her hand. “Give me your purse.”

Ileana clutched it against her chest. “No. This is ridiculous. I’m leaving.” She stalked toward her car. But as soon as she passed Keira, Keira snatched Ileana’s purse.

“I assume your keys are in here,” she said. “I’ll return this inside.” She jogged up the steps and brushed past Levi, heading inside.

Ileana sputtered in outrage. “You have no right to treat me this way. You all have some explaining to do.”

Lance holstered his pistol and motioned toward the house.

She huffed and marched back to Levi. “Are you really going to let them treat me this way?”

Levi looked at Lance, his expression unreadable. “Lance has his reasons. I’m sure he’ll explain them to us.” He put his hand on the back of her jacket and ushered her inside with him.

After one last look around, Lance headed in as well and bolted the door behind him.

“She has a gun in her purse.” Keira tossed it onto the kitchen island.

“Yeah, well,” Ileana said. “I’m a woman, traveling alone. Of course I have a gun, for protection. You’re one to talk, whoever you are. Everyone here has a gun except Levi.”

Levi didn’t bother to correct her on her assumption that he was unarmed. “You have a black eye.”

“Well thank you for stating the obvious,” she said.

He stepped closer, clearly concerned. “How did you get that?”

She arched a perfectly plucked eyebrow. “My husband’s fist. It’s not the first time either.”

Levi pulled Ileana to the couch and sat beside her. “You never told me or Sam that he ever hit you.”

“It’s not exactly something to brag about.”

“Do you need some ice for that?” Lance asked, doing the right thing when he really wanted to throw some handcuffs on Ileana and interrogate her.

“Finally found your manners, Lancelot?”

He gritted his teeth. “Don’t call me that.”

“Whatever. No, I don’t need any ice. Like I said, my… difficulties with my husband aren’t new. And they’re no one else’s concern. That’s not why I’m here.”

"Why *are* you here?" Lance asked. "And how did you know that Levi would be here?"

The sound of running water had them looking toward the kitchen area. Keira had just wet a paper towel under the faucet and was wringing it out. She pumped a few drops of soap onto it, then took it to Ileana.

"What do you want?" Ileana frowned up at her.

"Proof." Keira rubbed the paper towel across Ileana's black eye.

Ileana cried out and shoved her hand away. "What the heck? Are you a sadist or something? Why did you do that?" She gently patted at her eye. "That really hurt, you little witch. And you've got soap all over it."

"I've been called worse." Keira held up the paper towel for Lance's inspection. "No makeup. She's not faking her injury."

Lance grinned. "Smart."

Keira smiled back and threw away the paper towel.

Levi faced Ileana on the couch, his expression one of concern as she continued to wipe at her eye. "Some…stuff is going on here. I'm sorry you got caught up in it. Now isn't a good time for a visit—"

"It's three in the morning," Lance announced. "She's not here on a social call. Why, exactly, are you here, Ileana? And how did you know that Levi was here?"

Levi frowned at the suspicion in Lance's tone but didn't interfere.

Ileana seemed disappointed that he'd let Lance speak that way to her. But she also seemed to realize that refusing to explain wasn't getting her anywhere. "I'd hoped that Levi was here. But I wasn't sure. I'd already looked everywhere else I could for him. And I called a million times without an answer. Either his phone is off or broken. This farm is Sam's family's place. I was hoping against hope to find Levi here."

She put her hand on his thigh. "I'm so relieved that you're okay. Hudson snooped in my phone and discovered I was having an affair with Sam. He shot Sam. And he bragged about it to me." She dabbed at both eyes this time, which were shiny and bright as if she were holding back tears. "When he saw in the news that you were killed in a mugging, he was furious. He said he must have gotten the wrong guy. He's been on the warpath ever since, trying to find you. He thinks you're Sam, with you two looking so much alike and all. If he finds you, he's going to kill you too."

"You came here to warn me?"

"Of course. What other reason would there be? Hudson is finally out of town on a business trip. This is the first time I've been able to get away in months." She motioned toward her black eye. "Of course he gave me this as a parting gift before he left, a warning not to go anywhere."

Levi patted her shoulder. "You should have told me about him." He winced. "Or told Sam. We'd have helped you. He might be a big shot at the FBI, but he's still going to get what's coming to him. We'll get justice for Sam, and for you. I know you really cared about Sam."

She sniffed. "Of course I did. Not telling both of you about what Hudson was doing was me trying to protect you. I wanted to take care of it on my own. But he found out anyway. And I couldn't… I couldn't protect Sam." She sniffed again.

"Is that true, Levi?" Lance asked. "Ileana and Sam were having an affair?"

Ileana rolled her eyes. "Of course it's true. Why would I lie?"

"Levi?" Lance repeated.

Ileana stewed in anger but didn't say anything.

Levi nodded. "Like I said earlier, neither of us was staying low under the radar. He saw something in the society pages in the *New York Times* about her one day. He'd always...always liked her. But of course, when you two were together, he never would have dared to act on his feelings."

"I know. Sam was a good guy."

Levi smiled sadly. "He was. Anyway, he was lonely, you know? He just wanted to see an old friend, a familiar face, again. She agreed to come visit in Newtown and, well, things progressed from there."

"Ileana," Lance asked, "how did you know it was Sam who was killed and not Levi? As you said, the news reported Levi as the victim of the mugging."

She shook her head in exasperation. "My husband was bragging that he'd killed my lover. Then he saw in the news that Levi was killed instead and was furious. I needed to know the truth, whether it was Sam or Levi who'd been killed. And I wanted to warn whichever one was still alive to hide from Hudson. What do you think I'd have done? Nothing? Just sit on my hands while my husband killed another one of my friends? What kind of person do you think I am, Lance?"

When Lance didn't answer, her face reddened. "Good grief. We had our bad times, plenty of them. But we had good times too. I don't understand why you're interrogating me like this. I had to go to the police in Newtown and look at that awful autopsy photo to confirm it was Levi. And then, of course I knew it wasn't."

"Did you tell the police that?" Levi asked.

"No, no, dear. I don't understand why you let people think that you were dead instead of Sam, but I assumed you had a good reason. Part of me wondered whether you knew

Hudson had killed Sam and you switched places to try to keep Hudson from going after you too. After all, the three of us visited quite often in Newtown when Sam and I were an item. Hudson probably realized that when he snooped through my phone."

She sniffed again, although Lance didn't notice any actual tears.

"Once we get you somewhere safe, we need to switch that headstone in the cemetery," she said. "It's not right that your name is on Sam's grave. He deserves better than that."

Levi patted her shoulder. "He does. I agree."

Ileana motioned toward her black eye. "This thing hurts like the devil. Get me some ice. But first I have to pee, and clean the rest of the soap off my face. You're not going to try to stop me from using the bathroom are you?"

Levi held his hands up apologetically. "Course not. It's the last door on the—"

"I know where it is. Been here before." She glared at Lance. "Years ago, with my ex." She marched down the hallway and into the bathroom, slamming the door behind her.

Keira let out a long breath. "She's something."

Levi's chin raised. "She's a good person. She's obviously been through trauma with her husband and losing Sam. And it didn't exactly help that we held her at gunpoint when she got here."

Lance and Keira exchanged a long glance. He sighed and scrubbed his jaw. "Right before she arrived, Keira and I were going to explain that we believe Ileana may have used her computer programming expertise to hack into our OPI databases. With her marrying the head of an FBI field office later on, it lends more credence to that theory."

Levi shook his head. "No way. Whoever got that information is responsible, either directly or indirectly, for people being killed. Ileana would never want any of us hurt. That's why she's here. To protect me."

"Would you bet your life on that?" Keira asked.

Levi frowned at her. "As a matter of fact, I would."

"You saw her Mercedes out front," Lance said. "It's black with dark-tinted windows. Could that have been the car used by the shooter who killed Sam?"

His face reddened. "Of course it could have. Because her husband, Hudson, was driving it."

Lance and Keira exchanged another glance.

"What?" Levi demanded. "What aren't you telling me?"

Keira gave him a sympathetic look. "Lance and I were performing surveillance earlier, to see if you were here. Since Hudson Vale's name recently came up in our investigation, Lance tapped some resources and contacts that his company has with the FBI. Hudson was out of the country when Sam was shot."

"Levi," Lance said, "when Sam was shot, is there any possibility that a woman could have been driving the car?"

Levi's face turned pale. "I don't…maybe." He glanced down the hall.

"Ileana's been in that bathroom a long time," Lance said. "Keira, did you see a cell phone in her purse?"

"Ah, shoot. In her pocket. I noticed it when I searched her for weapons and didn't think anything about it."

They both drew their guns and took off down the hallway.

Lance busted in the door without even knocking. He swore when he saw the empty room, and the open window above the toilet.

Keira sucked in a sharp breath. "The mirror."

Written in toothpaste were three words.

You're all dead.

They whirled around and ran out of the bathroom.

Levi's eyes widened in shock when he saw them. "She's gone?"

"Out the window," Lance said. "We need to—"

"I'll stop her." Levi ran for the front door.

"Wait," Lance yelled, rushing toward him.

Levi threw the door open. The crack of rifle fire filled the house. Levi's body jerked as the bullets struck his body. He was dead before he even hit the floor.

"No!" Lance yelled. "Damn it. Not you too." He started toward his friend.

Keira jumped in front of him and shoved at his chest. "He's gone. There's nothing you can do for him. We need to get out of here." She tugged his arm, trying to pull him toward the back door.

He stood frozen, unmoving. Blood pooled beneath Levi's body. The door gaped open, revealing the moonlit front yard. And the sound of an engine starting up.

Ileana.

He started toward the door again.

Keira slammed her body against him, knocking him to the side a few feet, but he managed to keep his balance. "Stop it. She's getting away."

She slammed the flat of her palms against his chest, blocking his way. "Wait. Listen to me. What if Ileana wasn't the one who shot Levi? You saw what she wrote on that mirror. Do you really think she would try to take on all three of us without help? She's not alone in this. Her hired hands must have just arrived and hid out front. Heck, she probably gave herself that black eye to get Levi's sympathy. Rather than her being a victim of domestic violence, I'd bet money her FBI husband is in on this with her. His men are likely out front right now. We have to—"

Another round of gunfire shattered the night. Bullets strafed through the open front door. Lance and Keira dove behind the kitchen island, low to the ground. As soon as there was a pause, they both jumped up and ran out the back door.

Chapter Nineteen

The rumble of more engines had Keira and Lance turning when they reached the woods, looking back toward the house. Three SUVs with gunmen hanging out the windows were barreling down the long road into the farm.

"Good grief," Keira said. "How many of them are there? We need help. A lot of help."

Lance shoved his phone in his pocket. "I just tried to call Trent. They're jamming the signal. We need to get out of their jammer's range."

They took off running again, crashing through the woods, leaping over the pallet of blankets they'd left from their earlier surveillance. They'd almost reached Lance's SUV when a flash of moonlight on metal had both of them stopping and ducking behind a tree. More vehicles were roaring up the back road.

"It was an ambush all along." Lance swore. "I'll bet all Ileana wanted to do was confirm how many people were in the house before she signaled her husband to bring in his mercenaries. Come on, this way." They took off running through the woods, leaving the back road and the house behind.

"What exactly attracted you to that woman in the first

place?" Keira asked as she struggled to keep up with his long strides while scanning the trees for signs of gunmen.

He grinned. "I was young and stupid, and she had a figure."

"Men."

The sound of shouting off to their left had them jumping behind some thick pine trees.

Keira held her pistol in both hands, her lungs screaming for air as she tried to drag in quiet, short breaths to avoid anyone hearing her. Behind another tree, Lance mirrored her position, his chest heaving as he too tried not to make any noise. Very slowly, he leaned around his tree, then jerked back. He held up two fingers and motioned to his right. Then he held up two more and motioned to the left. She nodded to let him know she understood.

Could she and Lance take four guys out without being shot themselves? Possibly. Probably. She was good with a gun. And Lance, well, he was good at everything, as proven by his performance at the cabin. But eliminating four enemies when there were dozens out searching for them would only give away their location.

The sound of voices gradually faded amid shouts of a man somewhere behind them ordering someone to get some flashlights.

Lance leaned around the tree again, then straightened. He gave her a thumbs-up, then a rolling motion with his hand for her to follow him. The two of them took off in a jog toward the right end of the property in relation to the back of the house.

She was soon considering begging for mercy, desperately needing to stop and catch her breath. He was obviously in great shape, and their fast jog through the woods didn't seem to bother him at all. But she had a stitch in her side, her ribs were still bruised and she was gasping for air. There would definitely be more Pilates in her future, if she survived tonight.

Thankfully, Lance raised a hand and signaled her to stop so she didn't have to embarrass herself by asking for a reprieve. But when she saw why he'd stopped, she vigorously began shaking her head.

No, she mouthed, afraid to talk out loud in case any gunmen were close by.

He pointed at the building that housed the horses and nodded yes.

No, she mouthed again, shaking her head so hard her hair flew around her face.

Lance pointed in the direction of the house, mimicking a gun with his thumb and forefinger and firing over and over, reminding her they were severely outnumbered and had no choice.

And, dang it, he was right. They didn't. No matter how good a shot either of them were, they couldn't win against such overwhelming odds if they were discovered.

She glared her displeasure at him.

Sorry, he silently mouthed, then motioned for her to follow him again.

I can do this. I can do this. She silently repeated the phrase over and over in her mind as she followed him into the stables.

Taking everything one step at a time helped. She was the lookout at the door while he did whatever he needed to do inside. It gave her a task to focus on instead of wondering how in the world she was going to manage riding a horse when the closest she'd ever been to one before was at Lance's stables in Gatlinburg. Feeding a horse a carrot without getting your fingers bitten off was one thing. Clinging to its back without falling was something entirely different.

Sending up a quick prayer, she pulled her burner phone out. *Please let there be a signal.* She pressed the numbers 911 and listened. Nothing but static. Dang it.

The sound of hooves shuffling against the hay-covered floors had her turning around. She immediately backed up, bumping into the doorframe as four impossibly tall horses surrounded her.

Lance appeared between them and grabbed her hand. “Come on,” he whispered.

“Wait. Which one is mine? They don’t even have anything to hold on to.”

He grinned and whispered, “Saddles and reins?”

“Whatever,” she whispered back. “I’ll take my chances with the gunmen.” She backed away from the horses milling around and started for the door.

Lance tugged on her hand. “Come on. We’re not riding these horses. Those are the decoys.”

A moment later she was standing in front of a huge black horse with a saddle and reins, as he’d stated. But there was no way she was getting on it. “It’s huge. Way bigger than the others.”

“That’s why I picked him. He can handle both of us.”

“Wait. Both of us?”

“You didn’t expect me to ask you to gallop all by yourself when you’ve never sat on a horse before, did you?”

“Well, yes. I guess I did. Wait. Gallop? That’s the really fast gear, right?”

He chuckled and put his foot in the metal thing hanging from the saddle. Then he vaulted up onto the horse. She stared at him, at his hand as he reached down for her.

"Sorry, I can't. I just can't." She hurried toward the other horses that were docilely standing just inside the door.

The sound of hooves clicking and stomping against the floor had her whirling around. Lance leaned down with both arms and snatched her around the waist. He swung her up behind him without even slowing down. Keira let out a squeak of fear as she landed on the horse's bottom behind the saddle and it gave a light kick.

"Hang on," Lance called out.

She wrapped her arms around his waist, locking her hands together against him.

"Hang on," he repeated.

She let out another squeak as the horse leaped forward. The other horses, the ones he'd called decoys, bolted out through the doors and raced toward the house. Lance jerked the reins of the horse they were on, and it dug in its heels, rounding the building and then taking off in a run deeper into the woods.

Keira knew she should have had her gun out and watched for anyone after them. But even if she somehow managed to hang on with one hand to free her gun, she'd never be able to aim it while bouncing on the back of this beast. She'd likely end up shooting herself, the horse or, worse, Lance. She suddenly realized that every spaghetti Western she'd ever seen was a passel of lies. No hero could manage this jolting, bumpy roller-coaster ride and manage to aim a gun at any bad guys. It just wasn't possible.

Bam, bam, bam.

Her eyes flew open, her ears ringing. Lance was holstering his pistol, having just shot it. She looked off to their left and saw two bodies lying on the ground, their guns dropped beside them.

Holy moly.

She blinked in shock and immediately revised her negative view of those spaghetti Westerns. Or, rather, she revised her view of Lance. He'd already been amazing. Now he was a hero in a whole other way. Her earlier fears dimmed and she straightened a bit, still hanging on for dear life. But no longer convinced they were definitely going to die.

Maybe they had a chance after all.

Bam. A gunshot sounded close by.

Lance suddenly arched against her. The horse whinnied as Lance jerked the reins. Then they were falling onto the ground. Her breath left her in a rush as she rolled underneath a scratchy bush, headlong into a mound of pine needles. Gasping like a fish out of water, she desperately tried to make her lungs work again. Her ears were as useless as her lungs. All she could hear was a low buzzing sound.

The horse bolted past her, its hooves flashing in the moonlight through the branches of the shrubs surrounding her as it galloped away from the house, minus her and Lance.

Where was he? He had to be near her, somewhere.

Her lungs finally expanded in a rush of cold air. She coughed and gasped, everything hurting as she got up on her hands and knees. What had happened? Gunfire. She'd heard a shot. Only one this time. And it wasn't Lance who was shooting. Oh God, please, no. Lance couldn't have been shot, could he?

The answer to that was brutally clear when some men shouted about ten yards away, motioning toward something on the ground. A man, a tall broad-shouldered man with a dark jacket and short dark hair. Lance.

A sob rose in her throat. She pressed a hand to her mouth to keep from crying out. Four men. There were four of them, poking at Lance as if he were roadkill. He suddenly moaned and swiped at one of the men's hands. Keira had never seen something so wonderful in her life. He was alive. Lance had either been shot or knocked out from the fall off the startled horse. But he was alive. Which meant there was still hope. It also meant that it was up to her to save him. She didn't know if she could shoot four men quickly enough to avoid being shot herself. But she was sure going to try.

She clawed for her pistol as two of the men grabbed Lance's arms and legs, hoisting him up between them. Her mind reeled in horror when she realized her gun was gone. It must have fallen when she was thrown from the horse.

Three more men, each holding rifles, joined the original four. They seemed to be arguing about something. Then they split up, some heading toward the house, others going in the direction that she and Lance had been riding. And another…coming straight toward her.

She bit her lip against the urge to cry out in pain as she scrambled around in the leaves, searching for her pistol. Everything hurt. She didn't think any bones were broken, just badly bruised, like her ribs that were really hurting again. But that was the least of her worries. If the man didn't stop or turn away, she was about to be discovered. And then Lance would have no one to save him.

The gun was nowhere to be found. And the man was getting far too close, scanning the woods near her. He didn't seem to know she was there. But he'd see her soon if she didn't do something. She continued to flail in the leaves, trying to find her pistol. Something sharp seemed to slice into her hand. She sucked in a breath, then pulled it up out of the leaves. It was just a stick, but it was thick and sharp on one end where it must have twisted and broken from the shrubs as she'd fallen. It was also slick with blood from where it had cut her hand. Stealing herself against the pain, she grabbed it and swung it up and out just as the man peered over the bushes.

It jammed deep into his throat. His eyes widened in shock, his hands clawing at his bleeding neck. Then he slowly crumpled to the ground.

Keira stared at his lifeless body, shocked that she was the one who'd done that. She'd never once shot anyone in the line of duty. And here she'd just stabbed one to death. With a branch. Hysterical laughter started to bubble up in her throat. She swore and forced herself to draw deep even breaths.

Think, Keira. Think.

How could she save Lance against dozens of armed gunmen with only a tree branch as a weapon? The answer was painfully clear. She couldn't. She had to get help. But how? There were men all through these woods. How could she escape all of them and make it back in time to help Lance before it was too late?

If it wasn't too late already.

She reached in her pocket for her cell phone, relieved when her hand tightened around it. Maybe she was far enough away that the cell signal was no longer blocked and she could call Trent or 911 or both. She pressed Trent's number and Send, then listened. The same buzzing sound she'd heard before sounded again. The signal was blocked. She'd heard somewhere that text messages went through better than calls when signal strength wasn't strong. She tapped in a quick message to Trent and pressed Send. Then she sent the same message to Asher. But both texts popped up on the screen with red exclamation points beside them.

Text failed to send.

She groaned and shoved the phone back in her pocket. Despair like she'd never felt before flooded through her. If she could trade her life for Lance's, she would willingly do so. But she was under no pretenses that the men after them would take that trade. They'd kill both her and Lance.

Lord, please. Help me figure out what to do. Give me a sign.

A whinny sounded behind her. She slowly turned around. The horse that she and Lance had been riding stood only a few yards away, calmly munching on some brown grass beneath a tree.

Keira swore and looked up at the sky. "You couldn't have given me a different sign? Like maybe a truck?"

As if in response, lightning cracked across the night sky. And it started to rain.

"Okay, okay. I won't look a gift horse in the mouth. Ha ha." She pushed herself to her feet and slowly advanced on the scary beast staring at her as if she were a bug it wanted to squash.

Chapter Twenty

Lance glared at the no fewer than ten men crammed into the small farmhouse's main room, milling around as the worst aggressor stood in front of him. No doubt him being tied to a dining room chair made Ileana think she was safe. She certainly thought so, the way she kept smirking at him and pacing back and forth. But she wasn't that confident, or she wouldn't be staying out of reach of his feet.

One step in the wrong direction and he'd sweep her legs out from under her. He'd follow that up by slamming on top of her, chair and all. He had every movement planned. But it was his last resort. Because the one thing he knew for a certainty was that if he attacked Ileana, every man in the room would riddle him with bullets.

Since there didn't appear to be a way out of here with his life anyway, the only thing really holding him back was Keira. When the bullet had grazed his head, knocking him silly, everything had gone fuzzy. He'd managed to climb out of the fog when he was being hauled out of the woods. But he had no idea what had happened to Keira. For her sake, he was trying to hold his temper. Stall. Do whatever he had to do to stay alive. Because if there was even one chance in a thousand that he could do something to help her, to save her, he would.

No matter how much torture he had to endure.

Ileana glanced at her phone again, her still-beautiful face drawn with impatience.

"What's wrong, Ileana?" he goaded. "Not allowed to make any decisions without hubby's permission?"

She scoffed. "Hubby? Are you kidding me? That weak, useless excuse for a man?"

"Ah. So you feel the same affection for him that you once felt for me."

"Shut up."

"If he's so weak, why are you taking orders from him? Why did you feed him information about OPI? Why do you let him beat you?"

She let out an angry screech and motioned to the man closest to Lance. He slammed his fist against Lance's jaw, whipping his head to the side.

Lance held back a groan. And smiled. The man raised his fist again.

"Stop," Ileana ordered. "I need him conscious and able to talk. Break his jaw, and he won't be able to answer my questions."

"I thought I already answered your questions," Lance said. "There are more?"

She stopped in front of him, her hands fisted at her sides. "You haven't answered anything! Where's the rest of your team? Where's Brett? Melissa? Where's Jack? Tell me and I'll let you go."

"Where's Keira? Tell me and I'll let you live."

Her phone buzzed in her pocket. She glared at him before checking the screen. Then she smiled. It was that smile that had him going cold inside.

"Bring another chair over here," she called out. "We're about to have company."

It took every ounce of control that Lance had not to shout in rage when two men stepped through the back door opening, dragging Keira between them. A chair was brought over close to Lance. And Keira was quickly tied into it, just like he was. Her head hung limply. Lance watched in terror for her chest to rise. Finally, it did. Thank God. She was alive.

Ileana was suddenly there with a glass of water. She tossed it in Keira's face.

Keira jerked in her chair, blinking at the water dribbling down her cheeks. She blinked again, then looked around as if only just then realizing where she was. She groaned, and Lance could have sworn he heard her curse beneath her breath.

"Hey, beautiful," he whispered.

Her eyes widened. Tears sprang into them and she smiled, drawing his attention to her cracked and bleeding lip. "My hero," she whispered back. "Glad to see you still breathing."

"I'm hardly a hero. But ditto on the breathing thing."

"Well, isn't this sickeningly sweet," Ileana said. "Two little lovebirds right before they die."

Keira completely ignored Ileana, keeping her gaze on Lance. "I rode that beast to get help. Unfortunately when I got to the road, I didn't quite clear the fence."

He stared at her in shock. "You rode the horse? By yourself?"

"I'm pretty sure it felt sorry for me. Well, until it saw the fence. Then it decided to get rid of me and veer the other way. The horse went left, I went straight. Before I could get my feet under me, some of Ileana's jerks grabbed me. So much for my attempt to save you."

"Enough!" Ileana yelled. "I'm about to vomit. Let's get down to business. Our dearly departed Sam was nice enough to get cancer and decide he wanted to reunite with old friends before he died. That's what finally got the ball rolling again on the stupid OPI train and opened the door for me to find and eliminate the rest of you. I failed my uncle when things fell apart with that company. I finally have a chance to redeem myself now. All I need to do is find the last three team members. If you tell me nicely, I'll have both of you killed quickly. Continue to defy me and you'll suffer a slow, agonizing death. Your choice."

Keira finally turned and gave Ileana her full attention. "Don't you have to call your husband for permission to do any of this first?"

Ileana slapped her so fast Lance didn't get a chance to whip his legs out to stop her.

Keira ran her tongue over her freshly bleeding mouth, then smiled.

Lance was proud of her courage. But he wanted to shake her for angering Ileana further. He spoke again to distract Ileana from hurting Keira again.

"I don't know where they are," he said. "Who's this uncle you mentioned? Is he yours and your husband's mob contact? The one you both sold information to for years, causing innocent people to die?"

"Stop dragging Hudson into this. He's as moral and ethical as they come. And he never hit me by the way. This black eye was my doing, to get sympathy from Levi. Hudson would never hit a woman, even if she deserved it." She rolled her eyes, obviously not thinking of that as a compliment. "He never knew I was the one getting information. And the people who died were far from innocent. They were traitors, snitches, the worst of the worst. They deserved exactly what they got."

Lance made no attempt to hide his disgust. "How I ever

thought you were a decent human being all those years ago is a mystery I'll likely never solve."

She screeched her rage again. But this time, she didn't stop to direct someone else. She hauled back to slap Lance just as she'd done to Keira. But this time he was ready for it. He whipped her legs out from under her and crashed down on top of her, twisting so the arm of the chair slammed against her throat. He was almost immediately yanked back up, still tied to the chair. But the damage was done. Ileana's face was already turning blue as she made gagging sounds and clawed at her crushed windpipe.

Her men all seemed to be in a state of panic, converging on her and dragging her into the dining room. They placed her on the table and started shouting orders at each other, trying to figure out how to help her.

Lance had been twisting and pulling at the ropes behind his back ever since he'd been captured. With the fall to the floor and him and his chair being hastily set back up, the ropes had loosened enough that he was able to yank his hands free.

Keira stared at him, her eyes wide with concern as he made short work of the rest of the ropes and knelt down behind her to work on hers.

"Go, go," she whispered. "Get out of here before they realize you're free."

"I'm not leaving you." He yanked and tugged at her ropes, swearing at how tight they were.

"I mean it, Lance. Please. I can't handle seeing you die. I'd rather die myself knowing you were going to be okay. Go."

He tugged at her ropes, finally loosening them. "I love you too," he whispered, grinning as he yanked her up to standing.

"Hey, hey, stop!" one of the men yelled. He drew his gun.

Lance jumped in front of Keira, shielding her with his body.

"Wait," another man yelled at the first, shoving his hand up toward the ceiling just as the gun went off. "We can't kill them until she's done with them."

"Look at her," the shooter argued. "She's purple. She's not telling us anything."

Lance and Keira were already running for the front door, not waiting around as the argument continued behind them.

He threw the door open and they both ran outside. Lights flashed across their faces, making it impossible to see past them. The sound of dozens of guns being ratcheted and loaded had him glancing at Keira in frustration. "I'm so sorry."

She smiled. "Me too. I wanted to see how this thing between us ended. And I really wanted to find out what comes after the kissing part." She winked.

He grinned. Then they both raised their hands.

The sounds of men jogging toward them had Lance stepping in front of Keira again. She swore and tried to stand beside him. Just when they expected to be shot, the men passed them and ran inside the house.

Gunshots boomed. Glass shattered. Shouts and screams sounded.

"Get them out of here," a voice that Lance didn't recognize called out.

"We've got them."

That voice, he did recognize. He blinked against the harsh lights, then grinned when Trent and Asher ran up to them. Trent grabbed Lance's arm. Asher grabbed Keira. They all raced off to the side of the house, away from the gunfire that was already slowing.

Kneeling down behind the engine block of one of the cars

that had pulled up, the four of them waited until someone called for a cease-fire.

"All clear," someone from inside shouted.

People started running in and out of the house, taking control of the scene. Lance hugged Keira close to his side as they straightened. When yellow crime scene tape came out and someone began using it to cordon off the area, Lance and Keira looked at Trent and Asher in question.

"What's happening?" Lance asked. "Who are these people? How did you find us? What are—"

"Enough, enough." Trent grinned. "Ask Keira here. She's the one responsible for us getting here in the nick of time."

She blinked. "I am? What do you mean?"

"The text messages. We were already in the area because we'd hooked up with Hudson Vale to find Ileana and—"

"Wait," Lance said. "Ileana's husband? Isn't he the FBI mole?"

Asher shook his head, joining the conversation. "No. Ileana was the only mole. No one in the FBI was involved. She hacked OPI's computers and fed the info directly to a mob boss."

"Let me guess," Lance said. "Her uncle."

"Later you'll have to tell me how you knew that. Her relationship to him was buried under a web of changed names and forged birth certificates."

"It wasn't any brilliant investigative skills on my part," Lance said. "She told me a few minutes ago."

"Can we get back to these text messages you mentioned?" Keira said. "They blocked our cell phones. Nothing I sent could have gone through."

"They did," he said. "You must have gotten the phone out of the cell signal jammer range at some point, because the texts told us exactly where you were and what was going on.

We—us and the FBI guys—were trying to figure out where exactly this farm was located. But until those texts came in, we were flying blind." He patted Keira on the shoulder. "You did it. You saved the day."

"No, I didn't. You all did." She smiled up at Lance. "And you did. You gave us both the time we needed to survive. You're my hero, truly."

He smiled and pressed a tender kiss against her forehead. "That's debatable. I'm just glad it all worked out. Or has it? Trent, Asher, you said you brought Vale here. Does that mean what I hope it means?"

They nodded. Trent said, "We have all the evidence we need to put Ileana away. And her uncle. Hudson Vale, the FBI, they had nothing to do with anything that happened. He was livid when he found out what Ileana had done. Due to a conflict of interest, of course, there's another FBI guy running this scene. But Hudson is here too. He wanted to be there when she was arrested."

"I don't think that's going to happen," Lance said.

"No? Why not?"

"I'm pretty sure she's dead."

They stared at him in surprise.

"I'm not proud of it," Lance said.

Keira tightened her arm around his waist. "There were at least a dozen armed men inside—"

"Ten," Lance corrected.

"Dozens more outside," Asher added.

"Right," Keira said. "In spite of all that, Lance did everything he could to protect me. And he did. Ileana would have killed us both. And even with all those thugs around us, and him tied to a chair, he managed to take her down.

He truly saved both of us." She smiled. "But you two get credit too. You did arrive, as you said, in the nick of time."

They laughed, then sobered as a body bag was carried out the door, escorted in part by a very pale, defeated-looking man. Lance recognized him as Hudson Vale because of the research he'd done. From Keira's gasp beside him, he knew she did too. The man was moral and ethical, just as Ileana had accused. And in spite of what she'd done, which would no doubt end his career with the FBI, he'd ensured that justice was served.

An EMT ran up to Keira and Lance. "I was told you were both hurt. Do you need a stretcher?"

Keira looked up at Lance. "Your head is bleeding."

"It's mostly stopped now. You're black and blue. And your lip is bleeding."

"It's mostly stopped now."

They both laughed.

"We're fine," they told the EMT, laughing again when they said the same thing at the same time.

He gave them an odd look, then headed off in search of someone else to help.

"Hey, Lance. Catch."

He turned, and Trent tossed him something. A key fob. Lance looked at him in question.

"The only white SUV out here." He pointed. "Go on. You two have been through enough tonight. Head back to wherever you've been staying. Asher and I will catch a ride with someone else and we can talk tomorrow."

Keira frowned. "There aren't any hotels around here. You can come to the house Lance rented. It's big enough for all of us."

Trent grinned. "I don't think Lance would agree with you. Like I said, we'll catch up tomorrow."

"Really late tomorrow," Lance called out.

Trent laughed as Lance grabbed Keira's hand and practically dragged her to the SUV. When they reached it, he turned her around so he could look in her eyes. He cupped her face with his hands and stared down at her in wonder. "I know it seems crazy to say this, so soon. But I've never been more sure of anything in my life. Keira, I—"

"—love you," they both said at the same time.

"Wow," she breathed.

"Wow," he echoed.

They kissed, and when they broke apart, tears were streaming down her cheeks.

"Keira? What's wrong?"

"They're happy tears. I suppose this means you'll be asking me for a date now."

He shook his head. "No. I've decided against that."

Her smiled faded. "What? I don't—"

"I was thinking of asking you something else instead. Marry me?"

She stared at him, her mouth falling open in shock.

The confidence he'd felt moments before took a dive. "Or, if it's too soon—"

She burst out laughing. "Too soon? We've never even been on a date."

"Right. Too soon. I've been worried this whole time about going too fast, about you possibly regretting this later. I want you to be sure, even though I know that I am. I'll wait as long as you want. We can take it slow and—"

"Yes!" She smiled. "The answer is yes!"

He stared at her, his mouth going dry. "Can you repeat that? I'm not sure that I heard you correctly. My ears are ringing."

"Which part? The yes that I'll marry you? Or the part where I tell you I am madly, deeply, forever in love with you? There will be no regrets, Lance. We can have a long engagement, if you need that to feel secure about me, about us. But I've never been so sure about anything. I love you. With everything that I am."

He groaned and kissed her again. This one was scorching hot. He pressed her against the SUV, fitting their bodies together. He kissed her the way he'd wanted to from the moment he'd seen how bravely she'd faced the gunmen at the cabin. She was an amazing woman in so many ways. Whether she wanted to return to Maple Falls and continue to be a cop or move to Gatlinburg with him and choose another career, they'd work it out. The only thing that mattered was being with her and living the rest of their lives together.

Whistles and catcalls had them breaking apart.

"Get a room," Asher called out.

Keira laughed. Lance rushed her around to the passenger side of the SUV and hurriedly fastened her seat belt. Then he was in the driver's seat racing them back toward their rental house.

When they arrived, he tenderly picked her up and carried her up the steps to the front door. Pausing in the opening, he held her in his arms and looked down at the most precious person he'd ever met. "I know we aren't married yet. And this isn't our home. But I still want to carry you over the threshold."

"That's so sweet. Since we're skipping a few steps, I'm thinking we could skip another one. Let's start the honeymoon right now. That is, if you want to."

He cleared his suddenly raw throat, staring down at the

beautiful woman in his arms. “How did I ever get so lucky to find you?”

“Hmm, I’m not sure. But you’re definitely going to *get* lucky. If you hurry.”

He eagerly ran inside carrying her, both of them laughing the whole time.

* * * * *